RIVERBEND

A Novel by
GLENN A. BRUCE

SECOND EDITION SOFTCOVER
ISBN: 1622535782
ISBN-13: 978-1-62253-578-1

Editor: Robb Grindstaff
Cover Artist: Kris Norris
Interior Designer: Lane Diamond

EVOLVED PUBLISHING™

www.EvolvedPub.com
Evolved Publishing LLC
Butler, Wisconsin, USA

Printed in Book Antiqua font.

BOOKS BY GLENN A. BRUCE

Banana Republic: Richie's Run
Race!: A Hei$t Story
Riverbend
Rubric
The Man
Versions of the Truth

WHAT OTHERS ARE SAYING

"**The Next Patterson** – *Riverbend* captures and maintains your attention from the first chapter. I have about 30 authors on my list of 'must read,' including Patterson, Sanford, Kellerman(s), Parker. Glenn Bruce is now on that list! Can't wait for the prequel and sequel that will be coming out!" ~ **Robert C. Bales**

"**Let's Have More Les Moore!** – This was my first for the 'hard-bitten detective' genre... Enjoyed ALL the characters, even the bad guys, made me hope for more of Les Moore. Some scenes are not for the faint of heart. But even at page 423 I was asking for more, not less. Some parts made me laugh, other parts made me hungry. The Frank Sinatra theme explains it all. Good read. Lot of fun. Good job, Glenn Bruce!" ~ **Dennis Blasko**

"**Loved it!!!!!!** – OMG, what a read. This book kept me on edge and surprised at every turn and funny too. Even though it was hard to follow some of the technical details, I would recommend this book to anyone who likes to read a good mystery, thriller and comedy rolled into one. The main characters were well developed and made you want to know more and more about what makes them tick. The author did a great job of pulling you in and keeping you there right on the edge until the end. Great page-turner!" ~ **Sonja**

DEDICATION

For Wanda Webster,
the greatest agent ever, who believed in me when others
didn't and predicted that Riverbend would be a success – even
if it scared her half to death.

Introduction

"O that thou hadst hearkened to my commandments!
Then had thy peace been as a river,
and thy righteousness as the waves of the sea."
Isaiah 49:18

Prologue – The Rain

Dusk on the Boulevard, Sea-Tac Strip. Usual soft rain doesn't keep the hookers in. Nor does the *Times* headline.

RIVERBEND KILLER GONE?
Streetwalkers Safe for Past Six Months

Encouraged, they're out in numbers. Waving cars down from under brightly colored umbrellas, sequined purses full of cash and condoms, newspapers with the same headline. Whatever keeps thick makeup from clotting.

A late '70s Monte Carlo — dirt brown metallic, tan vinyl lifting up, rusted rocker panels — slows down. Steamy windows obscure the john's face.

But he's looking.

Lots of choices tonight and each Spandexed player knows her role well — a wave, a whistle, a smile, or a pucker. Pouting seems to be working well this week.

A black girl in an orange wig licks her teeth, but this john doesn't like darker cuts. He passes the Asians too, stopping at the built blonde with the blunt-cut staying dry under the bus stop. Her Frederick's of Hollywood high hemline is classy for latex, he thinks. Sunglasses at night add to the mystery.

She sees his blond hair in the smeary light and moves quickly, trumping the other girls, his window already coming down in hand-cranked spurts. "Lookin' for a date, honey?" she says low and breathy, thick with promise.

Everything is well-rehearsed.

He leans into the yellow crime glow, dull gray eyes set deep in a hard face that's seen more miles this week than a pencil-pusher does in a lifetime. Maybe he's a convict, maybe he's just a trucker; likely, he's not a kind man. Either way, his is a face no sensible hooker would ask for a smoke, much less a *date*.

"I'm lookin' for a lot more than that, honey," he says, a hint of the south.

"You're looking *at* a lot more than that, too," she tells him, eyeing his rolling rust bucket. "Sure you can afford me?"

"Not my car," he says, looking away, probably telling the truth.

They both watch a '76 Eldorado prowling low and shark-like in the night wet. This one's red as new blood with a white top and seats to contrast. For him, the classic speaks to opportunities unseized, achievements unrealized; for the hooker, simple nostalgia — good times gone forever, memories lying dormant in a past as dead as night.

This night.

Tall streetlamps backlight her high tease, obscuring the face, the bones. Makes him wonder if she's a he — out loud.

"Cost you to find out," is what he gets back over the constant shouting in his head.

"What if I don't like what I see?" he wants to know.

"Double your money back if you're not completely satisfied," she says. The practiced smile. "I *cum* with a warranty."

A sense of humor is good, he thinks. It'll make the night's work go easier. And hell, lip service from a trannie isn't so bad. There was that one in Tuscaloosa, gave better head than most women he's had. Besides, he doesn't *have* to fuck it.

Tonight is more about the Statement.

Still, something doesn't seem right. Maybe something else. "You a cop?" he asks, attempting to protect his civil rights.

"The question is, are *you*?" Never make the deal too easy; that's a dead giveaway.

"If I was a cop," he says, prepared, "would I show you this?" The thrift store pea coat comes off his lap.

If she's shocked, she doesn't show it. "No, you'd show me something like this." Black-laced thumb and finger come up an inch apart.

He laughs, stroking her ego — along with his pride and joy — making sure to make a big impression.

It's working. "What kinda plans you got for that telephone pole tonight, sweetie?" Better to get everything out in the open, up front. Standard procedure.

"I'll take what I can get." He's been turned down before.

This gets a thoughtful nod and the quick menu. "Straight for fifty, oral for seventy-five."

"There's a new twist," he snorts.

"Small mouth," she shrugs.

"Big down where it counts, huh?" He grins *knowingly*.

"Kids," the hooker lies, sensing where he's headed. Why not? This is not an exercise in truth; this is all about seduction, sealing the deal.

Capture.

It turns the killer on, thinking how she's got kids at home to miss her. He wants to plow ahead, so he nods behind. "I'll bet you're still tight back there."

He has the gall to wink.

She sighs, reads him her Hooker's Litany. "I don't do Greek, okay. No Greek, no golden showers, no shitting on people, no freaky stuff. I'll spank you if you want for an extra ten, but you don't spank me unless I ask. No ropes, no belts, no buckles. You mark me up, I lose business with the ones who just like to look."

"Hmmm," he says, looking — and still stroking himself.

"You keep that up, you're not gonna need me," she points out.

He throws his best smile — something between Elvis and the president, he thinks — and tells her he's "just keepin' the motor runnin', sweetheart."

It's her move now; they both know.

She looks up at the endless traffic pulling opaque domes of silvery spray two stories high and twice as long through the tired night, a rhythm as monotonous as it is disheartening, past the endless flat canyons of strip malls and car dealerships where once stood grand palisades of old growth redwoods; where entire families ate easy picnics in pillowy meadows; where Man once met Wild, and vice versa. Where Life once actually had meaning. It's gone now.

All of it.

She stares down at the missing door locks, rotted vinyl cracked and scurfing, and thinks, *This is what it's become, what it's all been reduced to.* But there's nothing this whore can do except go along for the ride and hope for some small piece of salvation, some scrap of saving grace at The End. God knows neither one of them deserves any.

She knows her time is up, so she says, "You gonna open the door, or are you gonna let me drown out here?" He smiles like President Elvis again and toggles the power locks.

She's in the car now.

He knocks the locks down and goes for an early handful. Fishnet knees slap shut. *Pop!* Like a small caliber report. "Sea-Tac Inn," she says. "First you pay, then we play."

"I gotta get the room, too?" He sounds more amused than angry, rumbling the old Monte into traffic that never seems to stop or even diminish out here, even late. Must be the airport or the strip clubs, he thinks, though he's never been to either.

"I don't do parking lots, honey," is all the more she has to say.

He takes the first curvy road off to the right by Walmart, parking lot still packed at 10:45. America can't get enough. She looks over to see what he's seeing, but he's looking at her.

"So, tell me about yourself," he says, playing The Friend — as if he cares — still playing with his Own Best Friend. Still with The Look.

She's got her doubts now.

"Look, I don't need this, okay?" she says, putting on being put-out. Just to see. "You give me seventy-five bucks, I do the deed, I'm on my way. I don't do talk. You want a girl that talks, go online. If you want the real live me, here I am. No talk, no kink, no rough stuff. Just a good time."

"Now, how can a guy have a good time without any'a that?" he *asks.*

"All right, let me out," she says, making it clear she's had enough.

"Whoa-whoa-whoa, calm down, sweetheart," he wheedles, assuring her, "It's a joke." Turning on what charm he has.

Slowing the car to a crawl.

Both of them look out at the flat-plane outlines of derelict warehouses, dark and crowding under a bottomless sky of ceaseless gray drizzle. No signs of Life. Might as well be Nowhere.

She keeps an eye on him. She has to.

He tells her, "I coulda had any one'a those nigger bitches back there for a twenty in the backseat. But I picked you."

Turns out he thinks it's a compliment.

She looks him over, one last time to be sure. He *can't* be the one she's looking for, not with a line like that. "I think I'm done for the night," she tells him.

But suddenly...

He's braking hard...

Reaching under the seat...

"Maybe you need convincing," he snarls like Bad Elvis.

Will he pull an automatic or a revolver? Maybe a long nasty blade with a serrated edge—the kind these redneck hunters and fucked-up vets like to flash for effect. *Don't turn your back on him.* Be ready for the flash, the slash, the report, the...

Wallet.

There must be three thousand in hundreds in there. Who'd *he* rob? She sighs inside, but his face has gone flush with ultimatum.

"Now, I can let you off right here," he says, and he's got that languid tone, dark and calm, the one to watch out for. The giveaway.

He tells her, "You walk back in the rain, don't make a dime and you look like shit, nobody'll even slow down for you, rest'a the night. By the time you go home to your dump, get fixed up and come back out again, all the dull hubbies have gone home to their happy little families. The only ones still out that time'a night don't make you feel too safe. You blew the night, instead'a blowin' me an' maybe one or two more, makin' your nut."

He makes everything sound so simple, so easy to choose.

"On the other hand," he says, "you stay and act nice, it'll all go easy." The old car idling, stale and sweet with age and mildew.

She's thinking.

He thumps his swollen pride and joy on the bottom of the steering wheel for punctuation—which should hurt and probably does. But then he probably *likes* the pain. He must, he's still pounding away. *Thump-thump-thump.*

Sounds like a pile driver down the street. A big Huey coming in over the treetops. A flat on the freeway. *Thump-thump-thump-thump.*

"So, we have a deal?" He wants to know, and he wants to know *now.*

Thump-thump-thump-thump-THUMP.

There's no choice really. Not now. Not here. Not for a hooker.

This hooker.

One hand goes around his shoulder, the other on his leg, red nails teasingly close. "Okay," he hears, watching. "Let's go for a ride."

The face that comes up is no longer the john.

Now, he's The Killer.

***

The old brown Monte takes the first left sideways. She's thrown hard, held hard against her door as balding tires hop old pavement, bite potholes, then launch for the highway.

A block away the whole time.

The stop sign's coming fast and the engine's going faster as the slipping old automatic drops second, hard, at 6,500.

He's not stopping.

She lets out a low growl of dread, leaning back, one hand on the rotting dash, one on the door, as the piece-of-shit Chevy flies up Warehouse Hill, front bumper gouging the last six feet of incline, mining asphalt then, released, kicking up near-vertical, hitch-plate throwing a fiery rooster tail back into the black left behind.

In the light, now.

He's tossed forward then back; she goes down then up. Heavy metal takes wing in the wet and—

—they're airborne.

Traffic rushes sidelong and fast as the old Monte crash-dives Lane One. Dead shocks pound a weakened frame made creaky with time and rust. Tires, cocked sharp and smashed nearly flat, scrape black in crusted wheel wells, flip the back end around and send the whole show straight into oncoming, everyone hurrying home for the Late News.

But the news is right here.

Panic, electric and sticky, spreads instantly—a simultaneous, psychic hot flash. *Your whole life! in front of your eyes! in the next second!*

The cold adrenaline rush of sleepy-warm innocence meeting some unnamable, un*think*able evil head-on in the rain on a dark night. Horns ridden long and loud to let the others know.

The Killer cranks hard—his killer crank harder and centrifugally flung—right then left, hands gripping over, pulling down, spinning back. No more time to blow. They could *both* die here.

His hooker directing. "Back! You're over... compen... sating."

Another bump like the last one and she might *be* a backseat driver.

Diving cars duck on rain-slick. Narrow misses. Except for the woman in the green soccer-mom wagon headed for milk. *Whump!* Sheet metal folds; headlights are extinguished; insurance rates climb.

No one stops.

Miraculously, the brown shit-heap emerges unscathed, looping the last coupe in the undeclared convoy, finding the right lanes. She relaxes.

He speeds up.

The Sea-Tac Inn's just ahead, diagonally across at the corner of the highway and State Road One-Something. He throws a hard left, back across the onrushing automotive tide, directly into the path of a late lumber truck, loaded and in a hurry.

Air horns shatter what's left of the hooker's calm. Eyes close behind dark glasses; wigged head pulls back; red nails dig into the rotting arm rest. Bracing for it, but not ready.

By the grace of a God neither knows, the truck blows by — another dip of chrome-coat and everything would have ended there — its powerful slipstream smacking the back window of the old Monte like a hateful squall as the brown POS sails off the sharpest incline on The Strip.

Can't see the road 'til you're on it! is what they say.

The brown barge hits hard, fifty feet out, then porpoises like a short trawler in a high sea for two long city blocks before puddle-slapping a sign that reads *Riverbend - 8.*

There's already nothing but what's waiting in the night.

Drives like a maniac comes to mind — wipers slapping fast but doing little — a sarcastic, "What're you tryin' to do, kill me?"

He swings and misses, swerving, screaming for her to, "Shut up!" His hand going in his jacket. This won't be a wallet and…

Out it comes. A nickel-plated .45 with pearl grips. *Nice.*

Warm muzzle at her temple, reached over, stretched across, driving with his free hand — badly, the whore notes — he's beginning to moan.

His hooker recognizes the inflection and sneaks a sideways glance as the first of his release catches the bottom of the steering wheel; the second drapes his shoulder; number three hits the headliner; four through seven go random, all hands-free, unassisted — proud and out of the ballpark.

He flashes a half-baked full-blown psycho smile in the green dash light, red face dripping white. He knows the end is near and thinks it's funny. But the Last Laugh never is.

Not really.

***

Dark waters flow deep and uneasy under the narrow bridge, its solitary light casting pointless hard angles through rusted girders.

Shadows wasted on darkness.

The sign says 'Riverbend, Population 144,' but everyone's long gone. It's a dead zone now, and everyone knows:

Like attracts like.

A dirt brown 1978 Monte Carlo with peeling tan vinyl roof and rusted rocker panels sits half on, half off the road under the grip of a perpetual damp that ever hungers for more. Bald tires will spin two full car lengths before finding traction.

So quiet out here, so egregiously forsaken, even the night feels sorry for itself, alone but for the rain. Always the rain.

Pop!

A flash in the woods. A single shot, its echo killed instantly by the thick night air. Then another, to finish the job.

Black water falls in on itself.

Chapter 1 – Riverbend

Les Moore arrived at 10:36 a.m. He'd received a call the night before in Coeur d'Alene where he'd been assisting sheriff's deputies with a bizarre rampage-style murder — twins in a double-wide. A great headline; the kind Local hates. Les picked up the message from his boss Phil Brinkman at 6:47 and was on a plane out of Spokane by 8:12.

His plain-blue rental — the Seattle field office was short a car — crunched onto what little gravel there was on the far side of the road directly across from fifty feet of yellow crime tape that had been draped between two orange highway cones cordoning off a long, six-inch wide black slick left when the brown Monte's bald tire failed to find purchase on the lush, green highway grass. Not a mountain of evidence, but someone thought it worth preserving. The Monte Carlo was long gone.

A bevy of local authorities, to use the word loosely, gazed at the blue Buick. Some FBI-bashing was in order. "Hoover's here, everybody shape up." Cigarette tips glowed red as tin stars rose fast and fell in snatches under tar-filled laughs. No one moved.

Then the door fell open, Sinatra spilled out, crooning "Nice and Easy" from the CD player. Smooth, effortless. A moment later, Special Agent Leslie Francis Moore shut the motor off and stepped out onto the blacktop, holster on — but empty.

A county sheriff's looie felt inspired to remark. "Must build 'em brave in DC, these days." There came more glows and a phlegmy cough followed by something wet and heavy hitting the blacktop. Then Les's other hand came out of the car, gripping his 1991 Ruger P-85 Mark-2 with the stainless slide — old school, heavy as hell, reliable as Job.

Fifteen-round clip.

"Maybe not," someone else cracked, and the Winstons went quiet.

A young cop from Bellingham who happened to have been driving past on vacation when he saw the hubbub and stopped to mingle with some of his own, scratched under one eye and asked, "Wonder, do they pay for those suits or just the dry-clean on 'em?"

"I hear they have the maid take care of everything," came the answer from down the line, and the row went aglow again.

Les checked for traffic and crossed. "Fellas," he said, nodding to the lineup of chiseled faces shaded against a nonexistent sun under wide tan brims and blue ball caps with stars on the crown. Most nodded back, extending professional courtesy only as far as they figured they had to. "Don't worry," Les assured, "I'm just here to assist, not to steal anyone's thunder."

"Just our evidence," a voice came back, low.

Les looked to his left. A young Tacoma cop with no business out there in the first place wore a smirk that said he thought he was clever beyond his years. He'd heard about the body in the woods on his radio at Denny's and called in a temp off-air to check out the action. So of course, he had to be the most vocal.

Some of the older Locals braced, but Les Moore was decades past letting a rookie uniform get to him. He shrugged and said, "What Wilstrong wants, his employees take."

He meant Bureau Chief Wilstrong, Hoover's positional descendant, and the first African American to hold the job. Tall, tough and highly regarded, Evertt Wilstrong had taken a *position*.

More nods, less grinning, and Les, grinning. Everyone takes orders, even Feds. "He doesn't want it, it's all yours," Les assured the kid and walked on.

Just back of the crime tape sat a coroner's van. Two beefy ex-jocks dressed in white—farm boys gone soft—reposed against the side, one on either side of the Hippocratic snake, Camel Lights dangling from their lips—a sight not wasted on Les. "Hey, you guys die of cancer, you can haul each other in before you get cold."

The one with longer hair looked up and said, "Huh?" The other never moved.

Les wondered if they were both having the same dulling daydream and started down the steep bank, catching his first glimpse of bare flesh through the undergrowth—probably a buttocks and lower back, smooth and pale, with red spatters.

The flash of a crime scene camera, a pinprick in daylight, and it all came back like yesterday.

***

Standing off to one side of the body, Major Frederick J. Bondini of the King County Sheriff's Department watched with three of his underlings — one of them a salt-and-pepper veteran from the Major Crimes Unit — as an attractive female M.E.'s assistant did her dirty work. From his canted view across the body, Bondini spotted "Les!" coming down the bank, and turned up a friendly round face. The two young sheriff's deputies — one of them a woman — shared a discreet look. They had heard.

"How are ya? What's it been?" Bondini asked Les. He knew exactly how long Les had been away, but he wasn't bringing *that* up.

"Three years," Les said, graciously, as if nothing else had ever happened out here. "I see they made you Major."

"Had to. No one around with more gray hair," Fred said with what sounded like a genuine laugh. "Here to snake my case?"

"You bet," Les replied about the same way, and threw an honest handshake. "Wife and kids?"

"Let's see. A broken leg, four sets of braces, two state tuitions, one out of state, new caps, facelift, partial, and a Volvo. Youngest one lost it on Old 82. Rearranged a row of mailboxes and a brick shed, but didn't pop a pimple."

Les gave up a chuckle. Raising kids was safe talk and never really changed, just variations on a theme. But that was as much banter as anyone got out of Les Moore. "I heard chatter on the radio," he said. "You think this may be him."

Bondini's deputies shared another muted glance as their boss's good humor evaporated quicker than a raindrop on hot summer asphalt in Arizona, which was exactly where he wished he was at the moment.

"That's right. You heard chatter," Fred Bondini said, having a way of making the simplest remark come out as a complex caveat.

So, the two of them, along with the two deputies and the MCU guy, a captain, watched in silence as the brunette forensics woman measured spatter trajectories on the dead man's back and shoulder.

Killer, killed.

"I guess we can rule out Personal Cause Homicide," Les said, expression never changing. He meant domestic stuff.

The killer's thin blond hair lay matted in back, red-going-black at the exit wound. He had been shot through the face, the eye — probably while on his knees — and left here, nude, to be discovered. No attempt at hiding the body or the deed.

Statement, indeed.

GLENN A. BRUCE

Bondini gave a quick glower followed by a snort of appreciation, happy to see that Les hadn't left his sense of humor wherever he had sent his body and mind those three years in absentia. Someone said Tahiti, but Bondini figured more like Outer Mongolia or the middle Sahara—some anonymous nether region where Les could loiter unnoticed until the pain ebbed, or he drank himself to redemption or death, whichever came first.

Wherever he had gone, his soul had remained here, in Riverbend.

Done with measuring, the coroner's brunette—a young Kathleen Turner with a dark rinse—stood, seeming to realize only then that Les was there. She looked him over.

Les Moore was still a very good-looking man. He had smallish features, calm dark eyes that could go stormy on short notice and laser through diamond plate if needed. He had straight teeth and a smile to match, when he felt a situation deserved it.

The pretty coroner lady said, "All yours," ostensibly for Bondini, but her eyes never left Les's. After letting the look linger a moment, smolder really, she smiled and started up the bank. Les kept his eyes on her retreat, as hopeful for something to admire as the rest of the men, but her lab coat obscured anything of real interest, so...

She removed the coat.

This brought into play some very thin slacks, tight and white enough to reveal her choice in panties. Only, none showed. A moment later, the alluring assistant M.E. crested the hill and the coat went back on. She never looked back.

Les grinned.

"Okay," Bondini pronounced, moving on. He had other things on his mind, one of them at his feet. "Ever seen 'im before?" he asked Les, rolling the body over with his boot.

Where his right eye had been, the killer now sported only a gooey black pit, his left eye clear and staring straight ahead as if still surprised in death that he had turned out to be victim rather than executioner. Otherwise, their Doe Boy, as Bondini liked to call unnamed male stiffs (or the more oblique Pillsburies—unless a situation called for the gender nonspecific DWIA, Dead When I Arrive).

Otherwise, the dead man looked like any other average guy asleep on the ground in the woods, naked—except for one prominent feature. He had the largest sex organ Fred Bondini had ever seen in person, his boss hog cinched up in a three-quarter-inch wide yellow ribbon looped into a bow, tips trimmed to perfect 45-degree angles.

Les stared down a moment then said, "Can't say as I have. But the giftwrap looks familiar."

Bondini glanced over at Les a long moment then told the others, "You guys take ten." The two deputies shared another look and one with the MCU captain. There followed a group glance at Les, then at Bondini, then the three of them left for the road above.

Bondini watched them hike up until they were out of sight, then he turned back. His eyes fell on his old friend. "Are you... doin' okay these days, Les?"

"Fit as a fiddle, Fred," Les said. "And that's not easy to say if you're not."

Bondini didn't seem to get a charge out of Les's alliteration. "Anyone can buy yellow ribbon," he said.

"But not everyone knows what to do with it," Les said amiably. "How to give the proper decorative flair, that Martha Stewart touch, if you will."

"I won't," Bondini grunted. "And you're assuming it *is*."

"Are you trying to say something, Fred?" Les asked. "Because it sounds like you are. Trying."

Bondini's glower cut deeper. "I'm asking, Les," he said softly.

"Well, go ahead, ask," Les said. Plain, emotionless, very FBI.

Bondini swallowed hard, keeping down what he really wanted to say. He hated that detached Bureau crap, what the agency did to men, taking away their hearts and souls, replacing empathy and humanity with *inductive reasoning and redactive response*. What the hell was that?

"All right," the graying major finally said, digging in. "I'm saying, you don't want him to be him more than you should want him to be him, do you?" When Les didn't answer, Bondini added, "He's gotta fit the rest of the profile, Les. The evidence. *All* the evidence."

Now, Les looked over. "You've got some?" he said. "Does the Bureau know about this?"

He was definitely running agency bullshit on his old friend. Bondini would have fired one of his own men on the spot for such impertinence, but he knew what Les Moore had been through. And he *was* a Fed.

And he was a friend. So, Fred Bondini just sighed, looked off and said, "There's some out there somewhere." He pined for it. "There's gotta be."

After a sorrowfully long moment, he looked back. "In the meantime," he said, "we've got a profile." He nodded down at his Doe Boy. "And we've got him. He'll match or he won't."

"You're guessing he won't," Les guessed.

"I'd like nothing better and you know it. But my gut on it is he won't. It's too easy." Reflecting on a thousand cases at once—a dozen years on this one alone—Bondini shook his head. "Call it an old law dog's hunch, but something ain't right. I got a Henry Li on this one, Les," he said glumly, referring to the famous forensic expert's often accurate hunches.

Les nodded and took a step around what had been a fit body before muscle and sinew became evidence. The killer's corpse wore alabaster skin, with the sharp lines of a blue-collar tan on his forearms and neck. Several dark moles stood out incongruously on his hairless chest and milky abdomen that could easily have been confused with dried drops of blood if one didn't look closely. His pubic hair was thick and fair, wet and peppered with ground litter, and he had a red birthmark on his left hip which resembled a crow in flight. Then there was that huge purple thing in the yellow ribbon.

"You're right," Les mused, "most of them aren't hung like him. You know, they have those little peanuts." He pressed his thumbnail to the first joint in his little finger. "Marjorie always thought that was what made them kill." He nodded agreement with his dead wife's assessment then concluded, "But this guy?" Les shook his head. "He did a sex show in Tijuana? He'd cause penis envy in the *mule*."

Bondini fought a smile. He wasn't going to let himself laugh until he'd had his say and heard what he needed to hear in return. This was more than the discovery of a naked Pillsbury found shot through the head in the woods, assassination style, at the Riverbend Killer's favorite dump site, in the exact spot Marjorie and Melissa Ann Moore's nude bodies had been discovered three years before, raped and mutilated nearly beyond comprehension. And this was Les Moore, husband and father, standing in the same spot, heading the investigation again.

Bondini had to wonder how Phil Brinkman had ever pulled enough strings to get Les back on the job, much less on this case, leading the Bureau's new TASK Force—Target Active Serial Killers. Christ, it even had a catchy name. Reporters were going to glom onto it like free food at a symposium on blunt force trauma.

Bondini knew the answer to his own question without asking. Les was that good. Policy becomes quickly moot and easily ignored when the brass wants a job done.

"I know what Marjorie thought," Bondini said in a steady tone, conceding without caving. "That's not what I'm saying."

"I know what you're saying, Fred," Les said. "And I'm not going to make a joke about it being a mountain of fertilizer even though the temptation is there, Major *Bandini*."

"I thought you said you weren't gonna do that," Bondini grumped, trying hard to see into Les's charcoaled soul. "Maybe I can't trust anything you say, anymore." His brow was as tight as a six-foot spring jack in a one-foot box.

Suddenly, Les was all Bureau — no angst, no anger, no accusation. No ambiance. He said, "You run your forensics, you'll get the results. The Bureau will assist and review. If he is, he is. If he's not, he's not. There's nothing I or anyone else can do about the truth other than accept it. Whatever it is."

Bondini felt hopeful but cautious. "And you'll keep looking?"

"Wherever the Bureau tells me to. Unless you give me a great lead. Which of course would supersede anything the Bureau might say at any time. But don't tell 'em I said so. They're touchy about that sort of thing. God forbid Local should get a leg up and squirt the first drop on the hydrant."

Bondini took the compliment well. He appreciated the analogy, old law dog that he was, and his brow loosened all the way down to his knees. He wasn't a hard-ass; in fact, he was a softhearted old fart in a sheriff's suit. He just didn't like anyone knowing it — with the possible exception of the man standing next to him.

"I know how bad you want him, Les," he said with respect and caution. He had a further thought, but it didn't find light.

Les said, "Enough to be sure this *is* him, Fred," his eyes a deep hard aqua, like a warm sea, and clear as a new purie. "Otherwise, what's the point?" He smiled and shrugged.

There's what Bondini had been waiting for: the old Les Moore — pragmatic, confident, detached; grinning with relaxed ease over a fresh corpse before he'd had his morning coffee.

Black.

Bondini's smile broke through, unabated. "You're back," he declared buoyantly, feeling instant, deep relief.

GLENN A. BRUCE

"Big as life," Les assured, with a matching grin.

"Big as *that*?" Bondini beamed down at the ribbon-wrapped leviathan, then actually *seeing* it, winced. "Lord God, look at the size'a that thing. No wonder she killed him. If I had to look forward to servicing that horse dick, I'da probably shot him too. Or shot myself so I wouldn't'a had to." He chortled contentedly and shook his round head.

Les only seemed to hear one word. "She?"

Bondini's joy sputtered; there was no sense pretending he hadn't said it, didn't know more than he was letting on. "Heels," he confessed. "Megan guessed about 150, 155, probably tall. Leggy."

Les threw him a *That's all?* look and Bondini shrugged honestly. So, Les asked, "Megan without-panty-lines?"

Bondini grinned broader than before, maybe than ever. "You're back, all right!" he confirmed, and swatted Les on his shoulder blade. Then he called up the bank.

"Hartley, get Heckle and Jeckle down here with that gurney, on the double!"

"Okay, Major," came a response, presumably Hartley's. His voice then shot off in another direction, "Hey, wake up—time to get your deceased," which was followed by a "Huh?" then an "Okay," then another voice, a woman's.

She didn't sound happy.

"Hold on, goddammit, I haven't seen the friggin' body! Jesus Christ! You Seatta-billies ever hear of a thing called procedure?"

Les looked at Bondini who looked at him and both shrugged with their eyes. A beat later, a dark blonde woman maybe a bit over thirty half-slipped, half-ran down the drop, gatling away. "Did you move him? You did, didn't you? You turned him over! Jesus. You just couldn't wait, could you?" She snarled from twenty-five feet away, apparently able to tell even from a distance that the dead had been disturbed.

As she shoved past them, eyeballing the corpse for signs she was right, the two lawmen looked her over, more as men than cops. Noting the opaque, impenetrable pantyhose hiding her calves and the plain gray business suit hiding everything else—hair pulled back, no discernible makeup—neither thought that with some fixing up she might pass for fairly attractive.

"Good ol' boys, God love you," she said, squatting down, and sniffed at the wounds, seeming to savor the nose, as if approving a fine wine. Her eyes were even closed.

When she opened them again, she caught both men staring at the white cotton crotch of her pantyhose. "Do you mind?" she demanded misanthropically.

Both men looked away.

She then rocked back on her heels, pulled a pushbutton ballpoint from her jacket pocket and poked at a flaky deposit on the killer's forehead. "Is this semen?" she asked, then answered, "Yeah."

Then she asked, "What's semen doing way up here? Anyone wonder that? Or is this fairly standard trajectory *out here in the woods*?" The last part had a mean twang. When it solicited no response, she made a snorking sound and went back to smelling the dead man's face.

Bondini turned to Les, his irritation on display for anyone caring to notice. "Who is this? Do you know this person?"

Les said, "Why do you always ask me? Maybe she's a vampire. Seems to like blood."

A short cackle bubbled up under Bondini's cholera and made him feel better.

Nothing seemed to faze their visitor. "Hell, this blood is nearly, *what*, fourteen hours old?" she said. "Vampires like fresh blood. Don't you read?" She was looking at Les. "Well, no, obviously not," she said, "or you'd know not to move the goddam body until everyone's had their chance at it."

"I only got here, myself," Les said in a thinly veiled way that pointed his invisible finger of blame directly at Local.

Bondini started to object, but the woman cut him off by informing Les, "No. I like the smell of Standard American load." Then she turned to Bondini. "Did you run powder tests yet?"

Bondini pinked up pretty good and looked away, damned if he'd answer, so she finished with Les. "That's what I like the smell of," she said, and bent down so fast she almost fell over, narrowly catching herself by jabbing her hand into the soil, rather than soiling the evidence. This time, she sniffed the killer's mouth.

"And garlic and beer," she said. "Probably pizza."

Suddenly, she was up in Bondini's face, again. "Are we looking into pizza joints yet?" It sounded confrontational.

Damned again, Bondini spluttered, "We'll wait for the contents of the stomach to come up." Then he heard what he'd said and added, "From downtown, goddammit!" and looked to Les for backup.

Les looked away.

It was time for Bondini to take back his crime scene. This usually necessitated yelling, so he bellowed, loudly enough for his loitering *lackeys* to hear, up above. "Who the hell let you down here? I told them no press until I told them!"

Realizing that sounded no better, Bondini decided to switch to his always effective rant-and-rave tactic, guaranteed to run off even the most determined scandal hound or bureaucrat. But the oddly disturbing young woman stopped him short.

"This gets me past 'em every time," she said, and held up her plasticized photo ID that read Special Agent Cyndra L. Baker, TASK Force. Three, large blue letters shown prominently.

FBI.

Cindy nodded toward Les. "He knows who I am. He's just being the arrogant ass Brinkman warned me about in DC"

Phil Brinkman, their bloated Bureau boss, had long since abandoned the Quantico Hole, six floors down, for a high-rise suite with a partial view of The Mall. An unapologetic career climber, he was feared by some and avoided by the rest, which was precisely why Cindy dropped his name. Phil Brinkman always got a reaction. Though in this case, not the one she anticipated.

Les said, "Well, I guess formulating *opinions* is easy when you're sitting behind a desk, checking boxes and filling in blanks all day. You know, someplace safe where you can't get shot at. Personally, I wouldn't know." He offered a smile that wasn't genuine.

Bondini followed with one that was. He hated Phil Brinkman, but then Brinkman was an easy man to hate.

Cindy shot a quick scowl at Bondini then told Les, "I wouldn't either, but so far, you're making Brinkman look pretty sage." She turned back to Bondini. "That means smart." She offered him the same approximate smile Les had given her.

Bondini's grin departed.

Satisfied, Cindy turned back to Les. "So, I think I'll keep listening to him."

Les shrugged. "Your life. Give it to 'em if you want. They'll be happy to take it." He'd already given one to the Bureau. It hadn't worked out. This one was his.

Cindy stared blankly a moment, then started up the bank, calling ahead. "Tell that forensics team to hold up." When no one replied, she shouted. "I *said*, tell that fucking forensics team to hold up! Somebody answer me, goddammit!"

An anonymous voice came back, "Yes, ma'am," followed by, "Tell Megan to hold up. The FBI bitch wants her." Some muted laughter rolled behind him, then an HP guy at the top of the hill added, "Maybe for a date," and a few more raspy law laughs trailed off. They'd all thought Agent Baker was a trifle butch for their tastes.

Halfway up, Cindy turned back and called down, "Did you find the car yet?"

Bondini looked away.

"Why am I not surprised," Cindy said, then continued dodging and slipping back up the hill, admonishing the hapless HP on top, "If I wanted a date with a woman, I'd be man enough to ask. Can't say it looks like I'd say the same for you."

Les and Bondini could just see Cindy through the leaves as she reached the top, looked both ways and said, "All right, who called me a bitch? Anyone have the balls to own up to that one?" There were no takers. "That's what I figured."

Finally, she turned on the steroid Camel twins. "You two wake up and go get the stiff, if it's not too much goddam trouble. And try not to drop him. We might need him for evidence. You know what that is, right? Evidence?"

There came a low, unison, "Yes, ma'am."

"And put out those cigarettes. Didn't your mothers tell you not to smoke? Those things'll kill you worse than a drunk in a pickup."

Together the two young body snatchers weighed at least five hundred pounds and could rip a twelve-cow barn down with their bare hands in under an hour, but they gave another unison, "Yes, ma'am," flipped their butts away — without a last puff — and grabbed their gurney.

They would not drop this body.

Bondini let go a string of unintelligible expletives, but somehow felt no better for it. He had a Henry Li about her, too.

"My new partner," Les said. "Looks like we're in for a lotta laughs."

Bondini wasn't laughing already.

Chapter 2 – Getting to Know You

An hour-fifteen later, Cindy opened the trunk of her tan rental to make sure she'd packed tampons. She hadn't.

The last HP was pulling off—the one she'd reamed earlier. He slowed his loaded Charger next to her.

"Sorry, ma'am, about before," he said. "It's just you came on a little strong."

"Yeah, I guess I did," Cindy allowed, her eyes momentarily adrift in happy recall. She had made quite an entrance. They'd be talking about her for days.

Women had to do things differently, Cindy had learned the hard way. Still, she heard the trooper's point, appreciated his candor and effort. "Sorry. I was pissed."

The young man nodded. "I understand, ma'am. There's a lot to be pissed about these days." And he drove off.

"There sure is," Cindy agreed, shutting her trunk, freeing up a view of Les in the open front door of his rental, staring off into the woods. He was not inviting intrusion, but Cindy walked over anyway and leaned against the rear pillar of the Buick.

"Which one you wanna keep, which one you wanna turn in?" she asked.

"Huh?" Les said, looking up, his face reflecting nothing more than an interrupted distant memory.

"The blue one or the tan one."

He looked at her, then the cars. "The Buick."

"Keep it or trade it in."

"Keep it."

Cindy nodded, looked to see which one was the Buick, then gazed into the trees with him, trying to see what he was seeing as a lesser mind-track made small talk.

"Les Moore. You get a lotta ribbing on that?"

"Enough to fill a body bag," he told her as if he'd said it a million times. Still, Cindy chuckled, and they both continued to stare ahead, though her thoughts were on trying to guess his, and his were his own.

"Why didn't you tell them I was on my way?" she finally asked.

"Didn't know you were."

"Brinkman didn't tell you?" She sounded surprised.

"Didn't tell me when."

"It's not that far from Portland."

"He didn't say you were *in* Portland." Les stood out of the Buick and stretched. "You'll find over time that Brinkman can't even get the behind-the-desk stuff right. I've seen him get stumped on whether to use one or two sugars in his coffee. Creamer sends him into an absolute tailspin."

He added, as if just figuring out, "Oh yeah. Those little boxes he fills in? Crosswords. Those tough *TV Guide* ones. You know, 'Blank's Island, with the Skipper and Maryann.' I don't know how he handles the stress."

Cindy knew Les was slumming comedically—much had been made of her new partner's wit—but she figured he was exhausted, too. If he was half as tired as she was, this was going to be a long case. And they had just begun.

"This job takes it outa ya, huh?" she said, trying her best to sound like one of the guys.

Les stared a beat. "Are you gay?"

Cindy felt like she'd been punched. Still, she took only a second to declare, "That's none of your fucking business." Les didn't look away. Surprised at how uncomfortable she felt, Cindy stepped away from the car.

Les pursued her. "Might make a difference," he said.

Cindy circled until both were on the double yellow line, faced off. "Why?" she asked, feeling more up to the challenge. "You wouldn't hit on me?"

"I wouldn't hit on you anyway. We're partners."

"That's a refreshing word," Cindy said. "Can't say as I expected it."

"I follow orders as well as the next guy." Les shrugged.

"That's not what Brinkman says."

"Yeah, but if Brinkman was alive a hundred years ago, he would've said the world was flat. In fact, I think he still says that. So, are you?"

"Flat? No."

"I can see that. Are you?"

Freely showing her effrontery, Cindy bucked, "What difference does it make? Are you?"

"No," Les said without hesitation and waited for her answer.

Cindy pursed her lips. "I have to say I find this entirely offensive."

"So you are," he surmised.

Cindy let several clenched moments slip by then said, "No, I am not." But she was annoyed to have given him the satisfaction.

"Good," Les declared, dismissing the entire dialectic. "We're dealing with murdered women most of the time, killed by men. I just needed to know." He then walked over to the black-burned tire slick and squatted, allowing his fingertips to idle in the clean coolness of morning dewdrops that still clung to the collapsed grass, shiny as polished onyx.

Cindy pursued him. "Should I be concerned you're heterosexual? For the same reason?"

Two could play.

"No," Les said in a way that indicated, without words or emphasis, he was done with this line of inquiry — and she should be, too. Then he turned back to stare into the disturbed tranquility of the dense wood, humidity hanging like someone's last breath.

Les might have been done, but Cindy wasn't. "So, are you over your... problem?" Her indirectness indicated more kindness and understanding than she had wanted.

"If you mean the impotency, yeah," Les said, and stood to face her. "It took a while, but the masturbation therapy helped a lot. You masturbate much? Out here on the road all the time?"

Cindy at least acted unfazed. "I didn't read that part of your file."

"Oh, so you *do* know what the word 'personal' means. Obviously, you didn't take *everything* Brinkman said to heart."

"Hey, I needed to know what I was walking into," Cindy said with as much conviction as she could muster. Then she added offhandedly, "You could've read *my* file."

"I did," Les said flatly. "Quick read." And he started back for the Buick.

Cindy bristled. "If you're referring to my relatively short service record —"

"Relatively short?" Les cut in. "Is that the new Bureau PC for nearly nonexistent? We are talking about one assignment, right? Playing a teenager? I mean, that part wasn't overstated?"

Unfortunately, not.

"Okay," Cindy began, indignant but choosing to display impatience instead. "I may not have the years you have, but I was never referred to OPR, either. And what there is on my record —"

"Is exemplary!" Les proclaimed, stopping in the middle of the road again to face her. "There's no one else with your background and extensive knowledge who *has* any more years. From what I hear, you're almost Robert Ressler and John Douglas rolled into one! Less some practical experience, of course."

Oh, he had to get that in.

"You aced hostage negotiation like basic math, explosive devices like Ted Kaczynski, handwriting analysis like a gypsy tea reader, and I hear you're pretty good on pretext calls, too. Fooled your own brother for a full hour, once. You know your weapons like you know your own face, and shoot like a man — highest 1 percent, as I recall. No, I couldn't ask for a better partner."

"So, what's the problem?"

"I didn't ask," Les said flatly, and turned for the car.

Then he added. "And as for the Office of *Professional Responsibility*..." He made the very concept sound as ridiculous and hypocritical as he obviously thought it was.

Cindy wasn't interested in anything Les Moore had to say about ethics, not after everything Brinkman had drilled into her about his lack of them. So, she sloughed his opinions off with, "Look, this wasn't my call. The Bureau —"

"...hates loners and loves suck-ups," Les finished. "I hear you give good politics."

Now that was offensive. "Says who?"

"Brinkman." Les shrugged, as if stating the dull and the obvious — which was how he often referred to their boss.

Cindy was pulled up short.

"Oh, he's loyal to no one," Les assured her. "You'll learn in time. We call it Brinkmanship. His pathetic attempts to keep us from 'bonding' and teaming up on him. You know: Divided we fall into line. United, we conquer his puny ego, knock him off his imaginary throne, and take over the asylum."

Cindy was decidedly not comfortable with such overtly seditious mixed metaphors uttered out loud — even if she and Les were the only living souls for five miles in any direction.

"But don't worry," Les summed up. "You're tops on Wilstrong's list, and he's the one who has to balance the EEO books at the end of the day."

Now, he had crossed the line. Cindy blurted, and she hated to blurt, "Are you saying my assignment to this case is political? Because I'm a woman? Because I'm a relative rookie? What?" Her voice was going up. A bad sign, which sounded like losing, and Cindy hated losing worse than blurting.

Worse than anything.

"Because you were second in your class," Les reported. "Which really pissed you off by the way, didn't it? Be honest now."

Cindy looked down. *Damn!* She hated looking down.

He went on. "Because you turned down instructor to be a field agent. Because you did your master's thesis at Columbia on *Serial Killing and the American Dream*, a thesis which featured yours truly, without so much as dinner or a cigarette, I should point out. Not that I'd take the cigarette, mind you — I gave them up two years ago — but it's the thought that counts."

Cindy continued not to look up. He was right. Over half of the five-hundred-plus pages in her thesis were about her new partner, even though she'd never met him or even spoken to him once. She'd asked, through channels, but he declined. Then, he disappeared.

"Because you're a woman," Les went on. "Because you're a *definite* rookie, and because they don't really trust me out here alone again, but they know I won't let you get in my way enough to stop me from actually doing my job, which is what they really want, because they know I'm the perfect pawn to pull it off, because I care too much for my own damn good."

He paused a beat, then smiled. "Take your pick."

A stupider person might have taken the smile for sincere. Cindy wasn't taking it for anything other than the facetious punctuation he meant it to be.

But she had the gnawing feeling he was right.

To try and stave off that sensation, more than to defend anything, Cindy tried a patronizing, "Look, obviously you read my paper —"

Les cut her off — at the knees.

"You're assuming a lot for an employee of the Bureau," he said with startling cruelty. "They must train 'em a little more slipshod than they used to. You know, you'll never make G-14 thinking like that. No posting at Quantico, no unit chief stripes, nada. Brinkman may be an asshole, but he's stupid and stingy, too. Not to mention a manipulative, corporate thug. Especially when it comes to promotions. Trust me on that one."

Cindy tried, "Okay. I know you're thinking—"

"Now we go for the wild assumptions!" Les pounced. "How'd you get this job? Your mother sleep with Hedgcock back when?"

Hedgcock. William H. Webster. FBI director '78-'87, when Cindy was born. Good reference, good disguise, good call. Instead, she went with, "My mother is dead," and left off the icing. Well off.

"Sorry, I forgot," Les said sincerely.

But in his unflinching barrage of malevolent cynicism and militant disaffection, Les had made Cindy's true position crystal clear. She was a babysitter, here to help the spoiled-genius-slash-returned-lost-child with his murder case homework; to keep Phil Brinkman informed in the event Les started straying too far afield; maybe even to keep him out of trouble! But more than anything, she was to stay out of his way. Cindy realized, right then, she had been given the short end of a very shitty stick she'd be expected to clutch tightly, with her gritted teeth, for a very long time. There would be no hope whatsoever of transferring out without her career path going up in smoke, and no one would come racing to her rescue if things got out of hand.

Hell, they were *planning* on it!

The still-waking awareness of her meaningless role in all of this ran through Special Agent Cyndra Baker like disease and made her ache. So thoroughly did this realization take the sting out of her counterattack that Cindy was able only to splutter an impotent, maladroit, "God, you're an even bigger asshole than Brinkman said!"

Which had nothing to do with what she was thinking or feeling, and killed her to have said anything so incredibly trivial. Hell, she wasn't even thinking he was an asshole. She was thinking what an asshole she had been for not seeing what Brinkman had done—burned her with her own damn Blue Flame. She had wanted this assignment too badly.

The story of her life.

Les gazed idly as Cindy struggled for some semblance of control. She's heard he loved befuddlement on others and likely knew that she was above a retort as lowly and uninspired as her last and that if Brinkman was openly calling him an asshole to her face, to his next partner, the mood in Washington must be dark and desperate — total chaos — and that he probably thought, *Perfect!* They'd leave him alone.

She knew she would.

"It keeps me going," Les said, grinning, and turned again for the Buick.

Cindy managed to sound... briefed. "They put me on this case because I know profiling. I know your work. I know I can help."

"You know a lot," Les said. But he didn't sound too impressed.

"I'm willing to concede you know more," she said.

Les raised an eyebrow. "Say, you do give good politics. Brinkman was right for once. Wow, this must be some sort of record for him. One in a row. You must inspire greatness in the disaffected masses. Brinkman right about something. Mm-mm-mm. Imagine that."

Cindy huffed, "Well, he was sure right about you," and turned away quickly. Now, she was huffing. Good God, this was humiliating. She was better than this. She had three brothers, for Christ sake!

"Oh, come on," Les said. "Brinkman doesn't know his ass from his face." Then, feigning contemplation, he said, "Come to think of it, they are pretty hard to tell apart. But you see my point." Then he added, "By the way, you know how to tell the difference? He shaves one, and the other has a nose."

Christ, Les could have been one of her brothers!

Cindy pulled back her smile before Les could notice. "The question is, do you see mine?" With this guy on a roll, she then felt the need to clarify before he made some crack about her ass. "My point."

"Which one? I lost track at the part where you said Phil was actually right about something." Les chuckled as if still marveling over such a disclosure.

At the Buick, Les hung his jacket in the back, closed the door and sat into the front seat, good to go.

"Okay, look," Cindy said. "We're getting nowhere fast here. I see what you're saying. I'll give it serious consideration. How's that?"

"Do whatever you like," Les said, reaching for the door while starting the car. "I've got a pressing engagement with a cheeseburger and a malted."

Cindy let the archaic soda shop reference slide past, stopping him, and the door, to try the sincere approach. "I admit I learned everything I know because I had a detached interest in the phenomenon in college. I studied it."

Les cautioned, "I wouldn't go there if I were you," and tugged at the door.

Cindy held tight—and went there. "What I'm saying is, I didn't learn it by living it when my wife and daughter—"

"See you around the pool," Les said and yanked the door free, slamming it shut and throwing the dark blue Regal in Drive.

Cindy stared, dumbfounded. "Don't you drive off while I'm yelling at you!" she ordered. But what came out was really more of a shriek.

A shriek!

Without looking, Les stood on the gas and tore away, slinging grass and grit on Cindy's twelve-dollar, low-heeled Payless pumps.

Beige.

"We're partners, goddammit!" Cindy shouted after him. "We're gonna have to talk about it sooner or later!"

The V-6 whined and strained, RPMs continuing to climb as the Buick crossed the narrow bridge, over the river that flowed ever-peaceful toward the sea.

No. Les Moore wasn't coming back to discuss it now or ever.

"Shit!"

Cindy kicked at the grass and made the frustration face she hated feeling on herself. "Shit, shit, shit, shit, shit!" The day had turned to total "Shit!" She kicked again.

This time, the heel of her right pump caught the edge of the pavement and broke off.

Cindy stared down at the orphaned heel, then up. Though she could no longer hear Les's rental, she could make out some chrome flickering behind the highway brush, having come out of the trees and rounded the last curve before One-Something straightened out those flat few miles back to the highway.

"Give good politics, my ass," Cindy groused. "If you only knew." She picked up the heel and put it in her pocket, boiling. "If you only knew!" she yelled after him.

What a dose of ass-kissing, brown-nosing, shit-eating politics she'd had to serve up for Brinkman under Wilstrong's watchful eye to get this job. Afterward, she threw up.

Cindy hated Phil Brinkman. He was truly the most awful, smarmy puddle of sexist, intolerant, uncaring human waste she had ever met. In her estimation, Phil Brinkman was only the tiniest notch above the abhorrent serial subjects of her much-heralded paper.

Of course, she couldn't let Les Moore know how she felt about their boss. Her secret loathing was the only card she had left.

Frustrated beyond her ability to cope, Cindy fell back against the tan Taurus four-door, just now realizing that everyone was gone. Cindy was alone in Riverbend.

Her focus returned immediately.

There had been sixteen women found along the half-mile stretch over seven years, plus the others up around Seattle proper. Belleview, Woodinville, Sequim. Down in Vancouver, up in Bellingham. Even one out in Coolee City. Who knew how many more might be scattered around?

Crossing the road to the slick, black tire marks, Cindy stared down into the thick Pacific Northwest forest below, seeing the nude body clearly in her memory—the spatters, the ribbon, the huge penis she'd had a tough time *not* mentioning while parading out her angry/tough act for Les and Bondini—and the air seemed to freeze around her in anticipation of the bad to come.

Cindy was certain that the guy they took away in the coroner's van wasn't the killer of Les Moore's wife and daughter, or any of the others. RB, as he was called within the unit, had proved far too smart to let himself get whacked here in his namesake, on his knees, naked and unarmed. If you were going to off the Riverbend Killer, in Riverbend, by the Riverbend Bridge, you had to be a lot smarter than whoever killed this poor schmo, and a whole lot less attached.

No, the body in the coroner's van didn't belong to Riverbend, and this case wasn't close to over. It was just beginning. For sure, this one would be tough, and tough on whoever was assigned to it. But the agent who broke it would be a hero.

Or, more specifically, a heroine.

This thought brought the first real smile of the day. Holding that notion, savoring it, Federal Bureau of Investigation Special Agent Cyndra Lynn Baker, TASK Force Second in Command—so what if there was no one else below her—got in her rented Ford and headed for Hertz. She had made the right decision accepting this posting. This was the kind of case that made careers, with the kind of stakes Cindy loved most—all or nothing. This case was perfect.

Yeah, she'd go all the way with Les Moore on this. If she didn't kill him first.

Chapter 3 – The Trailer

Fred Bondini's King County Sheriff's Department building was lavish considering that it had been commissioned in an era of much-ballyhooed cutbacks. He'd gotten the last big chunk of law enforcement money before all funding dried up, so the new edifice had every technological advance and modern comfort available—which made Cindy even more disagreeable when she saw the space he had allocated the TASK team.

"What was this, the construction site trailer?" she asked within four seconds of entering.

"It's quiet, it's got heat," Les said, without looking up from his files—Riverbend, no doubt.

He had catching up to do.

Cindy nodded emptily and glanced out one of the two grimy windows to see if the day still looked cold outside. If anything, it looked worse. So, she strolled around, as much as one can actually stroll in a single-wide, and took inventory, checking the back room first.

Storage. *Of course* this was the site trailer! Then she picked up the smudgy pot. "Our own coffee maker, wow. I wonder if anyone's carbon-dated this thing, yet." Cindy tried to see Les through the layers of residue. His image was murky and dark, hard to discern. *Kind of exactly like him*, she thought, and put the pot back.

"Yeah," Cindy said with mock melancholy, walking around, "these desks must have seen some great detective work back in the Great Depression."

Then she said, as if pondering the notion. "Didja ever wonder why, if it was so bad, they called it the 'Great' Depression? As opposed to, say, the Truly Awful Depression That Almost Destroyed the Country?

"I mean, I for one denote 'great' with, well... good stuff. As in, say, 'great sex,' or a really 'great' cheese dog. Not a depression. Even a really big one. *Especially* a really big one. I've been depressed, and it's no bag 'a bon-bons, let me tell you. And if it was *really* big?" She made a sound something like a turtle squirting eggs into a hole on the beach.

Les grinned but didn't take his face out of his work. So, Cindy said, "Hey, whattaya call the tiniest dick in the world?"

Les glanced up, his brow pinched as if to abhor a lowly dick joke from his new partner. Already? Most agents tended toward the same tired gags about autopsy blunders, racial inequities, botched suicides — and, of course, the always reliable dick joke. "I don't know," Les said, sounding disappointed, and turned back to his work. "What?"

Cindy said, "I don't know either, but maybe if we ask Brinkman."

Les looked up and said, "Don't try to get on my good side. It's too early on." But he was grinning as he put his face back in his file.

"Okay." Cindy chose the desk farthest away from him, facing the wall, where she could doodle in private.

***

Lunch thankfully came quickly. Cindy knew it was lunch because Les got up, stretched and left. When she went outside, the rental was gone.

After cussing her way to the curb, Cindy looked down the road, spotted a diner about a quarter mile off, and started hoofing in the omnipresent gray drizzle. When she was about halfway to the diner, Les sped past in the Buick. He didn't stop, didn't wave, didn't even let off the gas. Gray road spray roiled around Cindy like the ill wind she guessed it presaged, and she cussed him again. This was going to be a long case.

The Olympia View Diner, which had no actual view of anything, much less the mountains, had been built around an actual railcar. The menu was small, but the place was warm and cozy and didn't smell too greasy. In fact, it smelled pretty good, reminding Cindy of the scents that used to waft from her mother's kitchen. Salisbury steak and real mashed potatoes, sweet buttered corn off the cob and lemon angel pie. Mom had cooked a dinner like that every night for Dad and the boys, along with their friends and their friends' friends, for over a third of a century, until she got breast cancer and died.

The cashier told Cindy to sit anywhere, as did a passing waitress seconds later, but only one seat stood unoccupied, a stool at the counter between a 350-pound truck driver in a black "Southern Pride Don't Die" T-shirt—which sported a dead deer draped over the back of a rebel flag-clad monster truck—and one of the local cops Cindy had insulted at the Riverbend crime scene. The clock clicked 12:15. No one was getting up.

Cindy headed for the counter.

The trucker didn't seem to notice her, but Local did. He tipped his head a full quarter-inch in recognition as she sat. Cindy returned the nod in precise duplication then perused the specials, handwritten on a flap of robin's egg blue typing paper and clipped over the right side of the plastic sleeve menu. Liver and onions, pot roast and mashed potatoes, Buffalo wings and steak fries. Halibut.

Cindy had about settled on meatloaf when the cop offered a surprising bit of gossip.

"Two of those women had been sodomized. Repeatedly. Premortem."

Cindy turned toward him as the cop delicately wrapped some onions around a piece of liver and lifted it all to his mouth. "Excuse me?" she said.

"No bleeding," he said, and consumed the drippy bite.

Cindy stared, no idea what his point was, but sure he must have one—and that her blood sugar must be very low. A sharp voice stabbed through her clouded ruminations.

"What's your addiction, sweetie?"

Cindy spun to find a tall woman, about fifty, grinning at the cop who was grinning back at her. "What?" Cindy said.

The waitress pulled a shiny black pushbutton pen from her high tease of lacquered red hair. The pen advertised Mutt's Transmission Service and featured a cartoon bulldog wearing a studded collar and a toothy grin, holding a monkey wrench in his paw. The redhead tapped Cindy's list of Lunch Specials with the pen clicker. "We got crab cakes off the menu," she said. "Soup's potato cheese."

Oh, the menu. Cindy said she'd need another minute.

"That's fine, honey," her waitress said. "Shout when you're ready." And she hurried away for her next order-up.

Cindy took a long, deep breath, then turned to the cop. "You're talking about the victims of the Riverbend Killer, I presume." Now, she thought she knew why.

The cop nodded, sipped some iced tea, then put the glass down silently, apparently in no hurry to carry Cindy's half of the conversation as well as his own. All Cindy could think was, *Iced tea in this weather. Lunatics!* But she said, "So, I'll also assume you're referring to this guy's huge c —"

Cindy stifled her vernacular. "Unusually large penis."

The trucker looked over, mid-dunk, eyebrows up. For a moment, Cindy felt the compunction to edify for the fat man she didn't know — codependence from another life. "I'm a..." was as far as she got before she simply waved him and his opinions off and, catching sight of the waitress breezing toward her again.

"I'll have the vegetable plate," she called out, "steamed broccoli, corn, red potatoes, and a dry-salad-with-lemon." Her words got faster and closer together as the waitress passed by at hypersonic speed.

Big Red, as the regulars called her — she took the nickname as a sincere form of flattery — boomed back, "Gimme a minute, honey, I'm two short today." She then grabbed up four orders, balancing the hot plates along her arm as deftly as a circus performer, and sped off for The Caboose, actually a freight car annexed as a back room.

Cindy turned back to the cop. "So, you don't think our John Doe is Riverbend," she said, and cracked open a pack of saltines to stave off the effects of her plummeting blood sugar! She didn't want to mention that she shared that opinion. Not yet.

"Just a thought," was all the more the local cop had to say. He grabbed his check, stood, nodded a quarter inch in farewell and strolled to the register. Suddenly and mysteriously, he had finished his meal. Cindy watched as he laid down his money and stepped outside to hobnob with some other cops who all wore wide hats and big grins — guffawing at dick jokes, no doubt. Or sodomy.

Or Cindy.

Cindy grunted, turned back for more saltines and was jolted clean off her stool by Big Red slamming her plate of hot, steaming veggies on the counter as she sped past. "Coffee?"

"Tea. Hot," Cindy exacted. "With-lemon-please!"

Red didn't acknowledge, as she hadn't before, but steamed broccoli, fiesta corn, and mashed potatoes with brown gravy stared up at her as Red flew past in the other direction, dropping off the hot tea, plain salad, and lemon slices. "We're outa the reds," she said. "If you don't want the mashed, shove 'em aside. I didn't charge you."

"Thanks," Cindy said as she stared into the buttery white peaks topped with hot brown lava and thought how serendipity was a divine companion—at least when it came to saturated fat.

"That stuff'll go straight to your hips." The female voice was unfamiliar.

Cindy turned to see a woman in civvies, but something about her said cop—the lean build, stiff stature, and noticeable lack of a neck.

"Detective Lorman. Anne," she said. "You took my case." She didn't seem to harbor any anger over it, but neither did she appear to be wallowing in good cheer.

The sturdy female detective sat down where the truck driver had been—somehow, he had finished and left as well—and said toward the busy phalanx of waitresses by the heat lamps, "Dee, let me have the Chinese chicken salad, goo on the side." Big Red nodded as she loaded up her arms with more hot plates and took her balancing act on the road.

"Cyndra Baker. Cindy. Sorry," Cindy offered genuinely.

"Yeah, I know," Lorman said, followed by, "You ask me, every one of those murderous sons of bitches deserves to end up in a low, wet spot in the woods." Then she called over to Red, "And tea today, Dee, honey."

Red grabbed an already full glass of iced tea, plunked it down on the counter and sped off with a full pot of coffee for refills, three desserts in her free hand. Cindy watched in amazement. "How do they do that?" She'd known early on in college she wasn't cut out for waitressing.

"They got no conscience," Anne Lorman said.

Cindy looked at the waitress, then at Lorman, wished her blood sugar would come up, and shoveled a few quick bites of hot veggies. Then what Lorman meant hit her. "Oh, you mean serial killers. Right."

The detective gave a sidelong glance as Red banged her salad down, dressing on the side. Cindy jumped but was relieved to see Red whammed everybody's food down, even people she seemed to like.

Then Lorman said, "Oh, you mean Dee," apparently relieved to see Cindy wasn't a complete Zone Case. "Yeah, she's a hard worker. Four kids, every one of 'em worse than the last. I've arrested three of 'em myself, and more than once." She poured the entire contents of the side dressing on her salad and asked speedy Dee for more.

Cindy guessed Lorman's weight to be at least 140, 145, maybe 150—which made Cindy feel good about her own 118-pound frame—though most of Lorman's bulk seemed to be muscle, no doubt wrenched from countless hours in Bondini's new gym. She wore no jewelry.

"These cocksuckers," Lorman launched right in around a mouthful of, "crispies. I can't get enough of 'em. Dee, honey..." And she held up a few wonton noodles.

"Women..." she then said, shoveling in a good half-pound of salad from her tub of greens, "aren't safe anywhere these days." She *almost* chewed before swallowing. "But no serial-killing sonofabitch is gonna fuck with me and my forty. I'll blow his nuts off."

Cindy could see Detective Lorman's .40 magnum peeking out from under her light jacket. She also appeared to have a pair of forties above her duty weapon, Cindy mused, feeling both inadequate and happy she was blessed with somewhat smaller than average but gravity-defying breasts more like her Aunt Fran's than her mother's 38-Ds.

They had killed her.

Lorman suddenly stopped eating and said, "You know, I don't mind so much giving up the case before I even got it. That's why I didn't bother to go out there when I heard you people were here." She paused, rolling her tongue across an errant piece of salad on a molar. "What pisses me off is Fred Bondini continues to kiss the asses of every goddamned—"

Bang-bang! More noodles and dressing.

"Thanks, Dee. Don't forget Mikey's arraignment Tuesday." Red waved and picked up an order without missing a beat.

Lorman stared into her wontons. "You see," she said to Cindy, "we don't get many great cases out here. And we know what we're doing."

"I'm sure you do," Cindy said, noting the challenge in Lorman's tone.

"Yeah. And what I'm saying is—"

"You'd like us to keep our collective noses out of your case."

Anne Lorman looked her over. "Yeah," she said, then turned back to her salad and took three bites at once. "But I know you won't."

She went back to chasing crispies around her oily salad bowl.

After Lorman left, a few minutes later—her salad vat looking licked-clean—another young male cop came up and stood over the vacant stool. "She's all right," he said to Cindy. "Good cop. A little edgy when we find one of these Swamp Things, but..."

His shrug finished his thought.

He looked to be in his late twenties, handsome, five-eight or nine and trim; maybe Lorman's weight, maybe a few pounds more. He had dark hair, short but stylish, and was sucking a plastic toothpick carelessly.

"You're her partner," Cindy assessed.

He nodded. "Chris Hines." He didn't offer to shake. "Good luck," he said, then smiled around his toothpick, winked, and left.

Bam! Bam! Hot water and a bowl of lemon wedges.

***

Twenty minutes and a third cup of hot tea later, Cindy looked up from her walk in the Seattle drizzle to see Les speed past, again, headed back to the trailer. He didn't stop to offer a ride. If anything, he sped up.

***

Cindy didn't see Les around the hotel all weekend. Nor the Buick. With little else to do, Cindy reviewed the file he had dropped on her construction trailer desk at the end of business on Friday. His report of their hour in Riverbend was brief.

So, Cindy expanded his version of the events, taking all Saturday and most of Sunday to do so in her room. During breaks, she watched the same lousy cable movie over and over, four times by Sunday midnight, quoting bad dialogue along with the terminally half-naked actors the last two times, verbatim.

Cindy Baker had a remarkable facility for recalling trivia in great detail and had always thought such a talent would serve her well in police work. So far it had only made passing tests easier and watching old movies unbearable.

***

Monday seemed to take forever to roll around, but Cindy made sure she was at the trailer first to deposit her amended version of their report on Les's desk before he arrived. She arranged it just the way she wanted then sat down in the corner to doodle.

And wait.

When Les finally arrived — late, Cindy noted — he took his sweet time. Coffee. Overcoat. Briefcase. Bathroom. More coffee. Then out to the car, return with a file, peruse a few pages, out to the car again, once more to the bathroom.

"Jesus Christ," Cindy agonized to herself. Men and their tiny bladders.

After at least twenty interminable minutes, Les finally settled in and opened the reworked report, flipping through it in less than a minute, then pushing the folder aside. He said nothing.

So, Cindy was forced to. "Well?"

Les looked up briefly, then down again. "Sodomy, pizza, beer, possible killer other than the theorized prostitute. It's all here."

Not all, Cindy thought. She had chosen not to mention Detective Anne Lorman, or her partner Hines, as potential suspects. That's how career tracks got derailed — agents', not Locals'.

Les pulled a new file from his briefcase — it looked like that Sacramento Migrant Murderer number — and started reading, jotting a note here and there, never returning to Riverbend at all.

After two torturous hours of this, during which Cindy walked past Les to the bathroom four times — once when she actually had to go — Les stood, went outside again, and…

Didn't come back.

When Cindy looked, the Buick was gone. Again. She called him a prick, mostly because she had to, then turned back inside. The report was still on his desk.

Keeping a cautious eye on the door, and the narrow strip of window that allowed a sliver-view of the parking lot, Cindy moved closer, regarding the closed folder with great caution, as if it were alive. Using a pencil — not her actual fingers — Cindy lifted the top and peeked inside the file, her head cocked at an angle, as if checking for land mines.

The file appeared safe, so Cindy scanned Page One — expecting the worst — but nothing appeared to have been altered. Page Two seemed similarly unmolested, as did the next three pages. Finally, after a deep breath, Cindy turned to the last page and there was Les's signature. And what a signature it was. *Egotistical maniac.* She closed the file.

After checking outside again—still no Buick—Cindy went back to her desk. She couldn't say she felt good, but she felt better. In a really queasy way. What was he up to? What did he know that she didn't? How would this come back to haunt her?

She got up and retrieved the file.

For the next three hours, Cindy read the report over and over, looking for that one word which, removed or out of place, could invite her first letter of censure—or reassignment. She couldn't find so much as a moved comma. But Satan himself couldn't have come up with a more devious hell than having Les flip through those pages so fleetingly, so disinterestedly—then sign it and leave. Cindy knew he was out there somewhere, laughing.

Les and Satan.

***

At exactly 5:01, King County Sheriff Frederick Jonas Bondini came out the side door of his Super Station thinking life was good. He climbed in his new, roomy Police Special Suburban with leather, military-grade GPS, two onboard computers, and mini-flat-screens in the backseat (for whom?), compliments of the county, and mentally patted himself on the back. Despite his *Henry Li*, he was seemingly about to close if not the oldest, then undeniably the most publicly visible, case on the county books. It must be true; all the media were reporting it. Hell, they were shouting it every hour on the hour.

Whoever had killed his Pillsbury was the Feds' problem now. Bondini didn't even care who she was. Or he. Or she-he! As far as Fred Bondini was concerned, anyone who killed a serial killer should get a friggin' medal.

Sure, he'd look for the Killer's killer. Just not too hard.

Fred Bondini depressed the Drive button of his new, full-sized, luxury SUV, happy that the only lingering loose end was the killer's missing car, but certain it would turn up sooner or later, probably sooner. Once his detectives identified the make and model, color and condition, they'd have the vehicle in impound back of the station in a matter of days, if not hours, and he'd look good in the eyes of the Bureau, finding the final piece of the puzzle. He might even get a complimentary call from Phil Brinkman, the notorious ass-chewer from hell, who would have to eat some crow for a change and admit Local had been, "Very helpful on this one, Fred."

Imagining Brinkman's fawning unctuousness, ordered by Wilstrong above, brought a happy glaze, which spread like merry rose-colored glaucoma across Bondini's tired old eyes as he turned the corner and peered into his impound yard. As usual, there were a few cars and light trucks—mostly parking-ticket tows, a few DUIs, and one or two drug seizures—nothing out of the ordinary. So, nothing about the dented, ocher Monte Carlo with the balding tires, peeling tan vinyl top, and rusted rocker panels spoke to Fred Bondini at all. He didn't even see it.

Chapter 4 – Pittsburgh

The Pittsburgh Slasher seemed to know when some nurse was going to risk walking to her car alone in the middle of the night. Then he was there, and she was gone—another sad story beginning with "A woman's nude body" and ending with a local body of water. A later report would verify she had been an RN. There hadn't been an LVN or candy striper in the bunch.

Virtually nothing was known about this SK. Forensics had found a partial print on one of the earlier victims' cars some four years before, but the smudged pattern wasn't a match to anyone anywhere, or to any other case, so it turned out to be useless. Even the FBI's fingerprint unit, IAFIS, came up with nothing. The Slasher had evidently never been printed. Nor had he ever been in the military, applied for a driver's license, been arrested, or cashed a check. Apparently, he'd never been anywhere or done anything at all.

As far as Pittsburgh Homicide was concerned, he was a ghost—a flesh and blood apparition whose stock-in-trade were a scalpel and surgical gloves, both of which were readily available at any flea market in the contiguous forty-eight. So, they had nothing; no leads, nothing. The only consistent piece of "evidence" in every one of the cases was the conspicuous lack of any.

That's when they called Quantico to ask for help. "Send your best," the PPD captain had beseeched. Quantico called Brinkman, and Brinkman called the only man he knew who was up to the task.

This guy is good, Les Moore thought as he pored over the nurse killer file in his loaner, parked outside the front doors of the Pittsburgh Field Office. The clock said 7:00 a.m. 'in the Pitt,' as Les always called the city due to an earlier unpleasantness here with an M.E. named Stanley Demontovicz, a.k.a. Stan Demont, that had resulted in the unnecessary deaths of several women in a case Les was working.

Les was alone—the way he liked it—though the frigid damp hanging over his Bureau-gray Ford left a lot to be desired. Les Moore liked his days hot, humid, and bright as a late August day in north Georgia.

Good and extremely careful, Les nodded over the last page, not finding this odd in the least. SKs made a point of not getting caught; none of this "Find me! Stop me!" Hollywood crap; no clues intentionally left behind; no cat-and-mouse games with some dauntless detective; just death and more death.

These guys liked to kill. So, the good ones avoided capture — at all costs — and usually succeeded. The Pittsburgh Slasher was invisible.

Real good. Les smiled to himself. He so loved a challenge.

***

Frankie Morgan had been a creature of precise habit. Every afternoon, rain or shine, she pulled into Parking Lot B of South Side Hospital at exactly 3:24 — unless she was on the morning shift, in which case she arrived at exactly 6:24. This was because Parking Lot B was exactly five minutes from the Green Meadow Townhouses, where Frankie Morgan lived. She had chosen Green Meadow for that reason.

There were three stop signs on the nurse's commute. Les counted them each time he drove the route, turned off his loaner, got out, walked to her door, zeroed out his watch, turned back, started the car, drove back to the hospital, parked in Lot B, and walked up to her station on the third floor, then turned around and repeated the process again. Each pass came out the same, give or take less than fifteen seconds, whether he took the elevator or the stairs.

On his sixth and final pass, Les walked the 227 paces — the dead RN's approximate stride based on her height and weight — from her space in Lot B to the emergency room entrance she used, to her post at the CCU desk two floors above. As with each pass before, the trip took just over four-and-a-half minutes from door to door. Another nineteen steps and Les was at her station.

Facing Cindy.

***

"May I have a word with you?" she said. Some nurses looked up at her spuriously pleasant tone. Les had left Cindy in Seattle without so much as a handshake—although he did leave the Buick for her to return. "In private," Cindy specified.

"Sure," Les said amicably and turned to the nurses with a smile. "Ladies." They all smiled in return, then glared at the bitch who was dragging their handsome FBI agent away.

"What took you so long?" Les asked cordially as they left the nurse's station.

Three feet around the corner, Cindy unloaded. "Listen, you arrogant cocksucking sonofabitch, if you ever leave me again, anywhere, or proceed without me on any business whatsoever pertinent to this case or any other case we're pursuing, whether we are on the clock or not, I will write you up so fast your nuts will fly up in a fit of confusion, knot themselves around your neck, and choke you with your own goddam testosterone-fueled mutant *machismo*."

Les's eyes narrowed some, but he said nothing.

"Then," Cindy assured him, "I will watch with great pleasure as you squirm and attempt to explain to every superior up the line whom I cc—and I will cc each and every goddam one of them—as to why you are continually operating as if you are the only agent assigned to this case, which you are most assuredly not."

On the flight out, Cindy had reconsidered their previous conversation—the one in the road at Riverbend—and had come up with her own conclusions, mainly that maybe her situation wasn't as bleak as she had first thought.

"We know why I'm here and what will happen if I'm not," she said. This being her crux. "The alternative, I'm sure, is not appealing to you."

Les's scowl deepened discernibly, so she closed.

"The way I see it, you've got it pretty easy with me and you know it. So, unless you enjoy Phil Brinkman breathing down your neck and checking your shorts on a daily basis..." She paused.

When Les didn't respond—resoundingly—Cindy knew he had heard everything she was implying. She then felt free to smile with matching cordiality and say, "So, you wanna walk me through this?"

Les Moore eyed his new TASK partner a moment longer, possibly in a new light, then smiled, said, "My pleasure," and led the way.

Out in the hospital parking lot, he pointed up. "She did the deed up there, third from the end, fifth floor."

"What deed?" Cindy asked, as already over their skirmish as Les apparently was. "Who?" She squinted up at the drab building, which seemed grayer than the sky behind, and shivered. The weather was actually worse than Seattle.

"Frankie Morgan? Our victim?" Les said somewhat sarcastically.

Maybe he wasn't over their *discussion* after all.

"Yeah, yeah, heard the name," Cindy said with falsified impatience. "What deed?"

"Quickie at work," Les told her. "Only it wasn't such a quickie. The nurse she did it with said they went at it for over an hour. Seemed proud of it, sounded like."

Cindy was surprised to hear this. "She was gay?"

Les shook his head. "Male nurse."

Cindy felt foolish. "Oh, right."

"Funny, I never took you for a sexist."

"You took right."

"Well, whoever filled out the report was."

"A sexist?"

"Or impatient or lazy. Grossly incompetent. Either or all," Les said perfunctorily.

"Take my pick," Cindy said, matching his earlier zing. He only smiled.

"Okay," she said, slow and melodic. "You're saying?"

"Frankie Morgan wasn't a nurse."

"She wasn't?" Cindy was lost again. The report had said the victim was a nurse. So, she was a nurse. Wasn't she?

"Nope," Les said positively.

"Then... what was she?" Cindy asked, losing patience for real.

"A doctor," Les said calmly, watching for her response.

"Wait, back up."

"No need. You got it." He walked on.

Cindy followed and launched. "What kind of lame, lunatic asshole fills out an official investigation report for the Bureau and gets the career of the victim wrong in a case where the victim's career is the single, preeminent, most consistent modus operandi we've got on the unsub?"

Les said, "Oh, just your average, run of the mill, lame, lunatic, asshole Pittsburgh SAC."

"Holy Dick!" Cindy said incredulously, referring, as Les was, to the Pittsburgh Special Agent in Charge, Richard "Dick" Cleveland (Cleveland Dick of Pittsburgh, as he was known throughout much of the system; Holy Dick to the irreverent rest, due to his proud association with the Promise Makers, a radical offshoot of a fringe fundamentalist group which made the Christian Coalition look like the Chicago Seven). His ineptitude was well-rumored if not well-documented officially.

"None other than," Les said with dark delight and bent down over the edge of a parking island where he carefully began lifting pieces of pine mulch with his pen, peering under each one before moving on to the next. "You know, before he got religion and took up with that platinum Pentecostal babe, Dick was mostly a regular guy."

Grumpy again, Cindy leaned down to give Les some of his own. "Funny, I never took you for a gossip."

"Never take anyone for anything," Les ventured, and stood up, looking around. "Except a few bucks if you can get it. Nobody'll miss a few. Any more than that and they come looking for you at odd hours."

Cindy stood with him. "Rule Number One of the Credo?"

Seeming to dismiss some random thought unworthy of further consideration, Les stooped again and delicately flipped a few more pieces of mulch with his pen. "Numbers One through One Thousand. I stopped there."

Cindy squatted next to him again.

Les stood up.

Cindy stood with him. "Never take anybody for anything," she repeated as if this was a motto well worth preserving. "I'll write that down later," she promised with no hint of actual intent to do so.

Les nodded, approximating her absence of enthusiasm, and squatted again.

Cindy started to squat with him but, annoyed at how they seemed to be doing a bad impression of an arrhythmic carousel, stopped herself and blurted, "What the hell are we doing?" though her blurt sounded more like a bleat.

Les said, "Well, I don't know what you're doing, but I'm working a case."

"Listen, you arrogant blah-blah-blah," Cindy said with little conviction, "I'm on the case, too, et cetera, et cetera." She made a point of sounding too bored to review the details, then finished with, "But if you're looking for any telltale signs Holy Dick the Wonder Agent may have missed, you might try looking on the other side of the parking island where the abduction actually took place."

Les stopped poking. He looked across the island, then up at the building, over at the ER entrance, and back to the island.

Cindy offered a sarcastic smile.

Les stood and shot her a cold hard look. "I knew that," he said. "I was just testing you." Cindy's eyes got wide; Les's sparkled. "I heard Brinkman use that once," he said with a big grin then stepped across the island and squatted again to resume his compost exploratory.

"Yeah, right," Cindy said, and didn't join him at ground zero. "And anyway, I already picked over that spot. You know they issued me a pen, too."

Les grunted and kept poking around.

Until she said, "Found this."

Cindy reached in her pocket and pulled out a baggie with a well-gnawed blue Bic pen cap inside. Les shot straight up, came over, took the bag out of her hand, and held it up to the light.

"Someone chews a lot," Cindy said.

Les glanced testily at her, then gave the bag back. "Don't do that again," he said.

"What?" Cindy asked naively. "Go ahead and actually do something on my own? Without your *permission*?"

Les glared a moment longer, then walked off.

"I was going to tell you about it," Cindy called after him. "But you were so busy not telling me about anything, I couldn't get a word in edgewise." Les didn't respond, but from the hunch in his shoulders as he walked off, she could tell she'd gotten to him.

Cindy watched until Les was gone, then looked at the chewed-up pen cap in her baggie and grinned. She'd scored several points on a cold, gray morning in the Pitt—and it hadn't even hurt that much.

***

"He fucked up. That's what you're thinking."

Cindy stood behind Les who stood in front of the Pittsburgh Field Office coffee machine at three o'clock. He had just returned.

"No," Les said. "I was thinking they could use a better blend." The stench coming off Mr. Coffee lay somewhere between stale oil and fresh pesticide.

"And maybe a vinegar douche," Cindy opined.

Les nodded, then poured the entire potful into the trash, followed by the pot itself, the coffee maker and the brewing supplies. He then put four twenties on the cart and walked off. Cindy followed.

As they walked down a long hall, unadorned but for a single framed photograph of J. Edgar in his later years, stern and unyielding, Les seemed to have several thoughts percolating that he didn't seem inclined to share. Cindy couldn't help but wonder if sharing his process was something Les Moore would ever do without a howitzer to his head.

The image had some appeal.

Finally, he asked, "Anything new?" almost as if he had no real interest in an answer, just filling dead air with more dead air. Cindy thought this odd since she knew he was asking about Riverbend.

So, she asked him if he'd heard about the car being found in Bondini's impound yard. Les said, "Yeah," and laughed with his eyes. "He'll be living that one down for years. DMV turn up anything?"

Cindy told him the Monte Carlo was registered to someone named Sittenfeld, from Tacoma Heights. Les said, "Doesn't ring a bell."

Cindy explained why. "No record. Couple of speeding tickets is all. A DUI."

Les grunted as if he thought there had to me more. "Did you go over the Pitt list?" He was back on the local scalpel-slasher.

"Common names?" Cindy asked.

He nodded.

They were looking for any correlation between any of the victims and their unknown assailant. "No one matches up," she told him. "But he could be using an alias. I've ordered photo IDs from every collateral worksite."

Les said, "And every worksite around every worksite, and every service company servicing every worksite, and every government agency policing every service company servicing every worksite. Have I forgotten anyone?"

"Probably only a hundred or more—categories, that is—but I'll look into it," Cindy promised thinly.

Les stopped. "Are we sure we're looking for a man?"

"No," Cindy shook her head. "Not at all. Aside from the usual profile criteria."

But Les said, "It's a man," definitively, and walked on.

Cindy agreed, followed, and went back to her earlier premise that The Slasher had merely erred when he grabbed a female doctor. "She was wearing scrubs when she left," Cindy said. "He thought she was a nurse, but she wasn't."

"I don't know," Les said. "He's been precise up to now. Seven RNs in four years, three in scrubs."

"Still," Cindy led, "woman in scrubs, dark parking lot..."

Les mused, "Are you suggesting perhaps our Slasher is the sexist?"

"Me?" Cindy said as if shocked and insulted then said, "We haven't come that far as a nation, much less as a band of misogynistic psychopaths."

"Speak for yourself," Les said. Then he stopped short in the hallway, a look of recognition crossing his face.

This time, Cindy read his thoughts as if they were her own. "He's upping the stakes," she intuited.

Les looked at Cindy sharply, as if surprised—and not pleasantly so—maybe even that she had shared his thought with him before he had shared the thought with her aloud. Then he nodded.

Then he smiled. Despite Cindy's psychic intrusion, this was what Les Moore lived for—some tiny revelation that would change the course of an investigation and put him one step closer to his prey. It was clear on his face.

Cindy allowed, "Could be.

"No 'could be.' Is," Les said conclusively, and started for the door.

Cindy shot him the hard look this time. "Where do you think—"

"Men's room," Les said, assuring her with his eyes and a nod down the hall, his way of assuring her that he wasn't leaving the building.

Cindy gave a grunting reply and headed for their loaner desks in the far corner of the fourth floor. Les grinned and turned away.

Then he left the building.

***

Cindy didn't see much of Les the next two days. Every time she turned around, he was gone. When he returned, he always had an excuse that at least sounded plausible or was so indefatigably inarguable as to deny pursuing. Multiple variations of.

Cindy: "I thought you said you were going to the men's room."

Les: "I was. I did. I just didn't say which one."

Then he'd disappear again, and Cindy would find herself by herself, getting nowhere.

Again.

That's when she decided to take matters into her own hands.

***

Donning nurse's scrubs purchased at a thrift store (for anonymity), Special Agent Cyndra Baker, FBI, starting cruising hospital neighborhoods at night. Alone. Her action was unauthorized and maybe even crazy, but Cindy had three loaded weapons on her—one in her jacket, one under her jacket, and one under the ankle of her long johns—and she could shoot the fuzz off a peach at two hundred yards. A Slasher had no chance in range.

Then, one night, it happened.

Cindy had meandered down an unlit street near the Catholic hospital when a scruffy guy came up, dressed in a dark running suit, grabbed her arm and started pulling her into the alley. He said, "Don't fight me. Just come along and you won't get hurt."

Cindy jerked away, swung the Glock out from under her jacket, and yelled, "Freeze, asshole!" with all the power vested in her.

The man said, "Huh?" then, "What?" and looked as bewildered as he sounded.

"Don't move!" Cindy shouted at him. "Down on your face! NOW!" When he still didn't move, she hollered, "FBI! Get down on your face, NOW!"

The guy stared another dumbfounded second or two, then said, "Oh, fuck," sounding like someone who had just received news of a ten-year audit.

But he didn't drop to the sidewalk.

So, Cindy bellowed. "I said, get down! The joyride's over, pal!"

At least she was the one holding the gun.

The man in dark sweats just shook his head and sighed heavily, hardly the response Cindy would have expected from a killer named The Slasher who found himself in the sights of a special agent from the FBI's elite new Target Active Serial Killers team — bad TV dialogue or not.

But before Cindy could shout any other dynamic commands, there came a rustling from the bushes, the sound of running feet, then the squealing of tires and, seconds later, Cindy and her arrestee were surrounded by the entire Pittsburgh SWAT team yelling, "Put it down! Put down your weapon immediately and lay face down on the ground, arms out! Now!"

They were yelling at Cindy.

***

Cindy had walked into the middle of the largest joint DEA/PD raid in Pittsburgh history. She walked away with her first censure. Special Agent Cyndra Baker had broken the real Rule Number One, the one about 'Never Embarrass the Bureau.' Break it badly enough, and they'd break you.

Still, Cindy didn't think her logic had been all that faulty. If someone could surprise that guy in Riverbend, someone could do the same to the Pittsburgh Slasher. Only Cindy wouldn't have shot him in the head, of course.

There were laws.

When Les heard the story from Brinkman, he turned off his favorite Sinatra compilation and the two of them laughed for two minutes, unabated.

Brinkman's good temper vaporized the moment Director Wilstrong called from the Capitol coffee shop demanding to know why the hell one of his new Special TASK Force Agents had been running her own sting operation "with no jurisdiction whatsoever" — and got arrested to boot. Brinkman was forced into a fairly knotty explanation, given the din coming from the press.

Late night comedians had a field day. "I know why you're in such a good mood, tonight," Bill Maher quipped at the taping. "You heard about this woman FBI agent in Pittsburgh who arrested a narc by mistake." The audience was cackling long before he got to the punch line. *The Daily Show* killed. Seth Meyers dedicated an entire segment to it.

Cindy received the letter two days later, directly from the director himself. Les had the page framed for her and said he hoped it wouldn't be her last. "Rule Number One's a bitch," he said.

Then he asked her if she'd actually said, "'Freeze asshole, your joyride's over?'" Cindy could only cringe and nod and stare at the floor. Thankfully, Les kept his howling to a minimum.

Hearing Les downplay the whole affair made Cindy feel better, but not as good as the part where he said he was impressed with her "devotion to duty." Those words sounded positively exquisite coming from Les Moore—even if his truancy had driven her into that ridiculous position in the first place.

Nonetheless, Cindy was starting to see what Brinkman saw in Les. No one, no one, was more dedicated to stopping these maniacs than Les Moore. And by God, Les approved of her taking things into her own hands. More or less. For that, Cindy felt more or less pretty damn great!

Unfortunately, the ignominy of having blown it big time lingered like shrimp stink. "Learn and move on," was all Les had to say about it. And he never kidded her about her kerfuffle in the Pitt again. Although he did advise that if she wanted to try "anything like that again," some rehearsal might help. And he recalled the old axiom that sometimes you're better off asking forgiveness after than permission before.

Cindy shook her head and said she couldn't believe what a fool she'd been. Les shrugged and said, "Nobody'd be laughing if it had worked."

Cindy nodded at the sad irony and made a pact with herself. Next time, she'd get it right.

Chapter 5 – The Barn

Late showing in a second-run theater, somewhere in Iowa. Tom Cruise as a rogue detective out to stop the nation's worst mass murderer in a half-century did just north of a billion before coming here. America loves its serial killers.

In the last lonely row, a diehard pops open his days' old paper, panning for light under the dim glow of rusted first-generation high-hats in the black and moldy cottage cheese ceiling far above, long since a safety hazard. Only one headline catches his eye.

RIVERBEND KILLER FINALLY STOPPED
Murder Victim Victim of Intended Victim?

"Catchy," the reader mutters to himself. "This guy should be writing beer commercials."

> SEATTLE— *Prostitutes were spotted in record numbers last week as word leaked that the area's most infamous serial killer may finally be dead, ironically the victim of his most recent quarry, according to the King County Sheriff's Department.*
>
> *Sheriff's spokeswoman Sondra Veere was quick to point out that the man, Ralph Waldo Sittenfeld, 42, of Tacoma Heights, has not been positively linked to any of the 27 murders attributed to the so-called Riverbend Killer. However, she seemed "fairly certain" he would be by week's end.*

"'Fairly certain,'" the reader burlesques. "Someone needs to play catch up." He didn't expect to find anything new in the news. Just killing *Time*.

> *Federal Bureau of Investigation's Leslie Francis Moore, lead agent of the bureau's new elite Target Active Serial Killers (TASK) force, and the profiler assigned to this case, declined comment other than to say DNA tests were being run.*

"Run against what?" comes a whispery laugh. "Somebody knows something I don't?"

He runs his finger down the victims list on Page Three. A pause to reflect, a shake of the head, positive ID. Imaginary lines drawn through 11, 17, 20-22 and 25.

"Copycats," he gripes.

If you can't be original, don't bother. That's what his grandfather taught him — right before he hanged himself. Not much of a legacy, but the memory stayed with him like finding the body.

Numbers 12 and 13, Marjorie Moore and Melissa Ann Moore, get a nod, even though the numbering is off.

A related headline reads *County Sheriff Embarrassed by Killer Car.* A photo of the brown Monte Carlo in the impound yard shows an unreservedly unhappy Bondini walking away in the foreground. This gets a laugh and, with only column fillers left, the paper goes down.

There's a small crowd tonight, mostly teens and young couples, a few farmworkers — and one mismatch. A few rows down, an old guy, weathered from four decades of alcohol and five packs a day, with a kid, fifteen-sixteen, three earrings, an attempt at a pale mustache under black-dye hair — green camos and some ugly-assed post-Goth boots. Could be anyone's runaway.

But he's not.

"What have we here?" The Reader wishes he could hear what they're saying with all their gesturing toward the back. The lobby? Across the street? California? Japan? *Mars?*

The old one nods, hands over some money. *Ah, the snack bar.*

The kid figures he's developed a pretty cold I'm-no-one-to-fuck-with face that he flashes to anyone who dares look. He feels The Power and throws it from four rows down. Doesn't hear, "You're mad-doggin' the wrong junkyard pit bull, kid," and seriously misreads the smile that follows.

"What the fuck you grinnin' at, ya old faggot," the kid snarls, then laughs. He can smell The Man a long city block off. And, here in the country? Shit. Fucker stands out like a cow in a Cadillac shop.

No cop can touch him, he's thinking; not with his fake ID and *Grampa takin' me out to the ninety-nine cent show of a weeknight.* He's got the act down, ready to run. No one gets over on him, not anymore. *Look. I dare you.*

The Reader does, halcyon smile never leaving his lips. The kid's on his turf, now. Deceptively inert eyes let the punk pass then turn to the next paper, dated four days later.

The breaking story is more far-reaching than first reported.

> *SEATTLE — Police got an unexpected break yesterday in the ongoing Riverbend Killer investigation — one they probably didn't want. A computer wire search of known felons has turned up indications that the man identified as Ralph Waldo Sittenfeld, 42, of Tacoma Heights, found murdered along the Black River south of Seattle last week, and at first thought to be the Riverbend Killer, is in fact one Henry David Merfinridge, 39, of Phoenix, Ariz.*
>
> *According to police in Butte, Mont., Merfinridge is a principal suspect in the murders of ten young women over the past six months, all suspected prostitutes, in an area spanning Idaho, Montana and North Dakota, where, according to Alicia LeConte, representative of Call Off Your Old Tired Ethics (COYOTE), prostitution is decidedly not a boom business. Butte police say they don't know how Merfinridge was able to find ten prostitutes in this area in such a short time, but they are certain he is the Tri-State Shooter they've been tracking.* *(Please turn to Page 13)*

"Tri-State Shooter. Christ. They need the beer guy," the Reader mutters. He follows directions to page thirteen.

> **Tri-State Shooter Found Dead — Cont'd from Page One**
> *Using DMV records and trace evidence recovered from a 1978 Monte Carlo thought to have been used in the murder of Merfinridge, and later found in the King County impound yard (see related article), sheriff's deputies quickly traced the older Chevrolet to Sittenfeld.*
>
> *Armed with a search warrant, a Sheriff's Department Rapid Response (SWAT) Team swarmed Sittenfeld's house in Tacoma Heights late yesterday afternoon. What they found was both surprising and disturbing.*

"I'm on pins and needles," he says. But it's better than he thinks.

In a story that continues to offer one bizarre twist after another, K-9 dogs led police to a mound of freshly turned soil behind a crawlspace opening in Sittenfeld's basement. Excavation of the site divulged a grisly denouement – the rotting remains of Sittenfeld's decomposing body.

Police say Merfinridge left Montana sometime in August for the Sea-Tac area and apparently "lucked" onto Sittenfeld, a drywall installer who was "the spitting image of the Tri-State Shooter." Merfinridge then murdered Sittenfeld, buried him in his own basement and, posing as Sittenfeld's brother, planned to continue his murder spree into Washington State.

"So, now he's the Quad-State Killer. Tough break, Montana."

Area residents said Merfinridge did indeed bear a striking resemblance to Sittenfeld. Both men were of average height, blond and slim with "prominent noses and jutting foreheads," according to an elderly neighbor. When asked where Sittenfeld was, Merfinridge told the man, who has asked not to be identified, that Sittenfeld had been forced to return "back East to care for their ailing mother."

The neighbor confirmed that Sittenfeld's mother had lived in Boston, though he had thought she was deceased. The elderly man said he accepted Merfinridge's explanation because, "Henry David (Merfinridge) was the spitting image of Ralph Waldo (Sittenfeld), and who would name two people in such a similarly odd fashion if it wasn't the same mother?"

Police agreed.

The photo of Merfinridge from a bad check beef in his home state of Georgia doesn't ring a bell. Neither does Sittenfeld's blurry DMV picture or a location shot of the elderly neighbor, identified as Ernest Gore in the caption despite his text request for anonymity.

Scanning the background details from Montana—victims, cops, maps—the Reader makes a mental note of Sheriff Red Stimson's name, his county, and his role in the drama. *Might have to pay Red a visit someday. Shake things up.*

Myriad prospects come to mind.

Everything makes sense, now. Les Moore, back on the case, a body in the woods at Riverbend, some second-rate killer, and brothers killing brothers who aren't brothers at all. Killers killing killers.

This really is a perfect world. The airheads are right. You just have to sit back and let it all happen around you, then step in and do your part when your turn comes up. So, be prepared! The call can come at any moment.

The little punk is coming back now, stuffing popcorn, dropping some. "Sloppy," the Reader thinks aloud. "Not a good quality in your line of work, kid."

Then he leans back to enjoy the show, happy with how the evening will turn out—like the movie. Someone gets caught.

The lights dim. There will be no previews for the late show.

***

Poor Little Farm Girl doesn't fit in around here and wants everyone to know. The hair's too blonde, the roots too dark; seven piercings on display, and a few more. Makes her feel grown up.

She can't wait.

Her momma died a few years back—three, she thinks, though it could be four—and Daddy hasn't picked her up at work in over a year. She doesn't care; hitchhiking makes her feel "free."

Every night after the snack bar, one of the local boys is usually waiting outside the theater to swap some herb for sex. A fair trade, she thinks. Sex is her currency, her weapon, her addiction. Already.

Tonight, the boys are off somewhere; probably down at the reservoir drinking beer, thinking about skinny-dipping on a warm night. She's swum with all of them—once, all together, the only time she ever got more dick than she knew what to do with. She felt degraded and liberated at the same time; her single orgasm left her drenched and spent. Too bad she never found out how much she hates men. Poor Little Farm Girl, thumb out, Daddy at home, alone.

He'll sleep through it all.

***

A knocking lime-green pickup slows down and pulls off, gliding silently over the hardpack alongside the pavement. She doesn't recognize the old Chevy from around here, because it's not.

"Need a ride?" the skinny old man behind the wheel asks.

She's never seen him either, but she remembers The Kid from the snack stand. *His hair is so cool. He's so sexy.* She thought so the second he came up and asked for a small popcorn and she told him how she usually walked home after the show but didn't think anyone'd be there for her tonight. Then she gave him a free medium Dew.

He took the hint—right back to his faux pappy.

"It's awful late," the old one advises. "Not safe out, even around here."

"Girl can't be too safe," she agrees. But she doesn't mean it. Danger's half the fun; safe's none.

"Smart girl." They nod and say they'll, "Just drive on, then." Real homey, from "up around Conners." She's never heard of it. Never, because it doesn't exist.

"No," she stops them, as if just now reconsidering. "Kinda cold out tonight," she says, and climbs in with a shiver to prove her point, knowing that her tight little top will second the motion.

"Luke," the old man says his name is, laying the cornpone on thick. "An' this here's Li'l Luke."

"Shit." The Kid hates the Name Game. He wants to be Smash or Knifer, Cut'n'Loose or HangDog D. Anything but Luke. And *Little Luke? Christ a'mighty!*

But he does his part—the shy look-over, the cautious smile— thinking how she's small-town pretty and would probably go off with them for some regular smoke.

And she probably would.

"Wanna get high?" he asks.

"Sure," she answers. Always.

He presents the fattie he had waiting behind his other ear and smiles. In the spirit of cooperation, she punches the lighter in with her big toe—sandals already on the floor—and giggles.

He asks how old she is.

"Fifteen," she says proudly, a badge of honor.

"Sixteen, soon?" Gramps wonders, leaning up to look around.

"No, just turned," she says with even more pride.

She shifts her already full body toward The Kid. Two of a kind, she thinks, happy to meet one of her own in this godforsaken shithole of a nothing hometown.

"Wanna get a room?" he asks, making sure to sound uncertain.

"Sure," she says with no incertitude at all. She's already had everyone her age and twenty years older in the county at least twice— a few younger, but mostly as a favor to someone. She had VD once—

they still say VD around here—and herpes too. But she hasn't had an outbreak in a month. Had that kidney thing, but sulpha drugs did the trick. The clap was *stubborner*.

She thought she had HIV once, but it turned out just to be a bad flu. Had Buddy John beat up Teddy Joe for giving her AIDS, then said she was sorry she didn't have AIDS after all, soon as she found out; forget Buddy John was the one gave her herpes.

In the end, she's proud of her medical rap sheet.

The dash lighter pops. The Kid torches up and passes the blunt. She takes a deep hit, leaning back to blow whispered smoke in his ear.

"What about your grampa? He don't like to watch or nothin'." Not like she would really care, but it's the principle of the thing. She's at least got to ask.

If she only knew what Granpa likes.

"Naw," Little Luke chuckles, all down-home. Granpa's trained him well. "He cain't even git it up no more." They share a cruel laugh.

Granpa gives an appropriate snort out the window, thinking how quickly his teen liege took to The Life, and how sometimes the whole charade is just too easy.

To prove his point as they pass under the last light at the edge of town, she chips in with, "I know a place. Won't cost you a room, neither." She loves pushing the envelope, breaking the rules. *Bein' alive!*

That won't last.

***

Granpa pushes his grubby little .38 to her eye.

"P-please, m-mister. P-please d-d-d-don't." Poor Little Farm Girl can't believe she's been this stupid. She knew she might end up like this someday, just not so soon. And *not in some damn old barn!* She doesn't feel so grown up, now.

Daddy!

The old killer runs a craggy finger through her down. She never shaved or waxed, proud of her soft adulthood. Not like those porn whores the Boyz all love. Granpa scrubs the small tattoo just above with some lardy saliva to see if it comes off. But the happy cartoon mouse holding a tiny red rose is real. Real as this.

"Plea... ea... ea... ease. I'll do whatev—"

Granpa punches straight down.

Short, jerky sobs form a blood bubble from her nose that pops red on Crest Extra-White teeth. A familiar metallic taste fills her mouth and makes her think of Daddy again, of all those years and all he did to her. She never minded. His abuse gave her a reason to hate him more, and this awful place called home. A good hate that sustained her in all the nothingness that was her life here, fueling her rebellion and sending her on night rides to the reservoir with the Iowa Badd Boyz.

Now she knows: They weren't so bad; *this* is bad.

Poor Little Farm Girl looks to her young killer for deliverance, but he's already had his. Her wetness still with him. She had thought her life was so wild and free, so uninhibited, not like the boring boys around here.

Eyes closed, The Kid is already lost in other memories of those two young housewives from Mississippi with the dyed-green landing strips. What a surprise that had been! A lost bet between girlfriends. Their dares ended up in his pocket.

"Those girls from down Natchez, with they pretty green snatches," he kept singing while the old one howled the night away, carving them up after he'd defiled their dead bodies with his rancid sex fluids in that field by —

Bang!

The shot seems awfully loud, brings The Kid right back from his happy death memories, suddenly vulnerable in his nakedness. "Someone might come," he warns.

"Yeah, me," the old killer cackles, and sets his smoking .38 aside.

Poor Dead Farm Girl.

***

"Hey, fellas. What's up?" The voice is low and calm. New.

Gramps goes for the .38 without looking.

He doesn't make it.

The roar from the big bore .44 Taurus makes their two-inch Detective Special sound like a girly gun — louder than anything the kid's ever heard. A heavy hollow point catches the old death-fucker in the chest and blows a hole out his back nearly big as his head.

The wound slows him down substantially. But he'll keep scratching for his rusting Smith & Wesson. What else can he do?

Young Punk Kid recognizes 'that smiley faggot from the movies!' but doesn't move. That's a big gun. *Who the fuck is he?*

"You boys having fun tonight?"

The man from the last row sounds like he is, with his smoking magnum.

"Sir, uh..."

The kid wishes he'd kept shut coming up the aisle. He never would've said a word if he'd known acting tough would lead to this. Now, he searches for any lie that might save his useless life. "I didn't do nothin'," he tries. "I just... I..."

"Just what?" the man says. "Sat over there and played with that sorry little peanut a' yours while this sorry old bastard did all the dirty work?"

"It... it is k-kinda... k... k... kinda small. But m... may... m... maybe it'll grow some when I g... get older."

"You're not gonna *get* any older, ya stupid little fuck," the stranger says.

He shoves his barrel through thick, stinking air at the dead girl's motionless body. "You and Gramps don't know it's wrong to kill innocent people?"

"He... he... he... ain't... really... my... g... gran... granpa."

"Gee, how'd I ever guess?"

Punk kid shrugs. He doesn't know; doesn't have a clue. Sixteen suddenly feels like six. He wants his daddy, now. Too bad he killed him four years ago after setting fire to the church. He's been running ever since; turned it into a lifestyle. Like that old Woodstock couple he met in another barn once. Peace signs on their bus and they blew up a bank and killed a guard. No remorse. That was the only part he understood.

Granpa's almost to his gun now. Just any other old man hoping to stick around a little longer and live out his last years in peace. His fingertips graze the chipped brown wooden grip, and he smiles. Freedom is a breath away.

The second shot takes off half his head. The report is even louder than the first, somehow — the expectation. The kid shakes visibly.

"Wh... what... kinda cop... are... you?"

The old one's executioner snorts ironically and shakes his head over the dead girl. "Tits has only two T's by the way. You ignorant country fucks. One at the beginning, one at the end."

Dropout kid looks over. 'Titts,' his phony PawPaw wrote on her in her own blood — right after he ripped out the little nipple gold ring for a souvenir. Blood ran but she felt nothing. They laughed. Now, nothing seems funny.

"O... Okay. S... sorry," the kid says, trying for sincerity as best he can.

He wishes he could reverse time, play everything different, so he wouldn't be here. Or just run away like usual. But this time he knows he's up against it—and a wall of hay. No escape. Pressing back to feel the soft jabs in his back, to know he's still here and his life story hasn't ended yet. To think he still has a chance.

"Look at you, you're a mess," the one still standing says.

Tough kid hadn't even realized he shit himself. Must've been the Olestra. Looking down now, a tight choking feeling threatens to close his throat.

"And I'll bet you two thought you were real professionals," the man in control says, making it clear he despises their ineptitude.

The kid shrugs, helpless. Darting thoughts search his infected, desperate memories. There *must* be some way out of this. He eyes the door, the .44, and knows he'd never make it. Not after what he's just seen. Maybe a bribe; that usually works. Even the hardest bastards jump for a chance at young.

"I could do you!" he swears for all to hear. "Every night if you want! I'm good. I'm really good! And you can do me all the time! I can take it! I even like it sometimes!"

And sometimes, he does.

"Christ." The Killer scowls and raises his Taurus.

The shot sounds louder yet, pointed right at him. But this bullet isn't intended to kill, rather to make a point.

The point is made. This bullet blows every bit of his maleness off.

He screams, losing his head. Lots of "Oh God!"s and "Oh dear God no!"s, just like he heard from women across five states. He never thought he'd hear those lame words come out of his own mouth. Folly of Youth.

"Noooo!"

He's mad he can't stop what he knows is coming. He promises this new God he suddenly finds crowding his heart that he will live a better life from this moment on, if he can just be spared. But he knows the truth. If he gets out of this, he'll go right back to his old ways, probably kill even more to make up for his temporary lapse.

He suspects this new God knows that too.

"Pl... pl... ple... please, sir. Pl... pl... ple... please!" He doesn't care if he sounds like she did, like some pitiful girl about to die. He wants mercy.

He'll get none.

"You two make me sick," the man with the big revolver says.

"Wh... why?" the kid chokes out between sobs. "We ain't so... bad! Just n... normal people gone a l... little off."

Must be a new definition of normalcy, one this killer hasn't heard. "DNA everywhere. Semen, blood, feces. Vaginal fluids on you, in your hair. You came in her, didn't you?"

The kid nods but has no clue what any of this means.

"You probably pissed in here somewhere too, didn't you?" Another nod. Once on the wall and once on the steps, more for irreverence than relief.

"And what was this? Lunch?"

Granpa's killer stands over the remains of a sandwich in the dirt. "You were gonna leave it here, right?"

The kid shrugs. *Why not?*

"Hair, fibers, footprints. Hay and dirt on your clothes. Those are the same shoes you wear every day, aren't they?"

The kid nods, helpless. Lost.

"Tire tracks, gas and oil leaking out, coolant. Mud from here on your truck, on the floor mats, the seats. How'd you ever expect to get away with this?"

The kid manages only, "Have been."

"Well, it's a miracle, kid. A fucking miracle."

"You... you..."

The kid can barely speak now, the shock is so great, the bleeding so prolific, the pain so unbearably deep, coursing his body like bad drugs. Like those Angel Trumpets in Florida that year. Tears fall under muted whimpers.

"Dish it out but can't take it, huh?" the mysterious man with the big gun says, not hiding his contempt—and shoots the kid again.

The kid cries out. He can't stop what is about to happen—and does.

Another part of his body is gone—this time his shoulder—along with his favorite ink of the Grim Reaper holding a dripping, severed head with the kid's face. He designed the tattoo himself. What goes around...

"What are you *doing*?" he suddenly hears himself screaming in piercing, straight-as-an-unbroken-line-to-forever disbelief, reeling, only his adolescent meanness keeping him even remotely conscious.

The answer is simple. "Sending a message."

"To who?"

"To someone who will understand."

The stranger's serenity is what is so truly, deeply frightening. "You're the most fucked-up'dest cop I ever saw," the kid swears. A last, futile "Who are you?" echoes like an empty canyon calling back to him from his own beyond.

"Okay, kid," the one in control says, as if thinking, *What can it hurt at this point?* "Think."

Dying kid tries, but his thought process has been noticeably disabled by the pain and shock.

His killer helps. "I knew where you were going, what you were up to. Identified your victim before you did. Waited for you outside the theater. Followed you here. Think!"

A first flash of emotion.

Slipping away on an ebbing tide of wakefulness, watching the shores of This World receding — numb and floating — the kid struggles against the cold currents of his own immediate and unquestioned destiny to pull himself back in for one last grasp. He can't check out leaving a final great enigma like this unsolved.

A second later, his eyes go wide. "Oh, sweet Jesus!" A look of purest fear crosses his face. Now, he knows. "You're one of us."

The insult gets a scornful laugh. "Don't flatter yourself, kid. We don't even shit in the same hole."

"Then who the fuck are you?"

He can take no more. Even the crying has stopped. He just wants to know — and to end the pain, the fear, the dread.

He's about to get his wish.

"Well, kid, they call me..."

The young killer looks up expectantly but sees only the flash. So close he doesn't hear the report this time as the big slug splits the air and his forehead, brains and half his skull blasting out the back.

The sentence is finished. "Riverbend."

Chapter 6 – Yellow Ribbons

Brinkman phoned the hotel at a little past one thirty. Les and Cindy had just returned, well-mollified, from a lunch of cheesesteak sandwiches and tossed salad. Coffee.

Les took the call.

Two more serial killers were dead in a barn in Iowa, this time shot to death with their victim at their feet. At first, Local thought they had a mass murderer on their hands—until they ran IDs.

"These guys were a cunt hair away from capture in five states," Brinkman told Les. "Classic team. One organized, one disorganized." As if he knew anything about anything he was saying.

After a moment of silence, Les asked, "Signature?"

Brinkman laid out the scenario with a queer mixture of delight and foreboding. "Wide yellow ribbon, one each, double square knot with a bow, left-over-right loop, perfect forty-five-degree angles on the tips."

***

Cindy didn't know what Les had just been told, but the expression on his face would haunt her to the end.

Les let Brinkman prattle on for another minute or more before hanging up on him in midsentence—Cindy heard it—and heading for the door.

She looked up from compiling their first full suspect list in the Pitt and said, "Whoa there, sport. You're not leaving me here to deal with him when he calls back."

Les said, "Sorry," honestly, then walked out. The phone started ringing again before he got to the elevator.

Cindy could have yelled at him to come back or told Brinkman she could catch Les and then run after him, then not come back herself. Instead, she took a breath, picked up the phone and snapped.

"Christ, what the fuck did you say to him, Phil?" Cindy knew it was always good to go on offense with someone so offensive.

A moment of silence on the line was followed by, "This is Fred Bondini, King County Sheriff's Department. Is Agent Moore there?"

Cindy winced. "Sorry, Major. This is Agent Baker. Les just left." She could hear the elevator door closing. "I might be able to catch him if you like."

"No, that's okay," Bondini said. "I just called to—"

Her mobile started ringing. He asked, "You want to get that?"

"No, it's okay," Cindy said, certain the other call was Brinkman. "Les has your number?"

"Yes." There was a short pause. "How's he taking it?"

"Taking what?" Cindy didn't know; hadn't been told, yet.

There was a longer pause. "You said 'Phil?'"

"Yeah."

"Phil Brinkman?"

"Yeah."

"Jesus. I can only imagine what that idiot said." This was followed by a groan and more dead space.

The other line was still ringing. Cindy hesitated, becoming irritated at being left out of the loop again! "Yeah. Listen, can you hold a second? I better see who this is."

"That's okay. Just keep Les away from Brinkman. He might kill him."

"Okay," Cindy said with little enthusiasm for defeating such a plot. "I'll have him call you as soon as he gets in," she said. She started to hang up, but the Midwest girl in her felt a pang of guilt. "Look, Major, I'm sorry about the wisecracks out there."

"Not a problem," Bondini said magnanimously as the other line stopped ringing. "This stuff gets to all of us, sometime. And Les Moore gets to all of us all the time." He hung up.

Cindy gave a grunt of agreement and started for the door. Maybe if she could get all the way out into the hall before—

The hotel phone rang again. And rang.

Cindy hesitated, the Midwest in her acting up again. What if the other line *wasn't* Brinkman? Maybe it was Bondini again. Or Les. Or someone else with information for someone else!

Cindy snatched up the receiver and barked, "Baker," with as much brusque professionalism as she had in her, which was already getting to be substantial.

Brinkman didn't even notice. Just started in.

Cindy let him get a good ten seconds into his tirade then said, "Hello? Is someone there? Hello? *Hello?*"

***

Though she didn't expect to find Les anywhere near, Cindy spotted him downstairs in the hotel parking lot, sitting in their Pittsburgh Bureau loaner—which appeared to have acquired some new damage to the right front fender and left rear quarter panel.

The engine was off, and Les sat still as an old rock, seemingly mesmerized by the one imperfect pimple of plasticized leather that somehow finds safe harbor on the top of every steering wheel. Cindy thought he looked like one of those life-size statues that gives you the creeps because they appear so real, only you know they aren't, and that's what makes the whole thing so creepy. *Bronze people, Christ.*

The newly paved and lined lot was sandwiched between their buck gray Sheraton and the polished black Pittsburgh Field Office, which had significantly less sheen under a flannel sky, this day being as dreary as the last three—a stalled front—and cold as back home in January. Only it was the Pitt in September, and the air felt like the winter solstice.

Maybe Les was conserving heat.

Cindy glanced up at the Pittsburgh SAC's window on the sixth floor and there he was, Holy Dick Cleveland, imperiously peering out over his dubious duchy. *The nut.* He even waved. Cindy waved back halfheartedly and started for the gun-metal loaner, hoping Dick would disappear but doubting he would.

Les didn't seem to notice her approach, so Cindy leaned down and tapped the glass. Les didn't move, didn't blink, didn't seem to be breathing. And damned if, up close, he didn't look less real than those fake real people! Maybe he was a model for them in his off time.

Maybe he'd been shot.

"Les? Are you all right?" When her partner didn't budge, Cindy said, "Your friend Bondini called from Seattle. He wants you to call him back."

Still no response.

"He was worried about you. I guess I am too." It just came out.

Les finally turned and looked at Cindy through the lightly tinted glass but didn't speak.

"Are you okay?" she asked him again, a little louder, and chanced, "You want to talk about it?"

Dark thoughts seemed to be swarming him like killer bees. She could almost see them.

Finally, he turned back to the Naugahyde nub as a sharp smack of Canadian chill whipped Cindy's hair onto her bare face so hard it stung.

Fine, she thought, *he doesn't want to talk*. She wasn't hanging around some cold, dull parking lot waiting for him to open up; she'd heard the hotel had a sauna.

"Well, okay then," she said. "I'll be upstairs." She turned to go.

A few steps away, Cindy heard Les's window slide down. "Remember Nietzsche?" he said.

Who? Cindy turned back. "What about him?" Better.

"That thing about, 'He who stares into the abyss better be prepared to have the abyss stare back.'"

Oh, *that* Nietzsche, the one from college. "More or less."

Les spoke as if from the dark depths of a coma cave. "Three bodies. Barn in Iowa. One girl, two SKs."

To a talented special agent like Cyndra Lynn Baker, those nine words contained a massive amount of potential details — all in conflict. She decided to think out loud and hope for guidance.

"The girl... killed them?"

When Les didn't respond, Cindy reasoned, "No, okay, you said three bodies," sifting the info. "Well, she could have, if they thought they'd killed her, then she rose up, killed them, then died herself."

She looked at Les. He didn't move. "But that's not what happened," Cindy concluded.

Les shook no in confirmation, though his head barely seemed to move. This left only one possibility. "Someone killed them after they killed her."

Cindy suppressed any implication of a question. Les nodded, again without any discernible movement, and Cindy suddenly had the whole picture.

Merfinridge and Sittenfeld in Seattle, and these two in Iowa, different in so many ways yet one and the same.

A polar wind rattled through the hollow of her bones, making the real chill around her feel almost balmy. "Someone *is* killing serial killers," she said, almost in silence.

Two events made it official.

Les remained still as death in an Iowa barn. Then he nodded — so negligibly as to defy any theories on detectable motion.

"Fuck." If nothing else, Cindy was concise when she needed to be. *Someone's killing serial killers,* she repeated in her mind.

Fuck, indeed.

Without time to give it much thought, Cindy already knew the basic concept was rife with contradiction, especially to a TASK agent. Whom did they go after now? And why? And *did* they? Their stated mission was to Target Active Serial Killers, not active Serial-Killer *Killers.*

Or was it? Wouldn't that fit in there, somewhere? Technically? But who could she ask? Brinkman? Not likely. He'd as soon prefer everyone outside the Bureau was dead; his job would be *much* easier. Les? He was her partner, but would he even answer? And if he did, would his position be much different than Brinkman? Something in the vicinity of, "Who fucking cares? Let 'em all kill each other."

And what would be so bad about that? Really?

Maybe Cindy didn't have the whole picture. She started to ask what she was missing when Les filled in the blank. "He left yellow ribbons."

Only one killer did that.

"Details straight?" Cindy asked quickly. "Double square knot? Bow, left-over-right? Tips at a forty-five?" She'd read that line in the file at least a hundred times. Maybe a thousand. Les nodded yes for each particular.

At least now Cindy had an explanation for Les's stiller-than-winter-midnight stare. This case was now, abruptly, about more than babysitting. It was about everything she had asked Les about back in Seattle — in Riverbend — all rushing at her like a bullet train, Cindy standing on the tracks, unable to move.

Her heart beat faster.

She said, not asked, "You think he did 'em both." Iowa and Seattle. Then she specified, "All three killers, in both places." Les shook his head no. He still looked spooky.

"Okay," Cindy said, trying to catch up. "Tell me about the barn."

"Old man, sixty-five, and a boy, sixteen. Kidnapped a girl, raped her, killed her, raped her some more. Standard drill. Our unsub came along sometime after the party. Left nothing but a couple of big bore holes and brain tissue everywhere."

"You're thinking maybe Riverbend did Merfinridge, too."

Les shook his head no. "Ribbon won't match," he said plainly.

Cindy recalled the briefing she'd gotten from Bill Badler at National Center for the Analysis of Violent Crime—NCAVC. "Riverbend's signature yellow bows are fashioned from a wide one-of-a-kind impossible-to-find linen-laced antique paper ribbon that hasn't been manufactured in over fifty years. Probably something left over from his childhood: a mother he hated, grandmother he loved. Wherever he got it, it's unique. No one else has it or can get it as far as we can tell."

"Is that a guess, or do you know?" Cindy asked about the match.

"I know," he said quietly.

Normally Cindy didn't respond well to arrogance. But since she was standing before the legendary Les Moore who was virtually *never wrong about a fucking thing,* she'd overlook her negative reaction and minor doubts. He probably meant he had a hunch the ribbon wouldn't match. At least she hoped that's what he meant.

Cindy turned and leaned her back against the car, faced away, thinking, as she had done in Riverbend five days before. But this time, she did her processing aloud.

"Okay, so the hooker, the guy, whoever it was in Riverbend, thought he had Riverbend, so he left the ribbon to make a statement. But he had Merfinridge. All he knows is it's yellow ribbon—he's read that—but it's the wrong kind of ribbon, because only Riverbend has his particular ribbon. But Merfinridge's killer doesn't know that. So, he thought he had Riverbend. But he didn't.

"So, now Riverbend reads about him in the paper or whatever, decides to prove not only is he still around and active, but he can play the serial-killer killer game, too. So, he finds two SKs somehow, maybe lucks onto them, who knows, doesn't matter."

Cindy considered what she just said and decided, "No, it might." Then, she further decided, "For now, it doesn't. But he knows what they're up to, because it's what *he* does. So, he stalks 'em, lets 'em do their thing, then pops 'em, leaves his yellow signature and vanishes without a trace."

Les had to be impressed; he hadn't even trained her that much, yet. If he'd been in a better mood, he might even have complimented her, she thought. *That would be nice.*

"Problem is," Cindy said, shaking off her own desire for recognition, and brought it all together, "Merfinridge's killer got the presentation dead on, right down to the forty-fives. That was never reported."

This, of course, didn't mean no one knew about it. A lot of people knew — mostly law enforcement — but who knew who they had told, and then who they in turn told? Running these calculations pruned the list down to about four million suspects, give or take a few million.

Cindy said, "I thought they were some kind of fraternity." Serial murderers.

Now Les made the turtle-birthing squack.

Out of the corner of her eye, Cindy saw Dick Cleveland waving down at her, thumb and pinkie held to ear and mouth, wiggling. "Looks like Dick's got some problem with the side of his head. Dandruff or lice, maybe."

Les glanced up at Cindy who demonstrated discreetly on the side of her head away from the building. Les assessed, "Brinkman."

Cindy knew damn well who it was. "You wanna take it?"

Now Les chuckled.

Cindy joined him, pretending not to see Dick. "So, now we've got two serial-killer killers," she said. But she was thinking, *Jesus. There's something they don't teach you at the Academy.*

Les half-shrugged, half-nodded. Cindy would have preferred more specificity. "You think it's him?" she asked. "In Idaho?"

"Iowa," Les corrected.

Cindy shrugged. "I-state west of the Mississippi."

Les sat still for a long time. Too long for Cindy. And the answer that finally came gave her no comfort whatsoever.

"I hope so," he said as routinely as vespers.

***

After several silent, motionless minutes, Les started the car. Sinatra came up, wallowing about in some bleached-out over-sentimentalized mental keepsakes from his youth, when he was seventeen and wasn't life great.

Wondering who really cared and what the deal was with this Sinatra fetish anyway, Cindy asked, "What happened to the vehicle?" sounding irritatingly to herself like a common cop. "Looks like you hit a pole."

"I did," Les said. "Dialing my cell."

"With both ends of the car?"

Les nodded. "Then I backed into one of Dick's cruisers."

"You gonna tell him?"

Les shook his head no. Cindy nodded. She wouldn't have either. Holy Dick would have more forms to fill out than all three of them had fingers and toes.

Cindy watched as Les put the crinkled sedan in gear and drove slowly away, thinking how she had never seen Les drive slowly, anywhere. Her angst trebled.

And that Sinatra shit was already starting to creep her out.

Unable to take her eyes off the departing sedan, Cindy slowly realized that her mind wasn't racing as she would have expected. Instead, her thoughts felt stuck in neutral, locked up in some cosmically disagreeable Les-induced post-hypnotic killers-killing-other-killers trance-state.

Thoughts of thoughts.

She marveled for a moment at how Les had—*Yes, that's exactly what he did*—somehow fomented some weird cannibalistic mental behavior wherein certain thoughts prey on other thoughts and—

"Ms. Baker?" a mousy voice said.

Cindy jumped. Dick Cleveland's achingly timid, anorexic agent-trainee Angie had snuck up silently to stand next to Cindy—right next to her—twitching.

That wasn't a good sign. Ever.

Cindy looked back up the block with no idea as to how long she'd been staring at the empty street where Les had driven off what? two minutes ago? Five? A half hour?

A day and a half?

"Ma'am?"

"Cindy, please."

"Yes, ma'am. There's a call. For you. Mr. Brinkman. Up... there." Twitching and speaking in spurts, pointing up.

Cindy hazarded a look and there he was again. Dick Cleveland—
the sanctimonious sack a' holy shit—still as stained glass. Had he even moved?
Good Christ.

Dick looked in rapture, as if ready to reach down from On High,
grab Cindy by the throat with his hand (an extension of His hand), and
yank her up into his demonic little slice of sixth floor government
heaven in order to cast her directly into Bureau Purgatory. And...

Was he actually nodding?
Holy Mother.

Cindy turned away with newfound conviction. "I'm at lunch," she
said, and walked off before Twitchy could coax her back with sweet
cautions.

Cindy didn't look up to see if Dick was squirming in his window—
in his shorts—spluttering red, in complete disbelief and denial over
what he was *seeing down there!* But she knew.

She knew the type. Brinkman's type, if Brinkman ever found
religion. Not that any religion would have him.

Brinkman, on the phone, waiting.
Sweet Joseph.

***

Dick Cleveland's holy tirade was worse than Cindy anticipated.
He liked chewing out Brinkman's appointees' asses almost as much as
Brinkman liked chewing Dick's. An old bent from college. Cindy
managed to tune out most of it.

Brothers.

Her call to Brinkman was another story. But she stopped his
annoyingly meaningless diatribe about professional ethics—twice in
one week—by asking, "What the hell is this Idaho shit?" The gap in
Brinkman's verbal bombing run sounded about perfect, so Cindy
persisted. "I wanna know what the fuck is going on, Phil. And I wanna
know right fucking now."

"Dick left the room, huh?" Brinkman surmised.

"Yes, and nobody's telling me a goddam thing about anything!"
She made sure to sound annoyed, which wasn't difficult.

"Les didn't tell you?" Brinkman sounded even more annoyed,
probably by design. He didn't mention the Iowa mix-up. Probably
didn't notice.

Cindy rattled off, "Barn, two guys, a girl, yellow ribbon."

"That's about it," Brinkman said.

"Oh, come on, Phil. You have to know more than that."

Though Cindy knew that Phil Brinkman had a strict policy about case information—less was best, none was better; let his field agents sweat the details—she also knew that if she was supposed to keep a close eye on Les Moore, she at least needed to know what Les knew. And she knew Brinkman knew that, too. He wasn't good for much, but he knew how to cover his ample ass. Cindy simply appealed to his corporate survival skills.

Several silent seconds passed during which Cindy took a moment to assess the religious paraphernalia in Holy Dick's office. She couldn't be positive of course, but Cindy was pretty sure twenty-seven crucifixes in one government office, in a federal building, violated at least the spirit of separation of church and state. That Dick Cleveland didn't seem to care to such a massive degree made her question the efficacy of policy as edict.

She checked for hidden microphones in Jesus's eyes.

After what Cindy imagined to be a difficult internal debate, Brinkman finally decided to break his number one Rule Number One and tell Cindy what he knew, which was that initial thinking on the two male victims had them responsible for as few as four or as many as fifteen serial murders, so that police in five states were now showing interest in the grandpa/teen team.

"Very sloppy," Brinkman charged, probably because he had heard someone else say it.

And he had a theory about their murders. "Riverbend copycat or a rogue cop. You know how those cowboys are. Out in the sticks too long without meaningful social contact. No Land Management beefs to take up arms against. Their guns getting rusty from disuse."

Cindy only halfway listened because she couldn't stop seeing the look on Les's face in the battered detective loaner in the freshly paved parking lot below. She had endured almost all of Holy Dick's harangue before putting words to the image, and then, the replay only served to upset her more. Because what she had seen on Les's face, Cindy realized, later, was fear. Simple, sonorous fear.

She made the mistake of voicing her concern.

"What are you saying, Baker?" Brinkman blurted. "Les Moore *scared*? Are we talking about the same Les Moore here? Your partner Les Moore? We couldn't be. But then, how many Les Moores are there out there? How many we both might know? Why, the chances of that coincidence are staggering, are they not, Agent Baker?"

"You didn't see him."

"I've seen him for twenty years, and trust me, little girl, one thing I never saw on Les Moore's face was fear. Never. You got the wrong man or the wrong emotion. Period. End of saga."

Cindy chose to ignore the "little girl" sobriquet. And the rest. "I'm *telling* you—"

"No, I'm telling you, Baker. Seven times honored for bravery and heroics beyond the call of duty, highest clearance rate of any agent under my command, ever, one of the highest in Bureau history. A man who once dove under a moving train to save a cat? *That* Les Moore?"

Cindy was silent.

"I thought so," Brinkman said, sounding self-satisfied. "Different Les Moore. Still, you gotta admit, the chances were astronomical."

Brinkman had a high-stakes interest. He had to have put his fat ass on the line by bringing Les Moore back. If Les was scared, Brinkman's career longevity was in dire jeopardy. Better to follow standard Bureau procedure and deny, deny, deny!

Then ship them out to Iowa on the first available flight.

"What about our investigation here?" Cindy said.

"It's on ice with your stiff. This is much more *muy importante*. So get your pretty little ass away from Holy Dick—tell him anything you have to, except the truth—then find Agent Moore, and be in Iowa before I take my morning shit."

As if all of this wasn't bad enough, Brinkman had lacquered on his super-irritating *don't test me* tone, which he now reinforced with, "You did hear me. Right, Agent Baker? *En toto*?"

Cindy couldn't decide whether to wish constipation on him or a heart attack. She chose to flirt with the latter. "Are you aware, sir, that referring to my derriere as a 'pretty little ass' is not in keeping with Bureau policy, and in fact is tantamount to sexual harassment which—"

"Hello? Baker? Are you still there? I think this line got crossed or something. Can you hear me? Baker?"

Cindy stood, dumbfounded. He was using her own dodge on her.

With equal parts disgust and admiration, Cindy said, "Goodbye, Phil," then hung up and headed for the hotel to pack.

***

Back in DC, Phil Brinkman grunted, gloated, and decided to watch his mouth around Agent Baker in the future. He had plenty of other female agents under him who were willing to take any amount of his crap for a promotion—the thought of which made him go weepy inside.

He then took his *Men's Fitness* magazine into the executive restroom, stared at himself in the mirror and decided a) he had Cindy Baker right where he wanted her, which meant, b) he had Les Moore right where he wanted him, and 3) it was time to take off a few pounds—and he was serious this time. Starting next week.

Oh, and he better add some fiber into his diet soon; this constipation was killing him.

***

Two hours of searching later, Cindy finally found Les swimming laps in the Sheraton's indoor pool. The enclosure seemed to have a tropical theme, though the "Solarium" provided little in the way of solar effect, hovering gray skies making the high-trussed glass appear opaque, like wet slate.

The potted plants weren't convincing in any way.

Apparently unaware of anyone or anything other than the water and his place in it, Les rhythmically pulled himself from one end of the hotel pool to the other as easily and gracefully as "an otter with RSD. Repetitive spatial dementia." That's what he told people who made too much of a fuss over his aquatic addiction. A length, a turn, back the same, another turn, and again, strokes strong and measured.

He really does swim, Cindy thought, almost surprised.

She had only known him a week and a half, but already she didn't trust Les Moore as far as she could drop him off a low diving board. Which caused her to keep wondering, *Why is that?*

Cindy had heard that swimming was the only exercise Les got, other than running down federal offenders. No anger-venting power-racquetball, no shin-splinting night jogs, no weights. No, Les Moore wasn't like other agents — in any way — he had to *swim*.

Suddenly realizing she had just watched Les swim three full laps without breathing once — him, either — Cindy sucked in a quick chest full of warm, moist, chlorinated air and sauntered over as casually as she could to the deep end of the pool where a stylish stainless-steel ladder plunged past cobalt-blue Mexican trim tiles adorned with colorful stylized fish.

Or were they tacos? The yellow stuff did look a lot like cheese, and the green part could have been lettuce. Or was it seaweed?

Jesus, where's Diego Rivera when you really needed him?

As Les broke the surface and took hold of the edge of the pool, Cindy complimented, "You swim well." But the truth was, she knew nothing about swimming; Cindy could barely dog paddle.

"I used to compete," Les said with no bravado, apparently feeling better than when Cindy saw him last — if no more talkative.

She turned to check out the handful of tourists around the pool, thinking this was one of those awkward moments everyone must endure from time to time and gave it a moment to pass.

Seeing no one of interest, she turned back to find Les staring at a buxom woman in a sparse bikini, reading a crime thriller. Thinking her breasts were entirely — and perhaps unnaturally — too large, Cindy said to Les, "Wonder what she's reading? Proust?"

Cindy wondered why she was being so damned catty. It wasn't like her. The stress of this case must have been getting to her — after less than a week!

Les said, "Mack Carter's latest Sue Grafton rip-off, *Z Means Zed*. Before you know it, he'll be on *Absolute Assassins*, *Bountiful Bodies*, and *Cantankerous Cadavers*."

Cindy gave a grateful chuckle, and he looked away, giving her an opportunity to notice and consider for the first time how smooth and powerful his shoulders looked, despite his slight build. *Swimmer's body,* she thought. *It's true what they say.*

She also thought it looked like he shaved under his arms.

Cindy's brow furrowed and she shifted slightly to sneak a better look through the rippling water and fractured, dancing light. Les rotated. She stole a glance. He did.

Cindy hadn't seen a man with shaved pits since she caught an uncle with a soapy razor up under his arm at the kitchen sink when she was twelve. The sight had so confused her at the time she never asked anyone why he would choose such a feminine act. Later in college, one of her dorm mates, Anne Hutchins, said all the men on her mom's side of the family shaved their armpits, but she didn't have a clue why and never dared ask either. Cindy and Anne decided that male underarm shaving was some strange secret practice, like a masonic handshake, to which they would never be privy.

Being freshmen, recently released from the constraints of home and high school, they both let their armpit hair grow out—what's good for the gander is grist for the goose—just to see what it was like. They decided it was like having great clumps of wet hair under your arms and shaved before going home for Easter. Fuck the hippies.

Cindy now confirmed that Les also had a hairless chest—well-defined, but smooth—and his forearms were fairly unhairy for a man. She hadn't noticed before. His face, too, come to think of it. Maybe he had some Native American in him. Didn't they have smooth complexions and very little body hair? And weren't they—

Yanking herself out of this uncertain depilatory preoccupation by the short hairs of her mind, Cindy said, "Listen, Brinkman called."

"He wants us to go to Iowa. 'First thing,'" Les said, mimicking their boss's most recent hollow manifesto.

"Yeah," Cindy said. *How'd he know that?* "How'd you know that?"

"Brinkman has about two moves. That's one of them," Les said, then turned, ducked under, pushed off the wall, and glided halfway across the pool before coming to the surface to resume his assured strokes, obviously disinterested in anything Brinkman had to say beyond his order to vacate the Pitt, which Les was likely happy to do, given that nickname he had given it.

Cindy wasn't about to argue. The weather was too damn cold for anyone with skin. She watched Les's easy, steady stroking and, for some reason unknown to her at the moment—unreachable—she couldn't look away.

Chapter 7 – Iowa

Since all three bodies had long since been removed from the barn by the time Les and Cindy arrived, and there were only day-glow orange spray-painted corpse outlines in the dirt, the TASK agents had to rely on the work of others to interpret the crime scene — statements by the first officer on the scene, her partner, other responding officers, the first investigating officer, the sheriff's investigator later assigned to the case, the local chief, the paramedics, the coroner, the coroner's assistant, the two state investigators sent from the Criminal Assessment Unit at DCI, and the mildly mentally handicapped kid who found the bodies in the barn and thought someone was "playing murder."

Some of the reports were useful. The majority, not.

Then there were the "witness" statements. Most of the theater patrons remembered seeing the old man and the boy. No one remembered Riverbend. No surprise there; no one ever did.

As for the poor dead farm girl, most everyone in town agreed Sarah Jean Hoxley was a disaster waiting to manifest, a lost child with a dead momma and a disconsolate daddy.

They meant mean.

"It was bound to happen someday," they would say. They just hadn't thought it would happen locally, which seemed to be the only part that bothered them and which, in turn, seemed to be the only part that bothered Cindy.

"It's no wonder," she said of Sarah Jean's teenage angst and anarchy, and dug in her purse for some extra-strength anything. "Neanderthals," she muttered more than once.

In the end, the statements proved moot. Everyone knew who had killed the girl — and who had killed *them*. But filling in the blank with "Riverbend" was only slightly better than filling it in with "unknown assailant." The average Joe on the street knew more about weather patterns on Pluto than the police knew about Riverbend.

It all just made Cindy's head hurt worse.

***

Day Two. Since autopsy protocols wouldn't be complete for seventy-two hours, Les and Cindy were forced to rely on still photos and videos at the county sheriff's office. But for farm country — far from the progressive city forensics to which most agents become accustomed — someone had done a damn good job documenting every aspect of the crime scene. Almost too good. Each graphic, horrifying detail had been *lovingly* captured in crisp digital clarity.

"I think this videographer enjoys his work too much," Cindy said, quietly.

The two TASK partners sat sequestered in a small, unadorned viewing-room off the large, cluttered central office of the sheriff's wing in the old county building downtown, viewing a slow-pan, high-definition close-up of the Old Killer's head wound. The image then cut to the girl's areola, blood-caked and torn where the ring had been ripped away. There followed a tight shot of the ring itself on the barn floor, propped against a piece of golden straw, glistening under low, warm, late afternoon light so that the image resembled a carefully composed jeweler's ad more than the cold, clinical documentation of a crime scene. Except for the blood. Finally, the camera tilted up to reveal the girl's nude body sprawled out a few feet away, then ran in a low tracking shot across the dirt back to a close-up of her ruptured nipple.

The shot held.

Cindy cringed, shook slightly, and gave a low grunt.

"Yeah," Les agreed. *That had to hurt.*

Cindy added, mostly for her own benefit, "They said she might have been dead by then, but still."

She shuddered again and discreetly covered up her own sensitive nipples with her arms, tucking her hands into her armpits as if seeking the warmth there. "I don't even know how anyone gets that done in the first place," she said honestly.

"Valium, three beers," Les said.

"Three Valium and ten beers," Cindy said.

Les chuckled as the camera idled, luxuriating on the firm, young breasts and their wounds. Both agents sat silent for several moments studying the impeccably captured particulars of the violent crime, until Cindy said, "Do you think that's sexy?"

Les looked at his new partner as if thinking maybe she was enjoying her own work too much. "Not the *video*," Cindy griped. Then she said, quieter, "Nipple rings. Genital jewelry. That sort of thing."

"Genital jewelry?" He seemed amused.

Cindy bristled. "I just wondered if men find that sort of thing... attractive. That's all."

"I dated a dancer once," he said.

"You mean stripper."

"They say dancer."

"To make themselves feel better about what they do."

"No, actually, to make other people feel better about what they do. You know, judgmental types who might think less of them."

Cindy's glare arced up a few amps.

"Anyway," Les went on, "she had a pierced nipple. It was," he conceded, "interesting." He looked... interested.

Cindy turned away to scowl at a D.A.R.E. poster, thinking how she could use a Valium right about now.

"I draw the line at lips, though," he said. "And eyebrows."

"Tongues," Cindy threw in.

"That clacking on their teeth all the time?" he said. "Almost as irritating as Brinkman telling Polack jokes." The thought of either made Cindy's teeth ache.

"Or was it both her nipples?" Les wondered aloud.

Cindy's jaw dropped enough to show her distaste. "I'd think you could remember a little detail like that." Nipples are important to a woman! Any man who forgets them is functionally suspect. Cindy could remember every penis she'd ever seen up close. Every vein, wrinkle, bump, cleft, and curve. Les better have a damn good excuse for not remembering every inch of a girl he obviously screwed repeatedly who had metal rings in her tits!

Cindy looked back at the D.A.R.E. poster for distraction. *Maybe a quaalude.*

Les grinned and said, "There've been so many."

"Hundreds, I'm sure," Cindy snorted, fairly certain he wasn't serious.

The camera now moved to and lingered on the girl's vagina. Though neither had viewed a lot of porn for pleasure purposes—Les likely more than Cindy—she thought this video was shot better than any pornography she'd ever seen. And the girl was dead.

On screen, a pen reached in, held by the videographer, or perhaps by a cop—the hand wasn't visible—and lifted the inner labia away from the crown to reveal a tiny hole. another piercing.

"Look," Cindy said, again marveling at the work. "This guy is good. How'd he ever see that?"

"Both nipples, her navel, and her nose," Les said of his dancer. "Now I remember."

"Good grief. I hope you never tried to take her through airport security."

"We mostly took cabs," Les said. Apparently, he liked taking taxis; he was smiling.

Two quaaludes.

"What the hell was her name?" he asked the cosmos.

"What was her *name?*" This was worse than nipple amnesia!

"Lotus. That's it," he recalled. "She had a tattoo of one in her—"

Les looked at Cindy—then turned back to the screen.

Cindy stared a beat. "You're very... liberal, aren't you?"

"I'm a guy," Les admitted.

"Yes, you are," Cindy agreed without malice. Mention anything to do with sex to a man—if you're a halfway attractive woman with fewer than three kids—and he's drooling all over his hard-on before you finish the sentence, was Cindy's experience.

"We can't help ourselves," Les yielded. "We're truly pathetic."

"You sound proud of it."

"It's something."

***

At some point—Cindy wasn't sure when exactly, she was so involved in the video—Les stood and said he wanted to go back out to the barn. He said there were a few things he wanted to check out, then picked up his case and walked out. Just like that.

Like Les.

Cindy grunted but didn't turn away from the monitor as the camera now refocused on the Old Killer, panning his aged body as slowly as it had the girl, taking in every bit of filth, from the stringy trails of his body fluids to the crusting rivulets of blood and shriveling scraps of tissue, all with the same loving attention to detail.

Cindy thought, *How weird*. The footage was—

"Good stuff, huh?" the woman's voice came close.

Cindy spun to find a girl who couldn't have been more than twenty-three, if that. She was pretty, in a healthy farm-fed way, tall and a little wide, but she wore the weight well. From her intonation, Cindy intuited, "You shot this?"

"Yep," the girl said with a touch of West Texas and sat down. "I got there late in the afternoon and the light was spectacular. But subtle. Effective." She nodded each time as she pinpointed the correct word.

Eyeing this softly tomboyish college girl from Anytown, USA, Cindy still couldn't believe. "You shot this?"

"I do all the gore for Sheriff Tole," the girl said, apparently accustomed to new viewers' surprise.

Cindy wondered why. "Does it pay well? Way out here?"

"Oh, no. Pays shit," the girl said. "I'm actually a stringer. I pick up footage in six, seven states. More, if the story's good. I put on two thousand miles last week. Some of my stuff from the tornadoes last year? That cluster in Missouri? Got on network. Norah O'Donnell did the lead-in," she said with pride.

"I think I saw that footage," Cindy recalled.

The young woman nodded vaguely, eyes fixed on the monitor, her body jerking in short darts as she anticipated which way the lens was going to move next. Left-down, up-right, over, back.

"Look at this," she said at one point, leaning forward slightly. "This is my favorite part."

The camera traveled up behind the Young Killer smoothly. "I had to do it handheld," she said. Then, "Well, duh. Of course. I have to do everything handheld at the carnage fests. Not like I can set up track and a dolly." She rolled her eyes at herself then renewed her focus.

"Here it comes," she said. "The light was magnificent. I mean it. I was *so* lucky. Almost... almost... okay, and... here."

The framing of the next image was exquisite, as if she had posed the dead bodies for maximum effect. Warm late light filtered through gaps in the barn siding, transforming motes of dust into fuzzy columns of magic that highlighted the most important elements of the scene.

The camera played across the smooth naked bodies of the two dead teenagers, their arms out, fingers almost touching, Michelangelo-like, as if reaching back for life from the hereafter; the Old Killer's leathery corpse sprawled out to one side, poignantly tying the dramatic elements of the composition together with skilled artistic precision; even encrusted death fluids seemed to take on jewel-like properties as sinking orange rays refracted through them into her lens, making the composition, the *piece*, almost beautiful.

Cindy shivered.

"I thought about using a star filter," the girl said, "but the police frown on, you know, aesthetic embellishment."

That's okay, Cindy thought; the shot didn't need augmentation. She was held spellbound by this — dare she think — *gorgeous* picture. One of the most repugnant death scenes Cindy had yet encountered, and she found the footage arresting. The work made her heart sing and sink at the same time. She shivered again.

Goddammit, it was art.

The shot held and held. And held. The girl must've squatted, motionless, for two or three minutes to get the shot. Cindy's thighs ached just watching the —

"Nice shot."

The voice had come from behind them, shattering their silent meditation on the dead like a shotgun in a bedroom. Cindy jumped again and looked back reflexively to find Les. He smiled and a wash of calm spread over her like warm surf on a private beach.

Odd, Cindy thought, how he could do that. She turned back to the monitor.

The girl had never moved, never taken her eyes off the screen, captured by her own flawless composition, her classical use of Rembrandt lighting on death masks.

"Thanks," she said, far more interested in analyzing her work for the umpteenth time than seeing who was offering the compliment.

Les turned his attention to Cindy. "Coming?"

"Didn't know I was invited," Cindy said, already transfixed again by the shot on the screen which still hadn't cut.

"I figured, when you didn't come out," Les said. Even though she didn't look, Cindy could feel his smile on the back of her neck like a quiet breeze through cracked blinds.

She smiled, herself.

The girl sat up sharply. "Now," she said and, a millisecond later, the shot ended. Then she stood, said, "Damn, I'm good," and started out past Les.

"See ya 'round the pool," she quipped, farm-girl friendly. "Good luck on your case." She disappeared down a side hall. The video played on, more creative shots of lives lapsed.

"She does good work," Les said.

"Very good work," Cindy agreed.

"Nice girl," he said.

"Very nice," she agreed again.

"But some freaky shit, huh?"

"*Very* freaky shit," Cindy said, and turned the monitor off.

Chapter 8 – The Corn

After Les had paced the barn, Cindy had smelled it, and both had taken their own full set of pics from every angle inside and out, he asked her if she was ready for dinner, and she asked him how he ate so much but never put on any weight.

"Swimming," he said, and she accepted him at his word, noting how hungry she was.

As they got in their red rental, a midsize Dodge, and started back through cornfields flat and dulled by an early autumn, Les added how he didn't eat that much, just often. Cindy said she had noticed. He smiled and that went okay, but what she really wanted to ask him had to do with that other thing she'd noticed.

"Do you shave your armpits?"

Les looked at her, then back at the road, and grunted, "No."

"Yes, you do," Cindy said. "I saw in the pool."

He didn't answer.

"Why would you lie?" she asked him.

"Why would you ask if you already knew?" Les asked her in return, irked. "Isn't that just a lie masquerading as a question?"

He looked out at the corn plants whizzing by and said, "How many metric tons of that yellow death you think they grow out here every year?"

"Corn?" Cindy said, thinking she'd never heard of anything benign as corn being so heartily assailed. "You have something against corn?"

"Hate it," Les said.

Cindy said, "Good thing you weren't born a chicken. Why do you hate it?"

"I don't know," he said. "Why do you want to know about my personal hygiene?" He sounded piqued and threw her a complementary glower.

"Jeez, excuse me," Cindy carped. "You'd think after our conversation about genital enhancement, armpits would be fair game."

He didn't respond. "So, it's a hygiene thing." She made a statement, but it was really just another question.

"Yeah," he said. "A hygiene thing."

"Oh." She nodded. "I wondered."

A long minute passed during which Cindy was able to consider this new intelligence she had gathered. She wasn't bothered as much as she thought she might be, now that the subject was out in the open. She had her eccentricities; he was allowed his. So, she was sitting pretty well with it all until he asked:

"You shave your twat?"

Cindy felt as if she'd been splashed with a fjord-full of glacial runoff, right there in the red Avenger. "Do I... *what*?"

"Shave it. Your twat," Les repeated, as if this were a normal conversation. "Just wondered."

Cindy felt like her face looked like a walnut shell, pale, wrinkled, and brittle. "Are you in love with that word or something?"

"No. Not the word," Les said. "So, do you?"

Cindy glared at him long enough to blink three times, at regular intervals, then said, "No. I don't." Curt enough, but more than she wanted to give up.

"Mmm," Les nodded, as if a great mystery had finally been solved for him.

"And for the record," Cindy said, tightly, "I don't think it's the same."

"Mmmmmmmm," Les nodded again, dragging it out longer this time, as if this was even weightier.

Which made Cindy go gristly inside. She didn't like being messed with, unless she knew she was and could mess back. But with Les, there was never any knowing. About anything. And it was really starting to piss her off.

***

A mile further, Les hit the brakes hard. "How did I miss that?" He slid the sedan off the hardtop onto a dirt side road.

"What?" Cindy said, craning to look. Les flipped his head back, but she had already found the sign. 'Tattoos and Piercings by Garth.' The paint looked fresh.

The tattoo parlor was more of a shed, a twelve-by-sixteen premanufactured plywood box on concrete blocks with small, curtained windows on three sides and double doors in front like a miniature barn. Off to the left was a clean double-wide with dark, added-on wood siding and a small porch on the front. The half-acre lot was bordered on all sides by a large, spreading cornfield, recently picked and plowed under early. A clean 1960 Chevy Apache pickup, Caterpillar yellow, sat parked behind the trailer home by a rat Harley, left flat black for aesthetic reasons. A wooden garage that hadn't seen fresh paint in six decades leaned toward the nearest neighbors, a half-mile off.

Les and Cindy followed the rumble of Insane Clown Posse to find the owner of this idyllic little fiefdom inside his office, sterilizing the torture tools of his trade in blue alcohol and an autoclave. Garth Titan, as he called himself, was of average height, about five-ten, but weighed in at some 250 pounds. He had a wide, dark goatee, three days of stubble, with tattoos on his neck and shaved head. He also had enough metal in his face to cause radio interference in low-flying aircraft.

But Garth turned out to be a nice enough guy, and one of their better interviewees, even though DCI had been out twice to question him already. "Oh yeah," he said, "I knew Mouse pretty well." Then, he clarified, "Sarah Jean," and turned off the million-watt stereo.

Cindy's ears continued to ring.

Had Garth done her tattoo? "Yeah," he said. "And her ears."

"You tattooed her ears?" Cindy asked, not remembering.

Garth shook his head. "Piercings. Nine as I recall."

Cindy was thinking that the reports hadn't mentioned more body piercings when Garth showed, on his own ears, where each five *others* had been. One in the tragus — the middle nub that always made Cindy cringe about like eyebrow piercings — and the rest along the tops, in the cartilage. He had at least sixteen, himself. And a cork, size: huge.

Les peered behind a black curtain hung halfway back and found an old OB/GYN chair with stirrups. "What about her..."

Les glanced at Cindy. Cindy took in the chair and said, "Other piercings?"

After several silent beats, Garth nodded but said nothing.

"Is that legal here?" Les asked. "Her age?" Garth studied the lean FBI man a moment, then shook his head no. Les was gracious. "Probably a lot of kids want that these days," he said.

On this, Garth offered nothing more. So, Cindy tried. "When was the last time she came around?"

"Day before she was killed," Garth recalled. "She put some money toward a new piece." He showed them on his display chart that she had chosen a hummingbird on a rainbow.

Cindy's heart plummeted deeper. Her eyes ran over the walls covered with flash—hundreds of skulls and other sharp-edged images of death and dying—seeing nothing but the poor farm girl's dead body.

"Have you seen the photos of her killers?" Les asked.

Garth nodded slowly.

"Know 'em?" Les said.

Garth shook no, honestly.

Cindy added, "Never saw them hanging around?"

Another no.

"Did you ever notice anyone else hanging around?" Les wondered. "At a distance. Out by the road, or off in the corn. Someone you didn't recognize."

Garth's eyes revealed nothing more for a few seconds—then he lit up. "Now you mention it." He moved to the door and nodded out. "The morning she was here, Sarah—well, it was probably after noon, more like one—I took her deposit, twenty bucks, wrote it down in my log, and put it in the register." He added as a side note. "There's no refunds on second thoughts."

Les and Cindy nodded. That seemed reasonable.

"I was standing here," the ink-covered biker said, "waving g'bye to her when I saw something in the corn out there. They hadn't harrowed it, yet. Just a blur, really. I wasn't even sure I'd seen anythin' at all. But then I heard a car start."

He seemed to be done, so Les asked, "That was it?"

Enough to have been Riverbend, but Les showed nothing.

Garth nodded. "Sarah started her daddy's old truck—the muffler's gone—so I didn't hear anything else." Anticipating their next question, he said, "Didn't see anything, either."

Les looked at Cindy. Telegraphically, they knew exactly what the other was thinking. Riverbend had targeted the girl, followed her here, then to the theater where he was planning to take her after—until he lucked onto the Old Killer and his teen sidekick.

It all fit.

Les asked, "Was your sign out there earlier?"

"No," Garth said. "Someone run over it last week, mashed it up. I only got around to putting up the new one about an hour ago."

The interview was complete.

***

Over a quiet dinner back at their hotel—there hadn't been a restaurant open on the highway—Cindy silently reviewed the new information about Sarah Jean Hoxley and a germinating theory on how Merfinridge in Seattle and the grandpa-teen team here had met their respective ends. What was the relationship? There had to be one, and Cindy was fairly certain she'd inferred the correct correlation. The problem was who had done Merfinridge, and why?

Really why?

Trying to get to that, Cindy asked Les, "How do you think this guy felt, the one who offed Merfinridge, when he read that Merfinridge wasn't Riverbend?"

"We know it's a guy?" Les asked her.

"For the sake of this discussion, yes."

Les gave a thoughtful pause, answered, "Probably pissed off," and forked a cube of T-bone. He didn't eat much red meat anymore, he'd said, but steak had "jumped off the menu" at him.

"Is that what you'd feel?" Cindy wondered.

"If I whacked him?"

"If you'd planned the whole thing, the stalking, the execution, everything, and you found your man and killed him and got away with it—then found out he wasn't Riverbend at all, just some... Merfinridge."

"Who says he planned it?" Les said. "Maybe he just got lucky."

"No. He'd done it before," Cindy said with certainty.

Les agreed. "Still could've had an element of luck."

"So?" She wasn't disagreeing, just sticking with the subject.

"How would I feel," Les said by way of confirmation, accepting the premise. He looked off a moment, as if pondering, then settled on, "Shitty."

"What kind of shitty?" Cindy wondered.

"How many kinds are there?"

"Millions."

"Millions?"

"Lots. Answer the question."

"I thought I did."

"Be more specific in your answer."

"Why? Am I a suspect?"

"Hardly! Jesus, don't you ever do this?" *Kick ideas around.*

"Not with other people. Sort of like sex these days. Solo venture."

"Sorry to hear that," Cindy said, not quite facetiously.

"And your sex life is..."

"Not the topic of this conversation," she certified.

Les grinned, took a breath and exhaled slowly. "Shitty like... I had put a lot of effort into this, to make a point, do some good, whatever, maybe to avenge some of the women he'd killed, and I wasted the opportunity. Probably my one shot."

"Not wasted. Merfinridge was an SK," Cindy pointed out.

"Not the right SK," Les said.

"So, you think," Cindy posited, putting her partner's thoughts together, "whoever killed Merfinridge will try again."

She'd made a bit of a leap, but apparently the right one because, after giving slow consideration, Les said, "Yeah."

"So do I," Cindy said, eyes flashing.

Les chuckled. "Save us some paperwork."

"Not really," Cindy dissented. "Not in the end."

"Your point is it's still murder."

"Still murder."

"Still our job to stop them."

"That's why we cash a check every other week."

"Speak for yourself." Les grinned and speared his last piece of cow as Cindy laughed and picked up the three-sided plastic dessert menu to ponder the many wonderful possibilities found in combining fudge, ice cream, and brownies.

"I was thinking of a malted," Les offered.

"A malted," Cindy repeated. "How old are you?"

"Old enough," Les said dourly, and after a moment added, getting back to the subject at hand, "Whoever it was would have to be pretty smart."

Cindy nodded and shrugged. Maybe, maybe not, she was saying. Then, she asked, "Are you gonna eat your corn?"

"Take it," Les said, then sat back and watched as she scraped the offending yellow bits from his plate to hers.

"Well, think about it," Cindy said. "They know the drill, the signs. Like gay men picking up other gay men back in the fifties. They had to get together somehow, so they had subtle signs only they recognized. You see what I'm going for here?"

"Probably an official reprimand. What about gay women?"

"Them too," Cindy concluded. "But lesbians, I think, were always more... open about it."

"You know this or you just made it up?"

"Little of both," Cindy said, then shrugged. "Made it up."

She grabbed the menu again. "But women are smarter than men in general. And are much more courageous about their social and moral convictions."

"You're saying men are moral wimps."

"And intellectual thugs. But that's not the point. I'm saying men start wars and fight over women."

"Not gay men."

"No."

"And not over lesbians."

"Unless they don't know," Cindy cautioned. "But gay men," the point was, "don't usually fight over each other, because they're more in touch with their feminine side. Which makes them smarter, gentler, kinder. More likely to appreciate art. The finer things."

"And go into ballet as a profession," Les offered.

"Are we gay bashing, now?"

"You started it. Comparing gay men to serial killers."

"I wasn't comparing gay men to serial killers!" Cindy yelped. "I was just saying all secret societies or subcultures have subtle ways of identifying each other. That's not bashing. It's not even a stereotype. It's a fact. They have ways, they *have* to have ways, to, I don't know, you know... sniff each other out."

"Sniff each other out?" Les raised his eyebrow. "Yeah, that's much better. No one would object to that."

"You know what I mean," Cindy said, chasing the last kernel of corn around her plate.

Les picked up the dessert menu. "We really need to start eating in better restaurants." He showed her the triangular laminated card with prices which began with "Only" and ended with an exclamation point. Not exactly five stars. He put the card down and sighed, sitting back.

Cindy stared at him. "Is that it?"

"What? I haven't decided yet," Les said. "Give me a minute."

"You are so infuriating," Cindy said, huffing again. "You know exactly what I'm talking about every time I open my mouth, but you constantly and consistently act like you don't."

"Frustrating, isn't it?" He grinned.

"I'm not going to give you the satisfaction of an answer."

Les wondered, "Aren't they the same?"

"Serial killers and gay people? No!"

"Constantly and consistently. They're sort of... redundantly repetitious, don't you think?" He picked up the dessert menu again.

"I hate you," Cindy said. "You do realize that, don't you?" Les gave a careless shrug. "And no, they're not," Cindy said. "One refers to a time continuum, the other to action."

Les looked across the top of the dessert menu. Cindy thought he might be about to express how impressed he was with her etymological aptitude, but instead he said, "I'm sorry. Did you say something?"

"Oh," she said, almost admiringly, "you feint so deftly. Change directions faster than Emmett Smith on ten espressos."

"Who's he?"

"NFL all-time rusher. Dallas Cowboys." Brothers.

Les said, "I don't follow baseball."

"Hardy-har," Cindy said. "Are you going to ask me if I shave my vagina again?"

"Trust me. I would never ask a woman if she shaved her *vagina*."

"Why not? That's what it's called."

"Not by anyone interested in one."

Cindy stared a long beat, then said, "Point taken. Now, do you or do you not agree that a serial killer, perhaps only second to a cop, would have the perfect instincts to search out and find other serial killers? I mean, it's happened before."

"On TV."

Cindy felt a turtle squack coming on but said nothing.

Les stared at her with what appeared to be mild incredulity. "You just gave me that one, by the way. Impressively graceful capitulation. Slid it right in."

Cindy let go an anguished, testudinal groan and put her head on the table.

Their waiter appeared, heard her, saw her, then spun on a light heel and said, "I'll come back in a minute for your dessert orders." His S's came off his tongue and teeth, not his palate.

Les nodded toward the retreating waiter. "Why don't you ask him what *he* thinks of your gay serial killer analogy? Theory, excuse me."

"Just because the man has a lisp doesn't mean he's gay."

"You're saying he's not gay?"

"Of course he's gay, that's not the issue."

People were starting to stare.

"I don't know," Les said with mock concern. "You're pretty hard to keep up with. What was the question again?"

"Forget it," Cindy said, standing. "I'm going to my room." She grabbed her briefcase.

"Okay then, you're right. I agree."

"Too late," Cindy said, and sashayed out of the restaurant—and she did sashay.

Just before the door, she looked back and caught Les admiring her retreat. She turned away, grinning to herself, and thought, *He couldn't help but.* She still had it.

Chapter 9 – Back to the Barn

"Weekends off," Brinkman had told Cindy. She mulled it over, comparing and contrasting what the term meant back home in DC and out in Los Angeles—where she'd spent some time in special ops training—or in *what was the name of this town*?

Saturday morning had come, and the rental was gone. Again. Or was it still gone? Whichever, Cindy wasn't surprised. So, she called over to the sheriff's office and asked if they had an extra car she could use for the weekend. They said they did and ran one over within the hour. A few minutes later, just after eleven a.m., Cindy drove off in the soon-to-be-retired detective beater to play tourist.

By eleven thirty, she had seen everything there was to see. The town felt a lot like her own hometown in Ohio only flatter, if that was possible. Town center had ten or eleven right turns, two fewer lefts, however that worked out, and that was that.

There was the Prairie Memorial—fairly engaging for a plaque on a pile of rocks in the middle of nowhere—but within five minutes of reading the worn inscription, Cindy had already forgotten how many settlers had frozen to death in the winter of... *what year was it*? And, *What's the name of this town again?*

***

"I don't care if you didn't see him come in or not! Maybe he used the back door!" Cindy shouted into her phone at the young desk clerk back at the motel. "Now, ring the damn room!"

The poor kid had just been trying to help.

Thirty-eight rings and no answer later, Cindy hung up feeling no better than she had when she woke up. A movie didn't help; neither did a malted. Neither did asking for it by that name.

So, Cindy drove out to the barn.

***

On approaching the breezeway, Cindy noticed an awful lot of new footprints in the soft ground—lookie-loos out for a peek and some souvenirs, no doubt. Kids getting their snapshot taken in the fading paint outlines. *Look John Boy, I'm dead. Hyuh-hyuh-hyuh.*

Being out here didn't seem to be helping.

Brown blood stains still graced the dirt floor of the old barn, though not for much longer. Time, weather, and tourists have a way of disappearing hematic residue. Tissue remnants on the walls were more resilient, though no longer recognizable as tissue except to a trained eye. Cindy thought how the uninitiated voyeur might think some local hillbilly had wiped his boogers on the wall after fucking a sheep!

"Oh, Jesus," Cindy finally said out loud, "I have got to get a life," and started climbing around behind the old farm equipment and moldy hay, looking for anything to get her mind off Les traipsing around wherever without her again.

That's when she caught sight of it.

From high on a pile of graying bales, Cindy saw the glint of something on the ground, on the far side of the barn—the one angle from which no one had likely looked. Or maybe the narrow slant of midday light was different, in a different place. Maybe today was the only day of the year the sun would hit the thing at all, lying where it was, much less line up the reflection with her gaze.

She had to correct her path on the way down and over several times to hold the twinkle, but Cindy went right to the small mother-of-pearl inlay in some loose straw and squatted, eyeing it from all sides, noting its relevant position to the rest of the room, pacing out every tangent before touching it—drawing diagrams in her pocket notebook and jotting memos to herself. Only then did she pick it up with two pieces of straw and deposit it on the clean, shiny, foil backside of a gum wrapper for safe transportation and later observation.

She had carefully examined the victims' clothing in the evidence room with Les at the sheriff's station and clearly remembered that there hadn't been a western shirt. The girl had worn cutoffs with a tight, pink midriff top; the boy had word a black AC/DC T-shirt and black Levis; the old man had been wearing khaki slacks with a short-sleeved plaid shirt with a Penney's label. Had their killer worn a western-style shirt? Was it now missing an inlay?

Had this inlay belonged to Riverbend? Was it possible?

Cindy became so engrossed in studying the sliver of abalone, now nestled on a bed of crinkly silver Doublemint paper, the casual female, "Hey!" sent her rocketing to her feet and nearly out of her skin. The inlay went flying and Cindy went digging for her service weapon, drawing and aiming as she spun to find —

The completely unruffled videographer.

"Wow, don't shoot," the girl said, as if speaking to a kid pointing a banana, then walked past and stood on the dark smudge that still marked the spot where the Old Killer's road ran out.

Her heart rate elevated more than she would have liked — and her grouch factor elevated beyond that — Cindy caviled, "You're standing in the middle of a crime scene."

More like a traffic cop every day. This job was killing her.

"Yellow tape's gone," the girl said. "Free-for-all from now on. Wait till the local hay-suckers start coming out for souvenirs."

Cindy reproached her, "Doesn't mean there might not be some new evidence left around that we didn't find." And she bent down to find the new evidence she'd just found and dropped.

"I doubt it," the girl said. "They went over this place with a fine-toothed comb. I know. I was here nearly the whole time. I shot over three hours." She added a somewhat sarcastic, "Good times. Hangin' with the boys."

Then she said, "But it was good stuff, wasn't it? I mean, tell the truth, when you see other crime scene footage, it just doesn't look like mine, does it?"

"Yeah, no. It's great," Cindy said tersely, brushing off the girl and her work to focus on relocating the dusty inlay then carefully and discreetly getting the damn thing back on the foil wrapper.

"You're pretty wound up, aren't you?" the girl observed as she headed back outside for her new maroon Prius. "I mean, I don't see many cops being so jumpy." And she was gone.

Myriad responses rattled through Cindy's brain, but she refrained from unkind comment as she eyed the inlay closer, this time clutching it tightly when she heard the video girl returning with her gear.

"You wanna talk weird, though. You should've seen your partner when I shot *him*. Whooo!" She gave a spooky movie-vampire laugh and set her aluminum Halliburton case and nylon sport totes on the spot the poor farm girl last glimpsed life at the end of a snub-nosed .38.

Cindy instantly forgot about the inlay—and the video girl's careless intrusion on a crime scene, uncordoned or not—because the young crime-scene reporter was apparently talking about having videoed: "Les?"

Cindy hadn't seen Les on the DVD. So, why was this girl saying, "I came around the corner over there, rolling, and *Jesuswhatalook!*" She made her eyes go wide. Apparently, she had found his reaction comical. She opened her Halliburton.

"Wait, back up," Cindy ordered. "You shot Les? On video?"

"Well, yeah. I don't do stills. I need motion." As if any fool should know this about her, about her professional integrity.

Far from the point. "When?" Cindy said, moving closer. *That* was the point.

"All the time," the girl said—as if Cindy was completely stupid—and swapped out hard-drives on her camera.

Jesus, she's worse than Les! Cindy thought while saying, "No," with as much patience as she could fake. "When did you shoot him? My partner?"

"Oh. The other day," the girl said, rolling it off like one of her own dumb mistakes.

She lifted her new high-end, high-def camera up and said, "I was real wide, so my depth of field was constant, and I was getting this great moving shot of the old equipment over there. You know, to get that Norman Rockwell thing happening, then cruise over to where the bodies were for the Truman Capote *In Cold Blood* tag."

She stood in the middle of the crime scene again, on the Old Killer's cranial leakage, and said, "It was almost as good as having the bodies here, the day before, when the blood was still wet and still oozed if you put pressure on a wound."

Once again, Special Agent Cyndra Baker had been presented with massive amounts of information that needed to be processed quickly. And on a Saturday afternoon, for Chrissake. After six!

"I like to think of it as visual poetry," the girl went on, rolling a few seconds to test her equipment. She played the clip back, saying, "Do you think that's pretentious? I mean, not to say it, or put it on your reel or your resumé or anything, but to think it. Like... poetry in motion. You know, like that song by what was his name? What was their name?"

My God, Cindy thought, this recall disconnect was contagious. Damn straw-sucking... *What was it she said again?*

"I don't remember," Cindy finally said of the song and tried to shake off her Alzheimic hypochondria. "I can't remember any of that stuff since I woke up this morning."

"I know the feeling," the girl nodded. "Hits me all the time. Especially out here in BFE."

Cindy hadn't heard that one since college.

The girl turned her camera on Cindy and the little red light on front lit up.

Cindy said quickly, "Don't do that, please. I'm not on duty, here, okay?"

"It's okay, this is great," she assured Cindy, crouched low, circling, zooming in—narrow slits of high light from the cupola her visual fulcrum. "You're gonna love it. The light's unreal in here." She obviously wasn't going to stop.

Cindy quickly ran her options—and chose to step into the glaring bright light of the wide barn door. She didn't know much about videography, but she knew about...

"Backlight! No, no, no!" the girl shouted.

Cindy didn't move. The girl stopped shooting and looked around her viewfinder at Cindy with great displeasure.

"I'm sorry," Cindy said, without sounding sorry at all. "I'm trying to conduct a double-homicide investigation here."

"Triple," the girl said torpidly, and turned away.

"She's Local's problem," Cindy said. "The other two are mine."

The girl grunted and lowered her camera. "I thought you said you were off duty," she grumbled and, with her shot of the day ruined, started looking for the next great angle.

"And I would've thought you were," Cindy said, following along. "Sheriff Tole couldn't want any of this. Or are you... stringering?"

"I usually say stringing," the girl said, apparently never having considered that conjugation—or possibly horrified by Cindy's creation. "I'm just shooting for myself," she said. "I'm putting together a documentary about cops and killers, murder and birth. Life, death. The Cycle."

"Sounds deep. Listen," Cindy said with indifference and no pause, "I need to ask you a few questions about what you said before, about videoing my partner. When was that, specifically?"

"Last shot I made," the girl said. "I don't think it got copied onto the footage you saw. The card was full, and I had to switch it out. The guys at the department probably misplaced it. That happens a lot."

On further consideration, her memory became sharper. "No, what am I saying? It's not even on that card. I shot it last night. It's the first shot on the new card. Duh much?" She snorted with self-deprecating annoyance.

"Last night?" Cindy repeated. Grit roughed up her tone.

"Well, late yesterday. About this time, but a little later. Sunset. Just after. The lux on this camera is surprising sometimes. Like point-nothing, I swear."

"I'm sure it is," Cindy said, with no idea. More important here, much more important, was that another card of video images was floating around, which Cindy hadn't seen—and Les was on it. That, and he'd been out here without her again.

"Is there anything else on that card?" Cindy asked, her hiatal hernia suddenly feeling like she had drunk high-test then swallowed a lit cigar.

"Not much," the girl said, aiming her lens straight up into the cupola and rotating slowly, creating a kaleidoscopic image in her wide viewfinder screen that Cindy could see. "Some stuff out in the field, the flowers at sunset, some old machinery in that shed out there, maybe a few shots in here. I don't remember. Nothing good."

"Nothing... relevant?"

The girl lowered her camera and stared blankly at Cindy a long moment, then said, "No," succinctly, and set off for a new shot.

Cindy persisted. "What about Les?"

"Who?"

"My partner."

"Oh. Well, I told you. I came around there..." She pointed at the post of an old stall. "And he was... here. Give or take." She indicated a circle of about two feet in the air with her hand, some eight or nine feet from the stall.

"What was he doing?" Cindy wanted to know, trying to visualize.

"What, is he a suspect?" the girl asked, as if finding it unusual that one cop should be asking about another's actions at a crime scene — or anywhere else.

Cindy registered surprise, then laughed. "No!" she said, louder than she had intended, which only served to make it seem she was lying and he was a suspect and *why does everyone keep asking me that?*

"No," she said, forcing a curtain of calm over herself. "Not at all. It's just..."

Cindy tried to figure out why she *was* asking the question. When no answer came right away, the girl started videoing cracked bridles and curling harnesses on the wall. Dust-covered atmospheric stuff.

Cindy followed her into the dimmer light. "It's just..." she said, trying again and, this time, after a few seconds, found the rest of her query. "You said he was jumpy, and Les is so — usually so — in control."

"Yeah," the girl said dreamily, apparently seeing Les — the controlled Les — in her mind's eye. She stopped shooting. "He's sexy for an older guy, isn't he?"

Cindy said, "I guess so," brushing the innuendo aside. "He's my partner. I don't think of him that way."

The girl looked at her a long moment then snorted again. "Yeah, right," she said, and headed off behind the old stairs, camera at her side.

"Ex-*cuse* me?" Cindy said. But the girl had disappeared into the darkness at the back of the barn.

"Hey, wait a minute, hold on," Cindy instructed, carefully checking the inlay in the foil, then carefully wrapping the foil in a napkin left over from breakfast, then carefully slipping the whole bundle into her jacket pocket, then hurrying around the corner not so carefully to find the video girl squatted down, jeans around her boots — relieving herself.

She looked up and said, "Do you mind? I'm peeing." Her question had that turned-up thing at the end, like a pouty coed.

Flustered by the unexpected sight of the girl's bare skin and a puddle in the dust between her Nike hikers, Cindy spluttered, "Oh... No, sorry, I just, I was..." She turned away.

Country folk. Christ. No boundaries!

By the time Cindy realized she was hearing sneakers on old wood, the video girl was zipped and halfway up the stairs.

As Cindy took the top stair into the loft, a barn owl screeched and darted for cover. Both women jumped, but for different reasons.

"Damn!" the video girl shouted. "I missed him! Did you see where he went?" Her eyes shot round the dusty open loft—moldy hay, chicken feathers, some eggs.

Slivers of thin light.

"No," Cindy said, trying to see inside herself and figure out why she was so damn jumpy! "Listen," she chose to lie, "I've got things to do."

The girl gave her an *I'll bet you do* look. Maybe even an *I'll bet it has something to do with your partner and being naked* look.

Cindy felt pushed past her civil limits. "Goddammit, now look!"

The girl shot her a frightened look then turned away to grab some last footage and likely *get the hell outa Dodge!*

Agent Baker blocked her way. "I want to know what was so goddam unusual about the look on my partner's face when you caught him in your lens. It's a simple question requiring some recall and a small amount of critical judgment on your part, which is something we all do with everyone we meet, every day. Okay? So, what was it you were seeing?"

The girl looked extremely uncomfortable with this unofficial line of official-sounding inquiry—and Cindy's intentional gaze burning into her like a blowtorch through Glad Wrap.

"I just shoot it, I don't analyze it," the girl said. Which was probably true for the most part, since she seemed to view her work as art more than documentation, even if that was the precise job description.

She tried to look busy.

"Bullshit," Cindy charged. "You implied my reaction was minor compared to his. That he looked nervous or unsettled in some way. That was your implication, was it not?"

"I don't know," the girl said, becoming agitated, and sounding fearful.

"Just tell me. What were you seeing?" Cindy's insisted.

"I don't know!" the girl snapped—and appeared to search her mind for any detail she might have tucked away that would get Cindy off her back.

She came up with, "He looked... scared, I guess. Like you did before, when I walked in. Only..."

"Only what?" Cindy pressed.

"I'm thinking! Give me a second! I'm not good at this."

This college-aged girl simply didn't have enough life on her yet, despite all she'd seen, and abstract scrutiny wasn't her job. But she finally settled on, "More scared. Okay?" Then, she thought aloud. "Well, I don't know if it was so much scared, but like he had just... seen a ghost. Yeah, yeah, that kind of scared."

Cindy backed off. "A ghost?"

"Yeah, he was... kind of pale. Like someone who thinks they've seen a ghost. You know, and it kind of... scares the pee out of you for a moment, before you realize you haven't. That it was all in your head. But for that moment..." She nodded.

Cindy said, "So you're saying he then... looked as if he was okay?"

"Yeah, sort of, for a second," the girl said hesitantly.

"For a second. Then he changed again?"

"Yeah, I guess."

"And, what? How?"

"I don't know! I'm not a stupid psychiatrist!"

"Just calm down and tell me what he looked like," Cindy said, forcing patience into her voice. "You know what people look like when they're mad or happy."

"He wasn't happy."

"Was he angry? Frightened? Spacy looking?"

"No. I guess, sort of... angry. In weird way, though. I've never seen that look before."

Cindy had. On Les.

"Kind of scary, almost," Cindy offered. "Not so much that *he* was scared, but that whatever he was thinking about scared *you*."

"Yes!" The girl lit up. "Like, I didn't know what he was going to do next."

"You mean, like, maybe he was going to attack you?"

"Oh, no," the girl said without qualm. "I never felt any danger for me personally. But..."

"For someone else."

"Right. Someone else better look out." She nodded to herself, satisfied that she'd nailed it.

Cindy backed off. "Okay. Thanks." She had her answer. Not that it made her feel any better, but it's what she had seen before as well.

Now, she had third-party corroboration. Screw Brinkman and his paranoid delusions of confidence.

The girl said, "If you want, I'll bump you a copy and you can watch it in your room. You have a laptop right, a notebook, pad, something official?" Cindy nodded, so the girl said, "I'll put it on the tail of the rest of the footage and run it by the hotel. Then you can see it all anytime you want. Thumb drive okay?"

"Good, yeah, okay, thanks," Cindy said absentmindedly. The look had had the same effect on her—haunting, even frightening. *Somebody better look out.*

Yeah, that was it exactly.

***

The light on Cindy's phone was blinking when she awoke the next morning, Sunday. She had slept poorly again, but at least she was getting used to the bad dreams, if not being tired all the time as a result.

"Hello," she said softly and yawned. The desk guy told her he had a package for her and did she want him to bring it up. She did.

The kid who knocked at her door with the small manila envelope a minute later looked much younger than he had sounded on the phone—the same kid Cindy had reamed the day before. She didn't bring it up.

"She's pretty, huh?" the kid asked, seeking confirmation, or maybe just sharing.

Cindy opened the clasp on the envelope, saw the thumb drive and instantly understood his rhapsody. "Yeah, she is," Cindy said kindly and honestly.

He repeated, "Yeah, she is," then Cindy tipped him five bucks, mostly because of the day before.

She closed the door and took the thumb drive out. A Post-It was stuck inside to the front envelope flap with a series of numbers jotted hastily in a woman's hand below a typed label, which read: "Sorbel-Diggs-Hoxley Crime Scene Raw Footage—All."

"All" had been underlined. Cindy understood what that meant.

Still yawning, she walked to the computer, stuck the drive in, waited and hit the Play arrow. She recognized the barn footage from before and scanned to the numbers on the Post-It note, watching them carefully until Les's image filled her screen, frozen in time and warm light. He looked *exactly* as if he'd seen a ghost—and that ghost better look out.

***

At one o'clock, Cindy ordered the Sunday Trout Special and a Heineken. She had watched the footage six times. By two thirty, she had viewed everything on the drive two more times and was out cold in the warm room, lost in those dreams again. But this time, Cindy was killing Riverbend, instead of the other way around.

Somehow, that was worse.

Chapter 10 – Brinkman's Call

The ringing phone echoed like an out-of-tune steel-drum band in a Kristallnacht art installation. Cindy squinted into late afternoon light pouring in the motel window and tried to unglue her eyes. Several seconds passed before she guessed she must have dozed heavily after her Trout Special and the Heineken. *One beer? And I'm out like a sorority pledge after a kegger?*

The arrhythmic steel drums again. Cindy reached over.

"Hello," she groaned into the mouthpiece, feeling free to sound as half-dead as she felt.

What the hell, it was Sunday, wasn't it? And she was off, wasn't she? Why did she feel so—

"Where the fuck is Agent Moore?" Brinkman grunted with his usual aplomb.

Oh. *Him.*

"You have the wrong room," Cindy said with a husky rasp, then hung up and went straight into the bathroom to heave. She didn't stop throwing up until ten after ten, her phone ringing every half hour on the flip of the LED. Knowing Brinkman, Les's room phone was probably doing the same on the fifteens.

The last ring she heard came at ten thirty. Then Cindy was out like death.

***

When Les finally picked up at eleven, Brinkman grunted, "Where the fuck have you been?" Little had changed.

Les kicked off his shoes, said, "It's Sunday, Phil," and seriously considered hanging up.

After a moment, Brinkman said, "The bitch hung up on me."

Les was immediately intrigued. Could he possibly mean "Cindy?"

"Who else?"

Maybe something had changed. "How do you know?"

"I know."

"No, but I mean," Les said, "how do you *really* know?"

"Christ, Les. We're the FBI. We're not morons."

"Speak for yourself, Phil."

"What's that supposed to mean?"

Les knew Brinkman knew exactly what he meant. They had a history. Despite that, Les said, "It's supposed to mean, and in fact does mean, that on Sundays I'm nobody. Not an agent, not FBI, sometimes not even me."

"That's not what you said at your swearing in."

"We differed on that point."

Les peeled off his socks and evaluated his deep fatigue in the mirror, thinking he still looked good in a plain dark-green pocket-T and blue jeans. Not bad for an agent his age, especially one so exhausted. Weekends had become killer—no real work to keep an agent occupied—and now this. Brinkman on the phone trolling.

"So, Phil, is there a business-related point to this call, or is it purely pleasure? Because I for one am enjoying the hell out of it so far, especially the part where Cindy hung up on you. If it *was* Cindy. But I'm beat. So, is that all?"

"No, that's not goddam all, you arrogant cocksucking son of a bitch!" (So, *that* was where she got it.) "And it was her! She! Cindy! Baker!"

Brinkman was stewing. Les could smell the bay leaves all the way in Iowa.

After a moment, Brinkman said, "Fine," putting an end to something. "Do you know what they found floating in the river in Pittsburgh?"

"Probably a turd," Les said. "But if there's corn, it isn't mine. I hate corn, you know."

"You must be loving Iowa," Brinkman said leadenly. "So?"

When Les didn't bite, Phil repeated with sing-songy exaggeration. "What do you think they *found*?" He was bound and determined to see his little game through.

"Which river?"

"I don't know what fucking river and I don't fucking care! That's not why I fucking called!"

"Well, then why did you fucking call, Phil? I've got a long day of Bureau bullshit ahead of me tomorrow. Someone killed another SK out here. Two, in fact. I don't know if you heard."

"Yeah, well, someone killed another one here in Pittsburgh, too," Brinkman said. "There, you ruined the surprise." He sounded thoroughly disheartened.

Les asked, as if confused, "You're in Pittsburgh, Phil?"

"No, I'm not in goddam Pittsburgh! Here on the East Coast!"

"Oh," Les said. "So, how do you know?"

"Because I'm here! I know where I am!"

"I meant, it could have been anybody, so how do you know?"

"It was her room. It was Baker! I could hear the denial in her voice! Sorriest pretext call I've ever heard."

"You called her, Phil. And I meant the dead guy in the river. Water tends to rinse away trace evidence, in case you weren't aware of that."

"Yes, I'm aware of it. I probably taught you that."

"I doubt it," Les said frankly. "And for the record, there are three rivers in the Pitt. The Monongahela, the Allegheny, and the Ohio. They all converge at Three River Stadium. Or what used to be Three River Stadium before they blew it down. That's why they named it that. The Steelers played there, you know. The *Pittsburgh* Steelers. Unless they've moved across the state line while I wasn't looking, in which case they might be the Akron Retreads now.

"There's a lot of that going on these days, Phil. I don't know about you, but I find it disturbing. Whatever happened to tradition? Tradition. Who can root for the El-Ay Dodgers? I mean really, with a clear conscience. I know I can't. It just feels wrong. And *Dodger* Stadium? Please. In El-Ay, Phil? Dodger Stadium. It's insulting. Then, they implode Three Rivers on pay-per-view.

"Tradition, Phil. That's what I'm saying. Dead and buried. Welcome to my world."

After a moment Brinkman said quietly, "Are you done?" applying the thinnest veneer of aggrieved self-control he could muster, which was roughly a mile deep.

"No, I was wondering if you knew where—"

"I know where the goddam Steelers played!" Brinkman shouted. "And they still play there, only now it's called Heinz Stadium and it's a hundred feet from where they used to play!" An armchair quarterback of great repute—at least he bet that way in the office pools—Brinkman put a silent *So there!* cherry on top.

"Eighty feet," Les said. "But that's irrelevant. Do you know which river?"

"They built the stadium on?"

"No. Where they found the floater, Phil."

"It doesn't matter!" Brinkman was so agitated he checked his pulse. "You need to cut this little mouse and cat trifecta. I'm up to 140. My cardiologist will be paging me any second."

Les was so happy he folded his socks.

"It might matter, Phil," he said, and assumed Brinkman had no idea which river. "Clues, Phil. They're what make our world go round."

"Jesus," Brinkman moaned. "I don't even know why I bother calling you."

"Because you think you have to," Les said, taking his watch off, setting it on the bare nightstand—no books, no magazines, no glass of water—as free of clutter as he hoped his sleep would be, but knew it wouldn't.

Brinkman tried flirting with knowledge again, as if he did that sort of thing all the time. "So, we got someone killing serial killers here. Multiple cases now. Kind of a serial-killer-killer killer thing."

"I think you have one too many 'killers' in there, Phil."

"It's like that fucking TV show."

"Which one?"

"Every one! They're all doing it. What the fuck do they think we're doing here? What do we do here? Huh, Les? What the fuck do we do?"

"I don't know, Phil. You never really made that clear to me." Les felt the textured lamp shade. Anything was better than trying to help Brinkman get to his point. He waited.

Brinkman finally, stubbornly, said, "And the floater wasn't just anybody. It was our guy. And he wasn't floating by the way, he was sunk. In a van. On the bottom."

"So, how do you *know?*"

Les shook his head. There was virtually no sport to fucking with Brinkman whatsoever. He turned on the Weather Channel. Rain in Seattle. Rain in Miami. Rain in the Pitt. So, he flipped to ESPN-9 for some "Classic Curling Hi-Lites of the '90s!" Anything was more interesting than Brinkman playing detective.

"Okay, this is all preliminary," Brinkman said reluctantly. "The guy was apparently stalking some chick, some..."

"Doctor?"

"Yeah. Or, well, at least that's what they think."

"What who thinks? Holy Dick?"

"Don't ever let him hear you call him that."

"I'm talking to you."

"Yeah. Holy Dick."

Les said, "And what in his great prescience makes Dick think a) she was a doctor, b) the sunk-floater was our killer, and c) Dickie Boy would have ever thought about the doctor angle if I hadn't brought up the possibility?"

"He didn't mention that last part."

"Gee, I'm shocked, Phil. Didn't you and Dick do Harvard together? I can't remember."

"City College, and don't piss me off, it's late," Brinkman said. "I don't know why I ever agreed to having you back on this team."

"*Heading* this team."

"Even more un-fucking-believable," Phil muttered. Then he added, in an attempt at control, "Listen, I've got... company. Okay? I'm in the kitchen."

Les could scarcely imagine who would take time out on a Sunday night to be Brinkman's company. "So, you want me to call Holy Dick in the morning for the rest of the details?"

"Don't ever let him hear you call him that."

"I'm still talking to you."

Brinkman remained silent for several moments, then finally said, "Fine. Call Holy Dick in the morning. He'll fill you in." Brinkman always likened conversations with Dick Cleveland to the first day after hemorrhoid surgery.

"Does he know you call him that?" Les said, stripping to his shorts.

"I'm talking to you, you prick!" Brinkman yowled.

"You're shouting."

"I'm not shouting!"

"Yes, you are."

"Well, of course I am! You piss me off!"

Nobody got to Brinkman like Les Moore. Les could hear Brinkman letting the phone hang at his side a moment to gather his senses while Les fluffed his pillows and turned down his red bedspread.

He heard Brinkman sigh-cuss and raise the receiver. "Look, when you talk to him, act like I didn't tell you any of what I'm about to tell you, okay?" Les said nothing. "You know how he gets."

More silence.

Brinkman gave up. "There were prints. Preliminary match to three other scenes."

"Prints where?

"On the murder weapon."

"He killed her?"

"No."

"So, you've got a witness."

"No."

"Phil, what are you not telling me, here? The Pittsburgh Slasher attacks another woman, doesn't kill her, he drops the knife, she gets away, he ends up dead, but you don't have a witness?" He paused for effect. "Say, the woman? The intended victim?"

Risky business, this, Brinkman leaking details from Holy Dick's inside track. They both knew it, but Brinkman risked continued. "She got away. You said it. And who said anything about a knife?"

Les paused, blinked, then said. "Pittsburgh *Slasher*, Phil?" as derisively as possible. Brinkman was silenced. "And what do you mean 'she got away?'"

"She got away."

"She got away-away?"

"Yes! Away-away! She got away, okay!" When Les didn't respond right away, Brinkman said, "Les? Are you there?"

Three seconds had passed. "No, Phil, I went out for Chinese."

"Well, I don't know!"

"So, are you thinking maybe this is the same hooker who killed the Emerson-Thoreau nutball?"

A beat. "The who?" Brinkman said with forced irritation.

"Henry-David/Ralph-Waldo whatever. The one who got tagged in Seattle."

"Oh, Riverbend. Merfinridge, from Montana."

"Right. And now she shows up in Pittsburgh—"

"She?"

"The hooker. Only now she's a doctor, and she kills the Pittsburgh Slasher and throws his body in the river in his own van." Les made it sound as ridiculous as it did sound. Brinkman went quiet. Les said, "Well, Phil, you gotta admit—"

"I don't have to admit cock, Moore! This is weird shit going on, here. You know as well as I do. Four serial-serial murders in two weeks? I don't know what the hell this is! Do you? Of course you don't. Nobody does. That's the fucking problem!"

His blood pressure had to be up to 170 over 100.

"Technically, three," Les said calmly. Four bodies, three incidents. "Two were by women, one by a man."

Brinkman let go a stream of blurred-consciousness, repercussive challenges. "How do you know that? Have you determined that? I haven't heard that. Does Local know that? Does anybody know that? Has anyone told anyone that? Does the press know that? Why the fuck haven't you told me that if you know that, goddammit!"

Spinning out of control, Les thought. *Lovely.*

"Phil, calm down. Your heart." Brinkman was always saying he had a weak heart, and Les would send him into "pulmonary distress, infarcting all over the fucking place" one of these times.

"Don't tell me to fucking calm down! I can take care of my own goddam heart!"

Les heard his boss take a deep breath, making a conscious effort to calm down before his heart exploded right out of his chest and onto the wall. He said, "Anyway, Phil, I'd think you of all people would be happy with four SKs permanently out of the loop."

"Oh, I *am* happy! I'm happy as a fat dog in a fart clinic!"

Ah, a Brinkmanism!

"But I've got people to answer to. I've got the Old Man, remember? And he doesn't like questions"—Les mouthed the rest with Brinkman—"he likes answers."

In reality, Evertt Wilstrong was only five years older than Brinkman, so Phil both feared and resented him. Forget he was African American.

"And all he's getting is questions right now, Les, and he doesn't like that, so I don't like that, so somebody needs to tell me what the fuck is going on out there or stop cashing his fucking paychecks!"

Les pulled the covers up and turned the light off. If he wasn't going to get any more details from Brinkman, he was going to sleep. "Ask Holy Dick or send me back and I'll ask him."

Brinkman went quiet again, obviously weighing his options. Les knew exactly what he was thinking. If Phil called, himself, Dick would be catty and indecisive, baiting him to pull rank, which, if he did, would lead to a nasty series of memos back and forth between Dick, Wilstrong, and Brinkman. In the end, the quasi-litigious battle would come to naught, but Brinkman would have a smudge on his otherwise mostly spotless record, and Phil Brinkman hated smudges. Of any kind.

He finally said, "Ask him from there. Then call me. I'll be in late. I've got a... dental... thing."

"Company staying over?"

"Don't push my buttons, okay? I can still send you back to Reactive." He was referring to the Reactive Crimes Unit. Mostly follow-up work on stale, old homicides.

"If you're gonna demote me," Les said, "give me your job. I can use the time off. And hey, without ever leaving the office."

"Just find out what the hell Dick knows about this bitch and call me," Brinkman grunted, ignoring the dig loudly.

"Are we back to Agent Baker again?" Les asked. "And, Phil, should you be calling her that? Is this an open line?"

"You know who I meant."

Les rolled over on his side, ready to nod off. "Phil, for my personal edification. How do you even know it was a woman if nobody saw her, nobody talked to her, nobody knows anything about her, and there's no evidence?"

Les closed his eyes, ready to hang up—almost did hang up—when Brinkman said quietly, "Somebody saw her."

Les went bolt upright with the light back on.

"You just happened to leave out that somebody saw her? Are we in the same fucking line of work, here, Phil? Somebody *saw* her?!"

Brinkman said, "Okay, I asked you once, don't push my buttons! Okay, here?" He was really laying on his *I'm barely in control* conciliatory tone, the one Les particularly loathed.

"Okay!" Les shouted, drilling it. "Don't take me twice around the lake on this bullshit lack-of-evidence fishing expedition if you know something! Who the fuck do you think you're talking to?"

"Who the fuck do you think *you're* talking to?" Brinkman screamed back.

180 over 120.

"The lead investigator on this case!" Les hollered back. "The head of the goddam TASK team that you put together with me in mind! The same guy who's gonna save your ass when the Old Man starts pulling your shorts down to insert the goddam golden cattle prod!

"Now, you want to find out what really happened from Holy Dick? Who, I might remind you, is not one to share pertinent details unless he can somehow benefit from doing so, and who is also not one to miss a chance to squeeze your nuts by pissing and moaning to Wilstrong and making waves on your otherwise smooth approach to the dock slip marked 'Assistant Director' just to get back at you for not helping him cheat on his algebra finals at NYCC twenty-eight fucking-years ago!"

Brinkman groaned, probably experiencing tachycardia. Les Moore knew a lot about Phil Brinkman. Too much, as Phil saw it and said numerous times. He had to be wondering why he'd ever told Les about New York.

"Or," Les went on, with no sign of letting up, "do you want *me* to find out from him? I don't know, I thought maybe you'd like to tell me everything you know before I call that hypocritical, sanctimonious sack of holy shit" — if only Cindy had heard that — "and make it clear he is just that, and I'm bringing internal charges against him for withholding evidence in a case so very important to Bureau Chief Wilstrong, during which exchange I will no doubt mention how you put me onto him!"

Brinkman said, somewhat pathetically, "You're shouting."

"Yeah, and in three seconds I'm hanging up and calling Wilstrong my goddam self! Okay, Phillie?"

Les could hear Brinkman biting his lip, the gnawing sounds remindful of a lizard eating a beetle. He said, "Please don't make fun of me, Les. You know I don't like that." His voice was low now, soft and helpless.

"Phil. Three seconds, I hang up and call Wilstrong at home."

"Jesus Christ, Les!" Brinkman spewed, shouting again, himself — even more desperate and pathetic than before. "Where's your sense of human dignity, your professional etiquette?"

"Someone took it away from me in a Walmart parking lot in Seattle," Les said, with as much real vitriol as he ever wasted on a Phil Brinkman. "Three... two... one... Bye, Phil."

Brinkman blurted out, "Wait!" and took a short, gasping breath. He well knew a second was all Les would afford him. So, he told Les what he knew.

"Someone saw a guy who fit the description of the guy found in the river grabbing a woman in scrubs from next to a Porsche in a doctors-only parking space. I'm your superior for Christ's sake, Les!"

"Yeah," Les said, "And?"

"And you should treat me like I am!"

"Yeah, and what else about the fucking case, Phil?"

Brinkman had to have hated himself for violating his own rules of nonintervention—hated himself with a completeness few men know. "And..."

Les heard him swallow again, bracing to get his confession over with.

"And?" Les pushed him.

Brinkman said, as reluctantly as a twelve-year-old admitting to finding his mother's vibrator in her top drawer, "And... it turns out the doctor who owned the Porsche was a woman. But she was performing a difficult surgery right then and had gone two hours longer than anticipated. Her abductor must not have known because he was waiting for her by her car, jumped out of a van, grabbed her, and sped off."

"Okay," Les said with no patience whatsoever. "And?"

"It wasn't the doctor."

Les could hear Brinkman close his eyes. The sigh gave it away. He was so far in the loop he had become the loop—a fat snake eating his own tail. Just where Les wanted him.

"They found the van in the river, two miles away. And don't ask me again which fucking one again! The water was only six feet deep, so pretty much everything was washed out except about a hundred chewed-up blue Bic pen caps on the floor. Make sure you tell that part to Baker."

"Prints?"

"Only the dead guy."

"And the thinking is he's The Slasher."

"Hundred percent," Brinkman said. "But how he got the tables turned on him, no one knows."

"I know," Les said.

"Enlighten me," Brinkman said with substantially dulled sarcasm.

"Our boy from Seattle."

"This was a woman."

"Someone saw her pussy?"

"Les, for Chrissake!" Brinkman blurted. He wasn't concerned about the politically incorrect anatomical reference, but rather, "The witness was two hundred yards away, at least."

"So? And two bucks to a Danish, it's him and he's gonna do it again," Les said.

Brinkman paused as if thinking that a Danish sounded good right about then. Then he said, "On the one hand, I hope you're right. That he does it again. And again. And again. And again."

"Right, Phil. And on the other hand?"

"I don't know on-the-other-hand. I haven't figured out the downside to this yet."

"The press."

"Oh sure, they're gonna make us look like total idiots."

"Shouldn't be too hard."

"Speak for yourself."

"I was speaking for you."

"Okay, you're not going to get to me right now, okay? I'm not in the mood, okay?"

"You were already in the mood. Now we're passed that, Phil. Now you realize you're in much deeper shit than you imagined. Reading the report Holy Dick faxed to Wilstrong is your smallest problem."

Les had heard the paper rattle and had been saving it. He could see Brinkman looking down at it in his hand, fretting. He said, "Peggy cadge it from Dick's girl?"

Brinkman said, "I don't know what you're talking about."

Les then heard Brinkman's shredder running and said, "You know Cleveland's gonna dick around with Local, squabbling over jurisdictional bullshit. Who gets the evidence? Who does the preliminary interrogation? Who takes credit for what? Who catches the flak? With Dick involved, it's always a cesspool of backstabbing paranoia and shadow maneuvers to try and score points with Wilstrong.

"And God only knows the deal he'll try to cut with Demontovicz over the body. We need accurate, detailed and *complete* protocols, Phil. Not some we'll-leave-out-this-and-that bullshit agreement hammered out in the backroom of a sports bar overlooking the fucking crime scene. We know what the press does when they get hold of it. Think

Ruby Ridge, Phil. Wen Ho Lee. Valerie Plame. Whitey Bulger, and Operation Fast and Furious! Missing guns, fugitives, yellow cake, laptops, House Republicans, and Waco all rolled into one. Then multiply it all by a factor of ten. Then multiply that by ten and you'll be almost halfway there."

Les Moore knew that nothing made Brinkman's brain swell to the point of exploding and leaking out his ears like hearing about everything that could go wrong in the future—except being reminded of everything that had already gone wrong in the past. And all or any of that turning up in the nightly news. Phil Brinkman hated the press more than he hated pie having more calories than tree bark.

"On the other hand," Les offered philosophically, calming down, controlling the conversation, their progress. "A few of them might report it as a good thing. Taxpayer money and all."

"Might," Brinkman agreed.

"On the other hand—"

"That's three hands," Brinkman interrupted.

"There might be an octopus full on this one, and every one of them with a knife aimed for our backs. But the only one we have to watch out for right now is Holy Dick's."

"The bastard."

Les chased his calm. "But the press..."

"Those bastards," Brinkman said. Then he wondered, "What about 'em? What do we have to look out for?"

"They'll try to bait us into praising whoever's doing this."

"Oh yeah. Then *unnnh*." Les could see Brinkman miming the stab. "Right between the old shoulder blades," Brinkman added for clarity.

"Um-hmm," Les said. "And then you know what follows, what they say?"

Brinkman said, sounding cautiously worried, "Go ahead."

"We're doing the killing."

"Those motherfuckers."

Les said, "Next thing you know we got Woodward and Bernstein following us into parking garages."

Les knew that any talk of the press made Brinkman break out into an instant sweat. He viewed putting Special Agent Leslie Francis Moore together interacting with reporters as akin to sending a pyromaniac into an oil refinery with a flamethrower.

But he didn't have to worry. Yet. Les said, "And don't start referring everyone to me. Talk to OPA, tell them to expect an onslaught, and have them work something up. We don't want this getting the wrong spin so early on."

"Yeah, yeah, okay," Phil said. "I'll get on it. First thing in the morning."

Les could hear him sweating.

Brinkman hated talking to the people in Media Relations because the only time he had to talk to them was when something needed immediate, delicate handling. And even he would concede neither immediacy nor delicacy was his strong suit.

But Les knew what Phil Brinkman hated most was having to ask Les what to do, then having Les tell him, because he knew he'd hate what he'd hear, and he'd hate having to do it, but he'd have to do it anyway, because Les was always right. That's why he'd brought him back in the first place.

Still, Brinkman had to at least pretend he was still in control. "And you and Baker get your asses back to Pittsburgh, pronto!" he said as gruffly as he could muster after such a thorough browbeating. "And tell her to call me. I've got a few choice words to share. Pretext me, goddammit."

"Okay," Les said and hung up. He'd gotten all he'd wanted in the first place — to get out of the damned Corn State. The past came back in a synaptic blast of bad memories.

Les's parents had taken him to the Sweet Corn Festival when he was six or seven years old, where he had eaten corn on the cob, corn pudding, corn soufflé, creamed corn, candy corn, corn jelly, corn bread, corn pie, corn dogs, corn flakes, corn *everything*. Then he threw up sweet, yellow, lumpy corn vomit in a cornfield next to an Iowa highway for nearly an hour. He never ate corn again.

Another of life's little mysteries solved.

Life is a series of small epiphanies which hopefully make some kind of sense in the end. One of Les's favorite sayings. He amended aloud, "Or preferably somewhere short of the end," and got out his suitcase to start packing. He couldn't wait to see the look on Cindy's pretty face when she got the good news.

Chapter 11 – Back to the Pitt

The Agent Baker who opened Cindy's door was not the Agent Baker Les was accustomed to seeing. "What the hell happened to you?"

"Train ran over me," Cindy said, sounding like Death had been the engineer.

Les saw the beer bottle, then checked the trash to see if there were more. There were not. "You weren't kidding about one beer."

"I don't think it was the beer." Cindy flopped back on the bed. "Do yourself a favor and don't go for the Sunday Trout Special no matter how long it's been since you've had a nice piece of fish." She stifled a belch. "If I'd thrown up one more time, I was gonna call Guinness. The record people, not the brewery." The belch became unstifled.

Les said, "Where'd you park the beater?" One of the detectives had told him about Cindy's procurement, but Les couldn't find the car anywhere.

"Some guy's backyard a few blocks over. Paid him five bucks."

"Nice." Les didn't bother to conceal his esteem. Successfully hiding from Brinkman was no big deal, but ditching Les took some doing.

He peered into the bathroom, looking for signs Cindy had actually been sick. The little room was spotless. "You're surprisingly neat when you're violently ill."

"Thank you," Cindy said, keeping a bloodshot eye on him while he took in every detail of the room. "Am I a suspect in something?"

Les grinned. "I'm a suspect, you're a suspect, everyone's a suspect. We're all like in one big homicidal Dr Pepper commercial."

"You know," Cindy said, sitting up as slowly as possible, "I think maybe you're the sick one. And how old are you again?"

Les took the compliment well, ignored the dig, and walked over to the desk where he picked up the Post-It for *Sorbel-Diggs-Hoxley Crime Scene Raw Footage – All*. "She made a copy for us?" he said. Cindy nodded. He said, "Did you watch it again?"

"Only about a dozen times," she said.

"See anything new?"

"Just you," Cindy said, struggling to hold something dangerous down.

"She put that in there, huh? That was the strangest thing," Les said, thinking back. "I was standing there, looking at the blood on the ground, the stains, and I flashed back on..."

He went silent, staring out the window into the intensely bright prairie light.

"Marjorie and Melissa Ann?" Cindy asked.

Les nodded without taking his eyes off the distant horizon. *So damn flat,* he thought, idly.

"She said you looked like you'd seen a ghost," Cindy said. "I didn't think of that."

Les stared out at the flat fields around the motel, grass already starting to brown in spots from an early freeze. "Knowing he's still out there. Still active..."

He didn't need to finish.

Cindy stood shakily. "Yeah," she said with such kindness, lack of judgment, and true understanding that Les snapped out of his drift before ditching.

Still, "Thanks," was all he could come up with. And he thought Iowa needed more trees.

Cindy took a trial step or two — which looked like she was walking through quicksand on Jupiter. She steadied herself on a chair. "Where were you all weekend?" she asked.

"I took a drive," Les said. "Ended up sleeping in the car. Drove some more yesterday, got back around eleven — in time for the Brinkman Report."

"So that's why he stopped calling me," Cindy said. "Praise the Lord and pass the biscuits." She cast her eyes heavenward.

"I don't get any thanks for picking up?" he asked.

"Ehh," she squacked and headed for the bathroom.

Les said, "The guy at the front desk said you told them to... well, he didn't want to repeat the exact words."

"I'll have to apologize on the way out," Cindy said, loading up her toothbrush up with extra Colgate.

Les started for the door. "Need anything?"

"No. I think the worst is over. I'm just a little weak. Anything new I should know about?"

"Nothing much," Les said perfunctorily. "Someone killed the Pittsburgh Slasher."

He stepped out into the hall and started the sweep hand on his Rolex Oyster Perpetual—white gold with the President band. His one concession.

Before Rolie's sweep hand had made ten ticks, Cindy had her mouth rinsed, the faucet turned off, and was flinging the steel-clad, fire-resistant hallway door into the wall so hard it shook the whole building. If they'd been in California, guests would have been running for the exits.

Cindy stepped into the stale corridor air in her crumpled PJs, hair a tangled mess, eyes sunken, traces of Colgate in the corners of her mouth, but wholly alert. "What did you just say?"

Les marveled. "Nine seconds. If I could package that, sick people the world over would hail me as their king."

"You'd be a rich man—who did it?" Cindy said in one breath.

"They don't know," Les said. "But they think..." He paused, asking her as if he was actually concerned, "Are you sure you're up to this?"

"Are you sure you don't want me to cut your nuts off with a spork?"

Les grunt-chuckled at the imagery, then said, "They think... Well, Holy Dick thinks, a woman posing as a doctor got The Slasher to nab her and—"

"Then whacked him and dumped him in the river! God-*damn*-it!"

"In the river," Les repeated. "You know something about this?"

"Lucky guess. I don't even know where it came from."

Les eyed her a moment, then said, "Alpha state. You're zapped from food poisoning, conscious mind isn't getting in the way, and presto, you're a seer."

"Better living through projectile vomit."

"Whatever works."

Cindy looked at him, oddly. "You believe that?"

"About the woman doctor?"

"Alpha waves."

"Of course. Didn't you ever play with the biofeedback machine at Quantico?"

"No."

"So, you don't believe in it?"

"No, I absolutely believe in it," Cindy said. "I didn't know we had one at our disposal."

Adrenaline rush over and having returned to a pale shade of Kermit, she sagged against the tan metal doorjamb.

"Saying goodbye to your Alpha state?" Les asked.

"I feel like an old sponge," she said, closing her eyes. "So, we're back to the Pitt."

"First flight out."

"Which is?"

"Whenever you're up to it."

"I'll be fine by flight time."

"In that case, an hour and a half."

"Shit." Sagging, Cindy turned back into her room.

"Oh yeah, and Phil wants you to call him. Something about hanging up on him."

Cindy said, "I don't know anything about that," and closed the door.

Les grinned. Lying about lying to Brinkman. He might make an agent out of her yet.

***

On the plane, airsick bag in her lap just in case, Cindy showed the diamond-shaped abalone inlay to Les, the one she found in the barn.

"You look much better," he complimented her. "Even shaved your legs, I see."

Not sure how she felt about Les noticing this personal detail, Cindy confirmed, "I feel much better," and shifted her legs away.

"Why didn't you turn this over to Local?" Les asked, taking the tiny evidence bag into which Cindy had transferred the inlay.

"I forgot," Cindy said.

Les raised a brow at her.

"No, really," she said. "I was going to, today, but then..." and she used odd body language to sum up eating bad fish, vomiting all day, sleeping all night like a rock, getting jolted by unexpected news on waking, and rushing to an airplane to feel sick again after smelling airline food on a sour stomach.

Les nodded, apparently understanding perfectly, and said, "Could be any farmer or cowpoke who ever went in there."

"Or friend of a farmhand or anyone else," Cindy expanded. "A lot of people wear that stuff around there."

"I noticed," Les said with no discernible disdain. Then he advised, "Have the Pitt Crew send it in for forensics, cc the Iowa Locals, and promise them the results as fast as you get them. And be sure not to apologize."

"Why not?"

"Implies guilt. Just tell 'em you'll get the results to them ASAP, blah-blah-blah."

"That's my line."

"Seemed appropriate."

Cindy had to admit, "It's multipurpose." Then she smelled someone's jet bacon passing by and felt her stomach take a header.

To take her mind off her involuntary reflux, Cindy watched Les examine the inlay. She was struck by the realization that she had never seen anyone scrutinize evidence the way Les did. He seemed completely disinterested, as if he didn't have a thought in his mind, yet she knew that every gear was turning.

Biofeedback machine, Cindy laughed to herself. She would never have guessed.

But the truth was, as she would discover later, Les had almost lived on the thing for six weeks. Other agents played with the machine; Les mastered it. But that was how Les Moore did everything. Some former partners swore he could smell blood types.

"Hmmm," he finally said of the inlay, handed it back, then turned to nestle his head between the seat and window. "I'm gonna try to catch a few. The thought of having to sit straight-faced in that ridiculous taxpayer-financed tabernacle Dick Cleveland calls an office while he pretends to be on the same side we are makes me tired just thinking about it."

"You know, you'd think," Cindy mused, "I mean considering who we are, we could, I don't know, kill him or something."

Without looking up, Les said, "I'll cover for you, say you were in the ladies' room. 'Yeah, she went in to pee and when we came back, there he was, impaled on his cross, naked.'"

"Does he have to be naked?" Cindy said. "That sort of turns me off to killing him, if he has to be naked."

"Okay," Les agreed, sounding half-asleep already.

Cindy chuckled and scrutinized the inlay again, quickly getting lost in the possibilities—and partners who looked as if they'd seen ghosts, and bodies in barns, and young female videographers who made death look sensual. This was hardly the FBI she had expected.

Les rolled back. "I almost forgot. You want the rest of my omelet?" Before Cindy could pull away, he swooped up the congealed glop and stuck it under her nose. "Cheese and ham, I think. The pink stuff sort of smells like ham, doesn't it?"

Cindy tried not to smell *anything*, but it was too late. She managed to burp, "You bastard," then gulped it back down and bolted for the lavatory.

"I guess you weren't feeling much better, after all, huh?" Les called after her gleefully.

He slept all the way to Pittsburgh.

Cindy spent the entire flight in the lavatory, on the toilet, face in the sink, braced against some of the worst turbulence she had ever experienced on an airplane.

Then, all of a sudden, somewhere over eastern Ohio, the air smoothed out and Cindy instantly felt better. So much so that when she returned to her seat, just as they started their approach, and she saw Les was sound asleep...

Cindy tied his shoelaces together.

When they were parked at the gate, Cindy said gently, "Les, we're here," like a caring wife or mother. Then she stepped aside to watch him face-plant in the aisle seat across the way. *This* was the FBI she'd hoped for.

***

It turned out Holy Dick knew much more than he had told Phil Brinkman, his old nemesis. First off, two witnesses had come forward, not one. Of course, getting new info didn't surprise Les; he didn't trust Dick Cleveland as far as he could throw Benedict Arnold and the six feet of dirt holding him under.

The first witness had seen someone cruising the parking lot on foot earlier, checking out the Porsche. The thirty-two-year-old Hispanic man thought nothing of it until he read the papers the next day. He told police — Holy Dick — he had thought at the time maybe the loiterer was a car-thief who then decided against boosting the car when he "seen me sitting on the bus bench watching him."

But that was a full hour before the abduction, sixty feet away, and then the witness — who didn't have his glasses with him and didn't see much more than a blur around his favorite car, a 911 Targa — got on a bus and went home. So, the lurker he saw might well have *been* a thwarted carjacker. Although Dick's Witness #1 did have the stats straight. "Five-ten, one-sixty, dark hair, looked like. Clean shaven."

That described The Slasher. But for some reason known only to his deceptive god and himself, Dick had deigned to keep this testament to himself.

The other witness, a seventy-five-year-old woman whose ninety-seven-year-old mother had just died in her South Side Hospital room after a prolonged bout with liver cancer, hadn't been thinking crisply when she came downstairs to go home the last time, after her months-long vigil, and had gotten lost, ending up in the employees' parking lot.

Tired and upset, she sat on a curb and cried. A few minutes later, she heard voices and looked over to see a man she later ID'd as The Slasher dragging a "tallish woman" into a white van — the one found in six feet of sludgy Pitt water not far from Heinz Field with nearly a hundred chewed-up Bic pen caps, all blue, trapped and floating up against the roof.

"Would you say this woman was..." Cindy pondered how to phrase the question properly to this woman who could have been her own mother — if her mother had been black and alive — and was still visibly upset about losing hers. Cindy looked around the old frame house, everything antiquey, spotless, and in its proper place. Doilies.

"... Feminine?" Les finished for her. Cindy nodded.

The woman didn't understand.

"We mean," Cindy picked up, "could it have been a man in woman's clothing?"

"Oh," the woman thought back. "You mean like some sort of... transcendental herman-afro-dite or somethin'?"

"No, ma'am. Just a regular man, dressed in woman's clothing."

"What kinda regular man dresses in women's clothing?" she asked suspiciously.

"A man trying to lure the Pittsburgh Slasher into trying to kill him, so he could then kill the Pittsburgh Slasher," Les said to Cindy's chagrin. So much for policy.

"Oh my," the woman said. "I see." Though, it wasn't clear that she did. But, after several moments of pondering, and the posture to indicate the process, she said, "No. I don't think so."

Cindy made a note.

The woman went on. "I mean, it coulda been, I s'pose. Mind you, I wasn't close nor in the frame of mind to be noticing details. Took me a whole little while to figure out something had happened and I better call the po-lice, after I got home."

"You waited to call the police until you got home?" Cindy asked and looked over Holy Dick's file. She found no mention of such a vital detail and made a face to Les that said. *And this guy is Special Agent in Charge?*

"It's in PD's report," he said.

"Still," she said and shook her head.

The older woman said, not sounding belligerent but trying to make it clear that she *wasn't* sure, "It coulda been anybody. Man, woman, man-woman. I don't know. But I think it was a woman. She had real pretty hair. Of course, it coulda been a wig. But it didn't hang like a wig. If it was, it was a damn good wig."

She nodded. They nodded.

Cindy said, "What about the way he, or she, carried himself, or herself?"

The woman thought back then said, "Hard to say, happened so fast."

"You could go either way on that, too?" Les asked. The woman tipped her head yes.

Cindy let out a breath, "Well, I'm done. You?" Les nodded.

This had turned out to be a fairly typical eyewitness interview. Average person on the street sees something, isn't sure what, and their mind bends the event to fit old memories of their own. Investigators try to straighten it out, but usually only end up twisting it more. A good defense attorney can unravel even an excellent eyewitness's recollection in less time than it took to commit the murder.

They thanked her and left.

"Well, that was constructive," Cindy said as they got in their new Pitt-mobile, a black Chrysler product of indiscriminate origin.

"Leave it to Dick."

"Why does he bother playing this game if he doesn't have anything?" Cindy wondered with genuine ire.

"In case he gets something."

Cindy grunted and let it go. "Lunch?"

"Thought you'd never ask."

Les grinned and wheeled a U-turn that would have had Mario Andretti grabbing for the hand strap. Cindy didn't even flinch. She was even starting to like Sinatra on the stereo all the time. Tapping her foot to "Call Me Irresponsible."

"I'll tell you who wears a wig," Les said. "Phil Brinkman."

"He does not," Cindy said.

Les said, "And you're gonna pay for that shoelace thing, you know."

"I know," Cindy said, smiling.

She couldn't wait.

Chapter 12 – Predator

Gainesville, Florida. Gator country. That's fine with Predator. He isn't really human, either. Part of his brain stopped evolving with T-Rex.

Night is best.

Cruising a newsstand, he doesn't stop. Doesn't have to. He knows who's in the news. SKs have the public's imagination. His kind finally getting the coverage they deserve. The Brethren, he calls them. Anonymous even to each other.

We're everywhere. ABC, CBS, NBC, MSNBC, the WB, and UPN; Fox of course; A&E, Discovery, The Learning Channel, The History Channel; cable, broadcast, satellite, the internet, wiki, TikTok, Facebook; Cooper and Carlson, Amanpour and Maddow, Doocy and Doocy; *20/20, 48 Hours, 60 Minutes, Dateline, Primetime.*

Anytime. All the fucking time!

Where would the media whores be without him? They've all gone the way of The Killer. SKs even have their own web pages, now. Predator, too. He got two thousand hits last week.

The public loves us. What we say and do is gospel, because we control who lives and who dies. We are gods! We are God.

He's made The Leap.

It's finals week. A lot of stress in this busy college town. People's guards are down. Easy targets. A predator understands this, feeds on it.

This Predator is hungry.

He spots a coed idling along, face down, backpack full of heavy books, earbuds blasting straight into her brain likely already numb from a Chem 302 review.

College losers.

Nothing wrong with me, though. It's all of them who need weeding out. And right now, she's tops on his list. *Dumb skeeze.*

No one around on a dark street. He could pull over and cut her off, shove her into the trunk quickly. With twenty pounds on her back and those clunky shoes, she wouldn't be fast, couldn't put up much of a fight. *Stylish for Death Wear.*

He revs his V-8 to impress. "Hey! Look at me, bitch! Over here!"

***

All she hears is old-school Jim Morrison. Something about a killer and a toad out on a road, some chemical-inspired mutant-amphibian survival thoughts squirming around inside his genetically altered brain.

She took Music Interp 204, so it makes more sense now. Jim speaking to her *personally* about acting alone in life, being thrown a few bones by her parents and teachers. She can relate.

It's all acting. Every bit of it. Fakers and liars.

A car horn blows, close. She jumps, looks to see the creep in the macho-mobile.

What's his problem? That hat? That shirt?

She speeds up, careful to watch without looking directly at him.

Don't let him see your eyes.

A quick half-glance.

How did he get so close!

Why wasn't she paying more attention like her parents always say?

Her fucking parents. They'd kill her if she got killed.

He's on the horn again. And she reads his lips this time. *Want a ride?*

She has a bad feeling about this one but leaves in her earbuds so as not to reveal anything. A shake, *No.*

"Come on, baby," he calls, revving his engine.

Chicks dig hot cars, but not this one. She's into Proust.

When he glances away, checking his mirror, she cuts the corner on the run, racing for her safe house—Pizza Hut—packed with kids studying, kids laughing, kids drinking beer.

Kids looking out for each other.

***

Predator could whip the corner and intercept her, but someone might see, might remember the car. She's not worth getting caught.

Never get caught. The Brethren's unspoken Rule Number One.

A macho roar, the squeal of rubber and he's gone. She'll live to dread telling her parents about that "D" in comparative lit.

The next twenty-five victim-wannabes get passed by. They don't want it badly enough. "She's gotta want it real bad tonight," he tells no one, and looks up at the uncomfortable sky, seeing a clean abduction, a few hours of rape, some slice-and-dice, a quick trip to another county to dump the body, then back on the couch by dawn.

He feels better already.

Tonight's will be his third in town. *That makes six, doesn't it? Or is it seven now?*

He thinks he really needs to start keeping records. Maybe when he comes down. *No, wait.* He already does. Doesn't he? *Damn meth.* He does another hit.

The clock on his dash says 6:30. Always. The one who got away told the police, but she thought he drove a Toyota. She didn't know much about cars — just getting away from killers.

Lucky her.

Predator has worried about her for months and lain low. But The Urge won out, and he's back on the street. His fuse is lit.

He has The Power.

A bus stop and a cute blonde just asking for it in her tight little top. Sitting there reading *Catcher in the Rye* under a streetlight. Stupid-ass college kids.

He's happy he was never that dumb. He read comics at home where he was safe — except for his mother and her damn enema bag. The coat hangers.

Salinger. Shit. He didn't have time or interest. Guidance.

Around the corner, a man walking a dog.

A direct look. *Shit.*

Teasy little blonde bitch doesn't know how fortunate she is that he scared himself off. Holden Caulfield lives for her.

No, tonight's has to have that extra something special, Predator's thinking, because *Tonight is kind of special.* He sips his Michelob, laughing at his droll routines. He could do stand-up.

"Two serial killers walk into a bar... kill everybody and leave!" He laughs so hard he cries. Great stuff.

A cat darts. He swerves but misses. *Damn!*

Time for another snort of biker crank off the back of his hand and a new brew from his blue cooler.

Clouds tumbling over.

***

Just outside town, he sees her. Exactly what he hadn't expected. She's black. Of course! *Once you try black, you never go back.*

A laugh, a swig, and a snort.

She's tall, she's thin, *she's really asking for it,* jogging alone on this deserted road at night. *Who the fuck does she think she is?*

Yeah, tonight is kind of special.

***

She doesn't see movement in the shadow until the bat cracks the side of her head and something is stinging her face, the unidentifiable taste of dirt and grass in her mouth. Blood. If she had noticed the hot Mustang pass by a minute before, she might have thought twice when she caught a hint of chrome behind the old oaks and scrub. Spanish moss dripping, still in the breathless night.

He drags her, arms loose, gravel gnawing at her back.

She feels something, not sure if it's pain or something else. But the next blow pounds to the core of her brain and hurts like no pain she's ever felt before, like she's suffocating.

Then there's nothing.

***

The garage walls are soundproofed—black recording studio eggcrate foam inside, four-inch blue-board outside. He told the neighbors it was for his drums, and he still plays them out here once in a while to keep the lie alive. But the truth is:

They all died here.

Visqueen covers the floor and runs four feet up the walls, shiny and black—some simple evil in that—Predator laying her out, *admiring* her velvety skin.

"Hey, Hot Chocolate," he coos from too many B-movies, too much porn.

Outside, the wind is kicking up. Tomorrow will be cooler; he'll sleep all day. "It's all good, no worries," he assures her, removing her cotton underpants.

Little blue flowers.

She's starting to come to, eyes free-rolling, the way he likes them — awake enough to feel their pain. His pleasure.

Running a fingertip under her jogging bra. "Mind if I take a peek?" A false courtesy as he makes his plans. Lifting and separating.

***

Beer fumes fall like marsh gas, humid and heavy.

Good, she thinks. Lets him get his hand all the way up under so he's off balance.

Her knee comes up fast. He folds, testicles smashed flat against his pelvic bone, and she's up, racing for the door that's —

Double dead-bolted on both sides. He has the key.

Cornered, she hurls herself at him, fast and furious. He doesn't expect it, mad with meth, anesthetized. And he's not just fighting to save his life — he's fighting to take hers.

She doesn't see the blade come out, but there's no mistaking the icy point of entry. The hardened steel tip goes through her shirt and the little yellow songbird tattooed on her upper arm. Clean to the bone.

It's shock more than anything that drops her to the floor, sitting straight up, staring at her opened flesh.

He crowds over. "See, I didn't wanna do that," he says, sounding compassionate, conservative. Truth is he likes them whole for the autopsy, alive and awake.

She gapes at the hole in her brown arm, the breach. A rage she has never known runs white hot. "No cracker is doin' this to *me*."

She grew up outside Atlanta and had more white friends than black. Never uttered a racist slur in her life. She hears herself now and thinks, *Damn shit's ingrained so deep, we don't even know.* Disappointing for a twenty-three-year-old psych major and dying optimist.

"I already did it," Predator says, circling. "You dead, bitch." He layers on a nasty slurring ring, mocking a dialect she doesn't have.

The hatred in this small room feels bottomless.

She sees his bat; he sees her see it. She goes for the wood; he goes with her. His stiff blade finding its mark a second time, this time puncturing a lung. She's strong, but this one brings her down on one side, gasping, coughing red.

The disbelief.

***

"Now see, I didn't wanna do that, either," he says with the falsely ironic voice. But she wants to change the rules? He can go with the evolving dynamic of a counterattack. He's flexible—but not overly observant at the moment.

Her hand is still around the bat.

She's up, swinging as she rises. Polished timber, blond and hard, catches him above his ear.

He staggers back, well hit. If she wasn't dying, she could probably have powered through the soft part of his head for a home run.

Weak now, she only manages a double. He's dazed, not dead.

Poured concrete under scant plastic is the first thing he's felt all night, since that initial line of crank. Not even The Lumber. He knew something sent him to the floor, felt his head bounce, heard a dull thump somewhere, but he wasn't sure what caused any of it.

Until he sees her standing over him with the nicked stick of ash in her hand.

Trying to focus on the hovering Amazon, he says, "Oh my god, you're The One."

He expects to be going with God.

"Yeah, I'm the one," she says.

He wonders how the hell he could have chosen her, of all people, on a road outside of Gainesville on a Sunday night.

He's read all about it on the internet, on the Special Serial-Killer Killer Website. The One—that's what they're calling the SKK. Satan's little helper. He doesn't remember a single blog referring to a black bitch!

She raises the bat to finish it.

Him.

He sees the conviction, the cold determination in her eyes, and braces for the blow. But in his oblivion, he misses hers.

The bat clacks down at his side — and she follows, right onto him, toe to toe, nose to nose, like a spent lover. Motionless, barely breathing.

She's done.

"I guess you aren't The One, after all," he grunts, relieved. He rolls her off and rises. "Just the one for tonight." He hears a coarse chuckle, no idea if it's his.

She tries to lift the bat, but it only rolls away.

"Come on," he encourages. "It's no fun if you die now." He stuffs a rag into one of her wounds and ties off the other.

Then he goes for his tools.

***

"C-section, huh?"

It's the next thing she hears. And him snorting another line off her most memorable scar. In the snarl and terror of the moment, she'd forgotten about her baby. Coming back now, she can feel her nakedness, his violations.

And his knife under her back.

"You... mother... fucker..."

He dodges her stabbing attack in the nick of time, but the razored blade still finds his ear, slicing deep. Somehow, he knows the streaming blood is his. Seeing red pushes him past his self-imposed limits.

Her hand on the carved bone grip, his hand on hers, he plunges its full length into her throat. Gurgling is the only sound, until he loses his shit.

"You see what you did? You did this to yourself! Don't blame in hell!"

Blood on blood in blood.

Then he's laughing. "Hey, look at us," he says. "We're like a newspaper. Black and white and red all over!" Back to his low-rent stand-up.

His audience of one.

***

Light funnels around the last white face she will see in life. But the last face she remembers is small, brown and content. She finds comfort in the thought that her mother will care for little Benjamin, and that his white father, a law student who left at the height of his post-graduate-degree depression, will no doubt find someone to sue. College money for little Ben. Better than she could have done for him, alive. *See?*

Mama always says, *Everything works out if you let it.*

"What the fuck are you smiling about, you stupid black cunt! You're dying!" Gone are the droll routines, the laughter. He lost; they both know.

A last soft chuckle.

***

The Killer makes do for another hour, forcing himself to enjoy her the way he enjoyed the others as best he can until the pounding in his head becomes unbearable. He will forgo The Ritual tonight.

The storm has arrived. All the way to the dumpsite in slapping wind and spitting rain, he stares at the clock that always reads 6:30, sensing his time is running out. He knows about metaphors; comic books are full of them.

Fuck Salinger.

Chapter 13 – Gainesville

An early morning fisherman discovered Charlene Horton's partly submerged body at his favorite spot a little before six a.m. He threw up three times before he could get to a phone. Running two miles didn't help, but he was so upset he forgot his car. Some kids found his rod and reel where he dropped them, a half-mile away, and kept them.

They didn't know.

Gainesville police recognized the instant they saw the body that this was not Personal Cause, nor a robbery gone bad, nor a hate crime. This was their Predator. But he screwed up this time. The cops found blood and hair, fibers from his blue Hanes pocket-T, and a piece of her skin on the grass nearby with a piece of his skin still attached. In nineteen years on the force, Detective Allison Goodale had never been so happy to find a body.

***

Despite a line of meth to give him fortitude to overcome the pain from the beating he had taken at the hands of his spirited victim, Predator had used far less than his usual care in disposing of her body. He didn't drive far (the dumpsite was less than a mile from his house), didn't check the depth of the water (only twenty inches) and didn't weigh her down well (a jack stand from his trunk). The relentless hammering in his head had convinced him nothing mattered but getting back home as soon as he could.

On his way, he stuffed the plastic sheeting from the garage, drenched with their commingled blood, into the first dumpster he found. The vitiated Visqueen was discovered just after dawn by a "waste removal engineer" — as he referred to himself when he called the police on his work phone — who thought it odd right off that anything with so much blood would be in a dumpster directly behind the Happy Goose Daycare Center. He opened his 911 call with,

"Something's amiss in Toddlerland," which made him an instant suspect.

But his alibi checked out. He'd been receiving a Sanitation Worker of the Year award from the mayor and had stayed for the local *star-studded* party until the wee hours, then gone straight home to his wife and her visiting family. He wasn't a killer; he just had an unusual, if somewhat bent, sense of humor for a garbage guy.

Ironically, there was a butcher shop not two blocks past the kindergarten. Had the award-winning sanitation engineer found the bloody, black plastic there, he wouldn't have given it two thoughts. But Predator had been going crazy with pain. He was out of crystal, his head felt split in two, and he didn't even have an aspirin in his glove box. So, Toddlerland was tops on his list because it was the first trash bin he saw.

Finally, with the throbbing so bad he went blind for a few seconds, Predator crashed into a second dumpster, leaving it in the middle of the next alleyway with a streaky greenish-blue paint swatch for elated detectives to find within six hours of the crime. Two hours later, a sample was being couriered to the FBI's Paint Unit in DC for analysis.

All of this was bad enough, but ultimately none of it mattered because, after attempting to nap through several hours of unremitting pain, afraid he had a concussion and his brain was hemorrhaging, Predator walked into an urgent care clinic out by I-75 around ten thirty a.m. In order to be seen right away, he gave up his real name and a hundred-dollar bill with his prints on it.

An hour later, doctors released him with a clean x-ray, six stitches in his right ear—Charlene Horton had been a lefty—a strong warning to lay off the speed, and a scrip for twenty-one Tylenol IIs. Since he loved codeine when he could get it, Alan Hagganish, a.k.a. Predator, went away happy and drove straight to the closest Walgreens. He took five of the elongated white tablets at the water fountain, not ten feet from the morning pharmacist, then got in his car and drove home to the address he had just given in order to receive a controlled substance, ink still wet on the prescription register.

So, there was quite a trail.

When Riverbend read the article in a local edition of the *Detroit Free Press* somewhere in upper Michigan, he knew Les wouldn't miss it. And Les wouldn't.

Not for the world.

***

After Les and Cindy received the rest of the preliminary police reports and other forensics data the next morning by fax in their Pittsburgh hotel, the TASK agents were on a plane by 8:15, in the Orlando field office by four thirty local time, after a delay in Atlanta, and in Micanopy, twelve miles south of Gainesville, by 6:40, having barbecue, which Les allowed was "not bad." He'd had better, he claimed, while ordering a second sandwich before finishing the first.

With her stomach still raw from the trout and the trip, Cindy ate only potato salad, dinner rolls, and two ears of corn on the cob. Les tried his best to ignore the evil yellow stuff, called her a "closet vegetarian with latent carnophobia," and went to the men's room.

When he returned, Cindy stood, said, "You're right, that's good. Order me one for the road, would you?" and went to the ladies' room.

Les saw the three less-than-dainty bites in his sandwich, and grinned. First, she tied his shoelaces together, and now she chomped down on his half-eaten pig roll. Maybe this partner thing could work out after all.

***

By the time Gainesville PD — as good a group of local cops as Les had ever counseled — had arrived at Predator's house, he was long gone. But it didn't take long to find traces of the black girl's blood on the garage walls and Predator's in a crack in the cement floor under spots where the Visqueen had torn during their struggle. Police also found the bat with Predator's blood that had rolled under a cabinet and two of his autopsy tools which he had apparently overlooked in his fog of hurt, having simply thrown them in the trash. He had also dropped one of her low-cut white running socks in the deep grass alongside his driveway, then leaned against the sill of the blacked-out garage windows.

"He left a beaut of a thumbprint," according to Sal Tensio, the lead homicide investigator. Clean, detailed, and in her blood. Having gone through the National Academy program at Quantico, Sal wasn't worried about the FBI scooping his case. He was happy to get help. He'd worked with NCAVC on several occasions and always found them worth the occasional arrogance. They could usually point you in a direction you hadn't considered, and were usually right.

"Our boy liked movies," Tensio said, inside the small frame house, made dark with blackout shades on every window. He directed Les and Cindy to the killer's collection. Along with *Star Wars*, *Pocahontas* and *Seven*, Alan Hagganish had every *Faces of Death* DVD and VHS tape available through mail order, and there were plenty if a predator took some couch time to seek them out.

This killer had every title from every line by every distributor— twelve running feet of shelf space dedicated to death and gore. *Murder! Homicide! Autopsies! Morgues! Death Masks! Putting a Face on Death!* and just plain *Death!* with up to eight and ten sequels following each initial release. Predator was well-versed in his favorite subject before he ever left his living room.

Cindy couldn't imagine how anyone who sold such awful stuff could sleep nights. There were car accidents, gun accidents, tool accidents, accidents at home, accidents at work, accidents on the street, domestic disputes, employment disputes, mob hits, gunshot wounds, ax murders, stabbings, pummelings, hangings. Homicide, genocide, suicide, fratricide, patricide, and infanticide—one video was "all and only" dead children—all great stuff for passing time between murder-rapes.

He also had pornography, not out of the ordinary for an SK— nothing soft and sensual, no couples videos. (Predator had never been part of a couple—at least not for more than the few hours leading up to the bloodletting.) He preferred imported ultra-hardcore stuff bought on the dark web with fake names and money orders, delivered to anonymous drop boxes. The worst of the worst. Leather-masked S&M, chrome-spiked B&D, torture videos with whippings so violent they drew blood by the cup; nipples clamped purple with huge mousetraps, breasts run through with gleaming shish-ka-bob skewers, labia needled (live) with anything sharp and ugly, and skinny shaved guys suspended on chains attached to giant fish hooks embedded in their skin; German "housewives" being penetrated in every orifice with enormous objects, both live and inanimate, from fat, flexed fists to inverted champagne bottles to rusted car parts; old Asian rape tapes, which appeared real, not faked, as Sal Tensio noted; freaks, farm animals, golden showers, brown showers, even one with women in skimpy lingerie vomiting on each other—then licking it up.

And one snuff film from Peru.

Willing Victim was the first live-murder sex flick Cindy had come across in the field. She couldn't bring herself to watch it. Les and the Orlando team screened it at the Gainesville PD. Two of the six had to leave the room. One man cried. The young victim looked a lot like his niece, Pammie. He said he hoped he would be the one to find Alan Hagganish so he could "personally put six slugs in this diseased bastard's skull," then went to the downstairs range at two in the morning to practice. Emotions ran high.

Then there was the matter of the journals, found in a secret compartment in the wall. Included were graphic accounts of every abduction, rape, murder, and dump site, complete with digital pics and some videos—maps and traces of semen on several of the pages. In his haste to flee, with his death stash not out in the open, Predator had forgotten his death diaries.

Cindy read a few paragraphs in a corner while the others were marveling over the Predator's kit of surgical tools, bought at flea markets in the Ocala area or stolen during doctor visits. When she felt tears coming on, she handed the book to Les and took a walk. Cindy didn't yet have the calluses on her heart that the others did and wasn't sure she ever would. Not on that day.

Predator had written, but not sent, numerous letters to the dead women. Apologies, rants, accusations, love letters, hate letters, marriage proposals. "Dear Jane" letters filled with hurt at *his* loss, blatant admissions of guilt, pledges for restoration or "fresh flowers on your grave at least once a year, my sweet," which he may or may not have been making good on. (Stakeouts at local cemeteries had produced nothing.) All were written in his hand, and all of it ended up in the hands of the cops—virtual mountains of incriminatory proof. Law enforcement was certain Predator was as good as on death row the minute they found him.

Assuming they could find him.

***

In the following days, Cindy watched Les pull further and further back into his shell, brain working overtime, evaluating and reevaluating each and every piece of evidence for the one elusive tidbit that would bring everything into sharp focus.

As he had with Nurse Frankie Morgan in Pittsburgh, Les first put himself in the running shoes of the victim. By knowing her better, he could know Predator better. So, he picked through Charlene Horton's cluttered closets, read her mail, spoke to her mother, her professors, her young son, his father up in Birmingham, her sisters and her friends. In two days, Les knew more about the victim than anyone who had ever known her.

Only then did he turn his full attention on Predator.

Little pre-offense information was available. No one from Martin-Marietta (where he had worked and filed his disability claim after faking a back injury right before the plant closed years before), the university, or even his own family, seemed to notice much about Alan Hagganish in regular life, so they had little to offer police in the way of a construct. But a wealth of post-offense behavior could be extrapolated from the evidence left behind — where he'd gone, what he'd done, the order in which he'd done it, all of which provided valuable insights into Predator's methods and thought patterns, and where he'd go next, what he'd do, the order in which he might go there or do that.

The specific acts of violence that had occurred that night with Charlene Horton could be guessed at with a fair amount of certainty from autopsy protocols, especially when compared to others attributed to Predator in the past. A quick survey of the garage and some imagination filled in the rest.

The Florida Department of Law Enforcement, FDLE, had Predator already pegged for at least five murders. By the end of the week, that number — based mainly on a quick comparison between the journal and FDLE files — had risen to nine. Since the murders went back almost seven years, without more than a hint of any real evidence, Les knew they were dealing with someone who usually took extreme care and made few mistakes. That meant something had gone terribly wrong this time and that Predator must be stewing somewhere, maybe making plans to get even.

Maybe with another black woman.

Cindy saw the light go on. "Got something?" she asked from across the aluminum-rimmed wood folding table, their makeshift office at the Gainesville PD.

"Huh?" Les said, apparently unaware he had let anything show. "Oh, I was, um... just... You feel like getting a bite. I'm famished."

He led her in a different direction—to the other barbecue place he had been searching for when they had to settle for the *lesser* one in Micanopy. "I think I remember where it is now. We'll hit it before we move on. Now that you're better."

Cindy said okay and went back to her iPhone and Diet Squirt. There was something about Les when he was like this, something she didn't get or even like. Yet, for some reason she couldn't put her finger on, she couldn't hold it against him. Not in this job. Air traffic controllers think they have it bad. Les had his reasons, she told herself. Good reasons.

She knew she was lying to herself. She just didn't know why.

***

That night, they ate alone, apart. Cindy's appetite was back in spades and she had it in for some shrimp, almost a pound before she was done, smothered with the most delicious, horseradish-and-lime-laced cocktail sauce she'd ever tasted.

Les had directed her—correctly she noted—to the one Local who would know the best place to get fresh shrimp in town. He was right; the shrimp were magnificent. The hush puppies weren't bad either, nor was the slaw. The meal was Florida eating at its best, and Cindy wondered how she had survived without such standard delights all those years.

Les went for soul food—chicken, field peas with snaps, greens, two slices of the best sweet potato pie he'd ever eaten—and kept his eye out for other white guys hanging out where they normally wouldn't.

Or shouldn't.

***

"Wha'da fuck chu doin' here? Ain't chu somewhat off-*white* to be up in here, muhfucka?"

There were four of them, but two would stay silent.

Les looked up, unintimidated. After all, his Ruger was less than four inches from his right hand, which was resting on the edge of the yellow Formica table near his open jacket. Though he knew he wouldn't need firepower. Truth was on his side.

He said, "I'm looking for the piece a; shit who killed Charlene Horton. He's white too, you know."

"What's 'at s'posed to mean?"

Some of the attitude and most of the threatening dialect had vanished.

Les laid down a generous tip. "Food's good, here," he said. They nodded but otherwise didn't respond. Les stood.

"It means," he said, "if you see a white guy cruising around slow, maybe looking like he's got his eye on one of your women, call the police. Or call me."

"How we gonna call you? We don't know you from nobody."

This was the moment to flash his FBI ID. It was all about the timing.

All four men eyed the three bold letters but said nothing. Les said, "Call information in Orlando and ask for the FBI. Whoever picks up, tell them you want to talk to Les Moore. Less-more. Easy to remember, right?"

The tall guy with the huge Dolphins jacket and gold incisor finally smiled. "A'ight. I'm Mo," he said, and pointed at his short friend. "He's Less. Less than Mo."

Littler Less grinned and said, "Shit." But somehow the single word had three syllables by the time he was done with it.

"How ya doin', Less, Mo," Les said. He smiled genuinely and offered his hand. The shake turned into quite an elaborate process, but Les went with the flow smoothly. He'd worked Urban Nightmare before, as his old shift commander called midnight-to-eight in the Early Years. Back in Detroit.

"Jus' fine, my man, Les," Less said in a voice lower than Lou Rawls. "We see that boy, we take care of it."

"Take care of it by calling me," Les said, firm but friendly.

They sniffed and shifted, halfway nodded. But they didn't mean it and neither did Les. If these guys took down Predator, it was fine with him. He just hoped if they did, they were good, fast, and neat enough not to get caught, or if not, they were smart enough to know they weren't and would call him.

"Might be a Toyota, might be Mustang. Light blue-green metallic." The Bureau crime lab hadn't finished evaluating the paint type to determine the manufacturer yet.

"A Mustang or a Toyota? What the fuck kinda clue is 'at shit?" Mo sounded almost indignant.

"The only kind we got right now," Les said and shrugged.

"Some bitch gi' you dat shit?" Mo asked.

Les shrugged like *What're you gonna do?*

They all said, "Fuck" together and laughed, giving Mo a congratulatory series of local handshakes and gestures which then carried over to Les with a "Shit. You take care, my man. This ain't the nice 'n' white, ya know." Not around here.

"I'm aware. Thanks." Les didn't know a damn thing about current Ebonics proper, but he loved the language of the street, and he made no pretense of being able to speak it. Les Moore was truly color-blind, and it showed. He wouldn't have lived as long as he had, otherwise.

Mo and his bros looked like they respected Les's cool reserve, even if they probably thought he was crazy. Even the police stayed out of this neighborhood at night, unless they had a 911 call and came in a pack.

There was some more handshaking and other gestures, then Les headed for the register. "Hey," Mo said. "You picked good, FBI. Aunt Jo's is it an' all that, ain't it?"

Les smiled and nodded as he paid an indifferent Aunt Jo. The food was excellent, the bathroom clean, and the service fast, despite his pallor. "Couldn't ask for more," he said, again with the genuine warmth Les offered anyone who didn't put on airs. Real people, just trying to get by in a tough world. He turned back to the old woman and said, "As good as I've ever had and then some. Thank you."

Aunt Jo smiled—likely the first one Mo and the guys had ever seen her offer a white man. They returned to their local dialect around the video game, swapping comic reactions that Les didn't understand verbally. But he grasped the context. Les was all right for a white guy— and a Fed. Must've been that second piece of sweet potato pie.

***

As Les correctly figured, Mo and his friends wouldn't stay inside Aunt Jo's long. They were just posturing. Didn't want to look too interested in *the man's bi'ness*, even if one of their own had been Predator's last victim.

Les climbed in his FBI loaner sedan—an old Crown Vic that was getting the evil eye by several newer and younger black men without belts, not privy to the conversation inside—and he rode off slowly, watching in his rearview to see if Mo and Less Than Mo would go outside and tell their slack-hatted friends *wussup* the instant he was gone.

They did. And when Les circled the next block to sneak a sidelong glance, they were all heading out in their lowered rides garnished with bright paint, smoked windows, and purple crowns on the dash. Les had his search party, which would only grow. And they wouldn't cost taxpayers a thin dime. Might even save some paperwork.

Chapter 14 – Les's Posse

Six hours later, Les's phone rang. He was parked alongside a liquor store in what most whites considered the worst part of town. He'd already made friends with half a dozen of the regular milk-crate alkies who let everyone else know that Les was okay. "No-no, he out to gi' dat whi' man what killed dat pretty college guhl from 'lanta."

Many a sacked bottle was toasted in Les's direction, then conversation returned to old lies of insatiable big-assed women, the sorry state of Gators football that year, and how the ex-governor was almost as big an asshole as the current one.

"Disenfranchised my *ass*," they said. "I gotcher voter ID righ'chere." And they laughed long and hard into the yellow night.

"Yeah," Les said into his phone with a formal voice. Hey, it could be anyone.

"Where the fuck are you?" Brinkman said.

"Outside a liquor store in Gainesville. Where're you?"

After a few silent seconds to telegraph his dissatisfaction with Les's *attitude*, Brinkman said, "It doesn't matter where I am. What're you doing there?"

"Earning my keep."

"You're off the clock."

"I'm never off the clock."

"Go home, go to bed, let Local handle it. This one's theirs."

This was true. Predator hadn't crossed state lines, hadn't asked for a ransom, hadn't violated anything directly *federal*.

"They're overstressed and undermanned," Les said, not as an explanation. Then he wondered, "Phil, why are you calling me at one thirty in the morning to tell me this?" He let his eyes dust the bars on the window, the greasy parking lot, and the six 55-gallon drums overflowing with trash.

"Because I'm *not* telling you that," Brinkman said. "I just got woken up at one thirty by a call from the Orlando office, from Pete

Bassett himself, who got woken up at one *twenty* because some colored guys have been bugging his niece at the office for the last hour, demanding to talk to you and no one else, so he called—"

Les hackles rose high to overshadow any hope of finding a killer. "Did anybody who was so bothered by someone trying to help us solve this Predator case bother to get a fucking phone number, Phil?" He ignored the *colored* part. Brinkman who was as current as a bronze ax. And he answered to an African American boss on a *daily basis.*

Maybe therein lay the whole problem.

"Don't start with me, Les," Brinkman said. "It's one-goddam-thirty in the morning and I was sleeping quite soundly, thank you very much. At home!"

"So, they didn't."

There was a pause. "I don't know if they didn't or didn't. *Did* or didn't. And what're you telling colored guys to call you for in the middle of the night when you're not there?"

"I'm here, you're talking to me. Why didn't someone give them my cell number so they could be talking to me?"

"You know we don't give personal contact information out except in emergencies or unless there's been previous authorization by—"

"Phil, for Chrissake," Les snapped. "Don't quote me the fucking manual. Please, don't quote me the fucking manual." Les was mad at himself. Why hadn't he given them his cell number? Because he didn't expect them to find anything so fast!

He turned his self-loathing on Brinkman—all things considered, an acceptable transference—and hit hard. "It's no wonder you guys have gotten nowhere on these cases for the past three years and had to resort to taking me back to try and get you out of this deep, steaming pit of horseshit you're up to your noses in."

Brinkman was rendered mute, the way Les liked him best.

"Did it occur to anyone those guys might be calling with information on this case, and I might actually want to talk to them so I might actually have a chance to solve this for Local and get you guys out at least down to your *chins*?"

Brinkman managed to sound fairly belligerent. "I'm not in anything." A lie. "And how do you know that's why they called?"

Les physically threw his hands up in the air. "How do I know you're in DC?"

"Because I told you!" Brinkman said with all the indignation and recrimination he could muster, which Les took to mean that he wasn't at home in DC at all. Though once again, Les couldn't imagine anyone actually inviting Phil Brinkman to spend the night anywhere.

Les said, "Maybe you're calling me on a cell. I'm on a cell. Maybe you are, too. Maybe you're parked around the next corner staking me out." He looked down the street, but not for his boss.

"Now, why the fuck would I be doing that?" Brinkman barked with growing irritation to make it clear that he just didn't understand Les. Ever. Another perfect arrangement, as Les Moore saw it.

Les said, "I don't know, Phil. Why does anyone do anything?"

"What the hell does that mean?" Brinkman snapped. "Are you going guru on me, Moore? Because if you are, I want to know about it right now. You've only been back a few weeks and you are *not* going guru on me already. You understand me? My ass is the line here!"

Philosophy—any ideological discussion whatsoever—was one of Brinkman's pet peeves. He felt woefully inadequate (rightfully so) in any arena even remotely resembling deeper thought. So, he avoided intro- and *extro*-spection like rabies, baring his teeth at any mention of Things Deep. He was a *nuts-and-bolts kind of guy*, as he so often put it (even if he didn't know the difference between a hex-head and a carriage bolt), and he was very comfortable with that designation. There *were* no Larger Pictures to Phil Brinkman, no Definitive Answers. Ask him the Great Unasked, and well...

Just don't ask. Unless you wanted to see him melt like a slug in salt.

"I mean it, Les. You go guru on me, and I'm pulling the plug. Like that!" Les could hear Brinkman's fingers snap on the other end. Funny, Les thought, how loud he could pop those stubby, chubby digits.

But Les didn't take this threat lightly. Before he left the Bureau the last time, in the wake of the murders of his wife and daughter, Les had begun pondering the Meaning of Life. He made the mistake of confiding in Brinkman, even though he knew of Brinkman's distaste for things infinite or indefinite. Those weak-moment confessions led Brinkman to start the paperwork. Within a week, Les was off his temporary duty assignment, out on indefinite leave. Start talking that shit again and he was facing permanent termination.

The end of it all. Right here in a greasy parking lot in *colored* town.

"It's just a saying, Phil. Calm down."

As Phil didn't calm down even more, Les happened to see Mo drive past slowly, on the prowl. No mistaking the lowered spring-green Pontiac with the dark bronze windows and gold trim, twenty-two-inch chrome wheels with tires so thin there was barely more than a suggestion of inflation.

"I gotta go," Les said suddenly, cutting Brinkman off in midsentence and trotting to his loaner. "Tell Bassett to tell his niece to get a phone number next time, or not to hire family members anymore. Then quote the manual to him. That part about nepotism."

He clicked off and climbed in.

In less than half a minute, Les caught up and waved them over. Mo said they thought they'd seen the guy in an older silver Mustang, not a green one, but the driver had pulled away suddenly and they'd lost him.

"Was it a 5.0?"

"Would if it was me," little Less said in his deep basso and got five from one of his buddies in the backseat without looking.

Les's phone rang. "Yes, what?" He was busy.

Brinkman barely got out, "Les, don't you ever hang up on me like that again or—"

Les hung up on him.

"Where was this and when?" Les asked the guys. Mo told him about a half hour and gave directions. "Shit!" Les said as his phone rang again. This time he answered and hung up without listening, imagining Brinkman taking a blood pressure pill *wherever the hell* he was.

"We tried to call you, man," Mo said, put out. "FBI kep' sayin' 'He not in, he not in. You hafta call back in the mornin'.' Fuckin' broken-record bitch. Pro'lly don't know the diff'rence 'tween a Mustang an' a muhfuckin' Toyota, no how."

Brown hands slapped round.

"I know, I'm sorry, my fault," Les said. "I should've given you this number. I didn't think you'd find anything so fast." *And the Bureau would continue to be so incompetent.*

"'S'cool, man." It wasn't, but what could they do?

Les wrote his cell number down for them this time, still miffed at himself for not doing it the first time, then sped off.

***

Mo and Less were right behind him. For about three blocks. Then Les disappeared.

"Where the fuck 'd he go?" Less asked Mo.

Mo had no idea. "Damn..." was all he said. Talk about a ghost motherfucker. And this was their 'hood.

***

When her phone rang at 1:48 a.m., Cindy came straight up out of bed a clean foot, having left the ringtone on high. She'd been dreaming about working with her older brother Vincent, the fireman. Cindy had slid down an endless stripper pole then raced after the departing ladder rig, naked, and was trying to leap aboard the red platform while Vince yelled, "Hurry, Cindy! People are burning! Hurry! Faster! Helpless people are burning!"

Her phone screamed at her again.

Cindy jumped, heart pounding—then realized what she was hearing wasn't an actual fire bell. She muttered, "Jesus H," burped shrimp, and told herself, "I gotta quit eating before bed."

Cindy grabbed her glowing phone in the dark room. "Yeah?"

Initially irritated that anyone had called so late, in the middle of the night—even if they saved her from her nightmare—Cindy relaxed instantly on hearing Les's calm voice, then listened as he caught her up on the night's events. She could hear Sinatra issuing low in the background. The one about a hole in his head. She hoped lyrics weren't prophetic.

"You want me to come?" Cindy asked, mostly awake but comfortable in her warm bed.

"I didn't know you could do it on cue," he said. "But sure, go ahead. Just think of me if it doesn't spoil the mood."

"What?" His double entendre threw her for a moment. Then it hit her. "Oh, shit. Les. Goddammit. Don't do that." She meant that he shouldn't confuse her. Nothing more.

Maybe she wasn't so awake after all. She turned on the light.

He said, "I took the car."

"Huh? Oh. Yeah." *Of course* he took the car. "Do you think you're close?"

"I don't know. That was a long time ago. He's probably halfway to New Mexico by now."

"Why New Mexico?" Cindy's mind raced through empty files. "Did I miss something in the briefing?"

"No, I was... it was the state that popped in is all. Man, you were out of it. Did you have another beer tonight?"

"No," Cindy said, disabused. She turned on a lamp, stood out of bed, and started meandering around her room to get the blood moving and clear her head. She forced herself to focus on the decor, such as it was—the walls a faded peacock blue, sort of like her last room which had been a faded peacock green. The curtains were nicer in this one, medium tan with irregular dark blue shapes that were either supposed to be large leaves or small sail-cats, Cindy wasn't sure.

"So," she said. "What now?"

"Drive around and keep looking," Les said. "I just wanted you to know where we're at. That, you know, maybe we were getting a break here."

Cindy thought that that was the nicest thing Les had done for her yet. Maybe the nicest thing anyone had done for her *ever*. "Thanks," she said, keeping it simple.

"You're welcome," he said.

It would have been appropriate to say goodbye at that point, but Cindy wasn't ready. So, she asked a generic, "Where are you?"

Les said, "Not sure. Gangs must've taken all the street signs—killed the lights."

"Watch yourself," Cindy advised, knowing he likely didn't know Gainesville any better than she did.

"I'm fine," he said. "Just cruising."

Cindy kidded, "Looking for action?" and lay back down on the bed.

"Yeah. Action," Les said and laughed.

A short block later, he got some.

Bang! It sounded like a gun shot over the phone, maybe a shotgun. "Jesus Christ!" he said.

"What?" Cindy sat straight up. "Is it him?"

"No. Some asshole threw a brick at my car."

Cindy could hear the incredulity in his voice. Then she heard his power window go down and him yelling, "FBI, jerkoff! Throw another one a' those and I'll call in a fucking air strike!"

Cindy had to laugh. Until she heard a faint, "Fuck you, muthafucka!" followed by another loud thump and Les saying quickly, "I'll call you back."

"No. Don't go! Les!"

She heard a ruffling sound, as if he'd tossed his phone on the seat, then squealing tires, some pops in the distance and breaking glass, followed by four very loud shots, followed by indiscernible urgent shouting somewhere. The bridge scene from *Apocalypse Now* came to mind.

"Les?"

Cindy was up, standing next to the bed, heart pounding again. She got no answer, only the roar of the engine. "Les!"

He said as if from two feet away, "Hold on."

Cindy heard two more loud gunshots, more squealing rubber, and Les shouting, "FBI, goddammit! Cut it out! I'm on your side here!"

Musing how the old "Halt, FBI!" bit didn't work like it used to, Cindy caught sight of her naked body in the door-mounted full-length mirror. She didn't usually sleep in the nude. If ever there came a real emergency, she wouldn't be—

Bang! Another loud gunshot in her ear, followed by two more quick ones—*Bang! Bang!*—followed by more distant shouts and shots, more thumps, and more breaking glass.

Les muttered something about the "goddam Gaza Strip," then what sounded like a hailstorm of heavy objects pelted his car.

Cindy heard him shout, "Fucking lunatics! F-B-I!" followed by three more loud shots then the growl of a fully gunned police V-8, and some last fleeing squeals around corners.

A few seconds later, Les picked up the phone. "Still there?"

Cindy could hear him ejecting the spent clip from his nine and asked, "Are you okay?"

"Yeah, but Bassett's loaner just lost a few thou in resale."

She heard the familiar crack of a fresh clip finding its seat, then he said, "It gets tougher to do this job every year, I swear. No respect."

Les was apparently fine, and relatively unruffled, considering. If their positions had been switched, Cindy'd probably need a stiff one.

That, or a drink.

She ogled her own nakedness in the mirror, having forgotten about the narrower than normal home-wax she'd given herself earlier.

Just to do it.

"You gave me a scare," she said and, relieved, picked and preened. Having less down there really wasn't as weird as she had thought it might be. Growing up conservative in a family of law-enforcement-adjacent professionals, she hadn't—

Les was saying something.

"Huh?" Cindy said, groping for reality. "I said you gave me a scare." She sat quickly onto the edge of the bed, out of range of her mirror image.

After a moment of silence, Les said, "Really, it was nothing. Couple of crackheads with nothing to do. Did you get anything to eat?"

He wasn't reasonably unruffled, he was *completely* unruffled. *Unreal*, Cindy thought. "Shrimp. You want me to call it in?"

"No. I'm sure Local gave up on that street long ago."

"Okay," she said, only now noticing her fingers were—on their own, it seemed—idly tracing soft lines up and down her newly-smooth skin. Odd, since she didn't usually do that. But feeling herself felt... okay. Even natural. Even given the unusual circumstance.

Maybe it was her mood brought on by the strange dreams, or maybe the vicarious thrill of hearing Les's chase action over the phone and the succeeding post-adrenaline droop relaxing her so deeply.

Maybe she was horny.

This wouldn't take any time at all. *Yeah, if you want me to come, I think I can swing it.*

"Shit," Les said suddenly.

Cindy's hand jerked away from its explorative enterprise as quickly as if she were hearing her father at her bedroom door asking, "What's all that moaning in there?"

What was it this time? A whole gang? Zombies? A friggin' mortar attack?

"Les?"

"I'm getting pulled over," he said with a sigh.

"What?" *What a relief!* "You're kidding." A nervous laugh escaped her.

"Blue light special. Dopeheads must've shot out a taillight or something."

Shot out? "Les, you need to be more careful out there." She sounded like her mother—and cringed.

"Yeah, okay," he said absent a slant. "I gotta go. It's a young kid. He might think my phone is a gun and kill me."

"Okay, be careful with that," Cindy said, then added a hasty, "And call me back!" Which sounded entirely too needy, too teenage, too codependent—too everything she didn't want it to sound.

Fortunately, Les seemed preoccupied with not getting shot by a rookie. "Okay," he said. She heard him saying, "FBI. It's a phone."

The line went dead.

Cindy hung up and sighed. Les would be all right. If he could handle a brick and bullet attack in the middle of the night in an unfamiliar hostile neighborhood, he could handle a routine traffic stop.

Two minutes later—with some fairly vivid visualization involving Les's smooth body in a deep blue pool surrounded by a *real* tropical grotto—Cindy was relieved of a great deal of tension. She slumbered the rest of the night with nary another shrimp-induced dream of burning buildings or human suffering.

She slept so well it scared her.

Chapter 15 – Gators

"Christ, Les, what is it with you and cars?"

Cindy stared at Bassett's loaner under the Ramada's red-topped porte cochere. The older Crown Vic Interceptor, plain white with the police prep package, had at least twenty serious dents from bricks, a dozen bullet holes, and all three rear windows were gone, along with the passenger side glass. There were no taillights. It reminded Cindy of those hulks she saw on the news all the time in the Middle East. All that was missing was the smoke and burkas.

"The little prick gave me an equipment violation. Can you believe it?" Les showed her where the kid had written, "No taillights due to bullets." Cindy looked up, incredulous. "Just doing his job," Les said with only a trace of asperity. Then he wadded up the ticket and threw it in the backseat through a blown-out window.

"You're lucky you got out of there alive," Cindy said, walking around the wreck to the passenger side.

"SOP these days," Les said. "Watch the glass."

As Cindy opened her door with some effort and a loud pop, the hinge dented from a hit, Les reached through with a file folder and scraped the scattered shards onto the floorboards. "Okay," he smiled up. "Hop in."

Cindy did. The door popped again, closing no easier than it had opened.

Les turned the engine over and it backfired. "I think it may've taken one in the intake manifold," he said as the Ford sputtered and lunged out of the lot.

Cindy thought he sounded awfully happy about his night's drama, and when she looked over, Les was grinning like a new father. She half-expected him to hand her a fat cigar with a black band.

"It's the life, ain't it, Toots?" He beamed.

Toots? And so brazen! Not only had he not been unsettled by the attack the night before, he had apparently been invigorated to the point of well-saturated fearlessness.

Cindy forgave the appellative trespass as immediately as she now understood why Les Moore had sunk so low those years on suspension. Even if this work almost killed him, literally and repeatedly, he enjoyed it like no man or woman she had ever known. She had to love that about him.

Didn't she?

***

The big "Protect and Serve" clock in the lobby read four thirty by the time Les and Cindy got back to the Gainesville PD and were handed a message from Pete Bassett in the Orlando field office. He needed to trade cars with them — something about a lease agreement service period. A driver was on the way.

When the TASK partners entered the detective bureau, they found a lanky twenty-year-old with shaved sidewalls waiting at their folding table, reading a *Silver Surfer* comic. Les stared at the kid with some sort of x-ray intensity from ten feet off until the kid looked up. "Oh. You Agent Moore?" he said. Les nodded. "Got the keys to the sled?" Les tossed them. "These Vics are real dogs, huh?" He flashed a car enthusiast's knowing grin. "Zero to sixty in four miles."

Les nodded and said, "This one's running a little rough."

Cindy kept her smirk to herself as she sucked a last sliver of shredded pork from a molar, amazed at how good it still tasted.

She hadn't believed Les about "Samantha's Sugar Shack, The Pig Pickin' Parlor of Choice!" when he had mentioned it before, but there it was in all its plywood and screened glory.

No a/c. In central Florida.

The food was even better than Les had described and more than worth the two hours it took him to find it. "What'd I tell you?" he kept asking, barbecue sauce from fingertips to hairline until Cindy had to tell him to, "Stop already! You win!"

The comic kid said, "Your new one's a '96 Impala SS we got from a local sting. Search and seizure." He raised his eyebrows. "It *rocks*. Last year they made 'em. It's big but it's baaaad," he said, happy as kid in a candy-apple street rod.

Les said, "Zero to sixty in...?"

"Less time than it takes to tell someone what it is," the kid bragged. He had run the black beauty out a little on the Turnpike coming up—finally backing off at 145 mph. "Have a good one," he said conspiratorially, and walked out.

Cindy looked at Les, Les looked at Cindy, and the two of them moved to the window. From the second floor they watched the kid's gait go funereal as he neared the designated parking space, then walked around the trashed Vic twice, checking the license number on the key fob against the plate three times, then looking up at the building—paler it seemed, even from three floors up—before he climbed in.

Les's words seemed to echo in from another dimension. "You've got a great smile. Anyone ever tell you that?"

Cindy forced herself to snap out of her vision of Bassett's reaction as he stood in the Orlando lot with the lease termination agreement in his hand staring at what was left of the Ford. Then there would be the lease agent.

Suddenly, the whole phone ordeal was made worthwhile.

On looking up into Les's face, seeing the kindness, Cindy said, "Thank you," honestly. "I never thought so."

They were close. He said, "You think we oughta just fuck and get it over with?"

Cindy laughed out. "No," she said.

Les nodded agreeably, then he looked out, apparently feeling sorry for the surfing car kid. "Maybe I should call Bassett to warn him."

Cindy watched the battered sedan lug and buck out onto the divided four-lane and away. "Nah," she said like the *Ohia* girl she was, then turned back to Les, the devil fully in him at the moment.

"So do you," she told him. "Have a great smile."

Some moments passed, during which Les's smile faded and his eyes glazed over. Then that passed and he said, "Not for a long time." He looked younger than he had in weeks. "You brought it back."

Cindy didn't know what to say. No man had ever said anything remotely as meaningful to her by way of a compliment.

Finally, after a longer, even stiller moment, Les said, "I'm kinda beat. Three hours of sleep, half a ton of barbecue. I was thinking a swim, maybe a nap." He was asking.

Cindy said she was stuffed, too, and feeling drowsy. A nap sounded good, but, "I'll probably have dreams of chasing burning barbecue shacks down the street, naked, with my brother shouting, 'Hurry, Cindy! Brinkman's on fire! We've got to put him out! Hurry!'"

Les looked confused, so Cindy explained. "I have weird dreams sometimes. Especially when I overeat."

"Mmm," Les said contemplatively. "Well, if Brinkman's on fire, do us all a favor and don't put him out."

Cindy said, "Okay," and they left for the day. Their first date had gone well.

And it *was* a date.

***

The kid had been right. The SS wholly looked the part. Black on black, black windows, twenty-inch Pirelli P-Zeros on eleven-inch classic chrome Cragar five-spokes, big-block 5.7 liter tweaked up to four-and-a-quarter horses with a dealer-installed half cam, freezing cold a/c. On their way back to the motel, Les put his foot into it on an open stretch of 441 and it stood up like a champ.

Cindy had a notion that her nap could wait and asked Les to swing past the canal even though they'd already been there once on the way to breakfast and once on the way back from barbecue. This would mark their seventh visit to the body dump site in two days.

The sun hung low — humidity and temperature both mild after the passing front — as they approached the spot where Charlene Horton's body had been found. "I thought it'd be warmer," Les said, seeming to complain, but he stood patiently, quietly, while Cindy tried to absorb whatever the place had to give up, one more time.

A dark creek, fifty feet wide, ran nearly platted-straight for a hundred yards, right to left. Lined with cattails on both banks, it had several deep sinkholes under the surface which made the water even darker, in places black as obsidian, and every bit as slick. Someone said it was the tannin in the water; some said silt. Cindy didn't know and Les didn't care. There had been a victim's body in it. That's all that mattered.

At the end of the meadow, the creek turned into a thick hammock of tall cypress with its short forest of knotty knees gathered at the shoreline like a congregation of dysgenic gnomes. Then it ran off toward a lake, somewhere — Alligator Lake, someone had said.

Since the past summer had been relatively dry, the grass in the field was only ankle deep and not as green as it otherwise might have been—more gray. Across the broad field, behind them, stood a vigorous hammock of oaks, saw palmettos, scrub growth, and a few sable palms, their stiff fronds clacking faintly in a breeze that was light and faint with pine from across the paved road.

Les had parked the black SS about where Predator had parked his green 5.0 the night he abducted Charlene Horton.

Collecting vibes.

Cindy glanced over at her partner. At times like these, visiting a crime scene, especially a body dump site, Les often looked as though he'd just finished a satisfying meal and was lost in some blissful post-epicurean meditation, as if on vacation, instead of on the job.

The truth was, being at the place of someone's final demise actually relaxed Les Moore and often had the curious effect of making him feel better about life. Making an effort to find sense in such senseless loss gave him bearing in The Storm and had become the source of his constant renewal—what kept him going. But then, what was left?

Cindy's eyes slid past Les, down the bank to their left, where two black men fished, a hundred or so feet away. Neither said a word, nor moved at all, their eyes fixed on their plastic bobbers.

Cindy then looked to her right where two more black men fished with equal stillness, about a hundred feet in the other direction. She wondered if they knew what had happened here and were giving those awful events wide berth, some silent respect, or if these guys just fished where they fished and never said anything anyway.

Cindy's focus was next drawn to a small alligator cruising down the middle of the canal, a smallish four-footer, tail lazily swinging from side to side, leaving a tiny wake, but no sound.

"Do they usually do that?" Cindy said.

Les came out of his contemplative stillness. "Do who usually do what?"

"Alligators. Down the middle, out in the open like that."

Les saw the gator. "I don't think so. They usually stay close to the banks, if memory serves," he said. Then he noticed another, longer gator in among the cattails on the opposite side of the black-water tributary—then another, and another still. All big.

Reality hit. "She wasn't here any hour and a half."

"Un-huh," Cindy agreed, negatively. "They would've found her by then and feasted like there was no tomorrow. Like you and those ribs."

"I'm not that bad," he said.

"You obviously haven't seen yourself eat pork."

Les grinned and the largest scaly beast slipped noiselessly into the reeds.

Having not evolved noticeably in the millions of years since first appearing in primordial swamps, the alligator's primitive feeding (killing) instinct has remained perfectly intact. Show an alligator any weakness, any vulnerability, or just get too close, and its narcoleptic facade vanishes as quickly as your chances of survival. Appearing with disarming suddenness from seemingly placid waters, a gator snatches you unexpectedly, drags you down into its world, where it can control the kill, and no one can hear your screams. It ignores your suffering with cold-blooded indifference, has its way, then silently disappears in darkness, sated, until its urge to kill overpowers its desire to sleep.

Just like Predator.

"He was saving this place," Les said, close to the canal, apparently feeling the Killer's presence through the alligators. "In case he ever needed a quick dump site in a pinch."

Cindy agreed. None of this was consistent with his previous MO.

"Not by thirty miles," Les said.

Cindy nodded, going back to the garage. "He probably lost track of time. All the drugs."

"And she was a fighter," Les reminded. "It threw him off."

"Getting hit in the head with a bat."

"I've heard it'll do that."

Inspired now, Cindy cut to the denouement, seeing it in her mind. "He finally sees a clock, realizes the sun will be coming up soon, so he wraps her up, throws her in the trunk, and hurries to the closest place he knows he can get in and out without being seen."

Les said, "He was counting on the gators to do his cleanup work. By the time anyone found the body, it would be impossible to tell what he'd done and what they'd done, and everyone would assume she fell in or went swimming and got et."

"Et?"

"It's legit. Check your Scrabble dictionary."

Cindy said, "Yeah, I'll be sure do that."

She turned to look around, get her bearings, then started back for the Impala. Les joined her as she asked, thinking aloud, "So, why bolt?"

"He couldn't count on his plan working. Plus, by then, he'd messed up everywhere else: the dumpster, the clinic, the drugstore. Maybe someone even saw him somewhere, or he thought they did. Or maybe he saw the cops here and knew he'd better skip."

Cindy agreed. "He could've been surveilling the area."

"Either way, he knew if the body was found intact, he was toast. So, he packed a few things and lammed it." Les seemed to be radar-sweeping the entire county with ESP. Then he said, "But he didn't go far."

"If I was him, I'd be in Hoboken by now."

"Why Hoboken?" Les looked up.

"Just popped in. New Mexico," Cindy said as a callback. At any rate, "Anywhere but here."

Les looked around, *feeling*. "He's here. Somewhere. Knows his run is almost over."

"So, why split?" Cindy agreed.

"Maybe get in a last few hits," Les said. "Go down in a blaze of glory."

Having reached the bulbous but nimble SS, they pondered this dire possibility a moment in silence, each of them letting the concept settle in just right. Then Cindy said. "What I can't figure out, what I haven't been able to figure out all along, is why we can't find his car. It's not that big a town. And you're saying he's still here. I mean, we've got tag numbers from the DMV, color and body style. Why can't we find it?"

Without breaking mental stride, Les gave her one of his looks.

Cindy understood. "He got rid of those tags long ago. And the fender he crunched could be the only blue-green part on the car," Cindy said, confirming his thoughts and feeling foolish. "But the car is still registered to him. It's still a two-door Mustang." Before Les could give her the look again, she nodded. "Well, we don't know that for sure."

"It may not be registered to him, but we know it's a Mustang," Les said. "They're all two doors, by the way."

Cindy ignored the last part. "How do we know it's a Mustang for sure?"

"Mo said it was."

"At a distance."

Les shook no. "Guys know cars. And my bet is it's a 5.0."

"What's that, some engine thing?"

Les shook his head. "How can women spend their entire lives driving cars and not have any idea how an engine works?"

"I don't know," Cindy said, not missing a beat. "How can men spend their entire lives chasing women and have no idea how a clitoris works?"

Les let out a low chuckle. "Okay."

"Thank you," Cindy said graciously. "So, it's a five-oh Mustang. What else do we know about it?"

"It's silver."

"So your informant said. But it could've been light blue metallic, like the paint scrape. They've got crime lights over there. Might've looked silver."

"So, you *do* know about cars."

"We're talking about color. At night. Could've been white, gold, or light *green* metallic. Gray, pale yellow, cream, off-white. You said he wasn't sure."

Les grinned at his partner's powers of pigment perception. "Right."

"Like, what's that paint that looks all kinds of colors?"

"Pearlescent."

"Right. Although that's probably too flashy for him."

"So, it's not dark, is what you're saying." SKs usually preferred dark colors. Les thought a moment, then reasoned, "But we can't go around stopping every silver, light blue, green, yellow, white or whatever-colored Mustang in the county. It's the most popular production car ever built. There are probably a thousand like it in the city limits alone."

"But we can start running the ones PD pulls over or Traffic Control finds parked. Maybe find out which one was stolen."

"Can't hurt. We get lucky and spot a VIN that's not on the list and maybe we got him." Les shrugged *why not* and grabbed his phone out of the black Chevy. "I keep telling myself there must be a legitimate use for Parking Enforcement."

"Come on now, they work hard. They're our peers. Sort of."

"Not mine, baby. Not mine." He grinned wide and dialed Orlando. "Baby?"

"I'm gonna get you in court yet," Les said, then looked at his phone askew. "Busy?" Cindy rolled her eyes and shook her head. Then he asked, "They have naked court? You'd look good in that."

Cindy rolled her eyes even more but felt a flush down low. She said, as a distraction, "How do we even know Mo saw our perp? Could've been anybody."

Les flashed Cindy a look she didn't recognize, then said, "White boy cruising those streets at night?"

"College kid looking for dope," she suggested. "Husband looking for a hooker."

"Why a husband?"

"Seventy-eighty percent. What is it now?"

Les grunted. "No hookers around there."

"He doesn't know that."

"Sure he does. Johns know where the action is before they leave home. They've read about it, heard about it, know the street by name, the block. No. Not a john."

"But it could be a doper."

Les sighed then paused, considering that, then said, "No. Mo said they lost him in a flash, like he was there one second, and gone the next. Dopehead doesn't do that. He's looking to be seen, to score. A Predator vanishes."

"Okay," Cindy relented. "So, it's probably him. But he's in the wrong car."

"Wrong color at least," Les allowed. Then, he realized something. "Shit."

Cindy got it immediately. "He dumped the green one."

Les took a few steps away from the car. "Goddammit!" He paced a few steps then came back to pound the innocent Chevy.

"Okay," Cindy said, trying to calm her partner before he destroyed another Bureau vehicle—this time with his bare hands. "We'll find it. Now that we know it's out there, we can find it."

Les leaned on the black Chevy, face toward the ground. Then he looked up, as if realizing something, and turned his gaze away, back toward where they'd just been.

Cindy looked where he was looking, the wide creek with several sinkholes hidden under its polished black surface. "Fuck!" At least she hadn't been the only one to miss it.

Les ran the likely order of events. "He had blood in the trunk, too much to get out quickly and thoroughly. He hit the dumpster and left a paint chip. Maybe somebody did see him, he came back here, drove it in, down there somewhere" — he pointed — "and walked home where he had another car waiting. Goddammit!"

"A silver Mustang five-oh," Cindy nodded, willing to concede the color. She still wasn't sold on the make. "Are we really sure it's a Mustang?"

"Ford owners are very brand loyal, especially with Mustangs."

Cindy nodded, supposing this was so — even if somewhat stupid for a serial criminal.

Les punched in the Orlando office number again. The line was still busy. "Get off the phone, Denise. Talk to your boyfriend on your own damn time."

Cindy suggested, "Maybe you should call Local."

"Yeah." Les did and got through immediately. They said they'd be right out, dragging the canal within two hours and would continue all night if they had to. He advised them of the gators. They thanked him and said they'd bring Fish and Game along.

"Good," Cindy said. "As messed up as he was, he probably left all kinds of goodies for us." She hungered to discover them.

"Mmm," was all Les grunted, looking distracted again already.

"Where do you think he got the other car?" Cindy asked.

Les glanced up with a strange look, as if annoyed at his partner's powers of clairvoyance. "I don't know," he said, brusquely. "I was trying to figure that."

Both knew that Predator could have boosted another car on his way home. Cindy said, "Or maybe he already had it."

"That's what I was thinking," Les said.

"Bullshit," Cindy said.

"What? Really. I was." Les looked as honest as a seventh grader swearing he was telling the truth about peeping in the girls' locker room. He tried the Orlando office again.

Still busy. "Goddam nepotism." Les looked like he was ready to shoot his phone to teach it — or *someone* — a lesson.

Cindy said, "Are you sure you're dialing right?"

Les looked at the keypad and thought a moment. "What's the last four numbers?"

"Three-three-two-four."

Les's face pinched up even more and some indescribable, low profanity gurgled in his throat. Then he dialed again—this time *not* 3244—and got right through. Cindy laughed out loud, then quickly put her hand over her mouth, eyes skipping.

Les shot her a look then spoke into the phone. "Hello, Denise, it's Agent Moore. Could you plea—"

He stopped. Denise was explaining.

"I'm sorry, I didn't realiz... Don't cry... I didn't mean for you to get in... No, I realize this is an important step for... Right... Uh-huh... Yeah... And it's the government, yes. I under..."

Les looked to Cindy for help. She bit her lip.

"I'll speak to your uncle, I promise," he said into the phone, adding quickly, "right now if you'll put me through. And you have my cell number? Um-hmm... Yes, it's okay. All forgiven... Okay, thank you." Denise put him on hold. Les sighed heavily and put his phone on speaker.

Cindy said, "That was very sweet of you."

Les grunted gruffly, but when Bassett got on the phone Les told him not to be too hard on his niece. She was young, and trying to do a good job, and she didn't know, but now she did, and now she had his cell number, so it would all work out.

Bassett thanked him and said he hated talking to Phil Brinkman— about anything. Les said he understood well and told Bassett about their Mustang theory and Gainesville PD's plans to drag the sinkholes. Bassett said he'd send an extra agent up to sit on the site. Les thanked him and clicked off.

Cindy was grinning ear to ear.

"If you say I'm cute," Les warned, "I'm asking for a new partner."

Cindy's said, "You won't get one, but..." She put her fingers to her lips and pretended to lock them up and throw away the key.

"Cute," Les said.

"Oh, I can be, but you can't?"

"You're a chick," he said. She threw a look. "Sue me."

"I'm sure I will, sooner or later. You and Brinkman."

"Please," Les said. "Never use my name and his in the same sentence. It gives me a queasy feeling all over."

They climbed in the car. "Snack?" he asked.

"No thanks. I'm still fulla pig."

"Yeah. Me too." He gunned the hot Chevy in the gray grass, cutting a deep donut back for the hardtop.

All five fishermen turned to look and shake their heads.

"So, a five-oh is a V-8," Cindy said/asked. Les snorted and rolled his eyes. "Well!" she said. "I had to ask. I don't know!"

"At least I know what a clitoris *is*," he said.

"Couldn't prove it by me."

The words were out of Cindy's mouth before she knew she was saying them, and the look he gave her made her smolder and shrink — at the same damn time.

***

Les's cellphone was ringing when he got out of the shower. He ran a towel over part of his body and dripped from the rest as he rushed to his jacket to retrieve the ringing nag. "Hello."

It was Mo. They'd seen the guy again.

Chapter 16 – Predator's Predator's Predator

Gainesville, ten p.m. The good weather is holding so the sidewalks are choked. It's Ladies' Night.

What a night.

Predator's silver 5.0 rumbles low and menacing. He didn't see what he wanted outside the Halfway Club, so he came all the way to Big Rock Candy, a purple cinder-block affair with no windows and hyperactive yellow neon.

They can't see in through his tinted windows, but he must be one of them if he's cruising here. They flirt and giggle, waggle and wave, dressed to kill—putting it all on the line for a good time. Everyone wants some on a Friday night.

Stopping in the darkness of a one-way side street, the Killer finds a space across from the many *Great Deals!* of a high-miles used car lot, giving him a block-long view of the boulevard. He can check out everyone from here. The men and women, boys and girls, and...

His second awful epiphany in a week: *A girl!* And the younger the better. One that won't give him any trouble like the last time. Get her out in a field, kill her and rape her, then dump her body in the creek when no one's looking. Simple plans are the best plans.

Predator smiles, but the side with a dent like a Louisville Slugger has to fight for equality. He pops three Tylenol IIs and snorts a line he got from some skank on the other side of campus, the one with tracks on her ankles, in the white trash neighborhood. He hates her, too. He's better than them. Better than all of them. He's God!

It's a big responsibility.

Tomorrow, he figures to go Asian; maybe a Latina the next night; then a Hindu the night after. *A Hindu!* Still killing himself with his routines. *Stop, already!* He can't take any more.

Pain spiders his head. Only two TIIs left. *Damn.* He washes them down and throws out the empty Michelob that tinkles on the pavement. Precision and neatness don't matter anymore. Caution blown off with the decreasing wind. Still now.

One girl a night until they get him. That's the plan. He just decided. Right after the last blast of crystal snowplowed a tunnel of dim light through the murky blizzard of hurt in his head. He watches the street, stalks without moving—a gator in the swamp grass, silent, waiting.

And there she is.

What is she? Fourteen, fifteen? She's petite; maybe thirteen. Even better! The word raises a backwash of brain babble. *Petite.* He likes the sound of the word. It's reassuring. She won't fight back. Won't hurt him like that goddam black amazon bitch.

He starts the engine, leaves the passenger door cracked open, seat back. She'll fit on the floor, under the dash where no one will see.

Cutting through the mounded shadows of the car lot, he keeps his eyes on his little black prize. A dog barks. He ignores the warning.

Unfortunately, so does she. Predator's hands are around her neck before she breathes again, nothing she can do.

A second later, she's on the ground getting bashed in the head between two used imports with *Unbelievably Low Sale Prices!* Young bones still pliant, her head caves in on one side like a deflated soccer ball. She loses consciousness instantly.

Predator breathes fast and shallow. This is what it's all been about, right here on the street at night, people close enough to see and hear. But no one listens, no one knows to look.

She belongs to him now.

He drags his littlest victim through the overpriced junk, across the street to his rumbling Mustang. *Chicks love hot cars.*

He stuffs her in as headlights sweep left to right, ticking the chrome, filling in the shadows. Someone's coming, slow. A brother cruising for trim, a block off the Strip? Maybe a neighbor from down the street.

High beams crack hard, and he squints into them. They're far apart, so it's not an import, not a small car. Could be a police sedan.

Or the FBI.

***

Les and Cindy don't recognize the face from his DMV shot from a block away, but they don't need to. They know who's shoving a limp black body into a silver Mustang at midnight. He's white, he's here, he's at work. He's Predator.

Les floors it.

Predator dives over the roof and down into the driver's seat, slapping the shifter before the door closes. Wide tires howl and smoke, launching him into the intersection thick with night traffic. He's already past the limit.

"Jesus!" Cindy gulps as the killer jets across both lanes without a glance in either direction, without brakes. *So* close.

Two club-cruisers crack an offset head-on. Glass, plastic, and dueling Super-Bass spill out. Engines die, but the beat goes on.

Predator is on the other side.

"Easy, Les. Watch it..." Cindy braces as they sail into the sheet metal melee and...

Bam! Their long black Chevy clips the short end of an open flower truck. Rose petal rain brings on the wipers, slapping floral red and velvet wet. "Call it in!" Les yells.

"I got it," she shouts back, digging for her phone as the Mustang rounds a curve ahead and...

He's gone. An empty street now.

"There, there! Right!" Cindy catches a strobing red blip behind ornamental oleander and thick citrus. "Go back! Go back!"

Les has the beefy, low Impala in reverse before she's finished — before they've stopped — wheels hopping mad. "Call it *in!*"

Pounding! up onto the curb, *slamming!* down into Drive, *squealing!* around over the missed corner in a thick blue twister of smoke and discord.

Sixty on a side street — quicker than he can say it. The SS delivers as promised.

Cindy stabs at tiny bouncing numbers while Les throws them into a four-wheel drift around the next corner. Why didn't she save PD's number instead of memorizing it!

Slammed against the door by resolute g-forces, she loses her phone on the floor.

But Les guesses right. A block ahead, red lights slide left. The tweaked V-8 reaches deep, groaning, as Cindy retrieves her phone and misdials an escort service. "Slick Chicks, where *nothing* gets in the way of your good time. May I — "

"Jesus," and Cindy dialing again.

Fifty feet and closing fast, Les punches his brake foot to the floor. Good vibrations roll from the rocking ABS as he pinches the turn hard and tight—fragile adjustments to hold the arc, inertia taking them wide, using up every inch of room on the right.

Good thing. A small, late-model Japanese import, dark, blows by so close they nearly swap pinstripes. Cindy cranes for a look back and—

Wham! They're into a parked Humvee. Her side.

Good Thing Number Two: Humvees are heavy. The sideswiping SS glances off and keeps going. But Cindy has lost her phone again. "Shit!" Fingertips on the floor, feeling but not finding. Damn thing must be under the seat, out of reach. Stretching lower and—

"Look out!" Les is into another hard left.

Cindy sits up in time to crack her head on door hardware. Operative part of the word: hard. She lets out a sharp *Ummmmmfff.*

"You okay?" he asks but doesn't look. He can't.

"Yeah," she fibs, rubbing. There's already a lump. *Forget the pain; find the phone.* Wet eyes can't be helped.

Three more turns and they're back at The Strip, the 5.0 dead ahead, blasting back through the intersection like the only car on the road.

It's not.

Predator takes the front cap clean off a squealing Cadillac. Leaves a fender of his own, along with the rattle of scattering highway shrapnel and the sweet scent of spewing coolant as three other cars find sudden stopping points. Full contact.

Les on his horn, power-braking, inching through the night-grind. For once, he wishes he had blue lights.

"Okay, okay, you're clear!" Cindy lets him know from her side. He's already using all six hundred pounds of torque. Altered rice-rods scattered like jacks.

Cranked on crank, speeding on speed, Predator ducks into a narrow alley, so tight he's slapping chain link, side to side.

Racing for the finish.

A half-breath later, Les plunges the old, wide Chevy in. Wood walls and metal fence posts claw at the Super sedan under a rising geyser of sparks. Side mirrors pop off crenelated fenders. They might... get... stuck...

Precisely Predator's plan.

Les never backs off as something big hits the right-side A-pillar. *Wham!* Cindy ducking reflexively and...

Good things come in threes. She's out of the way when the big limb crashes through her window, snaps off four-inches thick, hurls through the cabin, smashes the rear window out.

Les reflexively reaches a hand over to keep her down in the maelstrom of bark and leaves, metal and glass, a hail of burning embers their swirling slipstream. The smell of hot metal. "You okay?" Crashing through what's left of a gate at the end of the run.

One galvanized post does a number on Cindy's half of the windshield, but they're free. A trace of taillight, two blocks up, skids off into the darkest part of town. No street life, no light.

No help.

"I'm good," she swears—and dares a look back. The wobbling limb, at peace now, would have taken her head clean off.

"He knows the route," Les says.

Predator must, to find that tiny access lane and race through with such abandon, such confidence. Knowing his car would fit and a wider one might not.

A chicane left, then right—a double—then tracking, as Cindy catches a glimpse of something dark and speeding a block over. Someone...

Pacing them?

A small red pickup appears from nowhere. Les can't miss. He catches the front brush-guard, spinning the little S-10 a full 720 before it comes to a stop, twisted.

"Where'd *he* come from?"

"I don't know," Cindy says honestly. She was looking the other way, for the other car, the dark one, one street over, that's gone now. Lost to the night.

She checks back on the people in the red pickup. "They're okay," she says, as the people get out and walk around. Gesturing.

Another right-left-right, onto the blackest street yet and—

"Shit!" Les slams the brakes, folding Cindy into the dash, then shouting. "Get out! Get out!"

"What?" *Is he nuts!* Gathering her battered senses.

"The girl! He threw her out!" Revving backward, black burn, stopping sharply.

Under the tire smoke in the dim glow of one remaining misaligned headlight, Cindy can barely see the little brown leg and pink shoe. "Oh my God!" Les almost ran her over.

"Out! Now! Go! Call it in!"

Cindy's out of the car and into the moment. "I dropped my phone!" Knees on pavement, hands under the seat.

"Forget it! Here!" Les tosses his and floors the black beast. "I want backup!"

Cindy gets out a clipped "Yes!" as the door nips past, slamming shut.

Screeching tires, a groaning engine, and Cindy's alone in the dark—no idea where—with the motionless victim. She punches 9-1-1 and drops to see if they need paramedics or a coroner.

It's hard to tell with no discernible pulse.

***

Les gets lucky and catches a hint of red in a wide city park up ahead. Over the curb, into the woods and *Crack! Clunk!* So much for the front suspension. Both tires flat, flapping and slapping—now, the back two—the disabled Impala rocking like a rudderless boat in a washing-machine sea as Les takes out park benches, trashcans, a wrought iron fence, the bark off an old oak, to fly out the other side, and...

And?

And?

Checking every direction. Nothing. *Where'd he go?*

There! In the rearview. In the bushes.

A crazy looping reverse, busted P-Zeros blowing smoke, and Les is out with his Ruger, ready to empty the clip. *One less Predator* is what he's thinking. And how that math would be so right. Creeping closer, Ruger ready. The driver's door is open, but...

The Mustang is empty.

Predator's on foot. As is Les, nerves on fire in the cool quiet. Funny how the air's so sweet. And how you notice.

***

A shadow moves, hedge leaves shuffle—Les's eyes like cat slits in the night—but there's nothing to see. The Killer's up in a tree.

They don't call him Predator for nothing.

***

No one ever looks up. He remembers the line from a movie. An unforgettable line some forgettable actor said to him from his fifty-five-inch Hisense. The concept made sense, sitting there on his couch at three in the morning, and he never forgot. He knew it might come in handy some night.

Like this one. Tonight will be the most special yet—killing a special agent. He knows who Les is. He read about Agent Moore when he read about himself.

"Predator." The whisper sounds close. He doesn't realize the word came from his own mouth, so he repeats it. "Predator." It sounds good. Final. He pulls out his .42.

He always had to be different.

"Don't hit the branch. Watch the leaf."

He still doesn't know he's talking to himself—thoughts crawling over themselves like snakes in a pit of flames.

No escape.

He aims where he knows Les will be. All paths lead to his tree. He knows because he's been here before. Practicing. Planning. Waiting.

Wanting.

Les obliges. Predator can see his feet. Death is close. He feels it. That something in the air that stings his skin and burns his eyes. Etches his heart like frozen acid.

His finger eases onto the trigger. *People never look up.* "Predator." It's sounding better all the time, whoever is saying it.

Another step forward and Les is open, the center of his chest dead in the Killer's sights.

Now.

***

The shot is so loud Les's heart skips two beats before he hits the ground. A quick reconnoiter scan of his body and he's...

Not hit!

He rolls up against the thick trunk, trying to get a fix on the shot which came from... *behind?* Must be backup. But where were the sirens? And how did they know where he was? How did Cindy know?

Footsteps. Someone running away!

A fleeting glimpse, a gray night-blur behind thick public brush, and Les is up in a breath. But he only gets two steps when he hears a rustle and finally looks up—just in time to avoid the falling body.

Predator stares up, looking confused as to why he's on his back, dying, and Les Moore is alive, standing over him, kicking the .42 aside, and—

Predator's dead.

Les knows without checking.

A car starts up and peels away into the night. A small, dark import?

Les's mind crashes in on itself like a Dark Star. What the hell just happened? How did he almost let himself get shot by a guy in a tree? And who shot the shooter? And who just saved his life and ran away?

Only one name comes to mind.

Chapter 17 – After the Fall

Little Janet Smiley didn't recognize the white woman at her bedside when she came to, but she could tell it belonged to a friend. Fortunately for what remained of her sanity, the eleven-year-old hadn't seen her predator's face, so that image wouldn't haunt her forever. Only the attack. Being grabbed from behind, dragged between two old cars in a smelly lot.

Then everything had gone dark, and she woke up in this room of unfamiliar colors and confusing sounds.

"How're you feeling?" the woman asked. The battered child tried to answer but couldn't find the strength or ability — which felt strange and scared her even more.

"You're safe now," the woman assured her. "You're going to be all right."

***

The little girl nodded ever so slightly — just enough to break your heart — as tears rolled down her brown satin cheeks.

The final chain of events gave new application to what Cindy's father always called Unconscious Good Luck.

"Would you like to meet the man who found you?" Cindy asked her. "He's out talking to your mother and your brother." The girl's watery eyes said yes, and Cindy left for the waiting room.

Les had been with the family for seventeen hours, on and off, in between answering queries put to him by Brinkman, Gainesville Homicide, and the press. Everyone was painting Les a hero. The hospital halls stood full of grateful relatives, miscellaneous well-wishers, and important leaders of the black community. Even Mo and Less Than Mo came by to thank him.

Then the news came out that Les had only *chased* Predator — someone else had killed him with a single shot from a .40 caliber Ruger KP-94 — and the halls went empty.

A goddam Ruger.

Riverbend had foregone his favorite big bore Taurus in favor of throwing off the Bureau. Les wasn't thrown, even if Brinkman was.

"Les, you're paranoid. Next thing, you're gonna have one of those bumper stickers and a Kennedy website."

Les was surprised Brinkman knew what a website was.

Pete Bassett called, as did Wilstrong. Even Holy Dick. Everyone at least seemed pleased Les was still alive. *Still on the case* was probably all of it.

No one mentioned the heretofore-hot black Impala SS sitting in a salvage yard in Orlando two miles from the Orlando field office. The comic-reading car kid had met the triple-A wrecker at the junkyard gate then later reported grimly back to his boss, "You don't even wanna know," and took the rest of the day off to mourn his loss.

***

A Subaru made front page news.

Police found the late-model, dark WRX STI abandoned a few miles away—no prints, hair and fiber evidence inconclusive, no blood, no DNA. The vehicle didn't reflect a pattern, a preference for make and model.

Riverbend had never used a rally car before. No one had, by NCAVC's calculation. Such a sporty ride was not the usual choice of transportation by SKs; cars like that attracted too much attention. (And therefore *none*. Precisely why Riverbend chose the WRX when he came to Gainesville, looking to stir up trouble in Les's life.)

He had shadowed Predator to stay one step ahead. Hadn't tracked Les at all. But he could have, and that was the point. If Riverbend could find Predator before Les, and be there behind Les when the fatal shot was fired...

Riverbend wanted a showdown—just not yet. He wanted to fuck with Les a while first. Mess with his head.

It was working.

***

In the wake of these events, Brinkman gave Les the week off and took one himself—presumably to celebrate. So, when the call came in that the Bayside Mauler—frequently, and incorrectly, labeled the Miami Mauler by those journalists with alliterative fancy—was found floating in Biscayne Bay, Cindy had no partner to offer counsel.

The new Cuban cop who had been ordered to call her in Gainesville had to say "weeda jellow ribbon tie aroun' his cuck 'n' bulls," three times, then "peenee an' his 'eh scrota sack" before she figured out what the hell he was talking about.

Cindy tried Brinkman at the office, at home, and on his cell. They all just rang. If he was alive, he wasn't picking up. Thank God for small blessings.

She then rang Les's room, knocked at his door, and checked with the desk. Nobody had seen him. For all Cindy knew, he'd blown the state. She'd have to handle this one on her own. The idea grew on her.

Then, she remembered Les had the car.

Cindy vowed not to let this latest irritation interrupt her good night of sleep, but she had a never-ending dream in which her brother kept calling on a cellphone, yelling, "People are burning, Cindy! Hurry!" while she desperately searched some anonymous hotel parking lot for a car to use while Les drove back and forth on the street in a shot-up topless sedan, waving and smiling at her while her uncle sat in the backseat shaving his armpits.

Les's armpits, that is.

The next morning, Cindy made arrangements with Avis. In less than twenty minutes, a young girl knocked at her door. "Ami, with an i," the cheerleader-blonde said merrily.

"How come you're so perky at 6:51 in the morning?" Cindy asked grouchily. "Are you on something?"

"Just high on life, ma'am. Rah!" Ami threw up her arms and cocked her head like a jaunty parrot. To Ami, apparently, all of life was a cheer.

Having only recently passed thirty, Cindy hated being called ma'am already. "Life with an i," she said peevishly, only slightly ashamed of herself.

Ami proved interminably chirpy. A wave of self-actualized awe swept over her perfect features. "Gosh, ma'am. I never thought of that," she said, then led the way down and out to the courtesy van where she pointed out with continuing astonishment that Avis was with an i, too, as if she couldn't believe she had missed such an obvious symbolic connection for the entire three weeks she'd been employed there. She called it "spooky."

Which was what Cindy was thinking about the girl's entire generation, and she and Ami were less than a dozen years apart.

As they swung around the hotel parking lot in the aging van, Ami grimaced at the old Van Morrison CD playing in the dash, left by another driver, and declared it, "Yucky," but said she couldn't figure out how to get it to stop playing. Cindy leaned forward and pushed a button.

The CD ejected.

Ami looked at the deck a moment, then giggled. "Wow. I've never seen one of those before. That was awesome."

She proceeded to find her favorite station on the radio, with a quick series of button stabbings, and Avis Full o' Life Ami funked to Ded G's monster hit from *Killin' Tymes*, "Ded G's Ded — Hot as Fuck" from three years ago that Ami declared "a classic!"

"An' we gonna kill the muthas,
an' we gonna kill the bruthas,
an' we gonna kill AWWWLLL the muthafuckin' uthas."

An' Ami knew every muthafuckin' word.

"Stop!" Cindy shouted.

Ami punched the radio volume knob to turn it off. "I'm sorry, I'm sorry! My bad! You hate rap, right? Please don't tell my boss Larry! He'll have my ass on a plate!"

Cindy said, "No. That's not... but yes. No. It's fine."

What wasn't fine was Pete Bassett's latest replacement loaner, a brown, well-used, two-door Chevy Cruze, returned to the parking lot.

***

Les answered the knock at his door looking relaxed and refreshed. Before he could say anything positive or cheerful, Cindy attacked. "Where the fuck have you been?"

She breezed past him into his room.

"You're sounding more like Phil Brinkman with every passing day, Baker," he said pleasantly. "Are you aware of that?"

"Fuck you *and* Brinkman. Taking a week off and leaving me to talk to 'jello ribbon 'cuck 'n' bulls' while you two are out, what? Rolling gays in a park somewhere? I hear it's a Miami tradition. Then. Ami with an i? Fucking Christ. There's no end to the good times."

Cindy flopped her briefcase, suitcase, and wardrobe bag on Les's bed then slumped into a hotel chair. "And please don't mention me in the same sentence with him either. Especially in a comparative manner — of any kind."

Les asked, "Did you start your period?"

"None of your business. And don't start that sexist shit with me. I'm not in the mood."

"So I gathered from your breezy entrance," Les said, scooping some cubes from the ice bucket. Cindy glowered, made a sound roughly like *Gyicht!*, rolled her eyes, and put her face in her hands.

"Rough night?" he asked.

"Yes, as a matter of fact," she said, still seeing Les and her uncle in the shot-up convertible police cruiser, shaving one another's underarms.

There was an extra vein of gristle in her voice when she asked, "Have you read the papers? Watched *Headline News* by any chance? Stayed in contact with the real world?"

"MTV? Is that still on?"

"I have no idea. And no, the real real world where bad stuff happens to... well, bad people, too."

"Whoever was responsible for that *Human Centipede* movie is dead?"

"No such luck. The Miami—" She caught herself. "The Bayside Mauler floated up giftwrapped at some kid's bar mitzvah party."

"Oh," Les said, filling in the missing gaps, "'Jello cuck 'n' bulls.' Cuban cop, Miami." He nodded.

Cindy groused, "Why do I get all the shitty phone calls when you're gone?"

"Because I'm gone," Les said, jovially pouring some orange juice from a quart carton into his plastic motel cupful of ice.

"You drink orange juice with ice?" Cindy said with cringy face to match her sour tone.

"Not by choice," Les said. "It was warm, from the car. I had no say in the matter." He grinned and lifted his cup in a toast. Cindy grunted and looked away.

"So, someone left us a ribbon," Les said. "I'd be correct in assuming we're headed for Miami?" He sounded positively ebullient!

"Well, I am," Cindy said. "You're off."

"A whole week," Les said, already seeming entirely too relaxed for Cindy's tastes.

And she now noticed: "Why are you dressed, and your bed is made?"

Les looked at the unruffled covers. "Maid's already been here. While you were sleeping in."

"Sleeping in? It's not even seven fifteen! Give me a break. Sleeping in. It's fucking Sunday."

"You really have a foul mouth early, you know that?"

"If you'd had to listen to what I had to listen to, and go through what I had to go through, you'd sound like me, too." Then she muttered, "Death rap at seven in the morning on a fucking Sunday."

"There should be laws."

"Aw, we can't enforce the ones we got," Cindy griped. All she'd really wanted was to be able to read the Sunday funnies in peace, in *bed*.

"Ready to hit it?" Les said, blithely sweeping up the Malibu keys.

"Only if you promise to hold down on the laughter and good times. It's a small car."

If he was this happy on the second day of his vacation, Cindy could imagine what he'd be like by midweek.

***

Cindy slept the whole way down the Turnpike except for a minute or two near Yeehaw Junction when an ambulance screamed by. "What's a Yeehaw?" she'd asked, seeing the exit sign.

"I don't know," Les had said, "but it apparently converges here." To which Cindy muttered something even she didn't understand and promptly fell back asleep.

Les listened to Sinatra.

When Cindy finally woke up, she was alone in the tiny two-door, parked under the high canopy of the Intercontinental Hotel downtown. A valet glowered, disparaged over the possibility of being seen parking such a cheap piece of Tokyo, Michigan tin.

When Les came back out, having been in the lobby checking them in, he had finally run out of steam. Cindy fully understood when he said he wanted to go straight to bed and did.

"Next time, you drive," he said in the elevator.

"It wasn't that far," she said.

"It's Florida," he said.

She couldn't argue with that perspective, and when the door opened, they split apart.

Cindy found her room, took a shower, had a bite in the bar — conch fritters and half an Amstel Lite — went back to her room, took in the view of the departing cruise ships from her balcony, figuring she'd be bored stiff in Miami within the hour and up all night, then lay down to watch TV.

Fifteen minutes later, she was out like a light. She didn't have a single dream about her brothers, or fires, or Les, or armpits, anything else she could remember, but she was amazed in the morning, on examining her pillow, at how much one relatively small person could drool in eleven hours of uninterrupted sleep.

Chapter 18 – The Confession

"I didn't realize how tired I was," Cindy said to an equally revived Les over a breakfast of eggs, hash browns, and Cuban steak.

"Killing wears on you," he said, digging in and closing his eyes while savoring the rich and unmistakable *bisteca* flavor.

"Haven't killed anyone, yet, but when I do, you'll be the first to know," Cindy said.

"Huh?" Les opened his eyes. "What?"

"What what?"

"What did you say?" he said around a mouthful of potatoes. "What did I say?" He was either hungrier or sleepier than he admitted.

Her fork raised with a drippy piece of egg on the shiny tines, Cindy said, "You said 'Killing wears on you.' I assume you meant all this killing around us is wearing."

Les grunted, as if musing over what he had said, or that he had said it, or something, then said, "I must be working too hard. I don't even hear myself talking anymore."

"Maybe." Cindy leaned forward in a conspiratorial way. "Or maybe," she paused, eyebrows up, "you were out killing someone last night. Maybe the... Damn!" She lost her acerbic rhythm. "What the heck's his name. I've got that Idaho thing again."

"Iowa."

"Whatever." She fought her way to, "Miami... Bayside Mauler," and she was back with the program, nodding like a TV cop.

"Yeah, it's all clear as new ice now," she said as if a bare bulb were swinging between them. "You slipped down in the middle of the night and whacked the Bayside Mauler. Uh-huh." Feeling buoyant, she flipped the egg for her mouth. Yolk landed in her eye.

"I was here, last night," Les said. "In the hotel. Two doors down." He sounded irritated.

Cindy had him going. "Okay, the night before last, then," she said, wiping her lower lid. *Why is my eye stinging? It's egg.* "When Bassett's

- 179 -

loaner was gone from the lot all night. In Gainesville? Uh-huuuuuuh." She nodded again, blotted, blinked. "Might have to check the mileage in-and-out on it."

Les stopped eating to stare at her.

"Come on, I know you did it," Cindy said, full CSI, thinking maybe the salt was stinging. Or the pepper. Yeah, it could be the pepper. Pepper would burn, wouldn't it? But then, so would salt. But there's salt in your tears, so how come salt burns your eyes?

When she finally looked up, Cindy found Les staring at her, his jaw slightly agape, some stunned something on his face.

Blink-blink.

"What?" she asked. Had she missed something actually important while engaging in meaningless albumenical colloquy?

As Les continued to stare, looking pale, Cindy started to get worried, her whole face scrunching up with each quickening blink. Goddam pepper eggs!

Blink-blink. Blink-blink.

"I'm... I'm..." Les seemed at a total loss. "How did..." he faltered. "How did... you figure it out?"

"Figure what out?" Cindy said, trying to figure it out. Blot, blink, *think!*

Les looked around as if to make sure no one was listening, then he leaned closer and spoke in a low voice. "The Mauler," he said. "That I..."

He raised his eyebrows slightly and nodded his head toward Biscayne Bay, outside the window. "You know. Came down here and..." His eyes went up, then he nodded out, then up and down.

Blink-blink. Blink-blink. Blink-blink.

Was Cindy's partner sitting across from her in the restaurant of the Intercontinental Hotel in Miami after an exquisite night of deep sleep telling her he had... murdered the Miami Mauler? Was this a... confession? Of homicide? Of being an unsub? Only now he wasn't unknown subject anymore? He was their sub!

Blink.

Les sat old-mountain still, mortician somber, rattler serious. Cindy stared back as stiff as she could ever remembered being. She even stopped blinking, even though her eye still burned.

Les was close, a foot away, his eyes locked on hers, staring deep inside her soul, when suddenly...

"Boo!" he shouted and grabbed her knee under the table.

Cindy jumped and screamed, her knee banging up under the table. Dishes rattled, a glass of water fell over. Diners stared.

Les shoveled eggs and *bisteca*. "God, you're easy." He was grinning from ear to ear—the long way around. "You've got egg on your face," he said, nodding over, then grinned and chewed and chuckled and shook his head and grinned some more.

"You sonofabitch," Cindy said, wiping at her cheek, barely unable to suppress her pleasure. Cindy loved to be scared. She missed her brothers.

"What, I'm not a cocksucker anymore?" he said, disappointed.

"Cocksucking sonofabitch little fuckbug bastard, you are!"

Les stopped chewing. "Fuckbug? What the hell's that?"

Cindy sighed. "Okay. The correct saying is, 'Eat shit, you little piece of fuckbug pie.'"

"Correct by whose standards?"

"My little brother Josh," Cindy said. "He was twelve at the time and had gotten grounded for doing something my next-up, Adam, had actually done. But typical of Adam, he couldn't leave well enough alone and he started goading Josh, being generally obnoxious."

"So, you come by this honestly," Les observed.

"Anyway," Cindy went on, "Josh snapped and came out with a beauty. They both got an extra week, and we had a handy new family saying which could be used in any number of rebuttal situations. It slipped out of my subconscious vernacular because I was so pissed off."

Les said, "Funny. You don't look pissed off."

Cindy glowered harder—through the matching grin that was already hurting her face.

A moment later, their egregiously bored waiter showed up and asked if everything was all right—as if he gave a shit.

"Everything's fine, thank you," Cindy said pleasantly. But when the wasp-waisted boy-toy slunk away, she made a face after him.

"I'll tell you who's a cocksucker," Les said, flicking his head after the departing waiter, who seemed to be working on his *plie*—elbow, hands, and heels—as he made his way back to the butter bin.

Cindy looked. "No," she said. "You know what I think?"

"What do you think?" Les said. "This should be good."

"I think *you're* gay and that's why you take me to all these gay-waiter restaurants." She flicked another flap of egg onto the end of her fork with a flourish. This time the slime landed on her blouse. "Aw, shit."

"I think you've gotten too much sleep in the last twenty-four hours," Les said. "All this alertness is affecting your judgment. And your aim."

Cindy dipped the corner of her napkin in ice water and daubed at her blouse. "So, you're not denying it."

"That I'm gay or I know all the gay-waiter restaurants in the country."

"I didn't say 'in the country.'"

"You implied it."

"No, I *implied* you're our SKK. I stated unequivocally that you're gay, and the gay-waiter places, blah-blah-blah. So?" She shoved her plate aside and started on her toast. Cindy always saved at least half her toast and jam for last so it seemed like dessert.

"Okay," Les said. "So, I may like to give a little head every now and then. Sue me."

Cindy snorted, crumbs flying, then admonished, "E-*vad*-ing," musically.

"Evading, denying. You've got quite a suspect, here," Les chirped.

"Still evading," Cindy said and sampled some pink jelly. "Wow, this is good. What is it?"

"Guava. And I'm not denying anything," Les said.

"False denial," Cindy mumbled, mouth full. "The other thing," she specified, and flipped her head to indicate the other thing's whereabouts.

"You want a statement," Les said, making a statement out of a question about a statement.

"That would be nice." Cindy hadn't had this much fun since their genital enhancement fiasco. "Guava is amazing."

"Yes, it is," Les agreed. "Okay, look, I'm not denying I killed the... Oh Jesus, what's his name? Now, *I've* got it."

"Iowa Dimwit Syndrome, IDS," Cindy nodded. "The Bayside Mauler."

"Him," Les confirmed. "I'm not denying that either." He poured more coffee, a pungent Cuban blend, rich and vaguely sweet.

"Either. Hmmm," Cindy nodded. "And so smug, too." This was the Les she enjoyed, not the scared one in Iowa. (Or Gainesville for that matter; but who could blame him after that.)

"Killing and cocksucking comes easy to us murderous gays," he said, breezily.

"Shut *up!*" Cindy checked around self-consciously.

"I'll tell you who's gay," Les said, topping her cup, now. "Brinkman's gay."

"Stop it," Cindy said flatly, and dunked her toast into what was probably the best cup of coffee she'd ever had. "What is this?"

"Coffee," Les said.

She scowled.

"No, think about it," Les went on. "Have you ever seen him out with a woman?"

"I've never seen him out, period," Cindy said.

"Well, neither have I, but you get my point."

"That he *is* out."

"That he's not out, he's in. Way in. That's what I'm saying."

"Brinkman's not gay," Cindy said plainly and dunked again, wondering if she could manage to smear some guava jelly on the toast and dunk it without losing the jelly in her coffee, and even if she did, would that be so bad? "And this is not regular coffee," she said.

"French roast," he said.

"No."

"So, how do you explain it?"

"The blend?"

"Brinkman's perpetual lack of a date."

Cindy thought for a moment. "Maybe..." Nothing came to her.

"You got nothin'. And you know why? He's gay."

"He's not gay."

"Well, he's not married."

"So?"

"So, look at Einstein."

"What about him?"

"Gay." Les shrugged as if everyone knew. "Common knowledge."

"You're outa control. Einstein was married."

"To whom?"

In perfect unison, they both said, "Mrs. Einstein," and laughed loudly.

At the next table, a couple from Albany, drycleaners down for a week before peak season, looked away. Floridians could be so *gauche*.

Cindy said to Les, "So, did you?"

"Kill whatsizname?"

"Yeah."

"You got a body?" he asked.

"Sure do," she said.

"Did I have motive and opportunity?"

"Sure did."

"Do I have a reason to want him dead?"

"For sure. He's an SK."

"Do I have the ability to pull it off?"

"Without question."

"Then I guess I did it," Les said, conceding.

"Then I guess you did," Cindy said. "You want the rest of your potatoes?"

"Naw, you can have 'em. I gotta go to the men's room," he said. "I'll pay up and catch you outside, Dollface."

"Dollface! Good God," Cindy groaned.

"See you in court," he said.

"Not if I see you first," she said.

Cindy looked around the room at the dull civilians thinking how they could never imagine having this much fun in the middle of a multiple murder investigation — and somehow it made her feel that much more alone. At least she and Les had each other.

Chapter 19 – Diamonds in the Raw

Around ten, Les and Cindy made their way over to Metro Dade but were told the Mauler was City of Miami's. They drove over there where they were told their stiff was back in the county morgue because, according to the pimply young pregnant girl in the coroner's front office, the city morgue was "kinda full." They'd had a run on autopsy requests.

"Holidays," she shrugged.

By noon, Les and Cindy had seen the body, the "jello ribbon," the "cuck 'n' bulls," et al., and Cindy had decided that Les wasn't a serial-killer killer and Brinkman wasn't gay, just pathetic. They could have been on the Turnpike headed back to Gainesville by one o'clock but decided to stay another day and enjoy Les's week off. Cindy even turned off her phone, but that only lasted four minutes. The Good Girl in her switched it back on while Les was looking the other way.

So, Les locked it in the trunk.

By two, they were laughing in the hotel pool and Les was teaching Cindy the butterfly stroke. She was limber and a game student, but the sight of her flopping in the water like a harpooned sea turtle was as funny a thing as Les could remember seeing. Ever. Some German tourists laughed so hard, one of them choked on her chocolate-covered papaya and had to be Heimliched.

"German guy, Heimlich," Les pointed out. And he and Cindy made for their rooms before something else unpleasant happened.

At eight thirty, Cindy had just stepped out of a shower when Les knocked at her door unexpectedly. "What's up?" she said, opening the door in a towel.

"Busman's holiday," he said, pretending to look around her at her ass.

"I don't get it," Cindy said, not sure if he was looking or leering, and further unsure of whether either would really bother her.

"There's more than one serial murderer operating in South Florida."

"The Strip Killer," she nodded. Then, "Oh no you don't. You are *not* getting me in a strip club on your week off."

"He's killed six women. All strippers. All on the third Wednesday of the month."

"So why are you smiling, you male pig. Besides, it's Monday."

"We've got two days to stop him," Les said cheerily. "Will fifteen minutes be enough for you?"

"Make it twenty," Cindy said. "I gotta trash myself up a little."

***

As Les and Cindy walked up to Diamonds in the Raw at 9:27 p.m., he said, "Now remember, we're husband and wife. At least dating."

"That's better than most husbands and wives," Cindy said morosely. Les chuckled and listened for her gait to change as they entered the red velvet-lined lobby.

He had been taught by his first field training officer, Brinkman's first partner, Harold "Hap" Lipton—truly the worst agent Les had ever known, but curiously, the best observer of human nature and idiosyncratic behavior he'd ever met before or since—to always listen for changes in someone's gait as you entered a new arena. If their feet faltered, they either had or hadn't been there before, according to Hap. This was the kind of maxim that made Hapless Hap, as the other agents called him, such a brilliant judge of character and such a lousy agent. He could spot deviant behavior in its subtlest form a mile off, but he had no idea what to do with the information.

Conversely, Les knew precisely what to do with data once he gathered it. He heard Cindy's steps slow ever so slightly and asked, "First time?" as if it were a real question to which he didn't already know the answer.

"How'd you know?" Cindy said, sounding surprised.

"Gut thing," Les lied. Not that it mattered.

Hap had taken early retirement, at the director's suggestion, before Les spent a full year with him. He wasn't an old burnout, like many said. Rather, Hap was pushing himself to his limit, right up to the last day. The problem was, Hap just wasn't a closer. He had the lowest clearance rate of anyone in whichever region he was assigned. But Les learned more from Hap Lipton than he did from his other five field training officers put together. So, Les always figured he owed him.

One balmy spring night about a year after his dismissal, Hap was found dead in an alley a few blocks from the Capitol, shot execution style, a single .22 caliber hole behind his left ear. He had no next of kin—Les was the closest thing to it—so Les got the call.

Even though Hap saw death as an Equal Opportunity Employer—"Doesn't matter a bit, Les, we're all toe-tagged side by side in the end"—on arriving at the DC morgue, Les lost his composure, ripping the "John Doe" tag from Hap's toe to scream at the young morgue attendant about, "This man's long and venerable service to the Bureau! The Federal Bureau of Investigation, that is. You may have heard of it. The FBI? No? Well, it's heard of you, I can promise you that. It's heard of you loud and clear!"

He wrote "Harold Mercer Lipton, <u>FBI</u>!" on a new tag, then tied the old one—the "John Doe" one—to the rattled kid's shaking finger, while continuing to rail. "There. How does that feel? How do *you* like being a dead nobody?" Les made sure the young morgue attendant could see his gun.

In his formal complaint, the poor kid stated that he didn't sleep for one very long, unsettling Kafkaesque month, lost to paranoid fantasies of midnight arrests and planted evidence linking him to Hap's unseemly death. After his complaint mysteriously vanished, he transferred to county zoning (which turned out to be worse.)

Les set out to find Hap's killer in his free time and quickly became convinced a small-time, self-professed Baltimore gangsta named Julio Charman was his man. Several years prior, Hap had been unfortunate enough to catch the little sociopath with a half-pound of Mexican brown, back when Hap and Brinkman were partners. Charman swore revenge and later bragged to his friends that, yeah, he had, "Got behin' all dat."

Two weeks later, Charman the heroin trafficker was dead.

When Brinkman—by then an ASAC on-the-rise—called everyone in and asked if any agent had an explanation as to why "one Julio Charman's useless body" was discovered in the same alley in which Hap Lipton's body had been found, with a similar, single .22 caliber hole behind his left ear...

No one spoke up.

Les Moore spoke up less than anyone—even when Brinkman eyeballed him. Maybe they were eyeballing each other, but Les thought it ironic how, if Brinkman had ever listened to Hap's advice on "reading eyes," he might have seen something so dark and disturbing in Les's hateful gaze he might have feared for his own life. Or at least opened an investigation. Not that he would have found anything. Les had been out of the country. He had the passport stamps and airline tickets to prove his whereabouts.

But Brinkman apparently saw and thought nothing. He certainly did nothing (which was hard for the untrained eye to distinguish from his daily routine), even if some transient misgivings might have passed through his diagnostics-impaired mind. But who cared what happened to a Julio Charman in an alley in DC? An eye for an eye, a life for a life. Brinkman hadn't cared all that much when it happened to Hap. Which only made Les's eyes go darker still.

But if Les Moore knew something back then, he didn't say; if he didn't know anything, he didn't say that either. And that was good enough for Brinkman. That much about Les and Brinkman had never changed. Les didn't talk much about cases; Brinkman didn't ask much—especially after Riverbend.

***

"So, which are we?" Cindy said. "Mates or dates?"

Les chuckled appreciatively and said, "Your choice."

"Mates," Cindy decided, and put her arm through his.

"Two, please," Les told the bulldog-faced guy with the long-deceased cigar stump behind the glass. "It's our anniversary."

"Congratulations, that's twenty bucks, and there's a two-drink minimum each," the man with no hair or neck said, taking Les's money. Then he buzzed them in, stuffed the wet butt back in his flat face, and returned to his Jackie Collins.

Having never been in a "men's club" before—not being a man and therefore figuring she wasn't invited, plus having no interest—Cindy clutched Les tightly. To the strippers and bouncers, the wheedling DJ, suspendered bartender, and barely clad waitresses, Cindy looked like a timid wife. So, it worked out.

Most everything in the place had been painted flat black, except the lit-up liquor shelves and polished brass rails everywhere. What was left was red and padded. The effluvium of stale liquor, fusty smoke, cheap perfume, and immutable Pine-Sol was close to overpowering. Cindy tried not to breathe—or look—and let Les steer her to a table away from the stage.

The moment their butts hit the chairs, a waitress arrived dressed in little more than a few strategically-placed straps of DayGlo orange Lycra. She was of average height, about like Cindy, but everything else about her was exaggerated, from the unnaturally high arches of her feet stuffed into acrylic five-inch platform-heels, to the chaotic explosion of light brown curls piled high atop her triangular head, to the boomerang-shaped eyebrows painted on the front of it. Her breasts were impressive—not so much large as implacable—her waist tight and narrow, her calves well-defined and bulging like a true gym rat.

Leaning close, rigid breasts perilously close to egress, the waitress—either about thirty-five, or ten years younger, and prematurely hard—reminded Les about the two-drink minimum. With hip-hop blaring, she hollered. So, Les hollered his order back directly into her ear. Then she turned to Cindy.

"It's very loud," Cindy shouted over the din.

"All the clubs charge the same," their waitress shouted, twisting in such a way that Cindy got a good view of the thick, peened shaft of pewtered silver running through her left nipple.

Cindy looked away. "Whatever he's having," she shouted, hoping Les had ordered white wine, and the waitress left.

Cindy turned to Les and started to shout, "Did you see that hunk of rebar in her—" but her train of thought and field of vision were suddenly and forcefully interrupted by a bald, naked black woman, squatting, knees wide, not fifteen feet away.

"Oh my god!" Cindy shouted at the stage—at the exact moment the music ended.

Everyone looked.

Without losing her more-bored-than-bored facade, the black girl, "Ebony," looked at Cindy and rattled the twin metal posts in her tongue, clacking them on her teeth in the momentary silence between songs. Then she hissed like a snake, picked up her tips—twenty dollars from a Latin guy who appeared to be only slightly taller than Topo Gigio — and left the stage.

When their waitress arrived with two scotches, Cindy poured them both down and ordered two more. Les said he didn't know Cindy drank scotch and Cindy said she did now.

At this point, the DJ threw on a marrow-jarring, music-free, rap-and-scratch number — extra heavy on the bass — and started shouting about a "Parade of Pussy!" as the dancers trudged out single-file, more or less, chewing gum, smoking cigarettes, and clomping gracelessly on ludicrously high heels while chatting idly about delinquent boyfriends, rent checks, and menstrual cycles as if they weren't nearly nude at all and men weren't staring at them like they were sides of beef, marinade in hand.

After a few moments of blinking disbelief, as if trying to make this comically awful dream go away, Cindy shouted, "They walk like horses," just as the waitress returned with their second round.

"They're strippers. Whattaya expect?" Nipple Bar yelled at her.

Les smiled, paid the girl — including a generous tip — and she left, throwing a last rankled glare at Cindy who, looking pretty much hopelessly lost, turned to Les for explication.

He said, "She probably thought you said 'whores.'"

"Ohhh," Cindy said, winced, and emptied her third scotch as the music stopped.

Before she could get any enjoyment from it, any respite, the DJ screamed — as if no one was closer than a half-mile away and he didn't have a five-hundred-watt microphone, "Gentlemennnnnn, welllllcummmmm Mistyyyyyyyyyyyyy Raaaaaaaain!"

He spun the Artist Once Again Known As What He Used To Be Known As But Now Is No Longer Anything at a volume roughly equivalent to a 747 taking off in a tiled bathroom.

"Does he realize I have my .40 and my .32 on me?" Cindy asked Les.

"Probably not," he allowed.

Two fat men applauded, whistled, and whooped like drunken Packers fans on Thanksgiving, and a few moments later a tiny nineteen-year-old in a jet-black Betty Boop hairdo, complete with spit curl, took the stage, miniature red Corvette in hand and pouted.

Her act.

Misty was no more than five-two or -three—on six-inch heels—with nearly nonexistent breasts and the narrowest ass Cindy had ever seen on a woman. Cindy said she looked like her little brother naked when he was twelve. Les said that was the idea, and Cindy appeared fairly appalled.

Misty rolled the Matchbox car around what there was of her chest for most of the song then peeled off her short-shorts to reveal a pencil-thin line of trimmed whiskers leading down to a medium gauge gold ring in her clitoral hood—which was obvious when she lifted her leg straight up in the air over some complete stranger's head.

Cindy's brain felt leaden. "I can't believe I'm seeing this." She'd heard of such unabashed nude antics of course, but seeing was disbelieving.

"Believe," Les said as Misty slid her red pumps four feet apart and put her palms on the floor, without flexing her knees.

"If she bends over any farther, we're gonna be able to see if she's dilating," Cindy said, but courageously didn't turn away.

Three minutes later—exactly—the song stopped as suddenly as it had started, and Misty stopped dancing midgrind. Though it really hadn't been dancing so much as moving in the vicinity of music. She picked up her six dollars in tips from the dance floor with a "Thank you" and a smile for each adoring cheesehead, then clomped—loudly for such a tiny person, Cindy noted—back through the curtain.

Les ordered two more and again tipped generously. He was on vacation.

After a few more girls had performed, Cindy began to loosen up, feeling the alcohol. "Well, let's get this road on the show," she announced and dragged Les up for the stage-side seating.

"We'll have to tip," he cautioned.

"It's how they make their money," Cindy said magnanimously and chose two seats that appeared to be mostly clean.

Les grinned. He liked Agent Baker a little drunk; the booze wore away at those sharp Bureau edges.

Next up was Amber, a tall blonde sporting a pageboy with a flair, and eyebrows of an identical shade. She had an evenness to her coloring, an amber-like hue running head to toe which made her seem synthetic yet alluring at the same time.

Kind of like her breasts.

She was completely shaved, no pretense of propriety, but unpierced and tattooless. The DJ hollered, "Hey Amber, what happened to all your hair down there?" and "She's one slick chick!" and, in case anyone still wasn't up to speed on what he was driving at, "She's bare down there!"

"Original," Cindy scoffed.

But Amber was classy for a stripper, and she could actually dance. She worked each eager, hungry face at the rail for ten or fifteen seconds, showing them exactly what they wanted to see while energetically moving in perfect rhythm to pounding early eighties rock. Was Les actually hearing "Sex Dwarf?" Thinking, *isn't this disco doll nice though?*

"What's the deal with this shaving?" Cindy shouted into Les's ear, breaking his Soft Cell flashback, her breath hot and scotchy.

For a moment, he wondered if she was back on his armpits, but then she added, "Do men really like it?" and he realized she was referring to Amber's glabrous labia.

Les shrugged. "See better," was all he said. Cindy nodded, seeming to accept his brevity and turned back to the stage as Amber now spun in front of Les, turned away, bent over, and grabbed her ankles — showing him everything God gave her and a little more — then dropped, spun again, backward somersaulted and rolled smack in front of...

Cindy — who only now saw the five-dollar bill Les had draped over the rail in front of her. She turned away, then back, then red, as Amber flipped both ankles back over her head, toes on the floor behind her and, smiling directly at Cindy, puckering her anus to the beat of the music.

Cindy finished her fourth scotch.

Finally, Amber crawled, catlike, on her stomach to the polished rail, grabbed up the five-dollar bill with her breasts smooshed together, then stood and slapped her ass on the final beat of the song. *Finis!* Everyone applauded.

Les said, "I think she's done this before.".

Cindy snorted in agreement and said, "I have to admit that takes some kind of talent. I'm not sure what. But whatever it is, she's got it."

The night went until one girl, Sunni Daze, bounced out to a bona fide high-energy, Bible-pounding, grit-slinging, down-home, holy-rolling, save-me-Jesus gospel number — and brought down the house.

Other dancers started clapping along, shouting "Amen!" and "Hallelujah!" as did the men, perhaps not even aware of Sunni's nakedness anymore. Cindy wondered aloud if that was Sunni's way of dealing with her chosen profession, hiding behind music so happy and upbeat, so distracting, that men couldn't just sit glassy-eyed, trying to get a close look at her uterine walls — they had to get involved. To participate.

Les allowed, "If it works."

Whatever her motivation, Sunni played her role for all it was worth, humping the rail, the floor, the air, all the while looking at the men with what could only be called classic bedroom eyes. She climbed the brass pole in the middle of the stage with the ease of a circus monkey then slid down without the benefit of hands, instead gripping it with her thighs only, corkscrewing down slowly, back arched, arms out, the envy of every fireman in the crowd, Cindy was certain.

When Sunni finally rotated to Les, she turned it up full blast, eyebrows high, eyelids at half-mast, a strange smile cocked up one side, down the other, with a pucker in the middle — sort of Scarlett Johansson meets Will Ferrell, with some Flipper thrown in, Cindy noted.

All of this would have been strange enough, but Sunni then let her smile creep up the tickled-dog side of her face to reveal four missing teeth — molars, two up, two down — which formed a gap wide enough to run a salad carrot through without brushing porcelain on any side. The whole scene spun from low sleaze to high comedy before the next drumbeat fell.

Les said, "Welp, can't top that."

Cindy agreed, and they were halfway back across the causeway before they stopped howling.

***

Anticipating a barrage of messages from Brinkman when she got back to her multihued, tropical-themed room, Cindy was pleased to find none. So, he really was on vacation. Cindy didn't think he knew how. Then she remembered her cell was still in the trunk.

Standing before the double, mirrored, closet-sliders, still tipsy, with any number of reference images still fresh in her mind, Cindy suddenly threw her hips to one side then the other in a spastic pseudo-exotic-dancer move and, before she knew it, was pulling her clothes off, tossing her top this way, her skirt that, moving to remembered music.

> *Sex Dorf,*
> *isn't he nice?*
> *Doing disco lattes*
> *with a lot of ice.*

Being sexy without appearing foolish was much harder than it looked, even half-drunk.

Maybe she was trying *too* hard.

> *Sex drawers,*
> *Are-n't they nice —*

"Dwarves!" Maybe if she got the words right. Maybe humming instead.

Hm-hmm,

Hmm-hmm-hmm-hmmm…

Unsnap the bra. And it goes... over the head... around the chin... across the breasts... between the legs and... *Ride it like a horsey!*

Cindy bent over laughing.

Then, she stood and... fling! Her best Victoria's Secret draped the lampshade.

Alluring disco dotties,

Hm-hm-hm-hmmmm…

Now the panties. Down-one-side-and-turn-a-round and... *downtothefloor*! Kick and... naked!

To a life of ice —

"Oh, *vice*. Life of *vice*! I get it." Spin-gyrate-drop-slither-and... undulate! *Yeah, baby!*

Cindy pulled a few moves that surprised her—a hip flipped at the chair, a tease tossed at the lingerie'd lamp, a half-lidded lip-lick.

Finally, with a sudden jerk, Cindy the amateur ecdysiast ran her palms up her ribs under her breasts, pushing them together while flicking her tongue, checking her moves in the mirror and... she looked every bit as ridiculous and unsexy as she thought she would.

"Okay, maybe not," Cindy granted and went to shower.

At least she had all her teeth.

Chapter 20 – Naked Fear

Morning brought clean air, crisp light, and a ringing phone. Before she remembered where she was, Cindy picked up.

"What are you doing in Moore's room at this hour?"

Cindy was bolt upright and trying to figure that out before the last word left Brinkman's mouth.

What *was* she doing in Les's room? And why was Brinkman already calling again? Wasn't he supposed to be on vacation, too? And didn't he have any other agents to bother on a regular basis? Any at all! Cindy looked around.

They had started out in her room...

***

Les knocked at Cindy's door. She opened it naked, fresh from her post-striptease shower. Les stared a loaded moment, then wrapped himself around her. She had his clothes off faster than he could have taken them off himself, and they were in each other's mouths before they hit the floral bedspread.

Sometime after three, they switched to his room and bourbon, the scotch having mostly worn off. Scrambling naked down the hallway, all Cindy could think of was some secret hotel video airing on The Voyeur Channel's *Caught in the Act!* She made a mental note to threaten someone downstairs in the morning, maybe confiscate their security videos. "FBI—hand 'em over!"

Les pretended to have forgotten his key card in her room—right after Cindy's door slammed shut—which only made her giggle that much more when he produced the card from behind him.

Once in Les's room, they didn't go straight for the minibar. There were priorities. Like doing it against the inside of the door, the wall, the mirrored closet, the bathroom jamb, on the sink, on the toilet, in the tub, the doorjamb again, the wall by the dresser, the dresser, the bed, the chairs, the table, and the windowsill. Then they had the drink. And what a wonderful drink! Cindy had always thought she hated bourbon, but—

***

"Baker?"

"Getting him up!" Cindy blurted, jarred from her trance. Then she cringed down to her toes. *That sounded awful.* Brinkman said nothing.

That sounded worse.

Cindy forced her brain to cooperate, against its better judgment. "He wanted to get going early today." *No, Mom, I wasn't in Doug Porter's tree house with Barry Fellicano, honest!*

"I came over to make sure he was up. Awake."

Much worse.

Cindy looked around the room for some cue card with her next line on it that would end this waking daymare—a Brando crib note taped in a corner, on a glass, a lampshade. Another actor's forehead! But Les was the only other one in the room (thank God), and he was still sleeping (ditto the God thing).

The answer popped in from nowhere. "And it's a good thing I did," Cindy improvised with unexpected panache. "He'd fallen back asleep after his wake-up call."

"I see," Brinkman said, not sounding like he was buying it. "You're sure you two weren't playing smoochy-puss down there in the tropic heat?" His tone and wording were no doubt derisive by design, only halfway meant to evoke an actual answer.

"Playing smoochy-puss in... No, Phil. I don't think so," she said, sarcastically. *We were fucking like rabbits in heat!*

Then Cindy remembered there actually had been smooching. Lots of it. Lazy, glorious, passionate—

"'Cause I can't have that, Baker," Brinkman said, authoritatively— or as close as he could get to it.

"Keep trying, Phil. Someone'll cave in someday," she came up with. Not bad while migrating out of a deep drift.

"Not bad," Brinkman said. "But not funny either. You two start fucking like rabbits in heat..."

Cindy shivered. Having thoughts even vaguely similar to Phil Brinkman was terrifying. Fortunately, having her hackles shoved up so far that her eyebrows stuck straight out quickly negated any panic. "Lawsuit, Phil. Keep thinking lawsuit."

Brinkman went on, entirely unfazed. "...and we're all chokin' our chickens out on the street with a sign around our necks, 'Will profile for food.'"

Intractable. At least Cindy was awake by that point—and realizing none of this was any of his business. "So, he's in the shower, Phil. What can I do for you?" She made sure to sound put-out.

"I don't hear running water," Brinkman said.

"He's on the toilet, okay? Jesus. Where were you raised?"

"Rochester," Brinkman said. "And when someone said someone was in the shower, they meant it."

"No, they didn't, Phil."

Cindy took Brinkman's silence to mean he was only now realizing this. A moment later, he said, "Anyway, we're pretty sure it's a man."

Cindy suddenly felt less awake than before. So, she threw off one of her most reliable official-sounding sound-bite bluffs, used mainly when completely lost. "Clarify."

"Your killer-killer."

"Well, yeah." Oh. Nothing new. "Riverbend."

"The other one. I thought you said you were awake."

"I haven't gone downstairs for my Starbucks yet."

"They got Starbucks there?"

"It's the millennium, Phil. They've got Starbucks everywhere. I heard they're opening one at the Maxwell House factory in Costa Rica. Did we ever really think it was a woman?"

"We think of everything. That's our job."

That was Cindy's job. She wasn't sure what Brinkman's job was.

Les groaned dully and rolled over in the sheets, revealing some of the lean, hard swimmer's body Cindy had found so inspiring. She felt a pang of something sweet in her loins, longed to be able to indulge it—then slipped into the bathroom and closed the door to keep from awakening Les or her lust.

"So, we're sure on this. It's a man," she said, wishing she could pee, but figuring holding it until she got a urinary infection *up to here* was better than giving Brinkman audio ammunition like that.

He said, "Not sure. Pretty sure. Still could be a woman. But we think it's a man. Dressed like a woman."

"What cinched it?"

"Computerized co-analysis of the pertinent data."

Cindy found herself momentarily startled that Brinkman could put together such a technical sounding statement, even if she wasn't sure it made sense.

"Body fluids? DNA?" What was he talking about?

"No. No hair. Nothing," Brinkman said. "He's a pro." Then, thinking better of it, he added, "Well, he's careful."

"Too careful."

"Never be too careful in that line of work."

"Hmmm."

"No, this was body-type stuff." There it was. But he expounded. "Compilation of all eyewitness accounts, crime scene reports and forensics data: gait, stride, limb and trunk proportions, imprint variations, height versus weight correlations." He had to be reading. "Buncha shit I don't get." Cindy heard the papers shuffling. "But it all adds up to a dick stuffed into some pantyhose."

"I get the picture."

"Cute, ain't it? You'll tell Les?"

"Tell him what?"

"What to look for. Wigs, large sizes, falsies, butt pads, shaved legs/arms sorta thing. Waxed, maybe. Smooth face."

How did he know so much about being: "Passable."

"Yeah. That sorta thing."

"And the clothes."

"Clothes," he agreed.

Cindy added, as they came to mind. "Beauty colleges, hairdressers, learn-to-walk-like-a-model schools."

"Yeah, those."

"Cross-dresser supply house mailing lists?"

"We're running them, but there are going to be tens of thousands of names. Lotta freakos around these days, Baker. In case you haven't noticed. It'll take months if not years to run 'em all down."

"Not if we cross-reference. Days and dates of opportunity."

"Cross-reference the cross-dressers. Good one, Baker."

Neither of them took the obvious Hoover shot. You never knew who might be listening.

Cindy sat on the cool, salmon-shaded tile and gazed at the toilet with longing. "Didn't mean it," she said.

"Didn't think you did."

"We all get lucky."

"Speak for yourself."

If anyone was destined never to get lucky, Brinkman was top of the list.

Cindy thought of Les's naked body and how lucky she had gotten, and swooned, still tingling with love endorphins. *Bottle those and buy an island.* Anyway, "It still could be a woman."

"But we think it's a man. Or a big woman. Not too big. Average big. About like you or a little bigger. About like Les if Les was a woman. Maybe not that big. Smaller than me. You get the picture."

The picture Cindy got was of a tall-short fat-thin man-woman, half-Les and half-Cindy with some Phil Brinkman and a few hundred thousand other people thrown in for bad measure. Cindy closed her eyes and shook her head. "You'll keep us updated?"

"That's my job."

So *that* was it. Cindy couldn't resist. "I always wondered about that. Your job."

"You've been hanging around Les Moore too much," Brinkman said and hung up.

Cindy peed and felt much better—about everything. Then she crept back into the orchid-cast room, quietly returned the phone to the nightstand, and slipped back under the passionfruit-tinted covers.

On feeling Les's warm glow in the bed, all thoughts of serial killers and mass murderers, male or female, quickly vanished. Cindy moaned contentedly, rolled over on her side to face his reclining body, and slid the arch of her right foot luxuriously up the solid, smooth curve of Les's...

Hairless calf.

Cindy's jerked away so quickly and violently she went sailing off the bed onto the floor and her hip, then scampered crab-like, backward across the floor, to the mirrored closet door and up against the glass under her many ass-prints from the night before—knees to her chest, arms wrapped around her shins, staring at the tall bed as Les moaned and rolled over onto his back, his hairless lower leg coming out from under the sheets.

Cindy waited for him, expected him, to turn his head and open reptilian slits to stare coldly at her, having heard her entire conversation with Brinkman through the bathroom door. He would have no choice but to kill her now.

Cindy reflexively scanned the room for her Glock 35 — rather than the standard FBI issue Glock 23 — then remembered it was back in her room.

Shit! No gun!

Now there was a Rule Number One for you. Never go anywhere without your weapon. Not even into a fellow agent's room. Not even for sex.

Sex! What had she been thinking?

Cindy looked for Les's Ruger, but it was nowhere in sight. Hell, he probably had his weapon under the covers, hammer back and waiting!

She watched him closely.

Les's eyes didn't open into slits or ovals or spheres. He didn't speak or even moan. He didn't reach under his pillow. He still seemed to be sound asleep. So, Cindy raised up on her haunches a bit to see over the edge of the bed and saw:

His goddam legs were shaved top to bottom. How had she missed that!

The sex had been hot, that's how. Who was paying attention to his legs? Other than his divinely toned muscles which —

Les groaned and rolled over to face her, the sheet staying behind, affording Cindy a full-frontal view of his sex.

She took two quick deep breaths, steadying herself and looked again to confirm that her eyes weren't playing tricks on her. He had shaved. Down there. Just a little off the sides, a trim. But who would do that? And why?

An SKK posing as a woman, that's who!

Cindy stood quickly. Too quickly. Her head swam. Bourbon on top of scotch. What had she been thinking? She bent over, put her hands on her knees and waited for the *mal de mer* to pass, checking on Les every two seconds until it eased up. He didn't move.

Now was the time to make a break for her room. Cindy turned to look for her key card.

Shit! No key!

She'd have to call down to the desk and have them send someone up to open her room. So, throw on something quick and —

Shit! No clothes!

What was that feeling in the pit of her stomach? Was it booze or adrenaline? No. It was fear. Raw, naked fear. Bad for reaction time, bad for decision-making. Bad for everything.

Shit! Fear!

Cindy stifled a groan so deep inside it felt like someone else's worry. Had she actually made love to Riverbend's counterpart without realizing? Her partner? The other killer of killers? Dear God in Heaven.

Mom, if you're looking down, I didn't mean it!

Cindy realized she was tasting Les, again. Only this time, he tasted awful, and it sent another wave of chilling dizziness through her, coupled with savage nausea. Cindy went clammy and her knees shook. Her head ached. Cold sweat beaded between her exposed breasts.

Shit! Exposed breasts!

Cindy spotted Les's shirt on a chair and started for it — then froze. Wearing something a Killer had worn recently, which had not been laundered in scalding water, bleach and...

Cindy turned to the closet. Maybe something clean wouldn't feel so disagreeable against her skin. She checked back. Was Les getting an erection? In his sleep? After four orgasms in as many hours? *At his age?*

The shaky, clammy, queasy, dreadful, sickening feeling gripped Cindy with unrelenting muscle. She had to find something to wear fast and get the hell out of there!

Cindy carefully slid the closet door open, watching her own image glide past, hoping for anything — shorts, polo shirt, robe. A large paper bag.

Instead, Cindy found herself staring at a pale blue garment bag she'd never seen before. New. Full.

Feminine.

There was no getting around it. She had to look inside. How could she not?

Hands shaking, Cindy took another stabilizing breath — which did no stabilizing whatsoever — then slid the zipper down as gingerly as possible, wincing with each tiny *zzzzwit*, never taking her eyes off Les —

Goddammit, he is. He's getting another hard-on!

The little fuckbug.

Cindy wondered about the dream he was having. Probably something involving Amber the "dancer," naked and bald-headed, picking up hundred-dollar bills with her twat as Les shot the Strip Killer, execution style, on the stage at Diamonds in the Raw while Misty

Rain shaved his balls and Sunni Daze sang gospel numbers through giant dentures, accompanied by Brinkman playing ukulele in a DayGlo Lycra thong.

No. That was the kind of dream Cindy had.

When she looked back at the now-open wardrobe bag, Cindy froze. A brilliant blue mini-sequined dress was exactly what she did not want to find — not to mention matching shoes and clutch. No way was she putting any of those on. Who knew how many men had been killed by Les in that dress!

Cindy looked at Les. He now had a full erection. She hadn't remembered it being so large. Suddenly, her ass hurt. And the sick feeling was intensifying, sweeping over her like putrid surf awash in raw sewage and rotting condoms, nausea rising rapidly in her throat like baking soda mixed with vinegar. She was going to be sick.

Shit. Sick.

Cindy made a cursory upward flip of the garment bag zipper and leapt for the bathroom, making it to the porcelain altar in the nick of time as a column of black, rancid vomit the precise width of her mouth, open as wide as it would go, shot out as if launched from an air cannon. Fetid cheese and fruit from their wee-hours snack — washed down with bourbon and followed by two bars of bittersweet chocolate and lingonberry bonbons — spewed like tangible bad memories from a poisoned artesian well.

It had seemed so wonderful at the time.

The second column surely should have emptied her stomach. But there was a third, part of a fourth, then dry wretches and bitter bile. Cindy groaned, put her head on the edge of the bowl and recoiled at the stench.

Without looking, she reached up and flushed, choking back a last few dry heaves. Her brain hurt, her senses ached. Her being longed not to be anymore.

"You okay?" Les asked from not three feet behind her.

Cindy spun on her knees, finding herself nose to head with his erection. The damned thing looked even larger.

Les looked at her looking at it and answered her unasked question. "Dreaming of you," he said, his eyes playing over her nakedness.

She had to wonder if the thought of killing her made him so potent, but he said sweetly, softly, "Nice dream. But I have to say, reality's even better."

"No!" Cindy yelped, and flew to her feet in one leap, stark sober alert and, remarkably, head not spinning.

So sudden was her move and sharp her tone, Les backed up. His erection seemed to flag in that moment.

Cindy glanced at herself in the mirror. Yes, she was definitely naked — and slightly greenish. She shifted her gaze to Les's reflection. He looked... disappointed.

Fortuitously, "Sick," was all that came out of Cindy's mouth.

Les nodded. "Quite a night," he said with fondness and empathy.

To which Cindy blurted, "Woulda made anybody sick," louder than she would have liked, her words clattering off the hard tile walls straight into her now-aching-again brain.

"Thanks a lot," Les said.

"I didn't mean it that way," Cindy said, her face falling to stare at the salmon-colored floor.

"I didn't take it that way."

Why was he being so sweet, so understanding? "I... guess I need to... go back and rest," Cindy told him.

"Sure," Les said, turning away. "I'll have them send up a key."

As he went out to call down, she stared in the mirror. Cyndra Baker, tacitly voted Female Agent Most Likely to Make Director by her classmates, sleeping with her prime suspect, never suspecting a thing. If there had been anything left in her stomach, it would have come up.

"They're sending someone up." Les was back in the doorway, a long sleeve Geoffrey Beene dress shirt in his hand. "This should cover the good parts. Though I hate to see that wonderful vision go," he said with genuine appreciation.

Pulling the shirt up her arms, Cindy half-smiled as if she thought he was giving her a compliment. At least his erection had mostly gone down. She stepped out past him, only then noticing that the closet door was still —

Shit! Open!

Had she actually spied on him, picked through his closet, his things, then left the door ajar? Projectile vomit looming, she hadn't had time to think it through, cover her tracks, zip up the —

Shit! Wardrobe bag!

Cindy watched as the pale blue vinyl came into view a... little... at a... time. First the edge... then the side, then...

The closed zipper. *Hallelujah!*

Cindy sighed and whisked past. She thanked God and promised to go to the big Methodist church next time she was back home instead of lying around reading the comics while watching Sunday morning political shows like she normally did, thinking how sometimes they were hard to tell apart.

At the door — almost free — Cindy turned back to say goodbye and found Les sliding the closet door shut, seemingly without a thought in his mind.

Both services and Sunday School, I swear!

"Get some rest," Les said, coming over, and hugged Cindy with those long, strong swimmer's arms which had held such promise. *If only...*

An unfamiliar emotion swept over Cindy faster and more violently than the nausea had. She began to weep.

Shit. Weeping.

"What?" Les asked, giving her stringy hair a gentle caress while hugging her the way only a real man can, a loving man.

"Oh," Cindy sighed, turning her head away. "Nothing. Worn out, I guess." Lying was definitely getting easier. Never a good sign. She sniffed and dried her teary cheeks with the back of a hand, not wanting to soil the cuff of Les's Geoffrey Beene.

"It was quite a night," he said and released her.

Cindy checked to see if he was being boastful, some macho triumph, but she saw only deep serenity. She had never seen anything like it in Les Moore's eyes. Hell, she'd never seen it in any man's eyes. Why the hell did she have to be seeing it now?

They heard the elevator ding open, and a uniformed female desk clerk stepped out, carrying a master key card. "That'd be me," Cindy said, managing a weak smile.

Les nodded, smiled and said, "It was fun."

"Yeah," Cindy said, and tried to see a cold-blooded killer in the eyes of this adoring, adorable man who had let his guard down so completely. This lovely man who had treated her with greater dignity and shown more respect and passion for her than any man she had ever known. She tried to, hoped to, glean a glint of intent, a hint of murder, a wisp of anger or resentment, bitterness or revenge. But all she saw was contentment. And love.

Shit. Love.

Chapter 21 – Sitting with It

Cindy went to her room and cried for an hour. Then, she got up and started putting the pieces together, ignoring the ringing phone. She'd wanted to talk to her dad to find out how the boys were but wanted to avoid Les even more. To hell with Brinkman altogether.

She got dressed then undressed, feeling better out of her PJs — even her skin felt hungover — then, spreading her files out on the bed, the table, the dressers, the TV, and the floor, went to work, murder by murder, memory by memory, file by file, nimbly flitting around the room from question to answer to hypothesis.

With the aid of a simple timeline for the SKK murders, Cindy quickly determined, if nothing else, that Les had been available for the ones that counted — Pittsburgh, Miami, and Seattle. Most of the hits would have taken lots of travel, by plane in some cases (e.g., flying from Iowa to the Pitt for The Slasher and back), with some clever covering of his tracks, but Les could have pulled it off. The question was: Would he?

Cindy went back and forth on this foundational argument all day long. She wanted to believe in Les, but somewhere among those jumbled thoughts, way in the back, she kept hearing Brinkman warning her, "Never trust the bastard." Of course, Brinkman would then go on to point out there was no one he trusted more to have his back in a "situation" than Les Moore. No one. "Just don't trust anything he *says*. The sonofabitch would lie to his own mother's cadaver if he thought it would move his case forward."

Brinkman was clearly a paranoid schizophrenic, but the sentiment had stuck with Cindy. Now, standing over her string of files and the SKK hit-line, it resonated like a spectral warning from a distant shadowy past she had all but forgotten and stabbed into her brain like a rusty icepick.

There was only one way to get rid of that feeling.

***

Brinkman returned her page in under a minute. "This isn't easy for me to say," Cindy started off.

"You're pregnant, having Les's love child, and you want off the case," Brinkman said. If nothing else, he knew how to fire an opening salvo.

So did Cindy. "No, I think Les is our SKK."

There was silence — then Brinkman laughed, loud and hard.

"I'm serious, Phil," Cindy said darkly.

"Baker, we have to stop yanking each other's tampon strings like this."

"Phil, this is no joke," Cindy said and ran down her theory — including Les's depilatory proclivities.

After several moments of quiet, Brinkman said, "He's a swimmer, you know. Since college. Or before. They shave their whole bodies."

"I know," Cindy said — and told him about the dress.

"Maybe it was for you," Brinkman said. Maybe he didn't want to hear any of this.

Cindy knew they were sailing quickly into dangerous waters. If she said yes, she was as much as admitting to an affair, which was, at the very least, against every rule in the damn book, not to mention extraordinarily embarrassing. If Les turned out to be their SKK on top of everything...

Holy Joseph-Fucking Mother of Christ.

Brinkman most likely interpreted the silence as validation, but thankfully didn't pursue it. His ass was on the line as well, so he offered, "Or someone else."

Cindy sighed relief. But it did beg the question, "Like who?"

They both knew that Les had no one in his life — with a capital No — other than perhaps Cindy. But if the dress wasn't for her...

"You think it's his?" Brinkman had never learned how not to ask a question.

"It was in his closet."

"Maybe he's gay," Brinkman suggested, playing off the obvious joke. But he seemed to have little enthusiasm for his own theory. And when Cindy didn't dignify it with a reply — or a counteraccusation — Brinkman moved on to his next hypothesis. "Could've been left by the last person who stayed in the room."

Cindy rolled her eyes loudly.

"Yeah, okay," Brinkman conceded, apparently able to hear them rolling long-distance. He sighed and allowed, "I think it's about as cockamamie an idea as I've ever heard, but, what the hell, it's a cockamamie world."

"So, you're telling me... what, exactly, Phil?"

"I'm not telling you anything, *exactly*, Baker. This is dodgy stuff. Lead investigator of my TASK Force accused of being his own suspect by his second in command. His *partner*."

He didn't add, "Who is a woman," but he didn't have to. Cindy was well aware of the politics. Which was precisely why she hadn't called Wilstrong. Better to run it past a numb-nuts like Brinkman than get thrown out on her female second-in-command ass over unprovable or even patently absurd accusations.

The word had a bad ring. "I don't think I'm accusing him, Phil. I think..." Cindy chose her words carefully—hell, this could be being taped "I'm thinking out loud is all."

Brinkman went silent for a moment—he too had to be thinking that they could be being taped—then he said, "Yeah. Well, if I had *thoughts* like those, I'd keep them to myself. But I'd also keep a look out. See if there was any... merit to what I was thinking."

"So, you're telling me to keep my eyes open," Cindy said.

"I might be telling you that," he said.

Brinkman! Cindy listened for clicks on the line as she was certain Brinkman was doing as well. "And I should, what? Call the press if I see something?" she said dryly.

"Yeah, right, Baker. Like I said, we have to quit yanking each other's tits." Brinkman hung up before she could say the L-word.

***

The clock read 6:30 p.m. before Cindy decided she was ready to talk to anyone else. She hoped it wouldn't be Les, but knew she couldn't avoid him forever.

A moment later, there was a knock.

Cindy looked out the peephole and saw Les looking in to see if her shadow fell over it. She considered her nakedness a moment, then opened the door anyway, but mostly hid behind it.

He offered her phone. "Thought you might want this back."

"Oh. Yeah. Thanks," she said, taking it.

"Hungry yet?" he asked with a courteous smile and pretended to be trying to see around the door. "I made reservations for two at Tres Palmas. I was hopeful." Quite charming for a killer. "Unless you're still sick."

He was offering her a way out.

Cindy realized she was starving. Where had the day gone? "Okay," she said. "Give me twenty." She didn't invite him in. "And no Sinatra. I don't think I can take any more of his whining."

"Not even 'Baubles, Bangles and Beads?'" Les said. "It swings."

Cindy's expression did not change.

"Okay," Les said, apparently agreeing to both stipulations—the one she mentioned and the one she implied. "I'll wait in my room."

"Thanks," Cindy said and shut the door. She moved away, then came back to look out the peephole. He was still there, waiting for her return. He waved then headed for his room.

Cindy cussed and went for a quick shower. No shampoo, no shave, no makeup. She'd smell better, but that was all. It was her turn to scare him.

***

Dinner was quiet, and Les pointed that out.

Cindy said she wasn't sure she'd wanted any more Cuban food. Les said that you can't ever get enough Cuban food and Cindy said he'd already said that and Les said he knew he had but still, you couldn't ever get too much Cuban food and wasn't this the best they'd had so far, and Cindy had to admit it was.

"I planned it that way," he said. "It's on an escalating scale. Wait till you taste tomorrow night's." Cindy smiled with something vaguely replicating sincerity, but her mind was already somewhere else—in Biscayne Bay and Three Rivers.

Riverbend.

Les said casually, "I checked out the nude beach today," as if making normal conversation. "Haulover."

That pulled Cindy up short. "What?"

"Nude beach," he confirmed. "Checked it out. Today."

Cindy stared as Les dipped a hard Cuban roll into a shallow bowl of fresh garlic mashed into sour orange juice, then slathered some on his avocado "salad" — thick slices of avocado covered with thin rings of strong onion — and moaned.

With an intentionally conspicuous chill in her voice, Cindy said, "Didn't you get enough of that last night?" and looked away — just now noticing how Tres Palmas looked a lot like Diamonds in the Raw with lights on. Red carpet, black walls, red chairs, black table, mirrors.

Thankfully, the wait staff was male and clothed and there were no brass poles.

"Different concept," Les said, slurping avocado. "Good onion, huh? Sharp." He added a spoonful of garlic-orange sauce directly into his mouth and moaned again as if entering Elysium.

Cindy stared a beat then said flatly, "How was it?" and forced herself not to moan over the orgy of delight raging in her own mouth.

"The beach?" Les said.

"*Nude* beach," Cindy corrected. *Little naked fuckbug.*

"Nude," Les shrugged. "Nude everywhere. For as far as you could see. Half a mile, at least. Nude, nude, nude, nude, nude."

"Men?"

"Mostly. And fat women."

"That's not nice."

"Not supposed to be. But true."

"Fat men?"

"Oh yeah. Except for the gay guys. They're all slim and trim. Makes you wonder. Is vanity a side effect of homosexuality, or are they just more self-realized? More in touch with their feminine side. Not just, you know, health-minded."

"Are you saying women are vain by nature, and therefore men who act like women somehow automatically develop an overactive vanity about themselves?"

"I didn't say they act like women. That's fairly clichéd and judgmental thinking on your part, Agent Baker."

Cindy grunted something unintelligible but malevolent then asked, "Suspects?" and pasted on the same patronizing smile Les was giving her. Dipped some bread.

How could anything taste this good?

"Couldn't say," Les said, pretending not to notice any of her visual commentary. "Hard to profile naked people. Everyone's about the same with their clothes off. That's why I like going. Like Dale Carnegie said, it's the great equalizer."

Cindy wasn't sure Carnegie actually said it that way and *presented* that she was not about to concede or agree with, or to, anything. She hoped she looked a lot like an eastern diamondback. Dark, coiled, and ready to strike.

Les said, "Very relaxing. You should try it sometime." And that smile again.

Cindy doubted out loud such a time would ever come. Les shrugged. His *camarones* had arrived.

"So," Cindy summed up. "Basically, a bunch of fat women and gay men. No babes, no murderers. Guess you'll just have to go back to a strip club tonight." She dipped a calamari in the garlic. *Jesus, this food is good!*

"Yeah," Les said, dredging a giant shrimp and dribbling garlic on his chin. Wiping it with his red napkin. "I figure if we leave by eight, we can cover them all. If we schedule it right."

Despite the protests of her taste buds, Cindy stopped eating. "You have *got* to be kidding."

"Tomorrow's Wednesday," Les said — the Strip Killer's impending date with destiny.

At least that meant Les hadn't killed him yet. *Didn't it?*

"Les, you're on vacation. Vacate!" Cindy commanded. *And give me a break!*

"Sorry, Sweetness. Can't."

Cindy understood him to mean not with an SK loose. But *Sweetness?*

Not feeling like fighting, or even joking about this latest diminutive trespass, Cindy just shook her head, turned her attention to the steaming paella in front of her, breathed deep, took a mouthful, and moved on to other serial brain teasers.

She thought how thousands of murders go unsolved every year, and how many of them might be dead SKs. Bodies found in a ditch or hung up under a bridge after a flood, dry bones unearthed in the desert by a big wind or a family dog — or maybe never found at all. If their victims were never found, not only would the victims' killer never be known, but the victims' killers' killer(s), would never be known either. DNA be damned. This SKK thing could have been going on a long time, decades, with no one having a clue.

That is, until one of them killed two others in a barn in Iowa.

Cindy's mind reeled at the killer koan. The whole notion was so neat, so... Les. And this didn't take into account how many other murderer murders might have gone down during Les's three-year mandatory hiatus or his fifteen-plus years of duty before.

Cindy finally looked across the table at her TASK partner. He was attacking a fish, a whole fish, crusty and fragrant with Cuban culinary magic, still crackling from the broiler, eyes closed.

That is, Les's eyes were closed; the fish stared at her.

***

By the time they got back to the hotel, after visiting a dozen strip clubs all over North Miami and up into Ft. Lauderdale, Cindy had had enough. By her estimation, they had viewed more naked female flesh in eight hours than she had seen her entire life, and that included locker rooms.

She said she still felt ill and wanted to "climb in and sack out for like two days," privately figuring that would give her plenty of time to sleep a few hours then get up and think more about Les's possible connection to this madness.

Les said she should, "Really have that throwing up thing looked at," and managed to sound concerned, but she guessed he'd likely had enough of her as well, since she knew that she'd been decidedly less fun than their last outing.

When Cindy offered no goodnight kiss, he asked if she was giving him the brush-off.

"No," Cindy said. But the thought crossed her mind that she probably was. Though breaking up with a killer was much harder than she ever would have thought.

***

At nine the next evening, the third Wednesday of the month, Cindy sat on her bed staring at her phone. All day, she'd been dreading Les's call saying it was time to go find the Strip Killer on his red-letter night. Her phone never rang. Then it hit her.

Things were back to normal.

"Goddammit!" Cindy kicked the Cadillac in the space next to the empty space where the ecru shit-box had been — setting off the Caddy's alarm — then she struck off for her rental. She'd planned ahead this time, stashing the plain silver compact on a different level of the parking garage.

With some difficulty and no notes, Cindy pried the location of three of the clubs from her clotty memory before she finally spotted Bassett's tan loaner parked a block away from Diamonds in the Raw.

By now, she was old friends with the pug at the door, but he still said, "Ten bucks," with as much verve as Steven Wright after shock therapy. He didn't remind her of the two-drink minimum.

Cindy found Les, turned away, talking to Nipple Bar in the corner. As Cindy approached, the curvy waitress — down from straps to strings tonight — noted Cindy's convergence with her eyes to give Les notice then slipped away.

"What took you so long?" he asked Cindy, the way he had in Pittsburgh.

"You had the addresses," she said and, because they were in a public place, chose glaring over shooting him. A tough decision.

"Never heard of a phonebook?" he said.

"I don't rip pages out of phone books. It's the way I was raised. Besides, I'll bet there isn't a single Yellow Pages in all of South Florida with the strip joint pages still in it, if there are any phone books at all. And again: How old are you?"

She wasn't about to admit that she hadn't thought of Googling strip clubs.

To prevent further interrogation on that subject, she pretended to scope out the room. "Seen anything?"

Eleven men sat fencepost-still, trying to look as if what they were doing was a natural, everyday event. Perhaps, pathetically, for some it was. None of them looked like a murderer; any one of them could have been.

When Les replied in the negative, Cindy asked if Nipple Bar had offered any leads for them yet.

"Not yet," he said. "But she's on task."

Cindy admired the way Les had selected the artificially endowed waitress as his second set of eyes. He told Cindy he always chose waitresses — never dancers (too unreliable), and never bartenders (could be the killer) — and they had to be the ones who most needed the job, who wanted to keep it. The ones who cleaned already-clean tabletops and straightened already-straight chairs during lulls in the customer flow; who took their work seriously, even in a strip club, and weren't into drugs; the women who always had a smile for the men, but never gave away more than a professional waitress's attention and good service with the least amount of chat time despite their minimal wardrobe.

And they never looked at the pussy. His target informant knew the men frontward and backward and wasn't interested in the dancers, professionally or privately — no lesbians, no bis, no undecideds, not for this assignment. At least at the present time, they should be too busy for sex, easy or otherwise.

As he had done in Gainesville with Mo and Less, Les chose perfectly. Nipple Bar as they came to call her — Bitsy to her few close friends (which was no one in the club) — worked "at least eight nights a week," by her own accounting, and she was there for the long haul. Bad hours and hard work, on her feet often till dawn, wearing next to nothing didn't dissuade her because the money was great. Four hundred dollars on a good night, a thousand on New Year's. And she didn't have to strip for it, just look like she might at any moment.

Being an informant wasn't as weird as she'd thought it would be, she told Les, and quickly began to look on his invitation as a challenge. Plus, it helped her pass the numbing long hours of ferrying drinks to loud lawyers with trimmed beards and their collars opened up to indicate how laid back they were.

Before Cindy arrived, the waitress had told Les about one regular who always gave her the "heebie-screebies." She described him as tall, six-seven maybe, with white hair and pale eyes, dreadfully sallow, like a pasty corpse himself, and always wearing the same outfit — black Levis, a dark blue shirt, and a white Stetson.

"Black and dark blue. No fashion sense whatsoever," she had said, adjusting the DayGlo lime Lycra floss over the metal rod in her nipple. Les said he thought the killer would be less conspicuous, and she went off to think.

When he later relayed the encounter to Cindy, she agreed. Their unsub was probably not a giant albino in a cowboy hat.

In Miami.

After Cindy had been there a while, the waitress returned. She set down two drinks neither had ordered and told them about a more average guy she had noticed. What had stayed with her was seeing him in his car after hours, watching everyone leave the club. She had recognized him by his bad haircut in the backlight of a car pulling out behind him.

"Frizzed," she said.

The Diamonds in the Raw waitress had shared a long look with the guy that sent chills through her and made her lock her car door even before pulling it shut. "But when I looked back, he was gone. Just like that. It was freaky." She wiped down their table even though it didn't need it. For the first time, she looked uneasy. He had scared the *bejeezus* out of her so badly that she parked closer to the building the next night.

Then, she forgot about him. Just another creepy patron in the shadows.

Les asked about hair color or other identifying characteristics. Their waitress shrugged, "Average. Brown." Then she recalled his ruddy complexion, as from adolescent acne.

Cindy nodded — that fit — and asked, "What kind of car?"

The pneumatic young woman thought back then said, "Mustang. Or a Toyota, maybe." Les and Cindy shared a look. "No," Nipple Bar corrected, "Camaro. That's what it was. Black Camaro. Now, I remember." She was sure; an old boyfriend had one.

"New?"

"No," she laughed. What a ridiculous notion. A loser like *him*?

Then, putting on her best strip-club waitress demeanor — the one meant to dilute the sticker shock of high-priced watered-down drinks made with bar brands — she said, "That'll be fourteen dollars," and asked Cindy if she was "enjoying the show tonight?" as if it was actual entertainment. Cindy nodded and smiled, lying again.

Easier and easier.

Les grinned at the waitress's fiscal ingenuity, paid her, adding two tens. "Keep it." As informants went, she was cheap. And very few gave him two scotches for his thirty-four bucks, watered down or not.

***

The rest of the night, Les and Cindy rode around looking for an older black Camaro outside the clubs, and a frizzy brown-haired average guy with bad skin inside the clubs. They even swung back by Diamonds in the Raw — which Cindy kept referring to as Oysters in the Raw, much to Les's muted pleasure — but found nothing.

Around three-fifteen, Les said, "What do you say we call it a night?" and Cindy said, "Fine by me."

They rode back to the hotel in silence, both of them probably wondering what the other was thinking and hopeful that the Strip Killer was home asleep, having gone to bed early.

***

Cindy slept until three the next afternoon. When she called the desk for her messages, the afternoon operator told Cindy that Les had checked out.

Cindy wasn't surprised. After her comportment the night before, she didn't expect to hear from Les until Monday morning, what would be his first official day back at work in Gainesville. She was right. But Les was right about the nude beach. Cindy found the whole experience very relaxing and shame-free, naked fat people notwithstanding.

Chapter 22 – The Cabin

Montana, deep in the woods, deep in the night. Les is in the news again.

> *THE NATION (AP) – Police in 12 states have reported a sharp upturn in serial-type murders. Sixteen bodies have been found over the past two weeks, from Maine to Arizona. Details are few, but an FBI spokesman said the killings appear to be related, if not attributable to a single assassin. Special Agent Rolf Peterson of the bureau's prestigious profiling department said the recent killings "may represent a response by known serial killers to the execution-style assassinations of six of their own in as many weeks." He declined to name suspects.*
>
> *FBI Director Evertt Wilstrong added in a press conference held in Millimuck, Wisc., yesterday (scene of the most recent grisly scene – see "Twin Teens" on page 14): "We are concerned this might be a form of retaliation by some of the 62 active serial killers we are currently tracking." Wilstrong refused further comment, but a top-level source inside the bureau said, "The situation is being examined carefully."*

"Not too carefully, though. It might stop." A familiar whispery laugh.

> *An extremist group, the Christian Action Militia Organization (CAMO), whose motto is "We're Armed and Dangerous for God's Sake," has taken credit for three of the serial-killer killings. However, the FBI is holding to their theory that a lone person, most likely a man to whom they refer internally as SKK, or Serial-Killer Killer, is responsible for the homicides.*

"Good call," the reader grumbles. "Those idiots couldn't kill each other with a hand grenade in a bathtub."

Several pacifist organizations including Amnesty International claim that the higher body count is a direct result of the FBI's "renewed presence and vigorous drive to rid the country of serial murderers through any means possible, possibly including murder itself." The FBI declined comment.

Similarly, the ACLU announced today they are calling for the "immediate resignation" of Leslie Francis Moore, lead investigator of the bureau's new Target Active Serial Killer (TASK) Force. Considered by many to be the nation's leading authority on serial murder, Moore was directly responsible for the deaths of at least two serial killers in shoot-outs. ACLU spokeswoman Freida Peeples says the organization is calling for Moore's resignation in order to "stop this surreptitiously sanctioned butchery and bloodshed."

"Gotta love the liberals," comes the mutter. "Leslie Francis." Throws the news aside. "Goddam girl names."

Turning his attention now to the young man bound naked in the corner, arms tied high, a two-inch blue rubber Earth stuffed in his mouth, held in place with duct tape.

The next to die.

***

Poor kid, just accepted a four-block ride. How he ended up here, bound, gagged, naked, in another state, with this nutcase is still not clear to him.

He remembers browsing the racks in an adult bookstore, drawn to the kinkier stuff, as usual—lesbians, dominatrices, S&M, bondage, *she-males*. Men. He'd gotten half a hard-on in the gay section, then discreetly slipped into the video preview room to drop a few tokens in a private booth, searching for the transsexual movie displayed at the entrance. The reel turned out to be less than advertised. The featured performer looked more like a he than a she—and a freakish he at that—with high bulbous cheeks, thick waist, shriveled scrotum, and a swarthy, dormant, uncircumcised penis. Hemorrhoids.

The desired effect was not had.

"All Girl Lesbian Pussy Party!" was better, if redundant. But those two guys on the next channel doing each other in an abandoned gas station was hot. So hot, the kid ran out of quarters and had to go back to the front counter for change.

He didn't notice the fair-haired man eyeing him—the same one who had watched him browse the bi-mags, earlier—hoping only that the coarse young clerk with the dragon tattoo on his forearm wouldn't notice the bulge in his "Ghakis"—what he and his girlfriend Melody call their Gap khakis.

When the kid returned to his booth, the *lesbians* were done, sitting around dressed, talking about how much they enjoyed filming their first girl-on-girl scene. So fake. But the two gas station guys had been joined by two others, and then two more. The six were having a grunting sweaty time, like men do on video. Moments later, the kid exploded into a Kleenex through a carefully planned hole in his pocket. He had wanted to get aroused, not arrested.

Or abducted by Riverbend.

***

The Killer pulls up a chair. "Think you can get it up?"

No response, above or below. Just wide eyes staring. At twenty, this *kid* doesn't understand any of this. Doesn't *want* to. Maybe if he closes his eyes, it will all go away.

He'll wake up in Melody's dorm room. She'll be making hot chocolate in the short kimono he bought her, the one that shows her ass. She'll laugh and say how he was talking in his sleep again then come over and curl up tight against him, the way she does, and ask him what he was dreaming. "Was it hot?" and "Was I in it?" Rubbing him the right way.

"Now look, you want to live, right?" the Killer says.

He's still here. They both are.

"Of course you do. You're young. You don't realize what a horrible place this world is yet. But okay."

Standing sharply and slapping the Kid harder than he's ever been hit in his life. "You don't have a *choice*, you dumb little shit!"

He's very close, seething. "You will achieve and maintain an erection, or someone will find you dead in a field, wearing panties and a bra, with your cock stuffed up your own ass!"

The Killer jumps back in mock horror. "What will your *friends* say? Your *parents*? They'll wonder what you've been up to all these years. Why, they'll think you're a... *queer!*"

He struts away, swaying his hips, wrist bent and eyebrows up like, *See, this is you.* He makes the Kid mad, but not hard.

"Maybe some visual stimulation."

The Killer digs in the kid's backpack and comes up with a glossy men's mag—like providence. "Hey!" *What's this?* But he knew, dammit. He looked.

"This shit does it for you, huh?" The Killer flips pages, shaking his head.

The kid remembers buying the skin mag at a liquor store two blocks up from the porn shop. Melody would for-sure dig the layout of the two blondes on a sunny hillside. The title said Spain, but it looked like Daytona that time they went on Spring Bre—

"Kid stuff!" the Killer declares, tossing the glossy magazine onto his matte *USA Today.* "Let me show you the real thing."

He's acting like a friend, a mentor, offering slaves, ropes, leather, and rubber, compromising positions, gaping orifices, faces in pain. The harder stuff.

"Hey, this looks like someone we know." He brings pictures over.

Venom rises in the Kid, a minor antidote to fear.

"Oh yeah," the Killer says as if realizing. "You!" More pages, even worse. "And look. Someone's *spanking* him." A stinging swat to sell the notion, then checking to see.

Still nothing.

"Let's try this," the Killer says, turning to his bag of tricks with the warning, "Keep in mind the consequences of a limp dick."

The Kid braces, but only DVDs come out of the bag.

"Which do you prefer? Boys and girls. Girls and girls. Boys and boys. Boys and girls and boys. Girls and boys and boys and girls and more of the same FUCKING BORING SHIT!"

Hurling it.

Plastic shatters against the wall along with what's left of the kid's composure. The State U junior wishes he'd paid more attention in Abnormal Psych class. Maybe he'd have an answer for this, some way to win back control.

"Pick one. In three... two..."

The Kid chooses, "That." *Bi Your Leave*, a costumed romp in the king's court. If this is going to work, he'd better make the leap to hard honesty. "All for one and one for all!" the slick cover promises. Two Musketeers grinning plastically across a fair maiden in modern hooker makeup.

"Ah, girls and boys and boys. Why am I not surprised?" the Killer says, coming closer. "Maybe it's that cute little earring."

The kid pulls back. He finds himself hating that earring—along with every fantasy he's ever had. He wishes the new neighbor boy, the preacher's kid, had never shown him *How* in sixth grade. He learned a lot that summer. Just nothing about God.

He wishes he'd never gone farther with his friends out on the pontoon boat on the lake that next summer, boys full of boys. Talk of girls as emotional camouflage.

He wishes he'd never pursued his best friend's girlfriend because she was the only girl he knew in eighth grade who would put out. You never forget your first—no matter how forgettable.

He wishes he hadn't kept a running count of all the girls he had in high school. The ones who loved him, the ones that didn't; the ones he didn't care about at all. Ranked and rated.

He wishes he'd never cruised the gay hangouts later. Men's rooms and dark footpaths back home, secretly hoping some friendly guy would overpower his dread with charm and a saucy line, or raw sexual aggression. Whatever would take the decision from his hands.

He wishes he hadn't let that guy touch him that time. That *man*. Feeling his own frightening lust for the first time, afraid of where it might lead him some day. Running away.

He wishes he and Melody had never bought realistic sex toys or giggled about bringing other lovers into their mix, talking about love but knowing it was something else. Something worse.

He wishes he'd never told her how he fantasized about men. About being raped by an anonymous forceful man in a cabin in the woods.

He wishes he'd never met her at all.

"Hey, this is hot," Riverbend says over his mini-DVD player. He came prepared.

"Her tits aren't real, but then whose are anymore?" A real pal now, a buddy.

He knows he's got It. Marjorie and Melissa Ann thought he was a kindly veterinarian when he stopped to chat them up about Ginger, their big, goofy golden.

Ginger died first.

The actors seem to be enjoying themselves on the tiny screen — it's why they call themselves actors — the men tending to each other while the woman tends to herself.

"Now, you see," the Killer interrupts. "*This* is what these movies are really about, right here. To ease babies like you into the scene. Make you feel more comfortable about maybe being queer 'cause there's a girl in it."

Probably true, because the forced scenario is getting a rise out of the Kid as he watches, feeling something he didn't think he would — didn't think he *could* — that if sex is all this is about, he can handle that. He might even try to like it.

He might not even have to try.

Yes! The DVD is working. It has to if this kid, this child, wants to believe he has any chance at all. College isn't for babes; it's for babies.

"Much better." The Killer's voice cuts like a new scalpel.

His hand is warm, but his touch is cold.

"We'll do this. We'll get this done," he encourages. "And you'll feel better for it," he promises. "All those nagging little questions in the back of your mind about what this guy-guy shit's all about. Now, you'll know. It'll be a big relief."

He sounds like a consoling older brother — and drops to his knees.

***

It all comes back like yesterday.

He was six; his stepfather, thirty-eight. "You tell and I'll kill you," the redneck driller had said. "Your mother too." He swore it.

And back in juvie with that black guard, to save his life.

They're both dead now. He made sure. *No one* makes a *fag* out of this killer and lives to tell. Not then; not now.

Riverbend rising.

Chapter 23 – Montana

By the time Les and Brinkman returned to work, four new serial murders had been reported along with two new suspected SKK hits. And one in Portland with no clues as to *what* it was. The New Orleans hit yielded some trace evidence implying that the Killer could have been a woman again — another pump print; left foot this time — and someone possibly saw someone who might have looked, perhaps, like a woman.

Maybe.

Then there was that messy one. Some poor college kid found in the woods near a burned-out hunting cabin in Montana — genitals cut off erect, cauterized, then wrapped with a yellow ribbon and lodged in his own rectum, apparently while he was still alive, his body slashed head to toe in what appeared to be ritualistic markings, then left lashed to a lodgepole pine to bleed to death. At that point, it must have seemed like grace delivered.

"Busy week while you were away," Cindy said as she met Les at Gate Four in Bozeman. "Nice flight?"

They had arrived, separately, on a classic Montana autumn afternoon — piercing blue sky running forever without a trace of white, pines as green as all of summer, mountains begging to be attacked with a good pair of hiking boots, some trail mix, and a copy of *Field Guide to Birds of the Northwest*, and air so pure and dry it carried no scent but clean. A glorious day to be alive.

"No," Les scowled, apparently unaffected by good nature. "And what's that supposed to mean?"

Cindy sagged. Were they back to this? She took one of those relaxing breaths that didn't seem to relax her anymore and said, "It means I wanted to know if you had a nice flight."

"The other."

He waited.

"I meant..." Cindy raced through a few options and chose, "Don't take any more time off. Too many people end up dead." Les grunted, took a few steps then turned back and threw The Look. "What?" she asked. What *now?*

"Did you dump me?" he said plainly.

Cindy had always been comfortable with the truth. She preferred it. But here in Montana, under the Big Sky — at least under the big roof of the Bozeman airport under the Big Sky — she felt decidedly uncomfortable.

After all that had gone down in Florida, Cindy'd had plenty of time to sit with it, to plot her charts and graphs, compare and contrast her data, but she'd come to no definitive conclusions. Brinkman's whereabouts were unaccounted for during the same periods — along with thirty or forty thousand other possible suspects.

The field was narrowing down, so why pick on Les? He couldn't have done the two in Iowa in the barn. And what? He scooted around behind himself in Gainesville, shot Predator, then pretended someone else had done it?

No. Gainesville PD had run a paraffin test on Les's hands and clothes — at Les's insistence — which turned up no gunpowder. Just Florida grit and trace polymers from Armor All on the Impala steering wheel (Bassett's surf-kid-detailer's good work).

Plus, three different people recalled seeing the WRX sitting by the park. One even saw it racing away while Les stood watching. So, he wasn't any more of a suspect at the end of the week than he had been at the beginning.

Before they fucked and got it over with.

Les waited for an answer. His body language made it clear he would stand there as long as Cindy needed.

So, she said, "No," and sighed at the floor. "It just looked that way."

She was finding it difficult to dump the first man she ever felt she could love for real just because he had a dress in his closet and shaved his legs.

But when no pale blue garment bag bumped around the luggage carousel, Cindy felt the worms of uncertainty at work inside her head again. What if he'd used that beautiful blue dress to kill in New Orleans where the heel print was found? She *almost* asked him.

"So, what was it then?" Les interrupted, apparently still not satisfied.

Cindy thought about giving a real answer then decided truth, here and now, would accomplish nothing, so she lied. "Nothing," she said, and lied again. "I was hungover." And again. "PMS-ing."

Easier and easier.

That should have ended it—men being squeamish about feminine *issues*—but Les kept staring at her. So Cindy said, "Car's out here," nodded toward the exit, and left.

She'd had a lousy flight, too.

***

Les found Cindy sitting in the passenger side of their rental Explorer 4x4, staring at nothing. Figuring he had to do something to perk her up, he tapped on the window and told her. "You drive."

Cindy looked up as if she wasn't sure she'd heard him correctly. Les had never let her drive once, even when she'd asked if she could. He'd always said he didn't ride well and got carsick. "Are you sure?" Cindy asked, her voice muffled inside the car.

"Sure," Les nodded, opening the back door and tossing his bags on the seat.

Cindy climbed out, walked around, and he got in, the seat still warm from her body. "Just take it easy," he said, and she did.

After a few silent miles, Cindy asked, "You think it's him?"

"I know it's him," Les said.

"Local isn't so sure."

"They never are."

"So, how can you be?"

Les shrugged to indicate he just knew—the expected response—and Cindy pointed out that, "Anyone can tie a yellow ribbon."

"Not like him. Not that ribbon."

Les was sure it would turn out to be the same wide, one-of-a-kind, impossible-to-find, linen-laced, antique paper ribbon as the others.

"Okay. But why a male?"

"We don't know he hasn't done males before."

"No ribbons before."

"We don't know that he always leaves one."

Cindy said, "Brinkman had the stills overnighted to me in Miami. I thought the kid behind the desk would need oxygen when I opened the envelope."

"Yeah," Les said. "You shouldn't do that."

Cindy looked mildly rankled for the mild reprimand and said, "Have you seen them?"

"I saw them," Les said, and nothing more.

"Maybe the nuts are right," Cindy said. "Maybe it *is* The End."

Les nodded. He had yet to rule out Apocalypse as cause.

***

When they got to the cabin in the Montana hills, Les and Cindy found nothing more than a foot of smoldering charcoal. The wood walls had been old and dry so, with the help of a few gallons of kerosene, the shack went up like a pine cone in a coal furnace.

An acrid stench of burnt plastic and insulation, scorched metal, and paint violated the mountain air in a way that spoke directly to the evil born there. Most of the trees near the black mound were charred, a few still warm to the touch. Smaller, thinner trees fared worse, foliage singed away, never to come back. Thankfully, Paradise Valley had had a wet fall, otherwise the fire might have run unchecked to Yellowstone, a hundred-plus miles south.

Heavy hemp rope—coarse and prickly, to deny fingerprinting—hung from the tree on which the Killer had left his latest victim. Blood was everywhere—soaked into the bark, the needles, the ground—and a sticky black trail led back to the cabin where Riverbend had raped, castrated, and begun his torture-murder of Jerry Carver the college kid.

Everything got worse when a name was attached.

"He did the mutilations in there," Red Stimson, the local sheriff, told the TASK team, pointing up at the pile of black rubble. "Then he dragged him down here and crucified him on this tree."

Cindy asked, "Were his arms out?"

Stimson studied her. "Ma'am?"

"Out." She held out her arms. "Like a cross?" She knew they hadn't been. She'd seen the stills. "The victim."

"Not really, no, ma'am."

"Was he nailed to the tree?"

"No."

"Then, let's not use that word," Cindy said. "The press can turn that kind of thing into a 'case development' before you can spell the words for them."

"Yes, ma'am." Red didn't tell her he'd already used the word several times with as many reporters back when Henry David Merfinridge's connection to Montana first emerged. Red had rued his name being mentioned in national news. Who knew who might read it and seek him out later? Seeing the kid on the tree had brought it all back. Who would do this?

But something larger bothered Red. "What I can't get my head wrapped around is why he did the mutilating in there..." Again, he pointed up the hill almost a quarter mile to the burned-out hunting lodge. "And then he dragged the body all the way down... here." He moved his finger, indicating the path to the tree.

Les said, "He wanted to make sure the evidence burned but the body didn't."

Red ran his tongue along the inside of his cheek. "I'd say that's the greater part of my point. That body is the significant piece of evidence." He said it as if wondering police work had changed over the past week? "Isn't it?" he asked, just to be sure it hadn't.

Les said, "That body's no evidence."

Red looked as if he couldn't believe what he was hearing. With modern forensics? They had to learn something. *Didn't they?*

Cindy said, "Agent Moore is fairly confident the killer, whoever it may be, knew exactly what he was doing, and would have made sure there was no real evidence left with the body. Other than the ribbon. And we're fairly certain that'll check out."

Red said, "Have you seen the stills, ma'am?" His pate wrinkled.

"I have," Cindy said. "And I've read the prelims. And at this point, I have to agree with Agent Moore. If the killer went to the trouble to burn the cabin so thoroughly, didn't even leave a footprint in all this soft dirt—no fibers, no fluids, no hairs, not to mention no trace of the vehicle he used to get in and out of here—"

"It'll turn up, but it'll be clean," Les threw in. He meant, *As clean as that Subaru in Gainesville.*

Cindy said, "You see our point," to the sheriff and shot Les a glare only he would notice. He turned away.

"I hear it, but I'm not sure I agree with it," Red said. "That boy's body was an awful mess. There has to be something. A man can't be that... angry and not make a mistake somewhere."

Cindy noted with compassion that the older man appeared both perplexed and unsettled. That gnarled face had seen a lot of life, if not a lot of bodies up here in these quiet woods. He deserved more than Bureau-speak, but she wasn't sure she knew what to say to assuage his confusion.

"He isn't angry," Les said, coming to her rescue. "Not anymore. He's having fun now. If he was angry about anything, it was only because he felt he had to murder a male to shake things up."

Red shook his head and sighed. "I've got a grandson his age up to Missoula."

Cindy knew he meant UofM but didn't think they needed to wallow in melancholic worries. So, she changed the subject. "When can we see the videos?"

"Right now, if you want," Red told her, shaking off his fears. "They're back at the station." When Cindy didn't respond, Red flipped his hands out as a question. "Are we all done here?"

Cindy looked around, took a quick assessment. "I think so. For now. You?" she asked Les.

Gazing placidly around the site, Les nodded.

Red then directed his still-extended arms down the path. "Well, then. After you, ma'am." Cindy reluctantly led the way. She hated to leave.

How fucked up was that?

***

For Les Moore, Jerry Carver's final resting spot possessed a disturbing familiarity, a *feel*. His skin stung, his eyes burned, and his ears rang. The smell wasn't just of wood and ash, plastics and metal. It reeked of being too late.

Riverbend had been here, all right.

Les felt his pulse quicken. Events were spinning out of control all around him, all across the country. All because he had come back. Come back to end this. But here it was, total bedlam all over again. He could tell, he knew, everything would only get worse from here on. And there was nothing he could do to stop it.

Not a goddamn fucking thing.

***

Back at the station, Cindy had a hard time with the crime scene videos since they offered little more than carnage in close-up. The lighting was awful, and no thought had been given to composition whatsoever. There was no sense to it, no order. No poetry. A few loose master shots, then endless gaping wounds. Cindy longed for the three-dead-in-a-barn video girl.

Les sat silently for forty-seven minutes, never taking a note, never seeming to have an opinion. He had no interrogatories for Red or anyone else. No plans, no projections, no profile. Even Red Stimson seemed to think that was fairly unusual, especially for the Feds. Cindy sat alongside in quiet agreement.

Then Les said suddenly, "Wait. Back it up."

Startled that he finally had something to say, no one moved right away.

Cindy said, "What? What is it?" and scrutinized the jerky, reversing images once the deputy found rewind.

Les watched closely then said, "Okay. There. Play."

He watched intently as the blood-soaked segment ran again. Then, "Stop."

The deputy hit Pause.

Les leaned forward, scrutinized the frozen image a moment, then erupted. "Goddammit!"

He stood so suddenly and violently that his molded-plastic chair flew all the way across the wide central room and slammed into Red's door. Les followed it then veered left and stormed out the main front doors.

Cindy watched him go then turned back to the monitor, searching. The next moment, she saw it. "Oh no."

There, in among the slashings on the kid's upper body—carved intentionally uneven to obfuscate the message for all but the intended receiver—was an inscription. Cindy wasn't sure he'd even seen it, at first—she hoped he hadn't—but there it was, clear as day, if you looked at the right angle.

"Hi Les #1."

***

As Cindy ran out after her partner, Red's deputy leaned close enough to the screen to smell the rotting flesh, squinted to help his astigmatism, then shook his head. Nothing but slice-n-dice wounds you wouldn't inflict on a coyote, much less a human being. No details. No symbolism.

Red didn't see it either. "Switch it off," he said. "Whatever it is, we don't wanna know. Don't concern us." Not a Killer and a victim from other states being investigated by the Feds. All Red had to do was cooperate; anything more was the stuff of sleepless nights.

Over the many years of law enforcement, it had taken to make Red Stimson's leathery face as lined as it was, the one thing he had learned better than anything else was the importance of getting your sleep.

Red went back into his office, closed the door, and called his wife Rosalee just to ask how her day was going.

***

Les slammed out the station door so fast and hard Cindy thought the glass would shatter. "Les, it isn't! It can't be!" she implored from behind, more trying to convince herself than him.

"Goddammit!" Les shouted at any god who would listen. He walked circles in the circular driveway, cussing at his demons and swatting stray thoughts like yellow jackets.

Cindy cautiously approached. "Les? Are you all right?"

"No, I'm not fucking all right!" he shouted. "What the hell's wrong with you? It's a goddam challenge! He killed that sonofabitch in Gainesville to save my worthless life for *this*." Les nodded quickly. "Well, fine. It's me and him now."

He turned on Cindy. "I'll find him, Baker. I *will* find him. And this... this..." He didn't seem able to categorize what they had seen or what happened or anything else other than by waving at the countryside around them, then concluding, "... will be *over*!"

He clearly didn't mean the pleasant afternoon.

Cindy thought Les was being arrogant, if not plainly paranoid, but she said, "Les, the whole country's looking for him," as if to encourage, to say, *Yes he will be found, so calm down.*

"They've been looking for *fifteen years*," Les shouted. "And they don't know anything more about him today than we did back then!"

Fifteen? That was at least five years longer than the Bureau's official count. "How do you figure fifteen?" she said.

"Because, as I keep telling you people," Les said back at her. "I know this guy."

Cindy hated to be lumped in with anyone, much less any group that could be reduced in nomenclature to *you people*. A group like that had to include Phil Brinkman. She started to object, but Les didn't give her a chance.

"I know where he was born, Baker. What his room looked like. The bicycle he rode. The belting he got for every little thing he did. The mailboxes he smashed. The ants he burned. The birds he shot.

"I know the women he's loved and the ones he's dumped, and the ones foolish enough to dump him. I know his mother, his father, his brothers, his aunts and uncles.

"I know how much he hated to rake leaves and take out the garbage. To do anything anyone told him to do.

"How he jerked off in the woods, the attic, the shed and in a stall in the bathroom at school between classes. How he beat up the kid who caught him, beat him to within an inch of his life and got suspended and didn't care, and would've done it again and *did* do it again until they had enough of him and he had enough of them and he quit and started thinking about his first *real* kill.

"I know when he smoked his first cigarette and when he stopped because it was slowing him down and might cause him to leave some trace evidence behind somewhere."

Cindy snuck in, "Sounds like a profile to me."

"Oh, this goes way beyond a profile, Missy. This goes right inside his twisted, fucking head. And I'm stuck living in there! Just me and him. Don't you see? Can't you hear it? Goddamnitall!"

As usual, Cindy only heard one word. "Missy?"

Les didn't break stride. "I can smell this bastard, Baker. I know what he eats, what he drinks, what he shits. What he reads, what he doesn't read, what he thinks, what he avoids thinking about!"

Cindy said, "Don't call me Missy." This time, she wasn't smiling; this was no *Toots*. "Ever again. I mean it," she said.

"What?" Les shouted, looking entirely lost and angrier than she'd seen him yet.

"You called me 'Missy,'" Cindy said quietly. "Don't ever call me that ag—"

Les leapt at her and shrieked, "Are you out of your fucking mind, Baker!"

"No!" Cindy screamed right back. "It's demeaning as hell!"

"I am telling you," Les seethed, appearing certain Cindy was not from the same planetary race as he, "I—know—this—guy!"

"I got that part," Cindy said, going flinty.

"No!" Les shouted so sharply she jumped. "I don't think you did. I'm saying I know him like no one else knows him, like no one ever will know him! Better than he knows himself. Better than I know myself!"

Fine, Cindy thought, noticing that a claque of cops had gathered to watch this unfolding soap opera from behind the double glass doors.

Red in his office, looking out his double single-hungs.

Cindy turned away, blocking them out. "Then why can't you find him?" she asked Les, as cruel as Cyndra Lynn Baker ever got.

"Because he's goddam smarter than I am, that's why," Les said with no attempt to mask his fear or respect. "Because he's better at this than I am, goddammit!" His glare, his entire mien, was like shards of broken mirror in desert sun.

Prone as Cindy was to taking people literally at their word, she said, "What do you mean better at it? Better at what?"

Les snapped a look at her, stewed darkly a moment, then said, softer, "You know what I mean."

"No, I don't," she said as a challenge.

Les stared another beat, as if contemplating a much-too-complicated answer—or shooting her with his vintage Ruger—then turned away. "Don't fuck with me, Baker. I'm not in the mood." Then he said again, as if she had, as if she could have, missed it, "I'm telling you, I know this guy. I *am* this guy."

Fine, Cindy thought again. "Then how is it he snuck up behind you and shot Predator without you noticing? Without you, if I may say so, ever having a fucking clue?"

Okay, she was capable of greater cruelty, after all.

"I don't know, goddammit!" Les howled. "And it scares the hell out of me. What was I doing, what was I thinking, how the hell did I let that happen? I don't know!"

He looked scared — for the third time in a month.

Shit. Bad things came in threes.

Les turned away then back. "But I do know this," he said, apparently resigned to some evolving new truth. "If I don't stop him, no one will."

Cindy stared a moment, trying not to show what she was thinking. *He really believes this shit.* Because, if he did, this was more disconcerting than the fear part. Megalomaniacs got themselves — and their partners — killed.

"All this?" Les said, gesturing at the mountains again, this time to indicate the cabin and the hanging tree. "He's putting me on notice."

Was that pleasure in his voice? Was he enjoying this? Had he lost what was left of his admittedly tenuous sanity entirely? This was, what, *fun* now? This... *this*!

As if answering Cindy's unspoken query, Les said, "In a way, it's a relief."

Ah, relief. It was a relief! So, why didn't Cindy feel relieved?

"Now, we know," Les explained. "It's like that old Leno bit. He's in the car with his mother and they have a flat, and his mother says to 'Check the battery, your father always checks the battery,' and he says, 'We have a flat tire, mom,' but she insists, so he gets out, opens the hood, comes back and tells her, 'Battery's fine, Ma, we got a flat,' and she says, 'Well, at least now we know.'" Les nodded. "Now, we know."

He paced some more then stopped. "It's personal, Baker," he concluded. "Always was. Now, it's just out in the open." Even worse, "And it ain't gonna stop until one of us is dead, because he ain't goin' to prison."

Did Les mean Riverbend wasn't going to prison because he wasn't going to let himself get caught or because Les was going to kill him first? Cindy preferred the former but asked about the latter.

Les said he meant the former but, regarding the latter, "We can only hope."

He nodded, as if agreeing with the voices in his head, and said, "There's no going back now, Baker. There's me, there's him, and there's a string of victims I will not be able to prevent no matter what I do. But there's a longer string after. Those I can prevent. Because I *am* going to stop him."

"Well, you're not going to do it alone," Cindy declared.

"I'll do it any goddam way I want, Missy!" Les exploded again, then turned away.

"You don't have to yell at me. I didn't kill anyone!" Cindy shouted after him, suddenly, acutely, aware again of the audience inside staring.

She wasn't sure, but it looked like they were exchanging bets.

Cindy settled on, "Just calm down."

"Just don't tell me the fuck what to do!" he yelled.

"Then don't fucking yell at me!" she yelled right back.

"Back off, Baker!" Les snarled. "Just back... fucking... the fuck... *off!*"

He put that I'm-nearly-out-of-control-so-don't-push-me male warning twist on it—the one that all sober women know not to challenge.

Cindy sighed heavily. "Les... all I'm saying is, it may seem personal to you—"

"Seem?" Les said. "*Seem?* The sick bastard carved my name in his most recent victim's torso!"

"Okay, it is personal!"

"You're goddam right it is!"

Cindy let a few beats pass, took a breath, then said what she really thinking. "Then maybe you should take yourself off the case."

Suddenly, the air around her took on the kind of chill that usually made her skin contract, that kind of polar breeze that produces goose bumps on an Inuit.

Les stepped in closed enough to fog her contacts. Cindy thought that if the sports fans inside were betting she'd be the first one to swing, they didn't know Les like she knew Les. He didn't care that she was a woman. That was one of main reasons she liked him, Missy or no Missy.

He said, "If you even hint at such a suggestion to anyone outside the two of us, I will hand you over to Riverbend personally to make sure I stay on this case."

Cindy processed this as quickly as she was able—and poorly, by her own estimation—finally sputtering, "You would do that?"

"You're damn right I would," Les said.

"After what he did to your wife and daughter? To that boy up there? To the fifteen or thirty or fifty others he's tortured and murdered and the fifty others we probably don't know about?"

"Because of all that! Yes!"

Okay, but, "Me?"

Cindy was Les's only friend in the whole world, with the possible exception of Fred Bondini, and they both knew it. "Les?" Cindy reiterated, "Me?"

Her voice was soft, but the hurt was loud.

Les had crossed a sacred line. He threw his head back. "No. Not you," he said, regret and apology falling over him like dismal rain. "I meant it... allegorically. Metaphorically. Whatever."

"You meant it as a threat," Cindy said. The sting of treason racked her voice.

Several quiet moments passed as the folks inside pressed against the glass, no doubt wishing they could hear what was going on.

Les looked at them then back at Cindy. "A misplaced threat," he said quietly. "I'm sorry. You're right. I should think about taking myself off the case."

Though Cindy had just suggested it, hearing it back sounded worse than anything anyone had ever said to her—even in a dream.

Chapter 24 – The Big Sky Proper

The voice that finally came from behind Les was soft and full of pain, but it was *his* pain, not Cindy's.

"No, you shouldn't," she said, recanting her suggestion that he leave the case. Now that she knew him better—or thought maybe she did—at least as well as anyone ever could—Cindy understood what quitting could do to Les Moore. What it *would* do to him.

"You'd never sleep another night," she said, knowing that was the very least of it. He didn't sleep now. She added with a small smile, "At least not until I caught him."

Les snorted the briefest of chuckles but didn't turn back.

"Don't worry, you're gonna get there first," Cindy assured him. "That's why you can't quit."

"I didn't say quit," Les said stolidly, turning back. "I said take myself off the case."

Cindy didn't like the lone wolf sound of that at all.

Les grunted—she hoped it was a chuckle—then he looked her over. "So, you won't say anything to Brinkman or the Old Man?"

Cindy said, "You don't think they saw it?" and nodded inside without looking.

Les shook his head. "It's different when it's your name carved into someone's body. You tend to notice little things like that."

"They might pick it up in DC," she pointed out.

"Not if some of the eight-by-tens got misplaced—say for a few years." Les's eyes were unflinching dark dots in a narrowing field of white.

Cindy blinked, otherwise motionless. Was Les asking her to do what she thought he was asking to do? Holding back evidence could mean censure, damaged promotion potential, maybe even suspension. Hell, they could both do hard time!

Cindy's strong inclination, based on her strong instincts for survival, was to pretend she never even heard him mention it—much less help him do it. But she didn't want to be out chasing Riverbend alone. And she knew that if Les Moore was off the case, Riverbend would never be found. How many more would he kill, and could that number even be counted?

Cindy knew without thinking any further that looking the other way while Les *misplaced* a few photographs was probably best for everyone—the Bureau, the nation, even Cindy—and being a part of the team that brought down Riverbend could undo a lot of censures, even strong ones. He was right again. *Dammit.*

"Okay," Cindy said. "But I don't know anything about it."

"Didn't think you did," Les said, finally allowing a full smile—and a caveat. "It's just in case."

"Well, whatever," Cindy grumbled. "They were all there the last time I looked, if anyone ever asks."

This shit definitely wasn't in the manual. That damn book was as sorely lacking as Cindy's sex life had been up until about a week ago. And look how that turned out!

Les nodded. "Fair enough." Still smiling, he started to walk away.

"Wait," Cindy ordered. "You have to promise me two things."

Cindy wasn't sure Les would even agree to hear her out—much less promise anything—but she had to say what had to be said.

After the usual interminably long Les-moment, he said, steadily, "Go ahead." His smile had dissolved like salt in hot water.

"One," Cindy said, fighting a tremble. "You will never think of me as anything other than your biggest supporter and best friend in this world, and thus, you will never speak to me like you did here today. Ever again."

Les said, "Is that one or two things? It sounded like both of them."

"Two," Cindy continued, avoiding his avoidance. "You will bring me along."

When Les didn't look like he fully understood what she was getting at, Cindy clarified. "I want to be there with you when you find him, Les. I don't want to be sitting somewhere alone, worrying about you. We're partners, like it or not."

She wiped a tear before it appeared and said, "I care about you, okay?" Then, an irony struck her. "In fact, I may be the only one other than Riverbend who does."

Les looked long and hard, as he always did, then grunted, "So, I read," obviously referring to her thesis paper, and turned away as if taking in the Montana majesty.

Then, something made him grin. He turned back to face her and said, "Okay. Done, partner." Then he said, "Lunch?" apparently finished with the whole thing.

Cindy had to admire Les's ability to move on—at least in conversation—but there was, "One more thing."

Les's newfound comity vanished. "You said two, which I think was actually three."

Cindy nodded. "This takes precedent over all of them."

"But I didn't agree to hear three. Bad things come in threes."

"Good things, too," she said, burying her own superstition.

"But usually bad things," he said, positively negative.

"Goddammit, Les! Do you have to make absolutely everything as difficult as possible? Just shut up and listen. You owe me that much. And anyway, by your count, this would be four. Christ."

Les sighed. "Go on." Any less enthusiasm and someone would have needed to check his wrist for a pulse.

Cindy almost didn't want to tell him now, but figured she had to, for a number of reasons. One, she'd made up her mind to clear the air (even if she thought what she was about to say was obvious); two, she wanted to see his reaction (even if she might not be able to read it); three, it might help with this sticky SKK problem she was experiencing (even if nothing else was); and four... *Aw, hell.*

"I'm completely and ridiculously in love with you."

***

Les didn't move again until he saw Cindy drive away with Red Stimson in his big, county-owned 4x4. Only then was he able to recall what had actually happened.

"Jesus, what the hell was I thinking?" Cindy had said, tears streaming, when Les stood there like a puppet without a petrified hand up its ass, lifeless, useless. "The only room you have for love is for the love you have for the hate you feel for Riverbend," she had said. "There's nothing left for anyone or anything else. Is there?"

Les hadn't moved. Hadn't blinked. He was pretty sure his heart had stopped, so he didn't bother breathing.

Cindy then sucked in the rest of the tears, along with what was left of her pride, and said, "I wasn't asking for anything in return."

Les continued to stare. He couldn't think, couldn't speak. He wasn't sure he was actually awake, even alive. Maybe this was one of those dreams Cindy always talked about, and he was in it. Because it was one thing to imagine it, her saying that, something like it, but something else altogether to hear it right there, so stark and out in the open.

Love. The word sent him into full paralysis.

"Okay, I'll settle for the first two and go get our stuff," Cindy had said. "Save you the blank stares inside. I'll get a ride back with Red— Sheriff Stimson—if we're done here."

Les remembered feeling about as opaque as new glass. He nodded then, and she walked into the station. Odd, he thought—standing alone in the driveway staring at the colorful flowers but seeing no color, gazing up at the formidable mountains but seeing no form—how being told something so life-affirming in the midst of life-denying acts of such unsurpassed cruelty as to defy definition could produce such utter devastation.

The world hadn't felt this heavy, this slowed down, since he buried Marjorie and Melissa Ann. Maybe this was even worse, he wasn't sure. Cindy was the first person since they had died to say she loved him. She blurted it out in the parking lot of a police station in Montana, under the Big Sky proper, after seeing his name engraved in a dead college kid named Jerry Carver. *Yep.* When life got weird for Les Moore, it went off the chart.

***

Around midnight, Les was finishing a bottle of Chivas by himself. A concerned bartender at Bette's Butte-E Saloon called Sheriff Red who arrived just as a fairly large cowboy insinuated that the FBI was full of incompetent mindless bureaucrats, most of them "pussy-boys." Les flattened him, much to the surprise of his smaller saddle buddies. Red interceded before the riot started and drove Les back to the hotel. He had his deputy follow in the rental Explorer.

"This stuff can eat right through a man's soul, if he's not careful," Red said at one point. The ride had been otherwise quiet. "I suppose he needs to try and push it back every now and then."

Les stared straight ahead, eyes drooping. Red wondered if Les even heard him.

Then Red said, "She's a pretty lady. Good woman."

Les looked over in a liquored fog—no doubt wondering how much Cindy had said on her ride with Red—then turned away to watch the ten-horse western town sliding by.

Red never took his eyes off the road.

"You married long, Sheriff?" Les said after a while, his compound consonants starting to slur.

"Thirty-six years," Red said with a mixture of pride for his bride as much as for his own endurance.

Les nodded wearily. "Well, lemme tell you..." Day school clowns danced past on a painted fence. "It can end too fast."

"Marriage?" Red asked.

"Everything," Les said.

A block later, he pulled himself up in the seat as much as he could and said, "I'll walk the rest of the way."

"I don't think that'd be a good idea, Agent Moore," Red said.

"I'm just drunk, Sheriff. I'm not a menace to society or myself. Don't even have my gun. Left it in the hotel safe. Just need some air."

He was swaying, stinking, and not a sight Red Stimson particularly wanted wandering around his jurisdiction, but he could see the hotel roof up ahead and figured even someone as plastered as Les could make it that far without incident. Hopefully, he was telling the truth about his service weapon.

He pulled over, though he took a few hundred feet to do it.

Les mumbled a thank you, opened the door and spilled ass over teacup onto the sidewalk. "I'm all right, I'm all right," he said, pulling himself up quickly. "Hit a slick spot." He laughed, thanked Red for the ride, and staggered toward the hotel.

Red heaved a deep sigh. He'd seen many a drunk in his day—too many—and it was something he'd come to detest. But when a man with Les's background, his record, his history—most men don't create an actual history in their lifetime—needed to get inebriated just shy of a coma to stay even, Red was willing to let it be. He waved his deputy alongside.

"Make sure those boys don't find him again before he gets inside and settled," Red said. "He might kill every one of 'em, and I don't need that mess. I got reelection comin' up. I'll keep an eye."

The deputy nodded and followed far enough back that his sloshed charge wouldn't know he was there. But at the hotel, Les turned and waved directly at him before going through the "Welcome to Holiday Express" doors. The deputy waved back wanly, parked the rental up front, walked the four blocks home and turned in.

Red Stimson had a hard time sleeping that night. He held his Rosalee closer than he had in years.

***

A bleary-eyed Cindy answered Les's knock on her door a half hour later. She had dozed off not two minutes before, following a torturous evening of feeling foolish and unprofessional—scanning the parking lot every five minutes for the rental 4x4.

The stench of scotch nearly knocked her over.

No words were said, and neither would remember whose tears came first, but she helped him in, closed the door, and told the desk to hold all calls, no matter what—or refer them to Les's room. Then she turned off both their phones.

Les cried himself to sleep in Cindy's arms just before four a.m., having talked nonstop the entire time. He'd given her an earful. A headful. Cindy wouldn't drift off until daybreak.

The beast was loose.

Chapter 25 – A New Man

Cindy came out of the bathroom quickly, but the ringing hotel phone had already awakened Les. He rolled over and stretched, still in his dark blue suit. The annoying *Bleedle-eedle-eedle-eedle-eedle... Bleedle-eedle-eedle-eedle-eedle* continued.

"Aren't you gonna answer that?" he said to her.

The suit was a Hugo Boss, though Les sometimes wore vintage black he had picked up here and there at estate sales and twice-around stores—Italian, with narrow lapels; the kind agents wore in the Bureau's Glory Days—just to be camp. Thin ties and a stern brow.

Without getting anywhere near the ringing phone, Cindy said, "It's Brinkman," and went to choose an outfit for the day, something casual for cowboy country. "I ordered 'No calls for any reason whatsoever until further notice.'"

The *bleedling* finally stopped.

Les started to get up. "You know," he said, "I could get to like you."

His head throbbed just enough to jar his memory—the walk, the bar, the fight, the ride with Red, knocking at her door, spilling his guts—

Cindy was telling him, "That isn't what you said last night." The wink in her voice sent a turbid wave of doubt rolling over Les's ache.

"What did I say?" he asked grimly, throwing open mental files only to find them empty or ransacked.

"If you can't remember, I'm not helping." Boy, was she happy!

Les looked around. The other queen-size was still made but mussed. His Hugo was rumpled, his fly down; fortunately, his boss was not out. Still, he had to wonder, "Did we sleep in the same bed?"

Cindy said they hadn't.

"It's probably best," he decided.

"I don't think it would have mattered much," Cindy said, settling on jeans and a loose white shirt. She wasn't being mean, just honest.

Les nodded. He'd drunk nearly a fifth. "What else did I say?"

Cindy leaned down with a sweet morning smile, fresh from a shower. "Keep working on it," she encouraged, and gave him a kiss on the cheek.

"You smell good," he said.

"You smell awful," she replied cheerfully, then went into the bathroom to flick on some makeup. "You might want to get moving, it's almost noon."

Les hadn't checked his Rolex but groaned when he did and got up. Apparently, another memorable night had taken him into its warm embrace then cast him aside. Whatever was lost was also probably best that way. Some things didn't need knowing.

***

In less than twenty minutes, back in his room, Les looked and smelled like a new man, even if he didn't feel like one.

In the shower, he remembered telling Cindy about his "failed marriage" — significant because he had never referred to that union as such. He'd always given the impression to anyone who asked — even if they didn't ask — that his marriage to Marjorie was perfect in every way. In reality, he'd known she cheated on him over a period of four years prior to her death.

With a cop, no less. A uniform.

Les had also heralded Melissa Ann as the ideal teenager, the perfect daughter, even though she had stopped talking to him when she was thirteen and stopped looking at him at fourteen.

"Acting out," the kid-shrink had categorized, with all the tenability of a deaf-mute doing karaoke. What a winner he had turned out to be; busted six months later for swapping kiddie-porn on the web — unclebob@hotteen. Marjorie blamed Les. Melissa Ann sunk deeper.

Les never said a word in his own defense — his guilt was so all-encompassing — and continued on as he had. He felt that one of their daughter's parents needed to be an adult, at least act like one, as boring and repellent as Melissa Ann might find it. Marjorie thought not, stating unequivocally her newfound relationship with her daughter.

"We're best friends again!" she would tell Les on their way to a slasher-flick or a bubblegum Slurpee.

What Melissa Ann didn't know, what only Les and his wife's parents knew (remarkably, they never blamed Les for any of what happened) was that Marjorie had never rebelled as a child or young adult. Then, facing forty, eighteen snuck up on her and sunk its teeth deep. Suddenly she had, "A ginormous amount of catching up to do."

So, Mom began dressing as daughter, shopping in the Young Miss stores. "Hanging out." Lots of "Oh, your mom's so cool," in the mall, and, "Yeah, I wish my mom was like her instead of so boring and hateful."

Marjorie wore halter tops and midriff-less shirts, funky hats, and cheap colorful earrings. She got her belly button pierced, her hair lightened and spiked, and started listening to alternative stations — watching MTV and understanding it, saying the youngish on-air hosts were "cute" and "hot." She talked about getting a tattoo. "Maybe a bitch goddess," she threatened Les, and laughed, but didn't follow through.

Thankfully.

Still, the post-adolescent transformation from ideal FBI wife to high school slut-again was something to behold, with poor Melissa Ann having nowhere to go but down. Mom was out-rebelling her.

Then Marjorie took to alcohol and pills, staying locked up in the guest room for days at a time after Officer Easy dumped her for a real high-schooler. Melissa Ann finally found a way to win by losing her virginity on a soggy mattress behind the AMC-16 — then losing the baby seven weeks later to pneumonia. So the doctors said.

So Marjorie said.

She then withdrew into a Judy Garland world of fuzzy self-deceit, drugs, and perpetually unavailable dreams. Melissa Ann checked out completely. Both of them blamed Les. The hatred had cut deep. Still, Les never uttered an uncharitable word about either.

Until last night.

Les stood naked, dripping, staring into the hotel bathroom mirror, remembering the day everything changed — the day Riverbend won round one and Les was nearly lost forever. How then-Captain Fred Bondini had stopped Les a few hundred feet from the Riverbend Bridge advising, "You might not want to see this." Less than a year had passed since Melissa Ann lost the baby.

Les assured Bondini he'd be fine and Bondini, against his better judgment, let Les pass. But when Les saw the nude bodies of his wife and daughter there in the woods by the Great Curve of the Black River, virtually bloodless after having been bled to death in Riverbend's rig, antique yellow ribbons around their necks, Les threw up—for the first time in all his years of law enforcement—and couldn't stop. He then screamed until he passed out, having blown a blood vessel in his head.

When he awoke in ICU, Fred Bondini was there. What the major-to-be saw in Les's eyes would haunt him to the end—that killer's cool, the void. The darkest place where no sane man goes and from which no man returns unchanged. He said those very words to Les, and Les nodded. Nodded because it was all true.

"Guilt like that'll get a man killed," Bondini had warned. "Sooner or later."

Les replied, "Better late than never," and Bondini walked out.

It seemed like another lifetime and a few seconds ago all at once. That sensation never left Les Moore once in three-plus years. All of it changed after a bottle of Chivas Regal and a midnight confessional in a motel in Montana when Special Agent Cyndra Lynn Baker held him close, nodded and said, "You're probably right."

A weight lifted instantly. Because no matter how many times Bondini, or Les's few remaining friends or fellow agents, or the damn string of endless Bureau shrinks, or anyone else assured Les it wasn't his fault, and no matter how many times Les nodded and agreed with them, saying he knew it wasn't... he knew it was. Given the choice, and Les was given the choice many times, he had always chosen career over family. Then he paid for it in a way no one ever wants to pay for anything.

Cindy had listened and accepted his grief, acknowledged his implicit guilt. She said, Yes, you are in pain and Yes, you are at least somewhat responsible. Yes, you could have made better decisions, and Yes, you have a right to blame yourself. All without saying a word.

She had simply agreed.

It took that for Les to be able to say, finally. "But I'm not completely responsible. I can see that now." Pain must be felt to do any good.

As he toweled off and dressed the morning after, looking out his window at the steadfast green mountains, actually seeing them for the first time, Les thought that to feel as good as he did after a night like the one before, he must have told Cindy a lot; must have bared his soul. Up to then, a mildly busy pattern on the sheets would keep him awake most of the night. But last night, this morning, he had lain unconscious till noon.

Something definitely felt different. Les couldn't put his finger on it, but he knew it was there. He felt lighter, better, *happier*. He just wasn't sure he was ready for happy.

***

When Les sauntered into the lobby fifteen minutes later wearing Levis, a plaid Pendleton, and some Tony Lamas, all new, looking strikingly at home against the rugged emerald hills outside the tall windows, Cindy was taken aback.

"Where'd you get those?"

She could not recall ever seeing a man look so sexy — especially in *cowboy crap*.

"Yesterday. After we..." Les flipped his hand around.

Cindy concluded, "Had our little discussion at the police station? In front of God and everybody?" Les nodded, though he didn't look like he thought she needed the embellishment. "You went shopping to make yourself feel better?" she said. This was too good to be true.

Les said squeamishly, "I guess you could say that."

"I've died and gone to Girl Heaven," Cindy proclaimed, then came over and put her arm through his. "You look great."

Les stared at the floor.

"You don't have to respond," she said. "It's a common, everyday unsolicited compliment. People make and accept them all the time."

"Well, in that case," Les said, "thank you. Takes some of the pressure off."

Cindy was about to nuzzle him when a cranky old voice said, "Oh, you're back."

Cindy yanked her arm out of Les's to find the crotchety day clerk scuffling in from the back room with the day's mail. She started to cover with, "Oh no, we weren't—"

"—planning to come back," Les interceded, composure instantly at the ready. "But I forgot my wallet." Cindy glanced at Les, but he kept his gaze on the clerk.

The old guy looked them both over a moment, probably thinking they didn't lie too well for FBI agents, then said, "You've had a few calls," and started to get the pink slips from their boxes.

"We'll pick them up later," Les said. And started for the door.

The old man protested that, "A few of 'em was fairly insistent."

"Well..." Les opened the door for Cindy "... if he calls back, tell him you've spoken to a lawyer and you're considering a federal suit for harassment and verbal assault on the grounds of dissemination of fallacious information for the purpose of threat."

Cindy saw the old man's cogitator working — then he made notes.

***

When Phil Brinkman called again, five minutes later, screaming to the high heavens about the clerk having let his agents leave without calling him back, the old guy calmly read back the prescribed remedy.

Brinkman was silenced — for five seconds. He then let go a debasing tirade about "Ignorant, redneck, boonie cowpokes taking advice from fat-headed federal employees headed for censure," which ended with, "Now put one of them on the goddam phone, you fallacious old fool!"

After a few quiet seconds, the old man said, "Go fuck yourself, you Washington dickhead," and hung up.

***

After a late breakfast, Les told a somber Red Stimson, "Oh, it's Riverbend, all right. That isn't the question."

They were back in Stimson's County Sheriff's Department building, a squat gray affair that stuck out like a dandy at a dude ranch due to its modern civic design — sharp angles and polished floors, a hip roof of dark slate over pale blue block walls.

"What is?" Red asked, no doubt wondering what other question there could be and how Les could possibly be so chipper considering the condition he was in the last time Red saw him.

"How to stop him," Les said matter-of-factly.

He walked off to review the material spread out in Red's conference room, looking for that little something he had missed — the same drill in Florida, Seattle, or the Pitt. Where did the Killer slip up? *How* did he slip up? And would they be lucky enough to find it and figure it out, all the while knowing the answer was probably no, they wouldn't.

"Did the body go out this morning?" Cindy asked Red.

"On the early commuter flight," he said. "Johnnie got him delivered on time. Should be in Quantico by this evening. If you want the specifics, John can tell you. He called ahead like you asked."

"No, that's fine. Thank you," Cindy said.

"When should we get some answers?" Red wondered.

"Day or two on the prelim' stuff," Cindy said. "Few weeks on the details and DNA fine points. Anything that matters, anyway."

Not that there would be anything, she was thinking.

Red nodded. They both watched Les poring over the evidence files on Red's conference table as if unaware of the world beyond. "Interesting guy," Red said.

"Yeah," Cindy smiled, never taking her eyes off Les. "Isn't he?"

***

Les and Cindy spent the rest of the afternoon with faces buried in files, then ate an early supper and slipped in the back way to avoid the front desk and messages.

Brinkman.

They split up for the night to rest, and Cindy fell asleep in a chair reading *Vogue* in her bra and panties. She figured she was allowed an occasional girl thing. Two minutes later, she peeled off the underwear. Much better.

The knock on her door at 11:50 sent her flailing onto the carpet. She threw a robe on and peered woozily out the peephole. "Jesus, what now?" she said aloud and opened the door.

"Feel like a midnight stroll?" Les asked, wide awake.

Cindy thought a moment, then said, "Not really," and yawned.

Les said innocently, "Not even to a burned-out cabin in the woods?" and obviously saw the lights flip on behind Cindy's drooping eyelids. "Shall I wait in the lobby?"

"Ten minutes," Cindy said. Then she flashed him and closed the door.

The night manager downstairs wondered why Les was smiling so but knew better than to ask. He'd worked motels most of his life.

***

Driving out the hardtop, Les commented on the good surface, recently repaved with good, crisp lines. Once they hit dirt and drove a distance, Cindy said she didn't remember the unpaved part being so long. Otherwise, neither agent had much to say, lost in their own thoughts and fantasies—which did not exclude the possibility of running into Riverbend out in the woods in the deep of night. At the logging run turnoff, both Cindy and Les simultaneously and discreetly felt for their weapons.

On the trail up from where the logging road ended a quarter mile below the burnt-out cabin, the bright moonlight was as luminous and sharp as Cindy had ever seen. Had they been out in the open, rather than in these pine woods, night would have seemed day.

Looking up through the broken canopy of tall conifers, Cindy could see that the big silvery-white disk was shy only the thinnest sliver of being full, and wondered if tomorrow night it might be a sliver past full, and did that ever hap—

"Don't stare at the light source," Les said quietly. "Use your peripheral."

Cindy blanched and ground her molars. Caught! Basic training, first-year stuff. Over the years, sunlight damages the center of the retina—the sides remain more sensitive, but provide less detail to the brain, just movement and shapes. Enough to save your ass in the dark.

If you remember to use it and don't stare directly at a light source on a dark night.

"If a subject should happen to be waiting in the dark for you," her Basic Field Tactics instructor told the class of new recruits, "you'd be giving him the upper hand for a few seconds. That could mean your or your partner's life."

Cindy muttered some silent self-recrimination, hating like hell to have to be reminded of something so rudimentary, and stopped taking in the sights. Now, she watched Les to see if he would pull his weapon. He didn't. Almost as if he knew Riverbend wouldn't be there.

Of course, someone else might be—and someone was.

Les's nine came out so quickly and invisibly as to defy natural law. Cindy followed suit.

"FBI!" he said clearly and loudly, one hand on his gun pointed ahead and one hand waving Cindy back behind a tree. She had no idea her pulse could accelerate so quickly.

Les commanded the unseen intruder, "Come out with your hands up. Now!"

Cindy could see nothing, hear nothing. How did he even know someone was there? She tried using her *fucking peripheral vision*, but her retinal lining was bleached from the moon and *totally fucking useless!* "Who is it?" she whispered.

"I don't know," Les whispered back.

Cindy checked behind them, in case the intruder wasn't alone, but she saw only dark night and moon shadows and trees.

She hoped they were trees.

"Want me to circle around?" she asked almost silently.

"No," Les whispered, moving his head around to detect any form or movement in the darkness. When he could discern none, he shouted, "I'm going to fire a warning shot to let you know we're armed. I won't be firing directly at you."

Because we don't know where you are!

Cindy fingered her trigger. This would be the first time she had ever used her weapon in a situation. *A situation!*

Cindy felt her heart slowing, her breath regulating, her mind coming into incredibly sharp focus—like those yogis who slow down their metabolism with a single thought. Maybe she was born to this after all.

Faith in herself restored, Cindy let her finger find the side of the trigger guard, her fingertip feeling its way to the Glock's safety tab in the center of the divided trigger.

Cindy remembered her weapons coach's warning to, "Never ever stick a Glock down your pants. It's too easy to shoot your nuts off. Or your lips."

He had looked directly at Cindy when he said the second part, but she didn't take it personally. She didn't want to blow her labia away by going gangsta and forgetting about Glock's proprietary "safe action system," that allowed for quick reaction time, but not for street stupidity. "Remember that football idiot," he had said, shaking his head. Cindy remembered—especially the blood stain on his sweatpants. On the news.

Les moved slightly. Did he see something? Hear something?

Pay attention!

And remember to count, Cindy reminded herself. Seventeen was the magic number. After that...

Cindy felt for her extra clip. Had she forgotten it? Of course not. The clip sat high on her hip. Had she remembered to load it? *Of course! Concentrate!* Her spare clips were never unloaded. The optional seventeen round clip. Seventeen plus seventeen.

Where are they? Who are they?

Crap! Somebody jump out and start blasting so we can get this over with!

Les shouted into the darkness, "I'm going to count backwards from three. Then I'm going to fire."

Was this in the manual? Had Cindy missed this tactic somewhere? Or was this just more Les Moore, doing it His Way? Yeah, he was a real Frank Sinatra out in the field. The woods.

His stage.

Cindy cradled the base of the Glock stock into her right palm and wrapped her fingers up and around the back of her left hand. For a moment—always when she raised her weapon—Cindy remembered being the only lefty in her class and how her next instructor, Lancaster Budrow, from Baton Rouge, had encouraged her time and time again to learn to shoot right-handed. "Reglah," as he called it. He said her "sco-ahs" were sure to climb. But righty didn't feel natural to her, so Cindy shot the way she wrote, left-handed.

"Three," Les said, loud and clear.

Cindy ran her mental checklist. finger on the trigger's edge, backup clip ready, gun cradled, feet apart, knees slightly bent, breathing out, relaxed. But... ready to kill?

"Two."

Les's muzzle flash would give away their position. Then what? Encountering bad guys in the field, in a dark wood where you weren't certain what you were shooting, or whom, or even where, wasn't anything at all like standing in front of a large-screen TV in Quantico with a Nintendo gun in your hand, or even with a real one on The Course.

Even if you were extra amped-up back then, somewhere in the back of your mind you knew your assailants weren't real—not Riverbend—and you wouldn't die, not firing blanks. But here, they'd be live rounds, fired to end a life—an imposing responsibility with potentially irrevocable consequences. Was Cindy ready to kill? Could she do it?

The answer came bright as the almost-full moon. *Yes.* The feeling was unmistakable — like nothing Cyndra Baker had ever felt before. A clear-headedness, empowering yet portentous. Precisely what Budrow had predicted, should the day come.

The day had come tonight.

Cindy clutched her calm and held it close, finger slipping across the trigger, ready and willing to pull if she had to.

"One!" Les said with sharp finality.

There came a quick, "That won't be necessary!" from the shadows.

The agents shared a look. The voice was female, and not entirely unfamiliar. So, when the young female videographer from Iowa stepped into the moonlight, both agents sighed unison relief. No one would have to die tonight.

Cindy put her gun away, all wound up with nowhere to go — and vented.

"What the fucking hell are you doing out here in the middle of the fucking night? You're damn lucky Agent Moore here isn't trigger happy or you'd be the next star of your own goddam video series!"

Mild for Cindy, but the already shaken girl was further unnerved. She'd experienced Cindy's wrath once before and likely had no desire to go there again.

"I'm sorry," she said softly, honestly.

"It's all right," Les assured her, holstering his weapon.

"It goddam isn't all right, either!" Cindy growled. "She scared the shit outa me!"

Then, thinking a few beats down the line, Cindy warned the motionless girl, "And that you keep to yourself. Or I'll bring charges of negligent invasion of a crime site with intent to commit..."

Les let Cindy sweat a moment before helping out with, "Criminal pejorative hindrance."

Cindy glared at him.

Les said, "And it was going so well." He had that irritating smirk in his voice.

Cindy hated when Les was onto her before she was onto herself. "I was going to say... malfeasance. I was quoting the malfeasance... ordinance."

"Oh right. The malfeasance ordinance," Les said. "Six-oh-four-one-dash-A, I think."

The girl could likely see Les's grin in the dim light. She had to have heard it. But she kept her mouth shut.

Cindy turned away in a huff, muttering something generally profane, so Les turned to the girl and said, "She's got a point."

"I wanted night video," the girl said. "For my portfolio."

Cindy spun back. "Your portfolio?" she barked, incredulous. "As in resumé?"

The girl protested, "It's how I get work!"

Cindy scoffed, "And it'll make a dandy student film, as well."

"Documentary," the girl said, thoroughly offended and maybe even hurt. "I thought you liked my work."

True, but, "That's beside the point, isn't it?" Cindy snarled. "The point is you, out here, at a taped-off crime site, again, in the middle of the night, with no jurisdiction from anyone. Isn't it?"

Clearly not a question at all.

"I have permission," the girl said quietly, surprising both agents.

"From whom?" Cindy demanded, eyes narrowing. There was that other thing she hated going around her.

"Mr. Brinkman? In Washington?" the girl said with Valley girl emphasis.

Darkness thankfully diminished the flare around Cindy's eyes as she tried to process this baffling revelation—only to find her mind sputtering like a chainsaw with water in the fuel-mix.

She opted out. "You deal with this," she said to Les and walked away.

Les said, "Okay," but Cindy could hear burlesque in the word. She gritted her teeth and kept walking—probably for the car, though she wasn't sure yet.

Montana was a big state.

***

Les said nothing for several moments, giving the girl some squirm-time. Even in the thin, fractured moonlight, she knew that her usual facade of control had been shredded like bare knuckles on a new grater after having almost been shot.

Finally, Les said, "Okay, here's the deal. We get first-generation dupes of everything you shoot anywhere, anything to do with us or our cases, automatically, without asking, you mail 'em off, pronto."

There was something both soothing and frightening about Les Moore, the way he said things and looked at you. Through you. A chill ran from the base of the girl's spine to her skull and back down with an awful tickle right in the middle. She ran fingertips across goose bumps risen in the night—not from the cold.

"Okay," she said, not about to bargain.

"No copies of copies or I subpoena your masters," Les stipulated.

"With HD that doesn't really apply," the girl said, wondering how old this handsome agent was really. "But understood and agreed to."

Les regarded her a moment. "Anyone ever tell you you talk like a lawyer?"

"It's my minor," she admitted.

"A crime-scene film-making lawyer. Boggles the mind." Les looked up at the cabin ashes.

"My parents don't get it either," the girl complained.

"I didn't say I didn't get it," he said. "I said it boggles the mind."

He turned back. "They mind you're gay?"

Those bumps ran the length of her arm again. She felt them on her back and thighs, inside her jeans. "I'm not gay," she said with an intentional edge. Used to it.

Les continued his unbroken gaze but said nothing.

Figuring there was no upside in lying to this guy, this FBI agent, she sighed then said, if reluctantly, "I'm bisexual. I know it's *tres* fashionable these days, but I can't help it. I like everyone. But I'm not promiscuous." She made sure to sound emphatic.

Les nodded, looked off and listened. Cindy had apparently gone back to the car. He turned back. "You think Agent Baker's attractive?"

The girl paused, considering many aspects of the question, then gave a *comme ci, comme ça* look. "Yeah, I guess. When she's not being mean."

Les grinned as if agreeing then asked, "Get anything so far?"

She knew he meant video. "No. I just got here."

"Well, let's have a look." He indicated for her to lead the way up to the cabin remains.

Before moving, she said, "You knew I was going to be here, didn't you?" Les shrugged, noncommittally. "How'd you know?" she wondered.

"Brinkman called," Les said without hesitation and started up the path without her.

This time, the bumps went from her head to her toes and back three times in less than a second. She couldn't recall ever feeling goose bumps on the roof of her mouth. The palms of her hands. Maybe it was hives.

She had lied about Brinkman. His was just a name she'd caught from one of her sources—some tyrannical asshole every agent in the field avoided talking to at all costs. He should have been a safe bet. How could he have called Agent Moore? Were they all psychic?

When they reached the pile of blackened rubble, Les asked her name. "Shannon," she said, waiting a beat to add her last name. "Creamer."

Les gave her a look she was used to getting, but all he said was, "Get much crap for it in school?"

"Enough to fill a body bag," she said.

***

Down the hill, Cindy thought that craving a cigarette was a bad sign—she hadn't smoked since eleventh grade—but the nicotine torture only lasted a few minutes. The moment she heard their voices moving, so was she. This time she would ignore the moon.

As bizarre as it seemed to Cindy in hindsight, the three of them stayed out at the crime site until well after two in the morning, shooting footage for Shannon's piece on *The Cycle*. At one point, Cindy sat on Les's shoulders, clamping a schmooze-light onto a charred sapling while Shannon directed from the ground, on her back, under the bloody crucifixion tree, all of them laughing. As bubbly as pink champagne New Year's.

That was when Red Stimson's young patrol cop came up on them with his gun out. Finding someone out here at the death cabin in the middle of the night had nearly scared his skin clear. His voice was still quivering when he asked, truly put out, "What in hell are you doing out here at almost three in the mornin', Agent Moore?"

After hearing the explanation, and reholstering, he said he'd have to call it in. He was right to, but the kid obviously felt embarrassed and insisted that he owed the Feds an explanation. "They told me to run by and make sure no one was tampering with the evidence," he said as he turned down for his car.

Tampering. Les and Cindy nodded.

***

After putting Cindy to bed around six, Les said he felt like a Danish and some milk. Cindy said he didn't look like either and rolled over to pass out with a soft smile on her face. Les kissed her hair, turned out the light, and went to pick up messages.

He couldn't ignore Brinkman forever.

Downstairs, he found a young girl behind the desk, teasing her hair to a peak higher than the "No Out of State Checks" sign on the wall behind her. Les asked where the old coot was and she said he'd called in sick from Ferdy's Tackle out on County 1540, by the lake, to say he was taking a week. She hadn't thought he looked sick.

Les grinned, took the messages, and went into the coffee shop for his cow-juice and breakfast bun. He only got through three messages before he canceled his order and made plane reservations.

Chapter 26 – Everyone's a Suspect

Les and Cindy stared down at Helen Miller's body, half-submerged in black Everglades muck, the dark blue cocktail dress from the pale blue garment bag bunched up around her abdomen—matching clutch and shoes off to one side. The Diamonds in the Raw waitress's throat had been slit from ear to ear; her eyes, tongue, and female organs gouged with something jagged and mean. Her implants had been sliced out and tossed aside, metal bar still in the nipple of what was left of her deflated breast—for ID, no doubt—and she had been scalped, a savage sight meant to send a message to someone.

Someone got it loud and clear.

"Goddammit!" Les shouted with surprising sharpness. Broward County Sheriff's deputies turned away.

"I'm sorry, Les," Cindy said quietly, knowing it wouldn't help any, but she had to say something. She felt—being here, seeing this, seeing him see this—like gravity had suddenly tripled. Maybe it was the heat or the humidity. Maybe she was coming down with something. Maybe it was all this goddam endless barbarity and suffering.

At least there were no yellow ribbons.

"It was for me, wasn't it?" Cindy said, looking down at the blue dress, blackened with crusted blood and chunky loam. "You went back and gave it to her after I was such a bitch."

Now she knew.

Les turned away. None of that mattered now. A girl was dead: his informant, an innocent, a friend. He stared off, seemingly without emotion.

Cindy knew better. "We'll get him," she said, trying to be positive in the mire of hate and homicide, lost dreams. She felt sorry for the girl, but almost sorrier for Les. You tried not to take each bit of human loss personally, out in the field, but it was hard; on the rare occasion you had actually met a victim before his or her demise, virtually impossible.

A sheriff's deputy came over with some paperwork. "Strip Killer, probably," he said, then nodded at the body. "She worked at—"

"It wasn't him," Les said flatly.

The deputy didn't know Les. He started quoting facts and figures and—

"It wasn't him!" Les shouted so loudly all work stopped.

Every face turned. The deputy went cold. Les looked at him with lifeless eyes and said softly, "It couldn't be." He walked away.

Cindy felt the need to explain her partner, at least his thought process—at least try. "She wasn't a stripper. She was a waitress."

The deputy weighed what she was saying. He was middle-aged, no rookie. Thick around the waist but still fit. He knew what he'd seen and heard, what the stats were. He looked the decomposing body over, then Cindy, then posited that the Killer, "Could've made a mistake."

"These guys don't make mistakes," Cindy said, remembering Pittsburgh and how everyone thought The Slasher had made a mistake with the first doctor, thinking she was a nurse, Holy Dick throwing elbows this way and the other to be at the head of that line.

The deputy's eyes narrowed. He looked after Les, retreating to their most recent loaner, a deep red, downsized Dodge. "He always like this?"

"No."

"I guess you're happy as a clam about that."

"Not really," Cindy said to the hardened veteran. "At least he's still got feelings."

***

Les had parked their Miami Bureau loaner on top of the dike with the rest of the law enforcement and press vehicles. The sky shone clear to the east, but out to the west a storm was building, high and dark. The rain would be here soon if the nervous air was any indicator.

Cindy got in the passenger side of the crimson four-door, sat quietly a moment, then said, "Les—"

He cut her off. "You know why I listen to Sinatra?"

"The Francis thing?"

Les hadn't expected an answer, especially that one; he realized right then how he had never thought about it before, both of them being Francises. But that wasn't it.

"No," he said. "Because he's perfect. It's all wrapped up tight when he sings. The pain, the pleasure, the pointlessness. The joy, the beauty, the tragedy. The getting out while you still can. All that Live Hard, Die Young stuff. The whole phony self-indulged Sixties Las Vegas Hollywood Rat Pack mythology. James Dean.

"Only Frank didn't go. He stayed past his welcome. Even when he couldn't remember the words, up there looking like a fool when he knew he was embarrassing himself and his audiences, sullying his good name, his legend, he wouldn't get off the stage. His own family was telling him it was time to go, but he wouldn't. He couldn't. He wasn't done yet."

Les nodded, agreeing with his own assessment. "You've got to respect that in a man. The willingness to go on even when he knows there's no point in it anymore. When he starts doing more harm than good, even to himself. You have to respect such self-destruction on a grand scale.

"The grandest," Les chuckled, more to himself. "You spend your whole life building it up then tear it down right in front of everyone. Jesus." He shook his head with admiration and lament.

"But it's because he knew something they didn't. After you're gone, the soured memories fade, and there will remain your best work. That's what they'll carry with them and talk about."

He looked out at the massive thunderheads, white and defiant.

"They'll even forgive you embarrassing yourself and them because, goddammit, you took it right to the limit. Right to the bitter fucking end. They had to drag you away kicking and screaming. And they'll remember that. That will never go away."

Les nodded then shook his head again. "The rest of it won't matter anymore. But the truth is, it never did. All that mattered was that you cared and didn't give up."

One very large raindrop smacked the windshield as heavy, humid gusts laid down the saw grass. "That's all he's saying. It doesn't matter, none of it. So don't let them kick you off the stage a second before you're ready to go. He's saying it because that's what he believed, no matter what words he used. That's what matters. Staying as long as you can." Les's head gave its own tiny flurry of nods, then he summed up: "The rest of it is shit."

Les went quiet then, staring off at nothing, the way he did. But he had made peace with something deep inside himself, right at that moment, working through it, seeing life through Frank's eyes, his words, his way. Sharing feelings only men can know—only men who have known great victories and defeats—but most of all, men who have survived despite the odds against them. Men who weren't done yet.

At least it felt that way in a red Avenger under a rising storm.

***

Cindy sat quietly digesting everything Les had said, watching the sky and thinking, *Fine*, she could accept all that—even as a twisted metaphor for whatever it was Les thought he was doing. Even if he was wrong.

Even if it was a lie.

But that wasn't what she was going to say before. "Les, about this—"

"I don't want to talk about it," he said.

Cindy could accept that, too. "I wasn't going to talk about her." Only Les Moore could have looked over with such a symbiotic mix of acute curiosity and total disinterest. She said, "Maybe this isn't the right time—"

"Hasn't stopped you before," he said.

Cindy looked to see if Les was being a jerk. He didn't appear to be, so she went on. "You know why I didn't say anything about the dress? When I found it in your closet."

Les looked out across the endless flat swamp, storm clouds roiling up, black now, closing in. "You think I'm the other SKK," he said with less bother than he'd give a drycleaner for missing a spot on the elbow of an old jacket.

"H... how'd you know?" Cindy forgot about the weather, the body, the condition of the body.

The situation.

"Wasn't that hard to figure," Les said with equal slack as two smallish women dressed in white lab coats wheeled the body-bagged waitress toward their van, up on the dike, trying, with some difficulty, to stick to dry ground wherever they could find it.

One of them griped, "How come nobody ever dies on flat ground?" to which the other said, "Florida, you'd *think*," and the other agreed and they both pushed harder on the uneven slope as the gurney almost tipped over, them with it. Finally, they crested the dike.

Les said, "Imagine the poor schlump's gotta tell her parents she was whacked. They're gonna ask who did it. Cop's gonna have to say he doesn't know. 'Might be the Strip Killer.' They don't even know she worked in a strip joint. It's gonna destroy them. Then, they're gonna have to ID the body. In that condition."

The two slight morgue women wrestled the gurney into their van while a large, powerfully built man, presumably their supervisor, watched passively, then got in to drive. One of the women flipped him off behind his back, and they followed him in for the ride back.

"Too hard on everyone," Les sighed with finality as the van took away his dead informant.

What was left of her.

"It was more than the dress, you know," Cindy said. "The... shaving. Your legs. And..." She nodded higher. "The rest."

Les stared at her longer and with more intensity than she would have liked — though less than she expected — then looked away. Cindy tried, "I know you're a swimmer, but—"

"I'm a suspect, too."

"Les," Cindy said reproachfully. "You're not a suspect."

"Everyone's a suspect, Baker. Even you."

Cindy sucked in a short breath of surprise and choked on some spittle. "Me? Why me?" This getting blindsided all the time was getting old.

Les said, "You had access to the files. You're smart. You know guns better than any three male agents I ever met. You know how to use one. You've been trained to kill."

He sounded detached, even disinterested, but went on anyway. "All the SKK hits were accomplished by a single gunshot wound to the head. No ligature strangulations, no knives, no clubs, rocks, beatings. No asphyxiation. No drowning."

He meant no muscle. Pulling a trigger didn't require great strength. Seduce the SK into a lonely spot somewhere, an alley, a field, a car, and bang, one shot, you're an SKK.

"We know which ones were Riverbend's," Les said. "But the others could be anyone." He shrugged with his eyes. "You were unaccounted for on most of those occasions, if you consider the exact time of death. You want them off the street as much as anyone. Maybe not as much as some of us who've been at it longer, but you're getting the burn. You can't avoid it."

And the bottom line: "The SKK could be a man posing as a woman, or could *be* a woman. Could be a cop. Could be you." He paused to let the veiled indictment sink in. "Motive, opportunity, ability. You're a suspect." He said the words dispassionately then looked away. All in the line of duty.

Cindy stared a moment—half dumbfounded, half angry as hell—then gazed outside as a smattering wave of raindrops rolled across the car, her mind stalking answers as to why Les would ever think she could kill someone for any reason other than self-defense—even a serial killer.

Finally, she chose to say, "I hope you're saying this allegorically, to put my... suspicions about you in perspective."

Les said, "Suspicions are the result of your investigative training working in harmonious conjunction with your intuitive impulses," quoting his own manual again. "We're all suspects, Baker. The sooner you learn that, the sooner you solve the case."

"And the sooner life has no meaning whatsoever," Cindy countered.

"Who said it had any to begin with?" Les said.

"You've been doing this too long, Les," Cindy said sourly. "You're starting to believe your own bullshit."

Les shook his head. "I will have been doing it too long when the last SK's been dead and in the ground ten years and I'm still doing it. Until then..."

"We're all suspects." Cindy said it. But she didn't like it.

***

After a few minutes, a female sheriff's deputy leaned into Les's window. "We're done here, Agent Moore. If you need anything, please call."

"Thanks," Les said.

When she lingered, smiling over at Cindy, Les added, "I think we'll hang out a little longer. See if we can make sense of any of it."

"Good luck with that," the tawny woman of midthirties said with joking cynicism. Then she headed off to make sure the rest of her team and the press got turned around on the dike without rolling off or falling in.

Cindy turned back, eyeballing the form-hugging brown department slacks that highlighted the woman's workout-tight butt— then saw Les scoping out the same view in his side mirror.

"Was she hitting on you?" Cindy said, feeling a fever coming on, for sure—and the possible need to have a few words with this honey-streaked *sheriff-ette*.

"I don't think so," Les said indifferently. "She had a ring."

Cindy hadn't noticed. Now she looked back and saw the large stone glint in a passing slash of sunlight as the woman waved a News 6 van back toward the hardtop. How had Cindy missed that?

Definitely a bug.

She and Les sat in silence for several minutes as the motorcade faded toward the highway and the city beyond. Large drops began hitting the plain red Dodge with solid thumps now, one at a time, each jagged splat the size of Cindy's fist.

Les broke the relative tranquility. "What if I *was* an SKK?"

Broke it hard.

Cindy's brain locked up. Again! And she was getting damn tired of it happening. Especially with such frequency! What should she say? What could she say? After a prolonged moment of doubt, she chose a simple but direct, "Are you?"

"I asked first," Les said. "We know you've seriously thought about it."

Had she ever. "Well," Cindy started off with what she fretted was a telling pause, "I wouldn't like it. I don't condone it. Don't think I could ever do it myself. But if you were..."

She chose her words with great care. "I'd probably love you anyway, fool that I am. But I don't think I'd want to know about it."

That wasn't so hard. She'd said what she really thought without emotion, clean and simple. Straight up. But she was thinking: *What the actual hell?*

Les allowed a pensive beat. Unrushed, he said, "What if you found out about it? Later, say?"

"Are we leading up to a confession here?" Cindy asked irritably.

"No," Les assured her.

"Then I guess I'd have to keep it secret," she said.

"Might cost you your job," Les pointed out. "If, say, Brinkman found out."

"Hell, if Brinkman found out, he'd probably recommend you for deputy assistant director over himself!"

"Nothing could ever make him that happy," Les said.

"He didn't believe it anyway," Cindy said, shrugging it off, thinking she would finally shock Les some in return, get him back. That he'd turn and give her The Look.

He didn't. He said, "But he told you to keep an eye on me nevertheless."

Les didn't sound surprised or bothered by her admission of suggesting him as their unsub to their superior.

"Yes," Cindy said, disheartened.

Les dropped the Nagasaki. "Then he told me to keep an eye on *you*."

Cindy's jaw dropped. Literally. Again. One goddamned annoying bombshell after another. "He... when?"

"Right after you talked to him and raised your concerns."

But... "Why?" Unashamedly flabbergasted.

"I told him I knew you suspected me. He said everyone's a suspect. I agreed. Could be a smokescreen, I said. You could be our SKK. Wanna make it look like me to keep the heat off yourself, so you tell Brinkman. He says it's bullshit, but go ahead, keep an eye on me." Les paused. "Then he calls me."

"He called you," Cindy said as if restating such a horror out loud in her own words might somehow make it untrue—at least make it sound untrue—while knowing that nothing could undo something so egregiously Brinkmanesque.

"This is unbelievable," she muttered. Rain on the roof now sounded like Tito Puente come back from the dead—angry.

"He's known me longer," Les shrugged.

"Better," Cindy bristled. "You're really saying better."

"I wouldn't say that, no," Les said. "He thinks he does. But, no."

Cindy felt betrayed, stupid, green—and definitely ill. Had to be the flu. Maybe meningitis.

"Okay, so what? We're watching each other now?" she said irritably.

Les chuckled. "Let's not get paranoid," he said. "I'm just doing my job here, Baker. Same as you. Don't waste your time worrying about me."

Rain beat the car senseless, sounding roughly like what was going on in Cindy's head.

***

Twenty minutes later, what was left of the fast-moving squall hung high over the Everglades, trailing sunlight sinking shafts of silver grace onto the wetlands somewhere far off. The line had passed, the storm over.

Cindy silently stared out the windshield at the slowly rolling cumuli while Les watched several small ibis and a giant gray heron picking over the death site for abandoned parasites. Maggots. One died and one dined. *You can't stop The Cycle even if you want to*, Les was thinking, the notion as depressing as it was voraciously authentic.

Finally, Cindy said, as if intuiting what Les was thinking, "He won't get me, Les."

Les didn't look over. He hadn't thought Riverbend would get Marjorie and Melissa Ann. How could he have thought that? They were a Lead Special Investigator's wife and nearly grown daughter. He had trained them almost as well as he'd been trained himself. Marjorie carried a gun—a Ruger, of course—and Melissa Ann carried pepper spray. Two cans. How could Riverbend take both of them out of a busy, lighted parking lot with no sign of a struggle, no one having noticed anything—no consequence for the abominable acts that followed.

No, Cindy wasn't immune. Six-foot-six guys going two-eighty ended up in shallow graves next to their raped and mutilated girlfriends. In Indiana, a cop and his wife had been hacked up and burned in their car in the middle of a town square at midnight. Why? So that Riverbend could prove he was capable of pulling it off. No one was out of his reach. Not the wife of a young strong cop, not the cop, not Marjorie, not Melissa Ann.

Not Cindy.

Les clutched his TASK partner's hand tightly, wishing such sweet moments might never end, but understanding they must. Sitting in that car, at that moment, felt like standing at the edge of the universe, hands extended Sisyphus-like, feet braced, back aching, pushing for all he was worth, knowing that sooner or later Time would simply roll over them like everyone else. Time was the only real enemy, and Time was on Riverbend's side. All he had to do was wait and Les would come to him. He had to.

Then Time would stop.

Finally, Les turned to look at his partner. Cyndra Lynn Baker was smart and beautiful. She was a dedicated agent with a great sense of humor and perfect breasts. He never stood a chance. He knew the first moment he saw her on that slippery slope outside Seattle, first heard that mouth in gear in Riverbend—where this all started and where it would all probably end someday.

"Cuban okay?" he said.

"Cuban's great," Cindy said, and slid closer.

He said, "I ever tell you the reason I eat all the time is I'm hypoglycemic?"

"No, but I wondered," she said. "I am too."

Les nodded and, holding Cindy close, wheeled out onto Highway 27 as the last drops of afternoon purgation fell over the Glades; he tried not to think of the dead waitress's butchered body, left out there in Cindy's peacock blue evening dress.

But he could think of nothing else.

Chapter 27 – 6-6-6

Six days, six bodies, six killers. Six-six-six. For many, this formula added up to The End. For Les and Cindy, it just meant more headaches with Phil Brinkman and the media, a lethal combination by anyone's standards.

"Goddammit, Les! Why can't you find these fuckers and stop them!" Three of the six had been credited to Riverbend.

"Press gettin' hot, Phil?" Les looked around at his hotel room. like any one of a thousand other hotel rooms he'd spent most of his last fifteen years in. This one was tan. Or was it gray?

He was pretty sure he was in Atlanta.

"They're roasting me alive every goddam day!" Brinkman brayed. "And I'm getting sick and goddam tired of it. Then! This six-six-six shit. Jesus Christ. You'd think it was the End of the World!"

"Maybe it is, Phil. Maybe it is."

Les looked out the window. Misty gray rain and, yeah, the buildings looked like Atlanta. Or Birmingham. Memphis.

Vladivostok.

Phil was attempting intimidation. "It can't be, not on my watch. You find them and stop them, or I stop signing your checks."

"I'm doing all I can, Phil," Les said.

"Well," Brinkman said, suddenly softer, vulnerable. "Do more." Then he added, almost pitifully, "Please. End this, Les."

Les had never heard Brinkman talk like that. Never heard him sound vulnerable. "What're you saying, Phil?" This was worth exploring.

"I'm saying, we all do what we have to do in times of crisis, Les. And believe me, this is a crisis."

"For America or for Phil Brinkman?"

"Phil Brinkman *is* America, Les. And don't forget it." A preacher in the Church of Me with a message. "And while you're not forgetting it, end this. Please."

Brinkman saying please twice in less than thirty seconds? They must be in the midst of a crisis, one that stretched coast-to-coast, all of Brinkmanerica.

Les almost felt sorry for his sorry boss. But the Bureau's lead TASK agent was tired to the point that he wasn't sure what city he was in or the color of his room. But he did feel fairly certain this conversation seemed to be headed into deeply murky waters — if circuitously so, per the usual Brinkman route.

Time to hang up and go to bed. "So, Phil. Who do you want me to take out specifically?"

A short pause was followed by, "What?" Brinkman sounded both confused and terrified. A nice balance.

"Well obviously, you're asking me to kill people, Phil. I was just wondering who you wanted me to start with."

"What the hell are you talking about, Moore!"

"Well, I mean, if I'm gonna be committing murder for America, for you as its representative, and I assume the Bureau, I want to be sure to get it right, don't I? God forbid I should screw this up and murder the wrong suspect first."

He rustled a magazine page loudly. "I've got a piece of paper and a pencil here. Go ahead."

There was a moment of silence which lasted so long Les thought either they had been disconnected or Brinkman had finally had The Big One. Then the silence ended.

"Jesus fucking Christ, Moore! Have you lost your fucking mind? We did *not* have this fucking conversation!" He hung up *forcefully*.

Les smiled, feeling much better. Until he saw the headline.

"6-6-6! Is The End Near?"

***

There followed two weeks of insane pressure. Television magazine shows had a field day; cable and streaming became clogged with SK "experts" and doomsayers. Nothing compared to the internet, which was on fire. Threads with thousands of posts ran 24/7. One had to wonder if anyone anywhere was getting any sleep at all. Eating.

The press drove it all, refusing to let up on the story, so Wilstrong never let up on Brinkman, and Brinkman never let up on Les and

Cindy. He called them as often as thirty and forty times a day, all of which they ignored. What was the point? They'd heard it all before. They were already doing all they could do. It just wasn't enough.

It never could be.

By the end of the third week, a new White House scandal grabbed the public's attention, and the press swam toward that scent, circling the political chum, ready to swallow whole any bloody chunks of rumor that floated into their field of vision. Brinkman started calling them the Cartilage Crew for their "lack of spine coupled with primal killing instincts." But, "In a way," he said in a rare interview with the *Post*, "I admire their single-mindedness." The off-the-cuff cut was as close as Brinkman ever got to actual wit.

Then he took another week off, during which another suspected serial killer turned up dead, along with three more victims, and the whole carnival cranked up full throttle again. Wilstrong rode Brinkman, Brinkman called his TASK team, Les and Cindy left instructions at the desk not to be disturbed, Brinkman yelled at the desk clerk, the desk clerk took time off, Les and Cindy took their hotel phones off the hook, Brinkman changed his number, Les took out his battery, and Shannon Creamer continued to get to crime scenes before Les and Cindy on a regular basis. Wildly, the videos got even better.

"You know," Cindy said on a flight back to Iowa for some follow-up, "ever since that six-six-six thing..." and she drifted off, indicative of their whole dilemma. The pressure was suffocating. Even Cindy was speechless.

***

Time passed as slowly and taxingly as their investigation. The work had become grueling, much of it spent in Alaska tracking the Oil Rig Rapist—really a murderer—so Les was never warm. He had fared no better elsewhere. Roanoke was cloudy and cold; Denver, polluted and cold; Los Angeles impossibly crowded and ridiculously unsafe, not to mention unseasonably unwarm; Minneapolis, dull and cold; Detroit, filthy and cold; New York, smelly and hot—for about an hour until a cold front passed through making it smelly and cold; Portland, rainy, foggy, and colder than Anchorage; even Jacksonville was near to freezing.

"Christ, Baker," Les said. "Florida."

He'd been cold for as long as he could remember. He could barely even recall what a hot day felt like—not since his youth, it seemed—those hot July weekends with nothing to do but enjoy the heat. Then he grew up and became a special agent, and he was never warm again. Someone told him he probably didn't have enough brown fat cells to metabolize his white fat cells into heat. Les told them he probably didn't have enough money to retire to Jamaica.

Stress was starting to be an imposing factor for both TASK agents. Cases like West Virginia's Virgin Rapist didn't help. He checked. If their hymens were intact, he raped them and killed them; if not, he just killed them. His tally was pushing ten, officials feared.

A psycho in Mississippi slashed, shot, stabbed, poured acid on, and finally burned his female victims. Some bozo on TV, purportedly a serial murder expert, said the killer obviously had "an issue with women." Cindy stared at the screen... and growled.

The TV panel then shifted their cumulative expert opinions to the Chattanooga Choo-Choo Killer. He raped his male victims then threw them under a passing train. The expert said it was again "obvious this killer's emotional development was arrested around the time he got his first Lionel set."

Cindy said, "Or blowjob," and switched off the TV and put her head under a pillow.

But they were everywhere. There was simply no getting away from the whack-jobs. And not just the ones getting paid to make asses of themselves on national television.

Wyoming's Cowboy Killer branded his victims (Circle SK, some were calling him); Detroit's Car Killer ran his victims down then carved the name of a defunct car brand in their backs (dubbed the Autonomic Assassin by alliterative types, the Edsel Enforcer by others and, Les's favorite, the Packard Punisher); New Mexico's Las Cruces Killer crucified his victims on cemetery crosses (Red Stimson nodded when he read it); and Baltimore's Bowling Ball Basher crushed his victim's skull with guess what (and each time the tabloids shouted "Strike!"). Plus, new victims of new killers were turning up regularly in Kansas City, Salt Lake, St. Paul, St. Louis, and St. Cloud.

To name a few.

In San Diego, following a streak of killings committed with steak knives lifted from well-known Los Angeles eateries, after which the female victims were left, nude and carved, along the freeway, the 405 Killer (alternatively, the Sirloin Slasher, the Five Star Stalker, the Au Jus Assassin, and last, The Actor, since he stole flatware) turned up naked in a downtown Diamond Lane skewered with spoons—slower and more painful—from Spago, Chasen's, and Musso and Frank (for nostalgia purposes). He was, thankfully, very dead. Especially after several early morning commuters ran over the body but didn't bother, in typical Southern California fashion, to stop or report it. An SKK using spoons to kill wasn't the strangest part, however. Chasen's had been closed for two decades.

Les got to LA before Cindy, so she felt compelled to ask him if he'd killed the Actor Nutcase. "Sorry, he was DWIA," Les said, his old friend Bondini's acronym for Dead When I Arrived.

Cindy nodded, then she and Les examined the overpass crime scene, the Valley apartment, the roadside dump sites, gave some empty suggestions, and went to Black's Beach. It was too cold to take their clothes off anyway, so they went back to the Embassy Suites and took a hot soak in the jetted tub together. They ignored the ringing phone— didn't even hear it anymore.

The 405 case and the SKK's identity, like the many others, went unsolved.

***

Then there was Chicago. The Windy Killer. When Cindy first heard of him, she wondered, "What? Farts them to death?" Windy, as he was called by the cops, had "only" killed three women, but one was the mayor's daughter and the other was a councilman's wife. No one knew if Chicago's newest assassin was incredibly lucky or frighteningly organized. Nor did they know which public official's next of kin would be next. So, when he offed the chief of police's homely niece across the state line in Indiana, Windy made the Bureau's Ten Most Wanted within twenty-four hours. He bumped Riverbend to Number Two, despite RB's much higher body count. Who wouldn't feel stress associating—even at a distance—with antisocial miscreants like them?

Les and Cindy were drowning in it.

Regular sex was helping, but also adding its own level of stress. The TASK lovers were mostly conscientious about abstaining from public displays of affection. Still, someone had to have seen something somewhere — a loving pat, an adoring glance, a held hand. But with the case load mounting daily, mushrooming out of control really, any fear of reprisal over the inappropriate nature of their inter-agent liaison and any attempt at stifling it took a back seat to bringing an end to the worst streak of serial murders ever to grip the nation.

Trying.

The TASK lovers agreed that if Wilstrong ever found out about their affair and ordered an end to it they'd move to a grass shack in Polynesia where no one had even heard of the concept of serial killing much less the act. And there they would spend the rest of their lives whiling away the days playing smoochy and fucking like bunnies, thank you very much, Phil Brinkman. Only, they knew they'd never enjoy a single moment in Paradise with the Virgin Rapist, Choo-Choo, Oil Rig, and the rest of them still out there.

Riverbend.

So, instead, Cindy and Les carried on in hotels, empty fields, deserted patches of woods, and lonely parking lots, secretly hoping to be attacked while enjoying their illicit pleasures — each one's service weapon and backup within quick and easy reach. They counseled Local PDs from Boston to Brunswick, Anchorage to Anaheim, Portland to Portland, bringing NCAVC's message and solid profiles to the martial masses. Their visits were appreciated, but nothing much changed.

In the midst of all the madness, Riverbend continued to kill one every few weeks, taunting and teasing Les to the point of distraction. He even went back to Montana to spell out "Hi Les" again in the charcoal remains of the cabin, thereby removing any doubt that he was watching Les and Cindy and knew they were headed back there as well for another look.

He *had* been there that night.

If Les and Cindy hadn't've had each other, the strain would have been too much. That they could find love at all amid this sea of death and perversion was a miracle, and one not wasted on either of them. Nor was it wasted on Wilstrong when Brinkman told him of their alleged affair, Only because he was afraid of being fired himself for not reporting it.

In a rare parting of the ways with Bureau etiquette, Wilstrong instructed Brinkman that neither one of them had ever heard that rumor. Further, they would continue not to hear it until such point as Les and Cindy failed to make headway—or ran off to Bora Bora—whichever came first. Then they would ignore it in hindsight.

Bora Bora was looking damn good.

***

Six weeks after the waitress from Diamonds in the Raw was found in Cindy's blue dinner dress, buried under two feet of Everglades muck, Broward Sheriff's investigators received a tip to look for another victim in the same area, by the raised Everglades dike.

They found a mostly decomposed body, a male, buried not fifteen feet from the exact spot Nipple Bar had been dumped. Forensics took a few weeks to connect the dots, checking and rechecking their findings, but their final report was chilling. The new body belonged to the Strip Killer. He had been killed before the waitress was murdered.

This answered the question of why there had been no more Strip Killings, but begged many more, principally: Who killed *her*?

Les's name came up.

The same middle-aged Broward Sheriff's detective suggested that since Les had purchased the dress and given it to his informant, he should at least be considered as a suspect.

Cindy went full-metal. She didn't just call the guy names, though there was plenty of that, mainly comparing the diminutive size of his penis to his brain, and how the two could be easily confused. She recited Les's entire illustrious career in detail, including his many contributions to "this very case," ending with the "extremely unlikely probability he would kill his best informant, you..."

The ad hominem tag ran on.

In a gap created when Cindy paused to take a breath, the detective said, "Maybe she informed him she knew he was the Strip Killer."

"Yeah, she was that stupid," Cindy snorted. "I'm sure you think most people are."

She knew his type—working hard for The People, all the while holding contempt for them as deep and swift as the Gulf Stream, five miles out.

"And then, let's see," Cindy continued as if the guy was denser than the muck in which the bodies had been found, "Les was even stupider. Knowing I knew about her, you knew about her, everyone knew about her, he whacked her in the middle of an investigation and carried her out in, what? his Bureau sedan, and dumped her in the swamp? Excellent profile, Sergeant. I see now why we're doing this work and you're selling tickets for the Fraternal Order dance."

The *lieutenant* glared. "He did more than whack her, lady. He turned her into Ballpark Frank material. She was real kielbasa stuffer, if you remember."

He shot a smirk at his buddies, outside his office.

Cindy got real close. "Are you saying my partner could do that to a woman?" Cindy was intimidating for a woman her size when her attitude was riled.

"Shit happens, Agent," the guy shrugged, pretending to be unfazed. "We gotta ask the questions."

Cindy snarled, "The question you should be asking is who killed the Strip Killer, you halfwit. Come to think of it, maybe if you had half a wit you'd be asking the nation's leading expert on serial crimes, sex murder in particular, who he thinks it is, instead of jerking off on me and everyone else in range with your asinine insinuations!"

"I'm just doing my job, ma'am." He sounded happy to fall back on the Universal Cop Out—the one Cindy hated as much as sleet.

"Yeah, so was bin Laden," she said, burning.

"I don't appreciate that, ma'am. I had a cousin die in 9-11."

"Second? Third? Fifth?" Cindy said because she smelled an exaggeration.

Of course, none of this mattered in a pissing contest. So, Detective Smartass aimed higher. "Then maybe Agent Moore whacked the Strip Killer."

Cindy's eyes went wide with mock surprise. "Oh, so now we're gonna bounce from one wild assumption to another. Make up your mind, detective. Is he an SK? Or an SKK? Maybe he's an SKKK! A serial murderer who kills for the Klan!"

Not bad on short notice, pissed off and running low on patience.

Sergeant Speculation wasn't moved. "Your partner did make the comment that..." He checked his notes. "The Strip Killer 'couldn't' have killed the Diamonds waitress. How did he know that?"

"Because, you pea-brained infantile moron, this is *his case*!"

"This is *our* case, ma'am. You people were invited in to offer opinions."

Cindy launched again, offering many more opinions while attempting to recount every significant—and insignificant—contribution Les had made to solving each and every of the hundred-plus murder cases with which he had been even tangentially involved in his celebrated career, as if she was giving a eulogy for the most-decorated FBI case-solving hero of all time—on the verge of nominating him for sainthood.

"What, are you sleeping with the guy?" the detective asked and aimed a smirk at his cohorts outside again. When he turned back, Cindy slapped the sweat right off him.

"Yes, as a matter of fact, I am," she said. "But that's none of your fucking business, is it? And if you had your head in your case files where it should be instead of up your own ass, or up other peoples' asses where I don't believe it has been invited, you might someday, and I stress the extremely dim likelihood of such event, but someday in the far future, you might surprise us all and possibly achieve one thousandth of what Special Agent Moore does every day of his life, you needle-dick pinhead! Now, get outa my fucking face!"

Cindy dressed him down with such venom and fury that, even though they were standing in his office, the detective left—and went straight to his captain to file an official complaint. He left out the part about them sleeping together, apparently agreeing it was none of his business. Nonetheless, Brinkman chewed out Cindy for the better part of ten minutes, until he heard how the detective had suggested that Les killed his informant, a woman, after gouging out her female organs, her implants, and her eyeballs.

Scalping her.

The detective just *thought* he'd caught hell from Cindy. Brinkman yelled with such unrestrained profane ferocity the man and his captain thought their speakerphone might melt. Brinkman demanded, and got, the complaint rescinded and the detective transferred off the case. "Or the entire Broward County Sheriff's Department Homicide Investigation Unit will never again get any cooperation whatsoever from the FBI on any case, much less from my serial crime experts in NCAVC! None! Ever! Period! End of conversation! *Finis!*"

He hung up so hard he broke his own phone.

All things considered, Cindy thought the Broward prick got off easy. No one asked for her apology.

Chapter 28 – Chicago

To demonstrate he was still in charge, Brinkman ordered his TASK team in for a "formal, in-person sit-down, stat!"

Cindy asked Les if that meant Wilstrong.

Les said, "That's the stat part," but assured her the director wouldn't actually be there. "Phil just wants to be able to say he called us in for a personal update, and he's satisfied with our SAC's assessment. 'The Bureau is doing everything possible, and we're hoping for a resolution in the near future.'"

"We are?" Cindy said, skeptically.

"It's a press release," Les said. "It's not supposed to be factual."

True to form, the DC meeting produced lots of the usual Brinkman gibberish—the "When I call, I expect"s and "Who do you two think you are?"s along with lots of meaningless references to "The Director," who, of course, according to Brinkman, "Has had it up to here with you two!" He raised his chubby arm as high as his ever-tightening suit would allow.

Then he gave Les a, "Christ, Les, what the fuck are you teaching her out there in the field? Pickle ball?" Cindy got, "And what the fuck are you doing out there, Baker? Ruining his passing game before the finals?" Then, for both of them. "What the fuck are you two doing out there? Getting your brains sucked out by free agent zombies?"

To the untrained ear, these random sports and B-movie-related rants made no sense. But to the enlightened, they were patented Brinkmanisms which by design defied response. He didn't want one. He just wanted to showboat a while. Finally done, he shoved a fax at Les and said, "Windy's dead."

So that's what this was all about.

***

Once again, Shannon Creamer beat them to the body. By the time Les and Cindy arrived, the young videographer had already shot everything having anything to do with the crime, even tangentially, and burned their copy. She handed the thumb drive to Les outside Windy's apartment, saw Cindy's scowl as she entered the well-culled crime scene, and trundled for her little Prius while she still could.

Les gazed around in simmering silence. The body was long gone, the site picked over. A dozen cops ignominiously tromped around with eight news crews.

So, the evidence was colder than the night—thirty-eight degrees by the time the TASK team got there, thirty-two hours after the body was discovered. While they rode over in the loaner, Sinatra strained to convince them how toddling the town was.

Les was so steamed he turned him off.

But if Les was livid, Cindy was over-the-top apoplectic. "Who the fuck..." was all he remembered hearing as Chicago police and Bureau field office agents suffered her harangue for what must have seemed a small eternity to them. That Broward County Sheriff's detective just thought he got it bad.

Les went around the corner for a hot coffee. But if he had heard the many phrases Cindy made up or borrowed from Brinkman's morning tirade, he would have been duly impressed.

***

Henry John Freeman—the Windy Killer—had been the target of a massive manhunt by the Chicago PD, Cook County Sheriff's Department, Illinois state investigators, and the FBI. But the SKK found him first—at home in his living room watching The Learning Channel. Law enforcement hid, chagrined, while the press swallowed a bottle of happy pills.

"Heck, he was easy," Les said to Cindy. "He must've read 'Serial Killing for Beginners.'" Freeman had made every unoriginal, predictable move possible. How the cops had managed not to find him was as much a miracle as the idiot knowing how to kill anyone in the first place.

The TASK partners went over files in a well-appointed conference room loaned to them by the Cook County District Attorney's Office. Even the prosecutors were afraid of where this one might go next—whose daughter.

Though there was no shortage of evidence this time, what stumped everyone was how Freeman's actions fit the SK MO to a T. But there, the profile ended. He was fifteen years younger than predicted, a foot taller, didn't own the car anyone thought he did— didn't own a car at all, which made his getting around town to kill people in such a big city even more unfathomable. He was dark instead of pale, fat instead of thin, a real weirdo instead of average, and obviously a total moron instead of a near genius. So, nothing fit.

Serial Killing for Beginners. Cindy chuckled.

Les said, "Jesus, he's got Ted Bundyism down to a science. Did you read this crap?"

"Pathetic, huh? This is Chicago. Holmes and Gacy land."

"Worse than pathetic," Les said, glowering, and read from Windy's journal.

"'Every *sense* I been a child, I been in pornogaffy.' Spelled with two fs." Cindy rolled her eyes. Les read, "'I use to steel *Payboy* from the garbij, then jack off on them at home in my mother underwears.'"

"Who's he writing to?" Cindy wore a pained expression.

"Us," Les said.

"Or Geraldo." Then she wondered, "Is he still around? He can't be. Maury?"

Les said he had no idea and read, "'Then I move to hardar stuff.' If that isn't our Ted, I don't know what is."

"Don't laugh. People listened to Bundy."

"I'm still not laughing."

"Yeah, but then you figure who listened," Cindy amended, mostly for herself.

"Politics makes strange bedfellows," Les agreed, recalling the visits by truckling Born Agains to Bundy's cell—led by that Orange Bowl Queen with the pasted-on smile, lacquered-up coif, and Tourette's-like penchant for spewing psalms and hate in the same breath—proving how they'd go to any lengths, stoop to any depths, slither through any sludge, gambol in it, consort with any teenage-girl-killing degenerate on death row, shake hands, stand together, smile for any photo op, anything to get proof, straight from the homicidal horse's mouth, that masturbation led to murder. *Proof!* that sex was bad.

He brought that up and Cindy said, "Hey, *Hustler* went on sale the same year Bundy started killing women. 1974. Sounds like proof to me."

"How would you know a thing like that?" Les said. "You weren't born yet."

"My dad read it to me for bedtime stories," Cindy said. "The history, not the magazine."

Les gave an honest chuckle and picked up where he left off. "'Then I move on to hardar stuff.' And get this, he actually wrote, "'Hardar. Get it?'"

"Oh, my dear Lord. Someone *had* to kill this guy."

"Probably whoever read this."

Cindy laughed, getting harder, herself.

"'I licked' — not *liked*, mind you. 'I licked kiling them. They made me had to kill them.' See there? He *had* to."

"Well, of course," Cindy said, straight-faced then grabbed the journal, found where Les had stopped, and took her turn. "He got they great pusies. They all nise and wet an pink al the time.'" Cindy held the book down and away. "Oh, my fucking dear Lord. It's like a porno version of *Mystery Science Theater 3000*."

"I love that show," Les said. He had watched it in motels everywhere.

Cindy shoved the journal back to Les and said, "You." He scanned some without reading aloud. "Wait, you're skipping," Cindy said.

"You don't wanna know," he said.

"Oh. Okay."

Les moved down the page. "I like them hores. They all hores, you know. All them. I like to fuck them al, then kill them and then fuck them agin. The hole of them. They all hores. Al them.'"

Les noted, "Not a w on the page," and looked down to continue. "'An I start with that niger tonight. She had die. I had kill her. She a black hore. And I had kill her.'"

Cindy picked up a photo of the first dead woman CPD had found, the black councilman's wife. She had been raped, sodomized, and left naked by the river with her throat slashed, a smear of Freeman's semen on her ample breasts.

"Janis Parkins," Cindy said, "Number One. Does it say where he picked her up?"

"He calls it 'Hooker Avenue.' Must mean Roosevelt and Cicero."

"What was the councilman's wife doing there?" Cindy wondered.

"File says charity work."

"Right. Peterman mentioned that." Rob Peterman was the local ASAC. A good guy, Les had said of him. Helpful. Cindy recalled, "Mainly women's causes. A lot with the underprivileged. Junkies, tough welfare cases."

"Hookers?"

"Hookers."

Les turned a few pages. "Here's Number Two, the mayor's kid."

Cindy found the picture. She was white, twenty-nine, with abundant cleavage. "Why do men have this... unnatural desire for large breasts?" She stared at the photo of the dead nude woman a moment as if not even seeing the death, just the addiction.

"I wouldn't call it unnatural," Les said.

"Depends on whether you're giving or receiving."

Without even looking up, Les understood and said, "Yours are perfect. Couldn't be perfecter."

As tired and not-in-the-mood as she was, as they both were, Cindy looked at him with a loving smile. "You mean that, don't you?"

"Of course. I never lie to my partner."

"Bullshit."

"Well, not about her tits."

Cindy rolled her eyes and shook her head.

Les moved on to, "Number Three," paging ahead.

"Wait. Where did he find Number Two? Ellen Milsap. She was a lawyer, you know."

Les started to crack a lawyer joke.

"We're talking about the mayor's daughter here," Cindy reminded him.

"Sorry. Old habits." He scanned back a bit. "Doesn't say. Just, he saw her on the street and knew he had to kill her."

"He knew."

"Hey, some things you just know. 'Tonite I was feling doun, so I know I had kill agan to fell god.' Feel good."

"Maybe God," Cindy said. "You know, you're right. It's almost as if —"

"He didn't write it at all. Just what I was thinking," Les said.

"Well?"

"Unfortunately, I think he did. Handwriting matches his check ledger entries. Close enough at any rate."

"This cretin kept his checkbook balanced?"

"Go figure," Les said. "But you're right, it's almost too perfect. Too sick. Too stupid. Too..."

"Serial killerish."

"Yeah," Les said. "Anyway, Number Three."

Cindy found the photo. The woman was naked, stabbed some fifty times and had very small breasts. "Julia Nardino. The niece."

"You're not gonna like this. If it doesn't make you paranoid about breast size nothing will. 'She sad her nam was Ashee but I'm not beleve her.'"

"Ashee?"

"Ashley?"

"What do you make of that?"

"Why did the police chief's niece give our boy a phony name? Probably out doing something she shouldn't've been doing."

"Drugs?

"Maybe."

"Maybe she suspected he was Windy and didn't want him to know she was related to a public official."

Les gave an affirmative grunt, made a note, and read on. "Let's see... 'She lye to me and was wear falses. Didn't even have no tits at all. So, I had stab her 50 time, one for each inch of tittys I wish she had got.'"

Cindy felt nauseated.

"She was fourteen," Les said. His daughter Melissa had been fourteen when she turned away.

Cindy said, "And the ACLU wanted this guy to get a trial and serve out the rest of his years filing appeals at taxpayer expense. Fuck me." Harder indeed.

Les said, "They didn't get their wish."

"No, they got Richard Speck and his hormone tits, laughing at them from the grave."

Cindy had made some kind of cryptic synaptic leap, but Les went along. "Great video, speaking of videos," he said, setting the diary down. "Did you see that thing?"

"It was disgusting."

"Sure, it was disgusting, but goddam it was inspired, don't you think? Waving his boobs around, takin' it up the ass, snortin' coke, and some sissy inmate taping it all, tellin' him, 'This way, Richie, now over there. I can't see! I gotta see your cock, Richie.'"

"Enough, Les." Cindy said, having soured on the whole subject.

"No, I mean, what was that guy thinking?" Les insisted.

"I'll tell you what he was thinking," Cindy said. "He was thinking, 'I killed those eight nurses, and enjoyed it. I made them suffer, and I made them beg, and I strangled them and stabbed them, and mutilated them, and almost got away with it, and I don't give a fuck what anyone thinks about me. I'm happy as a turd in a steel toilet that I'm sitting in stir for the rest of my sorry-assed life until they fry me 'cause I'm getting all the drugs and perverted sex I can handle while the parents of those victims have to see this video some day and relive the horror all over again with me sitting up here smirking and laughing about it!' That's what the fuck he was thinking and it makes me wanna puke."

Les sat back and said, "But what do you *really* think, Baker? Don't hold back."

"Well, it does, dammit! It makes me wanna *puke*!"

"Okay, but 'stir?'" He felt himself grinning. He couldn't help it.

"Well! It pisses me off! The whole goddam thing!" She stood up.

Les reached up, took her hand, and said gently, "That was my point, you know. I just said it badly. I'm sorry." Cindy looked at him with something resembling sadness. Calm acceptance of the worst of ·humanity.

"Speck's dead," Les said. "Windy too. If things keep going the way they are, there won't be any of them left in a few weeks."

"I wish I could believe that," Cindy said, looking more defeated than assuaged.

"You'd help it along?" Les said.

"You bet your ass," Cindy said, hard and clear as white diamonds.

"Well then." Les stood beside her, kissed her gently on the forehead, then held her close. "Let's go find who whacked this sorry bastard before he kills some innocent people by accident." Then he added, "But maybe after he kills a few more Henry Freemans."

Les pulled back to wink. "You get the first shot," he promised.

Cindy smiled weakly and said, "Okay." But Les knew it was gnawing at her the same as it was him. Those death-grip feelings of inadequacy, frustration, and rage would never subside no matter how much they hoped or wanted. Not until someone paid for these sins.

Chapter 29 – Killer Eyes

For two days, Les and Cindy cruised hooker hangouts and adult bookstores in a five-mile radius. Everyone recognized Henry. He was big news and, as it turned out, a regular customer. That is to say he visited often but bought only enough to keep himself from being blacklisted as a loitering cheapskate.

At store after store, the clerks all knew Henry. Hookers, too. They said he always stopped and talked, but never had enough money no matter how low they went on their asking price. So, they always told him to take a hike, especially when he started lurking in vestibules, watching them, muttering to himself. They hadn't been frightened, just annoyed — until the news broke.

Cindy contended that Henry Freeman was living out his fantasy of being a serial killer as much as being one and, purely by luck, she and Les stumbled onto the cornerstone of her theory. They'd gone into what they thought was a dirty bookstore near Freeman's apartment, which turned out to be a used bookstore with a few provocative titles in the window. The older hippie woman who ran the place said that yes, Henry was a regular there, too. "Always looking for books on serial killers. Nonfiction, preferably."

Freeman had studied the part assiduously in order to create his SK persona. That made sense. But the rest still didn't add up. There was no abuse in Henry's past, no animal torture, no violence, no arrests. No signs. There was a preoccupation with sex, though not deviant sex — no S&M or bondage, pain or blood — just the usual "whack-mags" as Cindy dismissed them. He didn't even have internet service, didn't own a computer.

Otherwise, most everyone painted Henry Freeman as a fairly typical underachiever — far too slovenly for even an average serial offender — essentially a dullard who lived alone, worked at CVS part-time stocking shelves, and had no aspirations of any kind. He ate at Subway almost every day and visited his mother twice a week. He loved pigeons.

Mrs. Freeman did tell the TASK agents that her son had wet the bed until he was twelve and hadn't had a date since high school as far as she knew. But otherwise, she was grievously confused as to how her Henry had become such a diabolic murderer without her having so much as a single clue.

"That's the way it often is," Cindy offered as comfort. The old woman stared at Cindy like she was fresh from a UFO, not consoled in the least, and went back to bed.

Henry wouldn't be visiting anymore.

Les allowed as how Freeman's hatred of women probably came as a result of their constant rejection of him from a young age. Later, he started objectifying his rage on hookers — since they were available — finally moving up to killing important women he read about in the many newspapers strewn around his apartment.

The last part was a bit of a stretch, but Cindy agreed, noting how most men can't deal with rejection or powerful women, despite their macho posturing and verbal smoke screens.

Les said, "Yeah, but I never kill the bitch."

"That's because you don't have the balls," Cindy said, without batting an eye, and went into the next adult bookstore.

Les chuckled in the late sun slant then followed her in to find her already flashing her badge and Freeman's photo, asking the young Puerto Rican kid working behind the counter unpacking sex toys if he had ever seen this man. He had.

Cindy asked, "Did you ever see him watching any women in here? Hookers maybe? Talking to them."

The kid said they didn't allow, "No hookers in here." A moment later, he laughed.

Les asked if he found something funny about the question. The kid said, "The last time I saw a woman in here was the boss's wife yellin' at him about forgettin' to bring home some chicken for supper." So, no politician's wives.

"How about anybody else?" Cindy said.

"What?" he said.

"Talking," Cindy clarified. "To anyone."

"Talking?" the kid said.

Something about his voice, maybe the youthful innocence that snuck in for a second, but the way he said the word, as if knowing something he maybe didn't want to share, prompted Les to raise his eyebrows at Cindy.

She said to the kid, "Yes. Did you ever see him talking to anyone else?"

Les threw in, "Or anyone talking to him."

The kid said, "People don't talk much in here. They're usually too embarrassed to even look at each other. Except the queers. They always talk about stupid shit and maybe show each other a hard-on in their pants."

Les mused, "Well, as long as it's in their pants."

"Yeah, I don't wanna see that shit," the kid said, unpacking the largest rubber penis Les had ever seen—according to the price, apparently sold by the pound.

Cindy looked then tore her eyes away and asked the kid, "How about following? Did you ever see anyone follow him in or out—you know, trying to be slick, or like he might know him, like they might know each other? Like a partner, maybe."

The kid gave this some thought, and something seemed to cross his mind. Then he glanced at them, and it was gone. "No," he said.

Both agents saw it. "No?" Les asked.

"No. I... I never saw nothin'," the kid assured. But he was starting to look sketchy, not hiding his worry well.

Les and Cindy shared an insignificant glance which signaled Good Agent/Bad Agent time. "How old are you?" Cindy asked, with sudden sharpness.

The kid looked more anxious. "Eighteen," he said.

"Yeah?" Cindy said, with more than a hint of disbelief.

The kid glanced at the front door.

Les casually moved that way while Cindy feigned idle indifference and played with a key ring on the counter—until she realized she was holding a small plastic vagina with painted-on pubic hair and dropped it like a spider. She snapped, "Do you have ID?"

Nice, Les thought. *Subtle*.

Before he could react, the kid made his move. He leapt over the counter, grazing Cindy's head with his shoe and sending her back into a rack of magazines and over. As he raced for the back door, she was swimming in smut.

Because Les had moved around the other end of the counter, the kid was out the back and gone before Les got to the quarter booths. By the time Cindy clambered to her feet and ran out the rear exit, Les was in the middle of the alley intersection, looking both ways, seeing no one but Cindy looking back at him. "You all right?" he asked her.

"I'm fine. Did we lose him?"

Les said he thought so then ran off to see.

***

Les returned ten minutes later to find Cindy sitting behind the counter flipping through Triple-X-rated magazines while two middle-aged men picked up the spilled rack.

Les looked at them, then Cindy. "They volunteered," she shrugged. "Must think I work here."

Les noted her plain gray business suit and doubted the assessment. Then he noticed the open porn omnibus in her hand, titled, "Asian Ass Masters—Collectors Issue." Apparently already a classic.

"I thought you said you don't find anything erotic about 'close-ups of busy genitals,'" he said.

"Do I look turned on?" Cindy asked dryly.

"About as much as ever."

"You should pay closer attention," she said then flipped a few full color pages, shaking her head. "I mean really," she said. "Look at the acne on this woman's ass. Would you fuck that? I wouldn't. I wouldn't even touch it."

"Don't have to touch it to fuck it," Les said, matching her aridity note for note.

Cindy uttered a low groan and tossed the magazine on the floor. Les's grin felt good on his face.

Liking what they were hearing, the men picking up the rack nudged each other with their eyes and their smiles widened. Cindy noticed and said with no emotion, "Yeah, thanks for taking care of that. FBI." She flashed her credentials.

The men left the store.

"You're a complex and troubling young woman," Les said with a mix of admiration, awe, and caution.

"I ain't that young anymore, Les. Not after hanging out with you for a few months." She started for the door.

"Wait'll it's been a whole year," he said, following.

"I can't wait," she said morosely. And she probably couldn't.

***

Two days passed. No one had been able to find the Puerto Rican kid, but Cook County Sheriff's Department had a body in a field south of the city. Thanks to a lack of traffic, Les and Cindy were there in twenty.

Everything was fresh for a change with no sign of Shannon Creamer, the video girl. Cindy had no one to yell at. It showed. She looked as pinched up as an old pumpkin.

Les chuckled to himself and took several deep, relaxing breaths. The beautiful, clear, autumn day smelled damn good, even for South Chicago.

"Death by ligature strangulation," the assistant ME said, sharing his initial evaluation. Les thanked him and they headed for the body, wading through a small sea of reporters who started shouting questions the moment someone recognized him.

Les said something in his barely audible reporter-answering voice. Everyone shut up and started asking everyone else, "What'd he say?" When they looked back, Les was on the other side of the crime tape with a grinning Cindy. She was learning the good lessons.

Les stood over the body. "Thrill kill?"

"Aren't they all?" Cindy said drolly.

The way the teenage girl's body was so carefully posed made it obvious to anyone who understood murder that the killer knew his victim. Various personal items had been spread in a circle around her — jewelry, tampons, address book, hair barrettes, purse — her clothes perfectly arranged. Her hands had been placed peacefully at rest across her modest chest. This murder had been thought out, carefully planned. Organized.

"Any pages missing from the address book?" Les asked the lead investigator.

"One," the woman said.

"That's your boy," Les told her.

Cindy agreed. "Any prints?"

"Not so far."

"There will be," Les said, looking relaxed, probably since this obviously wasn't anything to do with Riverbend or any other serial offender. "He left one somewhere in all this, probably on the address book," Les told the female dick. "Match it to a name on the missing page and you've got your unsub."

Les pointed toward several high-rise housing units nearby. "Probably lives in one of those." The woman cop looked and nodded, then Les wandered off to yak it up with a former Chicago Field Office SAC he knew from the old days. The graying, bearded man had heard the call on his scanner and dropped by to pass time.

After being introduced, Cindy hung back, thinking how even when you leave this job you can't leave the residue behind. She saw herself standing in a similar field, at a similar age, her hair as gray as his, wattles under her neck, liver spots on her hands, with no one waiting for her at home, no one in her life anywhere. Just a corpse in a field. The image felt as terrifying as the waitress in the mud. Maybe worse.

***

The Chicago field office had the Puerto Rican kid in custody, waiting at Les and Cindy's loaner desks. At first, the boy's uncle Ernesto, a short, mustachioed man in his early forties, the owner of the adult bookstore and delinquent chicken buyer, had said he didn't know who the Feds were talking about. "Musta been some kid off the street who strayed in and was rippin' me off."

But when Chicago ASAC Rob Peterman suggested that employing a minor in an adult bookstore might be a federal crime, the uncle was quick to bring "the little pinga" in.

Not quite sixteen, young Ernesto — Ernie G to his homies — was a good kid. He'd stayed out of gangs by working since he was ten. He grew a mustache at twelve and always looked older than he was, so he'd started working for his uncle at the bookstore at fourteen. He was already fairly callous when it came to sex, but at least he'd never owned a gun.

He gave half his money to his mother who worked two other jobs to feed Ernie and his three siblings, and the rest went into a college fund for himself. He had run because he was afraid of losing his job. His uncle had said if anything ever went down because of Ernie being in the store, he was back on the street and gang bait. As a result, during any shift Ernie worked, the place was clean, neat, and never missing so much as single condom. The local beat cops knew but never said anything. Any kid who wasn't a violent nuisance made their job easier.

"So, I hear you're Employee of the Month at Uncle Ernesto's dirty bookstore," Cindy opened.

Still the bad cop, Ernie assessed.

"Every month," Les added.

Maybe he was the bad one now. "You don't have to get smart with me. I'm here," Ernesto said with a sour face.

"You kicked me in the head," Cindy reminded him.

"I did?" The kid was truly horrified. "I... didn't know. I'm sorry. I wouldn't kick a lady in the head if I knew it, ma'am. Honest. I'm sorry."

"Apology accepted. So, what did you remember seeing before you unknowingly kicked me in the head and ran from two federal agents?"

"Doesn't sound like you accepted anything," Ernie said at the floor.

"Oh, she did," Les pledged. "Otherwise, she'd really be nasty. Trust me." He gave a knowing smile and got young Ernesto to smile.

Okay, he ain't the bad cop.

"Everyone in your family named Ernesto?" Les asked.

"A lot of us," Ernie G said.

"So?" Cindy prodded, wanting her previous question answered and making it clear the small talk was over.

Ernie said guiltily, "There was this one thing one night, late, just before closing."

"What time is that?" Les asked.

"Two," Ernie said.

"Two in the morning?" Cindy said. "Hope it wasn't a school night."

Definitely the bad cop. "Maybe, I don't remember," Ernie said, remembering well. He looked down again, then back up. "But this guy you asked me about—"

Les said, "The dead one or the other one?"

"The dead one," Ernie said, realizing what he said. "Okay, so you don't want him no more."

"Yeah, we got him," Les said. "He's not doing us much good."

Ernesto understood, but he remembered Henry Freeman well. He used to come in often, sometimes five times in a week, browsing his full thirty minutes without buying anything, then leaving. Only when Ernie said something would Freeman spend a few quarters in a booth.

"Ever have to clean up after him?" Cindy asked.

"No, he's very neat," Ernie said thankfully, though used to it. "Musta took it with him."

"How thoughtful," Cindy said.

"Tell me about it," Ernie said. "You should see what some of these—"

"No thanks. Go ahead," Cindy said.

Ernie said, "Anyway, that night, the dead guy, he'd run his limit, and I told him he had to leave, like always. He started to go then this other guy says, 'Hey, give the guy a break. He just wants to see some pussy.' So, I told him, 'Then he can pay for it.'"

"That usually works. These dudes don't any kinda confrontation in there. I have to call the cops and their families find out they're lookin' at gay shit, you know."

Cindy said, "But it didn't work this time."

"No," Ernie said. "He came up to me and gave me a look."

"The other guy."

"Yeah, him."

"What kind of look?"

"A look like I'll never forget it. That kind. Like he was dead, man. Or *I* was."

Les and Cindy shared a look then she said, "Okay. What happened then?"

"The dead guy left," Ernie said. "You know, he looked nervous and shit, guilty like they do, then he just walked out."

"Did the other guy follow him?"

"Not right away, but in a few seconds. He looked at me one more time the same, then the freaky look went away, and he smiled and said thank you like a real gentleman, then he walked out the door."

"And you never saw either one of them again?"

"No, neither one," Ernie said, happy and relieved.

"Do you think you could describe this man to a sketch artist?" Les asked.

"Like one'a those guys draws people in court?"

"Right," Cindy said. "Only now, we use computers."

"Oh, yeah, yeah, yeah. That's cool!" Ernie was excited to help. "I wanna learn to program in college, you know, like complicated graphics shit, CADs and all, virtual 3-D imaging. AI, you know. I'll tell you what he looked like, sure."

***

Cindy looked at Les, Les looked at Cindy, one of them picked up a phone, and a minute later, an agent trainee named Eiris was leading the happy young Puerto Rican kid to the virtual mug shot computer room upstairs.

Cindy hadn't felt this hopeful since she became a TASK agent. Les hadn't felt this energized since he got so close to Riverbend three years prior. They had an eyewitness who had seen Riverbend and lived to tell about it. Their first.

If it was Riverbend.

For a moment, Cindy's enthusiasm flagged. But when Les said he felt sure it was who they wanted it to be, Cindy felt it as well. Which brought up another concern.

Ernesto's life expectancy.

Les's feeling was that if Riverbend had wanted Ernie dead, he would have gotten to him already. If the kid had lived this long, Riverbend didn't care. But if they put cops around him and Riverbend saw them, he might kill Ernie to keep him quiet — or take it as a personal challenge and off him just to show he could.

"No protection," they agreed.

Apparently, for the first time ever, Riverbend had underestimated Les's detective work.

That caused Les great concern.

***

Les and Cindy later discovered the real reason Riverbend had left the kid alone. He knew something they didn't. Ernie, put to the test, could remember nothing but The Look. The warning. The kid got the eyes but nothing else.

He described six different killers, one for each facial shape offered, with every combination of lips, ears, and hairlines shown to him. He couldn't even decide on the hair color. The only consistent feature was the eyes, which Cindy had to admit were mesmerizing—even on a computer.

"Reaper eyes," she said.

Les held up the printout and, for the first time, looked into the last eyes Marjorie and Melissa Ann had seen. The vision—the thought—rattled him to his core.

Cindy saw it coming and tried to get the rendering away from him, but he was already shaking. "Les. It's okay."

She didn't actually expect her intervention to work, and for one long moment—a beat longer than she thought she could endure, as usual—Les stared through her as if still seeing those merciless blue eyes, and playing out a million brutal deaths in his mind, each one more agonizing for Riverbend than the last.

Then, suddenly, it all went away—as Riverbend's look had gone away in the adult bookstore—and Les said, "I'm okay. I just need a cigarette." He left the room.

The computer sketch artist looked up. "He smokes?"

Cindy shrugged. It was news to her—and not particularly good news. She hadn't thought her own craving for a cigarette was a good sign. But Les?

Cindy found him outside, smoking a bummed Marlboro Light, and hacking. As she approached, he tried another drag, coughed, then flipped it into the street.

"I can't even smoke anymore," he complained.

"If you ask me, that's a good thing."

"I didn't." He gave her another one of those looks.

"Les, we're going to get him."

Les stared a beat longer, said, "I know," then turned and walked away.

No one saw him for three days.

Chapter 30 – The Brinkman Theory

Brinkman had taken a long weekend and didn't hear about Les's disappearing act until Tuesday morning. But he couldn't have been happier. He had two more dead-SK files on his desk. Two!

West Palm Beach's Jupiter Killer, named for the north county gay beach hangout from which all of the victims had disappeared, chopped his young male victims into pieces about the size of flank steaks — which he then fed to wild alligators. All the Palm Beach County Sheriff's Department had was a few human bones found in the stomachs of gators caught by licensed gator population controllers, but someone found Jupi' anyway, hacked him up, and dumped him at Gatorworld. The cops had to pump the stomachs of six large adults to get enough to ID the Killer. The putrefying goo almost made the coroner sick.

And there was Boston's Star of David Killer. He liked to scorch a torso-sized six-pointed star into the flesh of his victims and leave them burning on the lawns of Catholic churches at night. Somebody, presumably an SKK, turned the tables on him and drove a wooden cross through his head, forgoing the heart. "Probably didn't have one anyway," the Boston PD press liaison quipped to reporters.

Between Boston's and West Palm's sickos, at least twelve fewer innocent people inhabited this world — not the kind of population control most people endorsed, even on talk radio. But when it came to winnowing gators and serial killers, callers were, if anything, ecstatic — both predators had been attacking too often, lately — and one culling got even better airplay than the other. Several major newspapers were hailing the killing of serial murderers as the best law enforcement tool since fingerprinting.

"Might even revive Nasdaq," Brinkman chortled over the phone.

"You're not gonna yell at me, Phil?" Cindy wondered.

"Are you kidding? Over Les being Les? C'mon Baker. Lighten up!" He gave it more than his usual balance of phony patronization and forced joviality.

Les telling her to lighten up was one thing, but Brinkman? Cindy hung up, her head filled with the deafening roar of a hundred warning flags flapping in a stiff wind. Something truly supernatural had to be going on for Phil Brinkman to be so agreeable.

His undisguised glee made Cindy think back to the day she pulled him aside to suggest that perhaps she should be removed from the case because she felt she was beginning to empathize with Les a bit too much. Starting to see his point of view.

Brinkman was so overjoyed he cackled, "No way, Jose!" then 'Hustled' his way down the hall, singing, "That's the way, uh-huh, uh-huh, I *planned* it, uh-huh uh-huh."

Cindy could almost see Brinkman discoing back in the seventies, shirt open, Capricorn medallion flopping around on his hairy chest between the wide lapels of his powder-blue polyester leisure suit, drinking Black Russians, and hitting on chicks with blonde afros and see-through platform shoes — as frightening a vision as Cindy had ever had.

An hour later, around sunset, Les called Cindy in her room and asked if she wanted to come over and fuck. "You've been hanging around Phil Brinkman too much," she said.

"Oh, I don't think that," Les said without humor or hesitation.

"You know what I mean," Cindy countered.

"You want some foreplay. I see," Les said.

"Don't put yourself out," Cindy said.

"Dinner do?"

"Give me ten."

***

As it turned out, Les wasn't interested in sex after all. After a long day with the press, the coroner, and a dozen different homicide detectives, what he really wanted was a dinner companion and some light banter about baseball or home improvements. Since Cindy knew nothing about either, she talked about the case. And talked. And talked.

Les listened, patiently nodding here and there, giving a thoughtful "um-hmm," in the spaces between — until she got to her Brinkman theory.

"Wait a minute. Go back a few spaces," Les said. "You think Phil-sits-on-his-ass-all-day-long-and-does-nothing-but-yell-for-coffee-and-lie-about-stuff-he-doesn't-even-have-to-lie-about-just-because-he-*can*-lie-about-it-Brinkman could be our SKK?"

Cindy nodded.

Les laughed so hard he cried.

At one point, he managed to spit out, "The man has trouble killing a spider in his office. He calls maintenance, for Chrissake! I've seen him do it!"

Cindy's hackles were up so far they shoved at the label of her new designer dress, the one she had bought just for Les, and that he had not mentioned once!

Under her cold and unrelenting gaze, Les finally settled down. "I'm sorry," he said, "But—"

He busted up again.

After a full minute of this, Les wiped away his tears with a coral-colored linen napkin—this restaurant actually had linen for a change—and said, "Well, what the hell. I needed a good laugh. Haven't had many lately." Conversations like this had to beat baseball and home improvement any day. "Phil Brinkman a killer. You're too much, Baker. Maybe you need a vacation. I hear Honduras is a good value right now."

"I've thought about it, believe me," Cindy said, because she had, numerous times. But the draw of these cases, of working with Les to figure them out, won out every time.

Les's demeanor reversed and he leaned up. "Granted," he said thoughtfully, "Brinkman's whole life is about death. I'll give you that. The man loves blood. You ever notice he doesn't really come alive at a party until the conversation comes around to the many ways people have been hacked up, burned, dissolved, shot, and otherwise dispatched from this 'good earth' on his 'shift'?"

How had Cindy never noticed this before? *Probably because you were too busy sucking up to get the job,* she answered herself with self-derision, then said, "I can't say as I've been to many parties with Phil." Not many really meant none. Who would want to?

"Well, I have," Les said. "Office parties only, mind you. But let me tell you it is not a pretty sight. Get a few chardonnays in him and someone's great-aunt Agatha Christie freak asking about the inner workings of the Bureau, and Brinkman goes absolutely funereal. He becomes a veritable fountain of gloom and doom. The man *loves* death. I've never seen anything like it."

Les nodded, agreeing with himself wholeheartedly.

Cindy pondered what Les was saying. The person he had just described wasn't any Brinkman she knew. "We're talking about the Phil Brinkman who almost passed out when he got a paper cut handing me my assignment to this case? I thought he was gonna have me call 9-1-1."

"Hey, it's your theory," Les said. "But you gotta remember, Brinkman doesn't live in a world of truths, or even half-truths. Just full-blown lies. He is one mendacious son of a bitch." Les chuckled then said soberly, "Never trust a word he says."

Now, *that* had a familiar ring. The obvious difference was that Les had told Cindy he didn't want Brinkman backing him up anywhere, anytime, situation or not. He didn't want Phil Brinkman standing behind him for any reason is the way he put it to her.

"See, you have to look at this from Brinkman's point of view, as if he *was* killing SKs." Les said, sitting back and putting on his Big Brinkman voice. "'Oh yeah, you shoulda seen the corpses. Piled a hundred deep!'"

Les returned to his own voice. "He's the only guy I know who can get a six-foot swagger from a two-foot tale. Truth is, if Phil ever saw a corpse up close, he'd probably pass out and never come to."

"Okay," Cindy acquiesced. "But who else has direct knowledge of every one of these cases?"

"You."

"Me?" she asked. Were they back to that? Les shrugged. Cindy said, "What about you?"

"Me too," he conceded. "And a hundred other people, if not a thousand or ten thousand. But not Brinkman. The man's not only a serious yutz, he's a complete nincompoop. I don't think he's ever seen an actual police file, much less read one. *Understood* it. I doubt he even knows what words like 'disinterred' or 'eviscerate' mean. Hell, I don't think he knows what 'deceased' means except as it refers to someone's career.

"To tell you the truth, I'm not even sure he can read. He just looks at the pictures. It's where he gets some of his best material.

"And," Les said perfunctorily, "quite frankly, I don't think he has the energy for it. Not to mention the heart, literally and figuratively. He's too weak and too lazy.

"You know what he told me once? His greatest goal in life was to find the perfect pair of Italian loafers. His 'quest,' he said. And it makes perfect sense, if you think about it. Operative word: loaf—from the Latin *lofus*, meaning dead weight.

"And there," Les tipped his head and smiled, "you have Brinkman in a nutshell."

Though she didn't want to, Cindy gave an abbreviated snort that vaguely resembled a chuckle.

Les shook his head. "He's crazy, I'll give you that. But not killer crazy."

"Crazy like a fox, maybe."

"Crazy like a loon is more like it," Les said. "But if you want to violate Bureau policy and start investigating your superiors without informing OPR..."

Les paused, then said, "I assume you haven't mentioned this to them." The concern in his nonquestion was apparent and real. They both knew the Bureau probably wouldn't investigate Brinkman, anyway—not on a case like this—but they'd fire Cindy in a heartbeat, meaning Les would get another new partner. After he'd trained Cindy so well.

She understood all that and assured him that she had not gone to anyone yet. Les said, "Good," sounding relieved. Then he said, "Damn good laugh, though," and finished his steak.

Cindy felt recalcitrant. "Well, I'm gonna look into it. To him."

Les shrugged. "Hey, it's—"

"My funeral, I know," Cindy said with little enthusiasm for further debate on that topic.

After sulking a few minutes, she decided to throw out another idea, one she thought Les would find less controversial. "I was thinking maybe we should canvass adult bookstores in the college kid's town. From the cabin. Maybe RB found him in one, too."

Les gave her an odd look, momentarily, then shook his head. "He was too young for the hard stuff. You go in those stores, you mostly see old guys like me."

His *old* smile wasn't convincing. Cindy doubted that Les had ever been in one except on business, much less hung around making mental notes on the other men around him. "I don't think so," he said, and finalized his part of the discussion with a dismissive shake of his head.

Cindy accepted his logic and let it go. "Just a thought."

Les accepted her shrug with one of his own.

Cindy, unable to let the other thing go, said, "Look, I'm not convinced it's Brinkman, okay? All I'm saying is, we're getting nowhere on this. It's like being in some parallel dimension where nothing ever happens, and it's not happening at warp speed. I'm afraid I'm gonna wake up one morning and I'm eighty-nine years old and I still don't know who done it. Bodies are piling up like the plague and we got zip."

Les nodded thoughtfully, then said, "So, how about you and I go up to my room and discuss this like the highly qualified team leaders we are, maybe screw a few hours, then solve the whole thing. Whattayasay?"

Cindy eyed him. "All but the last part. Call me a cynic." She stood and left the booth with, "I'll see you in a few. You'll get this?"

Les nodded, pulled out his FBI Visa—the one with a hologram of Hoover—asked for the check, and wrote in a generous tip. After he bought a bottle of wine to go.

Let Brinkman explain it.

***

When Les answered the knock at his door an hour later, Cindy was out of the dress and into sweats. As he surveyed her wardrobe with obvious disappointment—taking a moment to eye the bottle of sauvignon blanc chilling in his hotel ice bucket—Cindy said, "You don't compliment the new dress, you don't get any of what's in it. I gave you all of dinner and an extra hour." Les gave a pathetic sigh.

"Snooze, ya lose," she said and paraded in with a large cardboard box full of notes and visual aids, which she plunked down on his bed.

Les was happy he hadn't taken the lone Viagra he kept just in case. He hadn't thought he'd need assistance. Turned out he was right, if for an entirely different and disappointing reason.

Cindy started with her new time line. She had notes on some 240 murders in forty-seven states and had incorporated 161 of them into her presentation. She listed the rest as "possibles." With nearly a dozen probable SKs now dead, she also had quite a series of graphs and charts for them, as well.

Les complimented her on her artwork and spent the next three hours indulging Cindy's various theories, the most intriguing of which was Shannon the video girl, though he strongly doubted she had any inclination toward murder. "Just shoot 'em after the fact with her nonlethal lenses."

"Depends on what you consider 'nonlethal,'" Cindy said ironically. Then, she went on to Anne Lorman, the King County detective with whom Cindy had shared lunch—the buff and busty blunt talker who offered a few thoughts on serial killers and the Bureau in the Olympia View Diner in Seattle. Cindy relayed how Lorman had said she wanted to "blow the nuts off" every serial killer she could find and how they should all end up in "a wet spot in the woods."

Les asked if Cindy thought Lorman was serious, and Cindy said she did.

"Not just some macho cop crap?" Les suggested.

"I don't know," Cindy said. "She sounded pretty serious about it."

Les let that steep a moment then said, "No. Too obvious."

Cindy added, "She had a partner, Chris Hines. Young guy, handsome, fit. Good candidate for Team SK. Nice smile, convincing manner."

"You dated him or profiled him?"

"Ignored him, mostly," Cindy said as if proud of that accomplishment. "But there was something else about him, something intense and... distant."

"People say that about me all the time. I mean, when I'm not around to hear it, of course. Am I right?" It wasn't really a question.

Cindy said, "Okay, he's off the list. For now. But he also raises the idea of there being a team out there, not just a sole executioner, as it were. Or, at the very least, not just one SK but two or even a few. I mean, all this..." She waved over her voluminous *fileage*.

Les didn't disparage the notion. After all, he was certain there had been at least one or two copycat SKs. He went with, "What else you got?"

Cindy moved on, next enchanting him with the inclusion of Pittsburgh's medical examiner Stan(islav) Demont(ovicz), though Les seriously doubted "the incompetent dick-drip" could think of anything one-hundredth as clever as would be necessary to pull off any of the SKK hits. "He has a hard time tying his shoes in any particular order is my guess. Anyone else?"

This of course led to the Pitt's Dick Cleveland, Demont's "partner in crime," as Les always said. Dick showed promise, Les had to admit. He even lay back on the bed to stare up at the ceiling and float a delightful fantasy sequence in which Brinkman grabbed Holy Dick and shouted, "I warned you I'd get even for NYCC!" But in the end, Les didn't think Dick was much brighter than Demont and therefore a nonstarter.

Cindy said, "Okay," and moved on to Megan, the panty line-less assistant coroner. A lot of faith had been placed in her report, but what if she had fudged it to mask her own involvement?

"Too sexy," Les said. "She doesn't need to kill."

Cindy stared, blinked, muttered something vaguely unsociable about the opposite gender, skipped over two or three other possible candidates on her list, then returned to Brinkman.

"He doesn't have the nuts for it, I'm telling you," Les said, doubtless.

"Well, maybe not," Cindy said. "But there's something going on there and I'm gonna find out what it is."

"Well, when you do, don't call me," Les said. "The less I know about Phil Brinkman the better off I figure my mental health will be. It's already shaky enough. Just ask Phil."

Cindy agreed not to share her findings unless Brinkman turned out to be their unsub. Les said he wouldn't hold his breath. He then said he hadn't caught up from the weekend and he needed to get some shut-eye.

"Where'd you go?" Cindy asked.

"Nowhere. Everywhere. But really nowhere."

Turned away, Cindy mouthed it with him as he folded down his bedspread. Then he asked, "Could I interest you in a quickie?"

"Sure," Cindy said—and took her top off.

Les stood, staring.

"Well?" she said, "Are you just gonna stand there with your mouth open or are you gonna put it to better use?"

Les's mouth was open, true. Finally, he said, "I was kidding."

"I know," Cindy said, flipping her top back on. "So was I."

There was no way he was going to get any sleep now!

"Sweet dreams," she said, then took her box and left.

***

The next day, Les spent some time at the library, doing online research away from the many curious stoppers-by at the field office, and Cindy went shopping for a dress he'd notice.

She couldn't stop playing the many cases over in her head—the lists, the graphs, the endless combinations and possibilities—a stochastic rabbit hole she'd created for herself.

She finally decided it was just her shambolic lot in life not to have the answer, at least for the time being, until the TASK team's most wanted revealed him or herself. But she didn't figure there was a chance in hell of that happening any time soon. Maybe in her lifetime.

When Cyndra Baker was wrong, she was really wrong.

Chapter 31 – The Truly Unexpected

Les and Cindy found themselves in a new city. It didn't matter which one, anymore—death was the same everywhere—but it was Houston, and the weather was hot. *Finally!* Cindy was starting to think Les was right about the damned cold.

Riverbend had been hard at work, as had the "other" SKK. Or SKKs. No one was sure how many were operating at this point. It seemed killing serial killers was the New Thing, the hula-hoop of mass murder. It could have been a half dozen, ten, or even fifty out there, and no one would have known. But one thing was certain. If they kept going at this pace, Les might get his retirement wish early; the SKKs might use themselves up.

Or kill him doing it.

Les's Rolex read 9:02 p.m. He had a drink in the hotel bar, happy with himself that he'd managed to keep it to just one—and one more—and had walked out under the hotel lanai to finish his third. Rain fell in buckets. Warm tropical rain swept up on churning Gulf winds from the Yucatan. *Everything's steamy there,* he thought, and felt better for it. The heat had to be a good sign. Sinatra singing "Stormy Weather" in the smoky lounge of his brief melancholy.

Les watched shooter-sized drops fall like yellow diamonds past tall parking lot standards, thinking that a few more days like this and he might yet hand the case over to Cindy. She might even do a better job without him. He craved another cigarette but knew it would just choke him. On the other hand, he was already choking on the stench of so many rotting corpses lying about the landscape of his mind. Today had been little kids.

The girl was seven years old, raped then decapitated, her head mailed to her parents. The father would never recover, despite drugs and therapy. A twenty-four-hour suicide watch would go on for most of the rest of his life, if you could call it a life. The five-year-old boy had been split in two with a band saw, lengthwise, then UPS'd to each of the parents who were "Separated. Get it?" the cards read. The mother didn't wait for the watch to start.

Why can't Riverbend find this *maniac and put a yellow ribbon around his* vivisected *heart?* Les wondered, watching the heavy weather roll over.

He admired the storm's steadfastness and independence, its efficiency. Nothing stood in its way, nothing could stop it until it simply ran out of steam, all used up. *What was the name of this hurricane? Lesley?* Could it possibly be?

The citizens of Houston seemed thankful to be getting the long, outermost bands of the late storm. Maybe the pounding rain would rinse away some of the anguish and leave their city a little cleaner. Maybe make the Texas Two-Step child killer stand out better. First, he raped them, then he cut them into two pieces. How hard could it be to find a guy like that in a city purged of filth?

Les set his empty rock glass on a faux-stone bench between two of the thick veranda columns and stepped out into the downpour to let the big drops pummel him. The shotgun rain stung and felt good at the same time, like pain awash in pleasure, cleansing contrition.

Then he saw her.

Standing in the narrow grassy strip by the parking lot, soaked to the bone, wearing a blue dress. "I've been looking for you everywhere," Cindy called out over the rain. Mascara had run to her chin and her new 'do was a disaster, but she looked spectacular, nonetheless.

Les had barely said a word to Cindy since Nashville. He didn't feel like talk. Something had happened, something over which he had no control — maybe never had — as if the power was outside him instead of inside where he was only registering some unknown, indefinable sensation. Cindy had asked him if he was dumping her this time. He said he wasn't. "I don't think I am," is what he'd actually said.

He said, "You didn't look in the bar."

"Didn't know I should," Cindy said. "I thought you'd had enough of that."

"For a lifetime," Les said. "Trouble is, seems like another life already."

Cindy nodded wearily as if she understood well.

The rain fell like anger.

"Nice dress," Les said over the smacking roar, certain that if he could see her eyes, they'd be playing off the royal blue, as he had planned before. Sinatra now praising "The Way You Look Tonight" in his head. Too bad Cindy couldn't hear it.

"I got it for you," she told him.

"I figured," Les said, still offering no invitation. He wasn't even sure why, but there was something about them standing out in the stinging rain that was both romantic and tragic at the same time. Better to leave it alone.

Frank sliding seamlessly into "Rain (Falling From the Skies)," with some of "(That Old) Black Magic" thrown in—a medley ending with "Strangers in the Night." A perfect way to the end the night.

Maybe to end everything.

Les turned off the player in his head. Even music—even Sinatra— was dead to him.

"It's not exactly the same," Cindy said. "Fabric's different."

"Figured that, too," Les said. He had looked long and hard in Florida—during one of his extended absences—before finding the perfect color, cut, and cloth.

Cindy nodded and stood in the pounding rain a few more silent moments before saying, "I can take it off."

Les knew what she meant but went with, "Right here?"

"If you like." And she probably would have.

He chuckled but said, "I'm done for the night." After this day, and the photos of those two kids, then the morgue, the parents, he was numb, inside and out.

"I understand," Cindy called out. She probably felt the same, except maybe her hope was still alive. He hoped so.

"Thanks," he said and started back inside, passing behind the first wide column of the lanai. As the white concrete blocked their views of one another, Les thought how the pressure was getting to be too much, the whole thing getting to be too damned complicated—like before, when it all came crashing down in Riverbend in the rain.

Always the rain.

When his view opened up again, Les could see that Cindy hadn't moved. She looked small and vulnerable, yet brave, standing steadfast in the raging tempest.

GLENN A. BRUCE

He walked behind the last column, thinking it was awful to waste the dress and the moment, but a man had to do what a man had to do. And what Les had to do was sleep and recharge or he'd be no good to the aggrieved relatives of Texas Two-Step's tiniest victims or anyone else. Even Cindy.

When he came out from behind the final column, he glanced over to give a last smile before going inside, but—

Cindy was gone.

That fast.

Too fast.

"Cindy?" Les called out, moving toward the empty strip of motel lawn. He got only the rain in reply. If anything, the roar seemed to have increased. "Cindy?"

Les squinted into the frenzied squall, swiftly calculating the distance from where she had been standing seconds before to any exit in any direction. The rear hotel entrance was entirely too far; she would have had to break at a dead run, in track shoes, her key at the ready. Even then...

Les aimed his voice at the parking lot and called louder. "Cindy!"

Nothing came back but slapping waves of rain, pulsing with no particular rhythm. The irregular heartbeat of a furious tropical depression.

"Baker!" he shouted as an order and stepped into the parking lot, but he got no response. Just Hurricane Lesley howling at him, mocking him. His insignificance.

Les couldn't see fifty feet in any direction, could hear nothing but bawl and bluster. But he sensed the big Ford van coming. A second later, the brights flashed on, blinding him.

On raw instinct, Les threw himself down and away to roll behind a heavy redwood planter as *Wham!* the dark gray van took it out, showering Les, the broad walk, the thick columns, and the deep grass beyond with sodden potting soil, shredded azaleas, and golden splinters. Then the van was gone.

There was no doubt as to where Cindy was and who had her.

***

In the back of the windowless tin box, Cindy pitched helplessly on wet-slick metal, slamming side to steel side as the van jagged through the Marriott lot for the exit.

She couldn't believe how quickly and efficiently her abductor had gotten tape around her wet head and wrists and dragged her off. One moment, she was watching Les go behind a veranda column and the next she was yanked into blackness, completely immobilized, ankles, wrists, eyes, and mouth taped tight. Thrown into the waiting van.

She didn't have to see him to know it was Riverbend — or that she was on a fast track to permanent early retirement.

She was going to die.

***

The Killer saw the end of the alley coming a moment too late.

He'd gotten a streak of luck with this storm and had known the moment he heard its name what he had to do. Watching the storm's progress closely, Riverbend charted Hurricane Lesley's path up through the Gulf as it veered away from Galveston, headed for Beaumont — the eye passing directly over the courthouse before sundown, dumping over four inches an hour — no one on the street for five hundred miles around.

Before the first drop fell, he had stolen the storm-gray van, switched the plates and disabled every bulb but the headlights. Even now, he had them turned off in the thick, black night.

So, the T-bone alley caught him by surprise.

He cut right and slid left into someone's garage, the sudden impact throwing Cindy like a crash test dummy against the metal-ribbed side of the van. Riverbend shook off the jarring hit and kept going, the squeal and grind of sheet metal shrill as truck and garage tore free of one another. He then blasted out the end of the alley, hung a sharp left —

— and nearly head-on'd a big Mercury. The only other maniac out on a night like this blew by, doing at least fifty. He had to have been drunk. Didn't even hit his horn in protest.

"Fuckin' idiot! Watch where you're going!"

Riverbend sounded for a moment like any other road rager. Then his Killer's calm returned. *Slow down*, he told himself. There might be a cop out, somewhere.

***

Speeding out of the Marriott lot, Les clipped two parked rentals and a hotel courtesy van while wrestling a detailed local map from the door pocket. This loaner was another old corpulent Caprice Classic, metallic maroon, with spent shocks. No SS Impala upgrade, no Bluetooth, no *radio*—a bloated blob of automotive history headed for scrap.

Someone at Quantico was onto him.

Les lost sight of the gray van quickly and had no way of knowing whether he'd ever find it again in this colorless weather. All he had was the determination that he wouldn't stop looking until he did—and the sallow prayer Cindy would still be alive inside it.

So, Les plowed through blind intersections, one foot on the gas, one on the brake, hoping beyond all hope he would spot the long van without being spotted, himself—especially by some damn quota-conscious ticket-slinging blue-flaming rookie traffic cop. Dying in a fatal car crash before he could get to Cindy.

Before Riverbend could die at his hands.

No one would question that hit, not under these circumstances. Any opportunity at all, any clean shot, and Riverbend was taking one in the skull, maybe two. More likely an entire clip.

Fifteen in the head. What a symphony that would be.

***

Through her growing fog of pain, Cindy knew she had only one chance at getting out of her predicament—work her hands loose enough to get at the black nylon harness Velcro'd to the inside of her right leg, up high. Likely pressed for time as he was with Les so close, Riverbend had missed the thigh holster and what was in it.

Cindy almost hadn't worn the compact .32 caliber Beretta Tomcat under the new blue dress. But if she'd learned one lesson in Les's room that morning, it was to never, *never* be without a firearm, no matter where you think you're going or what you think you might be doing because you could end up in bed with an SKK.

Or worse, in his speeding van.

Cindy's New Rule Number One was to bring her weapon no matter what, no matter where. Put it in your pocket, under your vest, under your new blue dress. If you're naked, carry the damn thing at your side—or *inside*. Just *bring* it!

Now, if she could only get to the Tomcat before getting slung to death.

Bam! into the side. *Bam!* the back. *Bam!* the other side. Riverbend was navigating quick alleys. Every stop, start, and turn sent Cindy crashing into something hard and edgy. Pain on top of hurt. She could think of nothing but bracing for the next impact. Obviously, the Killer had left her loose for a reason.

***

Les trailed just two rainy blocks behind—not that he knew it. All he could see was an occasional smear of gray in gray on gray that he hoped was the van but could have been just more rain.

Ghosts.

On the first straightaway, Les grabbed for his cellphone to call for backup. Set up a screen, roadblocks. It might work, even with Riverbend. Les felt all over the seat, then remembered. He'd left his phone in the room, hiding from *fucking Brinkman!*

There would be no backup tonight.

***

Riverbend caught Les's headlights swing in behind him while they were weaving a particularly curvy section of his blueprinted escape route—then they fell away. Seeing the lights, knowing it was likely Les, didn't alarm him. He had planned for the unexpected—while accepting that you can't plan for the truly unexpected. He didn't expect that. But he knew you can't plan for that which no plan can possibly exist.

So, you leave wiggle room.

He cut through someone's yard, took the next short corner, then another, then sped up, certain of where he was, and where he was going. He didn't need a map; he'd run the course eight times each of the past five nights and had it as hard set in his mind as what he was going to do to Cindy.

First, he'd cut off a few of her toes, the big ones for certain, to make her unstable and in too much pain to run, while creating steady blood loss to weaken her. Then he'd rape and sodomize her—with sharp and abrasive objects. Abuse her in the basest ways he could think of, topping any horror he had ever devised before. These things would be expected of him. Finally, as she was dying, he'd drag her body over the floor of the abandoned dirt farmer's shack out in ag country, spelling out his favorite two words these days. "Hi Les."

Then he'd decapitate her.

After escaping in a dummied-up DoT truck he had waiting in the woods a short walk away, the Killer would send Les a postcard on which he'd have someone write something like, "Hey Les, *shacked* up with Baker, lately? She gives good *head*, huh?"

He'd then kill that person, the writer, and dispose of them. Neither that body, nor Cindy's head, would ever be found, and the truck would be burned to the ground.

Thoroughness was essential to being a Riverbend. But first, he had to get there, out to the open highway—and Les's headlights were back again.

The Killer sped up as much as he dared in the near total darkness and torrential rain, spreading out his lead incrementally, but crucially. Then he took two turns, skipped two others, made three more—and doubled back.

Riverbend was now following Les.

***

Cindy had given up on the unyielding wraps around her wrists and was trying to work the tape loose from her eyes. If she couldn't get to her gun to kill the Killer, she should at least get a look at him so she could describe him later. If there *was* a later.

Cocking her head and peering up, Cindy met only blackness. So, the task was set. She scrunched up her face—bad for crows' feet, but good for loosening wet tape—and the tape obliged. A flutter of street light caught her vision.

Yes! Cindy exaggerated her grimace-then-smile grimace-then-smile action—like that nutty facial-exercise woman she'd seen on YouTube, walking around Manhattan wincing and grinning like she had palsy of the palate—and the tiny slit opened as far as it was going to go. A shift of her body, a tweak of her neck, and there he was.

Riverbend.

A fuzzy view — slim, ragged, blurry — but Cindy could make out a vague profile, dark blond hair (that was new) backlit in a passing street light, and, in the rearview...

The eyes.

There was no mistaking those eyes — the same eyes from Ernie G's police renderings in Chicago. The kid had been right on the money. They were goddam spooky.

Cindy wanted more. She put her feet against the side of the van and silently pushed herself out to a spot behind and below the driver's seat, then turned her face to look up just as The Killer looked down and saw her looking.

The big Taurus revolver came up from his lap. *Blam!* It sounded like the forward mount on the USS Texas at Normandy in such tight quarters. Cindy screamed under the tape, hopping wormlike for cover behind his seat.

"Don't fuck with me, Baker!" the Killer shouted. "Do it again and I won't miss!"

To be sure he was making his point...

***

Boomf, boomf!

Les had stopped a few blocks over when his senses went cold. He heard the two last muffled big bore reports in the near distance *behind* him and was back in his sedan before the echo died.

***

Riverbend knew at once he'd been foolish. *Gunshots!* He pounded the steering wheel. He could not afford to lose control like that!

Goddam Les Moore!

If the Killer had thought for a moment there might be another agent like Les — say, right there in the van with him — who could second-guess his every move to track him down someday, he would have killed Cindy then and there. To hell with saving her for later. But she was only a woman, and women posed no threat — especially bound and gagged in the back of rape rig. Just to make sure, he snuck a look.

Cindy was still, and still in the same spot. "Are you hit?" he asked. Cindy gave a weak response to the negative, barely audible. *Good*, he thought, he'd humbled her. Maybe shooting at her was worth the risk after all.

A quarter of a mile later, Riverbend found his turnoff. From there, it was a straight haul out an old macadam road to the long, low bridge over the shallow bayou lake and, a few thousand feet past that, the ag shack. Ten miles to torture, ecstasy, and Sweet Release. He checked his rear views. Empty and black.

They were alone on the highway.

Chapter 32 – The Bridge

Something was wrong. Dead wrong.

Les slammed his brakes, sliding past the wide unmarked turnoff. Before coming to a complete stop, he ground the gear lever up into reverse, threw his right arm on the seat back and floored the dark red boat, backing into the dense night with little regard for anything other than figuring out where he was and why he wasn't seeing any road signs. Every moment lost in pursuit of Cindy brought her closer to her end.

Headlights appeared behind, coming fast.

Les slid his big Caprice off the road backward to the right as a car spun out and donuted past on the left, horn Dopplering the whole way. An older Corvette, so no one important.

"Sorry," Les said to the anonymous storm driver and swept up his map, quickly retracing his moves and the Killer's. "Here. Here. Over here. That was a decoy move. Back here. Over here. Doubled back on me. Then..."

Les looked up. He was where he thought he should be but, "Where's the sign?" This was a major cutoff, no others along this part of the road so, "There should be a sign."

Grabbing a flashlight from the dash, Les got out in the slingshot rain and tromped back through wet and heavy highway grass. He quickly located two square wooden stumps where the sign had been. A closer look revealed chainsaw marks and, with a swing of the light, the flat green board in a ditch, submerged under silt-rich runoff. Only one explanation came to mind.

Les started back for his car.

"Are you fucking crazy!" The driver of the spinout approached, tall and angry.

"Not really," Les said. "Just a little busy. Excuse me."

The guy swung low and from the left.

Les spilled him out in one sweep, all 245 pounds of him, then got in his maroon Caprice Classic and sped off before the door closed, slinging storm sludge and stringy road weeds onto the former college athlete. The lumbering Chevrolet caught pavement, spun a loose nautilus in the junction, took out the opposing stop sign and a fire hydrant, then raced away into the pitch-black rainy night, headlights off.

Seconds later, the only other idiot out in the night—the drunk Riverbend had seen before, in the big Mercury—smashed into the parked Corvette, totaling both.

***

A mile out the dark road, the Killer realized he was moving at a crawl, under twenty mph. He couldn't see fifteen feet. Checking the better of his rear views, on the right, he detected no headlights behind him so, deciding the need to extend his lead was worth the risk, he pulled the knob for his own and sped up. There followed great disillusionment.

The van's right headlight had been smashed out completely when he plowed through the redwood planter and the left one ended up severely misaligned from the garage mishap, pointing off nowhere in particular. All in all, barely better than no lights at all.

He didn't slow down.

***

A half-mile back, Les squinted into horizontal rain, headlights off, trying to identify the intermittent glow ahead. Was it a moving vehicle? a motorcycle? or just some incandescent anomaly? Hard to tell. He'd no sooner get a vague lock on the evasive glow than it would be swallowed in darkness and falling water. Les tried to speed up, but in seconds, wandered off the road every time.

Goddam rain. And it had felt so good, carried such promise. Hurricane Lesley. *Shit.*

Les aimed for the next streetlight, hoping it was on his side, realizing quickly it wasn't when he saw the semi-sized wrecker which had pulled out of the trailer park up ahead and was now *coming right at him!*

Les yanked to the left—it was closer—and ran off the road, plowing immediately into and through a blessedly flimsy rural bus stop. Corrugated fiberglass, tin, and two-by-fours exploded around him as the big rig blasted past to his right, air horns splitting the night.

(The now *very* awake driver had told his wife, minutes before, he was going to cruise for a call, hoping to pick up something on his police scanner so he could, "Maybe make a few extra bucks off this blow." He figured the tow would involve a grisly monsoon-induced wreck — bloody limbs hanging by sinew, a shoe on the highway — not a fistfight between a drunk and a well-known SMU running back he would happen on at The Cutoff.)

The churning wrecker wake sent a storm within the storm over Les's dark Caprice, rinsing most of the debris from the windshield as Les charged back onto the highway, never slowing down, never switching on his lights.

"Okay, the poles alternate side to side," Les mumbled, and aimed for the next streetlight, keeping to the left of it and hoping he wasn't headed for a ditch. Getting stuck out here without a phone was a no-go. His TASK partner would be on her own.

**

Cindy fought against the tape on her wrists with no success. Looped between as well as around behind her, she managed no movement, no slippage. She would have to try passing her wrists underneath her to have any hope at all of reaching her weapon. As she was slightly longer of limb than trunk, it might work.

Still blindfolded and gagged, she shifted onto her back, lifted up onto her shoulders and heels, and shoved her bound hands as far as they would go. Not far enough. She rolled onto her left side and pulled her knees up, catching fabric on the jagged, skidding Taurus-blown hole in the metal floor. Her new blue dress was ruined.

Reaching back, Cindy pushed her wrists down until they snugged up onto the widest part of her hips. The position reminded her of the time in Georgia when she had eaten nothing but pecan-cheese logs for three days and had to give herself an enema. The image propelled her hands like greased lightning past the offending orifice, directly behind her thighs.

And her Tomcat .32.

***

Without warning, Les was off the road, spinning out of control across the grassy flats of a broad curve. There had been no shoulder to alert him this time. Hydroplaning over wet turf, he fought for control, hands futilely palming the wheel this way, that way, and back, featureless scenery flying past in a rain-soaked blur as he spun endless, looping ellipses which finally deposited him, incredibly, back on the highway, just beyond the apex of the wide turn.

Backward.

Drawing on reflexes he didn't know he still had, Les steered into it, swung the floaty bastard around and finally got himself headed in the right direction.

"Jesus," he muttered, amazed he hadn't rolled it or struck anything solid, and finally took a breath. He'd averted another catastrophe. Now, to avert the main one.

***

Riverbend cursed at the night. He'd been searching for Unkle Urk's Produce Stand in the dim glow of the walleyed headlight off to the left for what seemed like an eternity, certain he should have come to it by now. Urk's was the last landmark he had felt a need to memorize because the bridge was less than a mile beyond it.

A mile beyond the bridge Cindy was his to do with as he pleased.

The Killer checked his speed: Thirty-five mph. No wonder! He eased up to forty... forty-two...

***

Les lost the elusive light again. *Maybe it's aliens,* he grunted in his mind. *Swamp gas.* If what he was seeing was a moving headlight, it was sure aimed off at an odd angle. Les pushed his four-door up to fifty.

Four seconds later, he hit the tree.

***

Working her hands up under her dress, close to her backup gun, Cindy touched thigh, then thigh holster. Another tickling stretch and she found the cold steel of her .32—made warm by her pressed flesh, her body heat, her *nerves*—and the coarse cross-hatch of pale alabaster.

Nothing had ever felt finer.

She took a breath, pinched the tip of the holster's Velcro strap and began to tug one... tiny... *sccrritccch*... at a time, until... the strap broke free. Her Tomcat was loose.

Bang! The van hit a jarring pothole, and the Beretta headed for the floor.

Cindy clamped her thighs shut and tugged her taped wrists up, burning to snatch her little Tomcat and... just caught it, a quarter-inch before it would have clattered onto the metal floor. Cindy was so relieved she let out a loud sigh of relief.

That, Riverbend heard.

***

He had just passed Unkle Urk's stand and felt almost giddy.

"Whatcha doin' back there, baby?" the Killer asked playfully. "Ride's been rough on you, huh?" He laughed, knowing the answer.

Cindy moaned again, sounding delirious.

The Killer responded favorably. "Don't worry. It won't be long now," he promised over his shoulder, as if updating the kids—then said nothing more.

He wanted to savor these last two miles before executing what he knew would be his greatest, headline-grabbing murder ever.

***

Holding the barrel, then the slide, Cindy painstakingly rotated her Beretta a sixteenth turn at a time until the grip lay in her palms. But how in *hell* was she going to get a shot from a position like this? She could barely see her target, much less acquire it. Lancaster Budrow never taught this one on the Quantico range.

The deep-tread truck-tire roar changed to a low hum. *Smooth pavement.*

Cindy guessed they were on a bridge. If she killed the Killer now, and he forfeited control, they wouldn't go far before hitting something solid and steel-reinforced. Her chances of surviving such a crash in the back of this tin box without a seatbelt might not be high. Still, higher than surviving whatever Riverbend had in store for her at the end of the line.

But what if they went over the side? Cindy wasn't a great swimmer. Her ignominious thrashings in the hotel pool with Les had cinched that. Now, out here alone, with her hands and feet duct-taped together...

Cindy ran her options. She could shout something official like, *You're under arrest! Pull this vehicle over immediately!* but he would probably just slam on the brakes, send her flying into the engine cabinet, take her little .32, and kill her with *that friggin' cannon* in his lap, then shove her out onto the bridge to be run over by the next blind driver in the storm.

None of those choices sounded appealing, so Cindy tried to come up with an alternative to attempting a clean shot from behind her back while craning over her shoulder to see what she was shooting at while lying on the slick floor of a moving vehicle in the dark with her eyes mostly covered and her hands taped behind her back.

Nothing came to mind.

So, Cindy went straight to Plan B, proving conclusively that you really can't plan for the truly unexpected.

***

Les saw the flashes and heard the muffled shots ahead from just behind the gray ghost.

After glancing off the tree a mile back, then demolishing Unkle Urk's Produce Stand, coming to a full stop under a hail of squashed tomatoes and busted cantaloupes, losing the moving light ahead completely, Les had decided the need for stealth was far outweighed by the need for speed. So, he turned on his remaining headlight and stood on the gas.

Multiple muzzle flashes now strobed the Killer's profile in the moving van's twisted and cracked outside mirrors. Who was shooting whom was not clear, but a second later, the big gray box jerked right then left, straight into the path of a two oncoming bright beams.

The Killer's van hit the left railing hard at a sharp angle and flipped into the air, giving the onrushing dark sedan just enough time and room to swing around and *under* it—

—directly into Les's lane.

Brakes!

The dark car swerved again, barely squeaking past. What the hell were all these nutcases doing out *in a freaking hurricane!*

Les slid his loaner to an angled stop against the right-side rampart, his eyes glued to the van as it rode up onto the opposite railing, straight up and down, scraping along on its grill for thirty feet—sparks, windshield glass, and loose parts spraying—until the leading edge of the roof caught a pillar cap, wrenched around, and the whole deal headed over the side.

They were going in.

Les was out of his car and to the rail before the boxy Ford hit water. In the darkness and still-driving rain, he saw a circle of foam squirt out as the van landed on its front roof at an angle, then continued over, pulled down by the heavy six-liter engine, water flooding in through the absent windshield as it sank out of sight.

Les stripped to boxers and socks in six seconds flat and dove in without hesitation. A near perfect swan, and he stuck it, disappearing into the black depths.

***

Cindy awoke disoriented, eyes and mouth taped shut. She remembered unloading her weapon, all seven rounds; she remembered Riverbend jerking and swearing, the van careering right then left; she remembered the crash.

She had felt the silent free-fall, the hard landing, the sheet metal roof gratefully buckling under her weight. She knew she had been knocked unconscious then came to when the first splash of cold water hit her face as the full-sized F-350 cargo van plunged for the bottom.

Filling up fast.

A moment later, all motion stopped sharply with a dull thud as the van bottomed out, hood down in the bottom mud, rear-end propped unsteadily against the corner of a submerged buttress. The chassis creaked, scraping, and settled. Still.

Cindy kicked frantically, mermaid-like—ankles and wrists still bound—until she found a pocket of air and snorted a grateful breath. But, unable to keep a foothold on the slippery metal slope, she promptly slid out of her air pocket headed for the bottom.

Back under.

***

The bayou water was colder than Les had expected, and pitch black. After what seemed like an eternity of finding nothing, he was forced to abort for air. Popping to the surface, he looked up. The remaining headlight of the battered red Chevy shone directly overhead.

He had drifted.

Les lunged ahead, swimming hard against the wind-whipped chop, then took the biggest breath he could stuff in his lungs and plunged straight down.

He would only get one chance.

***

Cindy stabbed for a foothold and shoved up, found air, and breathed it in. Her knee bumped the spare, and her face the twisted rear doors. *Good.* She knew where she was.

No! Bad! Doors meant joints, joints meant seams, and seams meant *leaks!*

Cindy heard air bubbling out and felt water creeping up her neck to her jawline. Turning her head, she grabbed as much air as she could get before it covered her nose. Seconds.

She had seconds.

***

Les's hand hit something hard and slick—smooth here, twisted there. The van, for sure.

But where was he on it?

He found a handle and yanked hard. The doors moved, then stopped short with a faint *clink.* Riverbend had chained them shut. *Damn!*

Les started to swim away when he heard Cindy calling from inside.

"*Mmmmmm! Mmmmmmmmmmm!*"

Then, "*Un-mm! Un-mm! Mmmmmmm mmmmm MMMMMmmmm!*" And repeating, "*Mmmmm mmmm MMMMMMMMmmmmmmmmmmm!*"

Having experienced Cindy's abstruse quasi-verbal communications before, Les understood instantly. *No! No! Not these doors! Try the others!*

Lungs aching, he swam deeper, his hands never leaving the van this time. He found the driver's door wedged in mud, lodged shut, window up. No time to check for the Killer. Assume that if he doesn't attack, he's too dead to do it, and move on.

Time was running out as quickly as Les's air.

He felt his way around the roof to the passenger side—blackness and chill making this harder than he ever could have imagined—only to find the passenger door twisted worse than the other, glass gone, but impossible to open.

The side doors were his last hope, but he found them bent as well. He had no choice but to make do. Grabbing the front one of the two with both hands, he put a stockinged foot on the passenger door post and heaved with all he had left.

Once, twice...

***

The hand that took hold of Cindy's leg and dragged her down was stronger than she had anticipated, the motion more violent. Up felt down. Reason told her everything was okay—Les wouldn't try to drown her—but adrenaline argued she was being dragged deeper.

In her oxygen-starved delirium, Cindy suddenly thought it more likely that Riverbend had gone up for air and come back down to get her. She started kicking, struggling, fighting for her life—upsetting the van's delicate balance.

It creaked again, then started over onto its side.

***

The wind had increased, making the chop higher, but the rain had eased off. Up on the bridge, the other car had backed up and parked behind Les's boaty Caprice. Someone had a strong flashlight out, scanning the black waves on the opposite side.

Les shouted, "Over here! Over here!"

The man trotted across the bridge and flashed his light down, finding Les, then Cindy. They'd gotten out just before the van rolled over onto its side to rest on the muddy bottom. They would have died down there.

The beam passed over them. Les shouted, "Hold it steady!"

When it came back and settled, he saw the tape on Cindy's mouth and ripped it off.

She greedily sucked in two lungs full of air and said, "My hands!"

Les reached down, found the tape, and tore it loose while treading water for both of them.

He shouted up at the stranger. "Do you see anybody else?"

The light left, searching. Cindy was obviously still scared, fighting the water and Les, pulling them under.

He told her, "I've got us. Relax."

"My feet," she said. "I can't help."

She reached down, Les helped, and they got the tape off her ankles.

The guy on the bridge shouted down that he didn't see anyone and asked if they could make it to the bank. "Over there, to your left, about two hundred feet."

Les said, "Okay," and, having drifted enough to get a glimpse of the cruiser parked behind the red Chevy, realized the man was a cop. In the chaos of the moment, he hadn't noticed the low-profile light bar or markings before. *My luck, he'll probably give me a ticket for stopping on a bridge.* He started for shore, Cindy clinging tight.

"I shot him, Les," Cindy said, her voice a shaky mix of stress, relief and cold. But under it all was pride. "I think I may have killed him."

"I hope so," Les said.

Because if she hadn't, they just *thought* things were bad before.

Chapter 33 – Habeas Corpus

Wrapped in a towel in the turnout at the end of the long, low bridge, Cindy noted the damage Les had inflicted on their most recent loaner when he leveled the vegetable stand and battled a southern mahogany. "What is it with you and cars?" Her first words since being fished out of the water by the county cop.

Les was relieved to hear anything coming from her, but especially a joke. "You had me worried there for a minute, kid," he said, still not confident she was okay.

"Kid?" Cindy said irritably.

She was okay. "Term of affection. Guess it dates me," he said. That and hearing Frank in his head, swinging "Luck Be a Lady."

Walking off with the same sad smile—Frank from his stage in Never-Say-Never Land, Les from a battered Texas windscape.

The bayou dawn was breaking dull and gray, but thankfully warm, heavy with the scent of shredded flora in the misty drizzle. Mud covered what could be seen of the road. Hurricane Lesley had come and gone. Texas had survived the storm, but Cindy had survived Riverbend.

She smiled, then as quickly paled, looking out over the dark water, thick with black lowland runoff and littered with hurricane flotsam—lumber, bleach bottles, pieces of Styrofoam ice chests. A mannequin, face up, one arm reaching heavenward.

"Could've been worse," Cindy said to Les, in the muddy turnout. "You could've been me."

"Or," Les said, even worse, "I could've been me without you now."

Cindy shook her head. "I wasn't gonna be the one to go first."

Strange how comforting those words were to both of them.

Back on the bridge, searchlights pointlessly scanned the sound as sheriff's divers worked the water and wrecker drivers waited their turn, idling by the rail, swapping stories with cops the way they always did, as if they were equals, but knowing they weren't. Only fate, pure coincidence, put anyone on a bridge at dawn under these circumstances. Even tow truck guys knew that.

"As scared as I was," Cindy said, "and believe me, I've never been more scared in my life... I knew somewhere deep inside it wasn't going to end like that. It wasn't my time. Somehow, you were going to find me, and I'd be okay."

"You had a lot more faith in me than I did," Les said.

"Always," Cindy said, and gave him one of those smiles he had come to cherish, even if he never said so.

"There's another reason it was better this way," she went on. "Rather than the other way around."

"Yeah? Why's that?"

"As you may have noticed previously, I don't swim all that well."

Les broke a full grin. "You call that swimming?"

He laughed and she laughed, and they felt an ease slip around them, a welcome buffer to what was still here, but silent now.

Les looked at her long and hard, almost as if he'd never seen her before. Agent Cyndra Baker was wet, cut, bruised, battered, exhausted, and pale; her hair matted and sticking out straight to one side like Wile E. Coyote's head after coming out of an Acme vice. But she had never looked more beautiful. No one had.

It hurt so bad, he had to walk away.

***

By daybreak, the rain had stopped, the wind had dwindled to a stiff breeze, and the divers had determined that Riverbend's body wasn't in the van or the general vicinity as could properly be searched in the present conditions. Cindy's elation fell out from under her.

What if she *hadn't* killed him? What if he had survived the crash and gotten away?

Then, one of the divers from Corpus brought up the only piece of real evidence his team would recover from the wreck—a double-yoked gray cowboy shirt missing one diamond-shaped mother-of-pearl inlay.

Cindy's still-cold blood went thick as winter. She knew without sending the shirt to DC that the inlay held in evidence would fit the empty button cup perfectly.

"He was going to leave it on you," Les said, close to a whisper.

Cindy stared blankly. "It's gonna get weird now, isn't it?"

"Real weird would be my bet, Princess," he said, and headed back to see if the divers had noticed anything not necessarily meaningful to them but that might be a goldmine to a TASK agent.

"Princess," Cindy said fondly. He hadn't tried to get her into court for too long.

"Ma'am."

The man's voice was behind her. Cindy jumped, despite the forty plus local, county, state, and federal law enforcement officers loitering about, along with a growing drove of reporters.

"Sorry," the older paramedic apologized. "I was just wonderin' if you was ready to go the hospital, ma'am." A real Texas gentleman.

"Not without Agent Moore, thank you."

"Uh," the craggy-faced man said, looking down the bridge at Les. "He's the one told me to go on an' take ya, ma'am."

"He did, did he?" Cindy grimaced and stood to go after Les.

Pain racked her entire body. She stopped and looked down. Everywhere she could see skin, she saw bruises; where her skin wasn't scraped, it was missing altogether.

Forget the ruined blue dress.

Cindy let go a groan, then looked over and saw Les joking with the divers on the bridge. She couldn't help but chuckle. *All this, and he can still get it up.* He'd be okay without her.

"All right," Cindy said and accepted the craggy Texan's hand to steady her steps.

***

Les waved at the departing ambulance then turned back to the county cops and told a pretty good dick joke, which made them all laugh and forget their miserable lives for a few seconds. Knowing it had once belonged to Cindy made it even better.

***

Cindy slept for two days, nearly straight through. The meds helped. But she was more exhausted than anyone knew, including

Cindy herself. The stress of getting kidnapped, shot at, beat up, car-wrecked, and almost drowned—not to mention nearly killed by the worst serial killer in American history—had worn her out.

She hadn't been sleeping much, anyway. *Who did?* Out in the field for months. Add to that the general stress of the work and her manifestly bizarre relationship with Les, and it was remarkable Cindy didn't sleep for a week.

Les looked in on her several times, but never interrupted her slumber. The few moments she was awake, Cindy was thankful not to find Les sitting at her bedside. She felt like crap and figured she looked it, too.

On the third day, Cindy sat up fully awake when Les came in. He advised the agent team in her room to take five. The two, Ellie Portman, a tall, thin woman, and Chick Thinnes, a chubby, shorter man—they had acquired the doubly transposed nicknames of Portlyman and Thinchick—were happy for the break, even if only to pace the sterile hallway.

"Good news," Les jumped right in.

"Texas Two-Step is dead?"

Les stared at her, somewhat blankly. "How'd you know?"

"I didn't," Cindy said, equally astounded.

"Oh. I thought maybe you slipped out from under anesthesia and the watchful eye of our twelve friends here and whacked him."

"Yellow ribbon?" Cindy asked.

Les nodded.

"Has the lab typed it yet?"

Les said they hadn't.

Cindy grunted some ambiguous affirmation, then asked if he actually had twelve agents watching her.

"I'd 've had twelve more," Les said, "but Brinkman put the brakes on the second dozen."

"That wacky bureaucrat."

"He's flying down to see you tonight."

"Oh, Jesus. You gotta get me outa here!"

Cindy tried to move, but pains from parts she didn't know she had stopped her short.

"Nope. Doctor says a week, it's a week," Les ordered.

"A week! It's just some bruises."

"Just some bruises?"

As Les came closer, Cindy grimaced. She knew how bad her condition was, how lucky she'd been. Trying to divert him, she asked if they'd found anything else in the van once they got it out of the water.

"This," Les said, and produced her .32, cleaned, oiled, and test-fired.

Cindy's face lit. "My little Tomcat! Ohhhh." She racked it, checked for rounds, then held it close like a pet.

While Cindy was fondling her favorite weapon, Les pulled the sheet back. Something stopped her from stopping him as he lifted up her gown to gaze on her nakedness.

"That's more than a few bruises, Deary," he said.

"'Deary'? Really?"

Cindy shoved her gown back down and put the stunted Beretta on her hospital tray by her disregarded institutional red gelatin product.

"I thought you were gonna do something nasty," she said, disappointed.

Les said, "You mean like maybe a... touch-up?"

He pulled a new can of Barbasol and a fresh disposable razor from his jacket pocket.

Once Cindy got her jaw up and her cackle out, she asked Les if he was *out of his mind!*

"No. I don't think so," he said. "At least not by any contemporary clinical standard."

He walked to the door and stuck his head out. "Thinchick?"

Chick Thinnes came closer. He showed no offense at his nickname.

"No one comes in here while I'm questioning Agent Baker," Les told him. Thinnes asked about doctors. "Not doctors, not Cooper. No one." Cooper was the Houston SAC. "Not until I come back out this door and say something to the contrary. She's only the second person ever to be alone with Riverbend and live to tell about it. Got it?"

Thinchick said, "Yes, sir," and Les knew he meant it. Chick Thinnes was a solid agent; Ellie Portman too, top-notch. Both had been flown in from Washington just to protect Cindy. Les had insisted.

He closed the door on them — and put a chair under the handle.

Cindy said, "That only works in movies, you know."

"We're a movie," Les said. "What can I say?" Then, employing his best brusque bedside manner, he said. "Okay, hike it up, Hootie. You're getting scraped."

"Hootie?" Cindy said with a wince. "Have you no shame?"

Les pretended to ponder that briefly, then said, "I doubt it. No."

For the next hour, Cindy marveled at the gentle, loving way he shamelessly depilated her from toe to ankle, ankle to knee, knee to thigh, thigh to... neck.

"Oh my *God*, I can't believe you did that," she said finally, feeling very naughty.

"I can't believe you let me," he said, feeling very erect.

Cindy noticed. "You're not going to try to use that thing on me in here, are you?"

Les groaned, "No, I guess that'd be pushing our luck."

"Yeah," Cindy agreed. "So, let's go in the bathroom!"

She was out of bed like she'd never been in it, wounds and all. She had his pants to his ankles before he had the door locked and had pulled him inside her before he got turned all the way back around.

"It doesn't hurt, does it?" he asked to be sure.

"Are you kidding? It feels wonderful."

"I meant your bruises."

"What bruises?"

***

By the time Brinkman didn't show up, around eight thirty, Les and Cindy had already snuck into the bathroom two more times—once to wash her hair, but it got out of hand. Les then went out for Chinese. The hospital cuisine didn't look like, well, cuisine.

On his return, Les excused the watchful agents from the room and found Cindy in the bathroom again. "Meds kickin' up your digestion?"

"No. I keep going in there and staring at it."

"It... as in *it*?"

"I lay down, feel *it*, want to lift up the covers, but your friends are always here, so I excuse myself, go in the bathroom and stare in the mirror for five minutes. Then I come back, lie down, feel it, and it all starts again. They must think I'm nuts."

"Nah. They probably just figure you need Imodium."

Cindy told Les that Brinkman had called to cancel. "Something about Interpol." They both snorted laughs.

Les then produced some exquisite Vietnamese food and asked Cindy if she was ready to talk about her kidnapping and near-death ordeal. She was, and they talked until dawn.

No new light was shed on who Riverbend might actually be other than he was blond, which Les seemed to know, which in turn surprised Cindy because that wasn't in the file.

Other than hair color, and the Killer not appearing to be misshapen or deformed in any noticeable way, Cindy couldn't definitively describe anything else about him, since she hadn't gotten a full frontside view.

Les was concerned that the reverse wasn't true, but Cindy assured him Riverbend hadn't gotten a good look at her, either. He'd grabbed her from behind, flung the tape around her face and tossed her in a dark van. The rain was blinding, her makeup was streaked, and it all happened fast. He would know her hair color, her general features, spying from afar, maybe. But up close, where it might count someday, "He wouldn't know me from Eve."

"The African one or the Bible one?"

"Either."

"Okay." Les nodded as if he was satisfied even if he wasn't.

Cindy then asked if the Killer had shown up anywhere yet—dead or alive—and Les said no. Neither had Riverbend sought medical help, as far as they could tell, which meant a) Cindy hadn't shot him after all; or b) she had only nicked him; or c) he was dead.

"Maybe our SKK found him," Les said, with little fire for the idea.

"You mean me, or the other SKK?" Cindy asked.

"Yeah, well, you or Brinkman."

"Fuck you *and* Brinkman. And your horses and each other."

"Feeling better, huh?"

"If I was feeling better," Cindy, said, "I could come up with a lot better than that. And *you're* the one who had opportunity. What's to say you didn't find him down there, slit his throat, and shove him downstream for the crabs to eat?"

It didn't sound like a real question, but Les answered anyway. "No knife. Besides, I was a little busy at the time."

"Yeah. And did I ever thank you for that? Formally?"

"No."

"Oh." And she didn't thank him again. Which only made him grin wider. He knew she was grateful—and thankful his allegiance had been to saving her life rather than avenging his dead family.

Cindy said with intentional conviction, "I'm certain I hit him, Les. Positive. I had to 've. I emptied the whole clip."

She went on to say that Riverbend's reaction had not been one of fear or shock at the sound of a gunshot. He yelled and recoiled, then crashed the van. Someone as seasoned as Riverbend wouldn't lose control of a rapidly moving getaway vehicle because of a loud sound. Even gunshots. Even seven.

Les said he was certain of her "markswomanship abilities. Or is it markspersonship, these days? I can't keep up."

Cindy said definitively, "He's *dead*, Les. Dead and floated away."

"Habeas corpus, hon," he said. Three days had passed, and The Killer's body had not turned up anywhere downstream. Les had called every coroner from the bridge to Galveston.

Cindy's voice fell to a whisper. "I want him out of the game, Les. I want him dead. Send him home to hell."

"I'll do my best, honeybunch."

Cindy was so focused, wanted it so badly, she didn't even complain.

***

If anybody understood Cindy's desire to know that Riverbend was dead and gone, it was Les Moore. Getting Riverbend out of the game had become his entire raison d'être. But he couldn't help noticing how Cindy had finally dropped that silly be-kind-to-murderers crap and was cutting to the chase. *Don't just get him off the streets, Kill the bastard. Kill him now!*

Maybe she was one of their SKKs after all. The thought crossed his mind—and how he finally had a real partner after all those years of operating alone.

All good things come to an end.

Chapter 34 – To Hell and Back to Hell

All uncertainty as to Riverbend's fate was wiped away within the week when a family of five were found dead in Utah, their bodies laid out to spell "LES." The Bureau tried to keep that part hush-hush, but someone leaked it, and all hell broke loose again.

Riverbend's message seemed clear: He wanted Les off his back and was willing to do anything to make it happen. He had to. The pace was killing him.

In a rustic motel outside Salt Lake City, the Killer savored a rare Bud longneck while considering a life of killing ease with Les Moore out of the way—and changed the bandage on his shoulder. Cindy had hit him, all right.

Fortunately for him, the slug went through the fleshy part of his upper arm, missing the bone. He had needed medical help, stitches and antibiotics, but it had to be so discreet as to be invisible. The whole operation was classic Riverbend.

First, he bought the cheapest rattling piece of imported claptrap thin-gauge sheet metal he could roll out of a *No Money Down!* lot—using an assumed name with full ID—then he drove it, sputtering and stuttering out to a deserted stretch of highway outside Durango and ran it off a bank into a tree.

The veteran highway patrolman who responded to the scene remarked how he was amazed someone could survive such a bad crash. He'd never seen anyone walk away from a "twisted piece of Japanese crap like that" with so few injuries, and none of them serious. Though he thought the shoulder gash looked bad.

It did, because minutes before, Riverbend had intentionally reinjured his shoulder on a jagged piece of twisted import wreckage to obfuscate any telltale signs of the gunshot wound imparted by Special Agent Baker. He then added a few other injuries—a bruise here and there, a few scrapes and cuts for verisimilitude—but never felt a thing. The Killer had trained himself to be impervious to pain in case he ever actually needed to be.

His powers of dissociation were strong. They had to be to kill with such icy indifference. He simply applied the process to himself momentarily to good effect. Then, he "staggered" up to the road to be "discovered" by the first passing motorist.

The lawyer from Purgatory called it in on his cellphone — then gave Riverbend a card and hurried off to personal injury court.

When the trooper asked if he wanted an ambulance, Riverbend declined politely, even bashfully, saying he didn't have much money and wouldn't be able to repay the ambulance system — something he "just wouldn't feel right about." No, he'd hitchhike to the nearest doctor and "get some stitches or whatever."

The HP was so impressed with Riverbend's manufactured humility he gave the Killer a ride into town and dropped him at the door of the closest urgent care — with advice on how to get free medical care. Then he suggested the Killer think about suing the car dealer.

Riverbend said there were "too many frivolous lawsuits filed in this country these days" and he "wasn't raised that way," but he'd "give it some serious thought." The trooper then thanked *him* and left. The Killer paid in cash and made a clean getaway into Utah.

But as Riverbend sat in his crummy motel room outside Salt Lake with the lumpy beds and pissy shower, changing his bandages, he thought this was a lot of work and how life had been much easier before Leslie Francis Moore came back to dog his every move.

He continued to discount Cindy as a challenge. He'd have killed her easily had he gotten her out to the cabin — Tomcat notwithstanding. Anyone could make that mistake in a hurry. He'd patted her down. *What? Did she have it in her pussy? Christ!*

No, if Cindy ever got too close to him again, he wouldn't be so elaborate. He'd pop her and get it over with. In the meantime, he wouldn't be worrying about Agent Baker.

Les, on the other hand, was a worthy adversary. This, however, was a lot like Les and partners. Riverbend hadn't asked for one. But he got one anyway.

***

"Les," Brinkman said soberly over the phone, "we've got a problem."

"No, we don't, Phil," Les said, stripping for a shower in his hotel room. The decor didn't matter. Not anymore. "Either you and Wilstrong want me off the case or you don't."

Cindy looked up from a sheaf of faxes and grisly printouts—a whole family—as Les said, "Just say the word, Phil." He was naked now, his voice careless. His manner.

"It's not that easy, Les, and you know it," Brinkman said. "I've got three dead Mormon kids and their parents spelling out your *name*. Something's got to give."

"Well, it's not gonna be me, Phil. Not after all this. Not after we've come this far."

"How far have we come?" Brinkman said with his usual lack of panache. "Do you know something I don't know? Are we nearing closure in this case? Talk to me."

Les thought the three questions through, and opted to answer with a simple, "No," ignoring this new "Talk to me" thing altogether.

"We're nowhere. Is that what you're saying?"

"Well, philosophically speaking, we're always somewhere, Phil." Les could hear Brinkman's brain pruning up as if he'd left it too long in the Great Pool of Thought. "But as far as the case is concerned, like I said: No."

Brinkman heaved a great sigh. "I'll get back to you."

"You do that, Phil. And have a nice weekend."

Brinkman grunted as if to impart that he was damned if he was going to have a nice anything, and he hung up.

"They want you to resign?" Cindy asked, standing, dropping her robe, and pressing her naked flesh to his.

"Not yet," Les said, then kissed the top of her head and went to take a long, hot shower. He didn't even think how much he still loved the smell of her hair. Even dirty.

***

Cindy stared at herself in the desk mirror without seeing her nakedness at all, thinking, *Ever since that damn 6-6-6 thing...*

Again, she couldn't complete the thought.

The next day, three coeds were found dead outside Santa Cruz. Their unclad, decapitated, and delimbed bodies had been placed side by side in a field with the letters "l-a-W" carved into their torsos, one letter per body.

The rest of the parts were laid out above, on the ground, to spell out the now familiar, "Hi Les!" complete with one head dotting the i and one under the exclamation stroke. The third head, complete with yellow ribbon around the severed neck, Riverbend had overnighted to the fucking president.

That's when Les quit.

Cindy wasn't having it. "Les, you can't give up now! He's leaving specific clues!"

"You call that a clue? His version of the 'law?' He can't even get his case correct," Les grumbled.

"That's it, that's it!" Cindy said exuberantly. "He's making mistakes! We've got him running. He's scared."

Les stopped packing. "Two things Riverbend never does—get scared or make mistakes."

"So, you explain it," she said as a direct challenge. Cindy did not want Les off this case. If he went, she'd be out there alone—or worse, with a new partner *she* didn't ask for.

Now, she understood.

"I don't feel like explaining it," Les said, sounding tired. "Eight people are dead in three days. An innocent family that had nothing to do with any of this, and three coeds who had less to do with it, not to mention their whole lives ahead of them."

"So? Whattaya goin' soft on me, here? You're letting a little death scare you off?"

"A *little* death?" Les said, unable to grasp her callousness. "Brinkman's right. You've definitely been hanging around me too much."

"Les," Cindy pleaded, "we're getting close. I can feel it." And she could. For the first time, she could *feel* Riverbend!

He was close.

"Then I suggest you run, not walk, as far away in the opposite direction as you can possibly go. And stay there."

"No," Cindy said plainly. "I'm gonna get this bastard. I'm gonna take him down." She swore, sounding like a TV cop again, much to her chagrin and Les's pique.

He said, "Apparently, you've already forgotten your little van trip last month. He almost killed you, remember?"

"*Almost*. Operative word." Cindy remained defiant, resolute, fearless.

Les went to the phone and yanked it up. Cindy didn't like the way he did it and moved closer. "What are you doing?" she said.

"Having Brinkman take you off this case."

"The fuck you are!" Cindy grabbed at the receiver. He dodged away. "You can't do that!"

"It's for your own good," Les said, deftly mimicking composure, and started to dial.

Cindy swatted his phone onto the bed. "Do not, do *not*, patronize me."

"I'm trying to save your life," Les said, trying to make it sound that simple.

"Bullshit!" Cindy hollered. "You want me off the case so you can stay on!"

"Baker," Les said, low. "Don't make me dislike you now. We've come so far."

Cindy ignored the Brinkman refrain. "Oh yeah, I get it now. You want me off the case so you can leave the Bureau and keep working it on your own. Outside the law. Cute, Les. But it won't work!"

Les gave her a brief, cold stare, then returned to his packing.

Cindy stalked him. "Les, goddammit, don't do this. Any of this!" She felt tears coming but would rather have taken another van ride with Riverbend than show any weakness, any emotion but outrage. Les continued packing as if disavowing her presence.

Cindy slammed the case shut, almost catching his fingers. "Les," she said, trying to at least sound calmer. "This is not you. This you I'm seeing here? In front of me? Giving up? Packing and going home? This is not you. This is not the you I know."

"Ah-ha!" Les roared, raising a finger. He reopened his case.

Cindy slammed it shut again. "Hilarious," she said flatly and reloaded. "Les, don't let 'em get to you. It's the press. They're always whining about something, looking for a way to sell papers and beer. That's all this is."

"It's a little more than that, Babydoll."

"Fuck you." That was for the name-calling. The larger truth was, "People die. Happens all the time."

"Not on my shift."

"Oh, please. You're gonna make me use you and Brinkman in the same sentence again."

"They're dying on my shift, left and right, Baker! Innocent people. Every one. And it's my fucking fault!"

"Oh, don't be ridiculous." Cindy scoffed and turned away, feeling some actual disgust at his descent into an ego abyss.

Les sounded totally committed to his premise. "Baker, listen to me. If I do not take myself off this case, Riverbend is going to keep doing this, not once a week but twice a week. Then three times a week, then every fucking day. And I cannot have that on my conscience!"

"He's not doing it because of you," Cindy said contrarily.

"That's exactly why he's doing it! Because I'm on the case. Because I'm on *his* case."

"No," Cindy said. "He's doing it to get you off the case, so he can slow down and go back to one a month, or one every few months, or whatever his schedule for killing is. That's what he's doing. Getting you off his back!"

Of course, Cindy couldn't know for sure — she was just vamping — but as usual these days, she was dead right.

"Well, he's succeeded," Les gave her. "I'm off the case." Direct and pragmatic. "Finito!"

"'Finito'?" Cindy repeated, incredulous. "You *are* turning into Phil Brinkman, I swear. I'm very disappointed in you."

She sat on the far side of the bed, faced away from him.

"Good try, but it won't work," Les said. "I couldn't become Brinkman if you surgically removed the hair from my head, grafted it onto my back, did reverse liposuction, and gave me a full-frontal lobotomy."

Cindy refused to laugh.

"And don't try sulking. That won't work either."

"Leave me alone," she said, having soured on the whole conversation.

Cindy felt abandoned. Every woman hates it when a lowly man makes her feel trivial. *Disposable.* How that unkind man has the ability to make a decision to just go and seemingly not care a whit about it. Or her. *He's made up his mind; let him go.* Every *Cosmo* Cindy had read since she was eleven years old had said the same thing, but that never made it easier. Old Helen Gurley never let a man do that to her. Cindy'd bet on that.

Les's hands found her shoulders. Cindy had been so lost in anger and self-pity she hadn't noticed the bed moving when he crawled across to her. Now she pulled away and fought the tears she wanted to shed.

"Don't cry," Les said softly. "I'm not worth it."

"You're telling me. You're a pathetic, sorry bastard." Cindy made sure to sound tough and held the tears in harder.

"What happened to 'cocksucker.'"

"You're a quitter. That's worse. I hate quitters."

Les touched her again.

This time she only pulled away enough to punctuate her point, but not enough to remove his hands. She said, "What really pisses me off is I never figured you for one. Boy, was I wrong." She tried to sound as indignant as possible.

"Hey," Les said, making light. "We're all wrong about stuff from time to time. Especially people."

Cindy said, "We're the highest-paid, most highly skilled profilers in the world. We shouldn't make basic mistakes like that."

"I'm not your basic guy."

"You can say that again."

"I'm not your basic guy."

His further attempt at lightening up didn't work. Cindy snorted angrily, refusing to laugh *or* cry.

Les sat next to her and turned her reluctant face to his. "Okay, two thoughts," he said. "One, we're not so highly paid. And two, SKs, Riverbend in particular, are the best profilers on the planet."

"So? That's not news."

"But it's what I'm trying to tell you," he said, turning tender. "It's why I want you off the case. Why I'm getting off the case. He's got my number, Baker, and he's got yours. And that's bad for the public welfare."

Cindy heaved a heavy sigh, knowing he might be right.

"You know I'm right," Les said as if reading her mind. "Gainesville, then Houston. Me, then you. At least think it over." He patted her on her knee. "Okay, babe?"

"Babe?" How low would he stoop?

Les stood. "I'm feeling very Hollywood lately. Thinking, hey, if it's good enough for those Mafia snitches, it's good enough for me. Sell my story, make a few mil, retire to Florida. Send you a postcard of a girl in a bikini riding an alligator in an orange grove. 'Weather's great. Wish you were here, *babe*.'"

Cindy looked at him. "You're a sick puppy, Les. You need professional help."

"Been there, done that. Didn't work out. Still nuts." He made a funny face that wasn't all that funny and went back to his packing.

After a minute or two, Cindy stood and came over to him. She reached out to touch his chin and smiled slightly. Then, without warning, she slapped the piss out of him.

"That's for everything," she said.

He looked shocked and his eyes went red and watery. She hadn't held back.

"Stay out of my case," Cindy said flatly, then she walked out, leaving the door open.

"Real funny. Getting the last laugh," Les called out. "Leaving the door open!" But this time there was no laughter, no happiness, no response.

This time, he was definitely dumped. Cindy knew she'd made that clear.

***

When Peggy—looking as pale as she had only once before, four years prior, the time she had to inform her boss of his mother's passing—silently placed the fax on Brinkman's desk, he knew what it was without looking and just nodded. Peggy left, quietly closing the door so he could be alone to grieve and consider a new career.

Les had somehow found a fax machine and officially resigned in writing. Now, Phil Brinkman was on point, and he hated going first at anything, except the dessert queue on a cruise ship. From this point on, his ass would be on the line.

He was already deflecting more heat than he thought he could tolerate, from Wilstrong to that new network news anchor herself. In person! Even the goddam *president* had called wanting to know what the hell was "going on out there?"

Hey, the guy'd only gotten a *head* in the mail. What was the big deal?

Brinkman hadn't known what to say, so as usual, he lied—this time about how they were close to getting a break. He got away with it for the time being, but the awful truth was that the Riverbend Killer might never be caught. Hundreds could die, and all of the blame for anything that went wrong would land squarely on Phil Brinkman's round shoulders with a resounding splat.

Peggy held all of her boss's calls the rest of the day and he went home early—the first time in the twenty-two years she had known him. He sat staring out his brownstone bay window at the seasonally dead trees, getting more and more depressed as the day died and darkness prevailed. Les Moore was gone for good. His only hope was Cyndra Lynn Baker, his personal choice for Number Two. What the fuck had he been thinking?

***

Five hours later, on a dreary and cold late autumn afternoon, Les Moore swung open the door of his Seattle home and stared in from the front porch, rain whipping in around him. Everything was still the way Marjorie left it. During his three-year descent into hell, Les had managed only to destroy one room, the family room, where he had the fondest recollections of lounging with the family, back when he knew how to lounge and he still knew what a family was—back when Melissa Ann was just learning to walk.

That long ago.

He annihilated every memory, reducing furniture and paneling to splinters, then burned it all in the back yard. The fire department issued him a citation, but no charges were filed, and nothing made the papers. Fred Bondini saw to it. Les then had a contractor come in and rebuild everything exactly as it had been, and he never went in the den again.

Les stood there on the porch, looking in, for a good five minutes until his ruminations were interrupted by Bondini's voice, welcoming him home after sitting across the street in his big SUV, watching and waiting. Cindy had called him with a heads-up, hoping that maybe his old friend might talk some sense into him, or at least convince him to stay at home.

Out of her way.

Les said, "Hi, Fred, thanks," without looking, then went inside and closed the door.

Bondini stared at the door a minute or two, deeply concerned but helpless, then got in his Police Special Suburban which still smelled of new leather, turned off his phone, and took the long way back to his new superstation, thinking maybe the fanatics were right. Maybe the end *was* near. It was for Les. That much he knew for sure.

Not much had mattered before. Now, nothing did.

***

On Monday, in Phoenix, Cindy met her new partner—sent by Brinkman despite her protests that she didn't want one. Brinkman pointed out her dangerous similarity to her former partner, and Cindy hung up on him.

A handshake and a "Your room's down there" was all she accorded the new guy. Then she went back to her room and her work, with every file she'd ever garnered spread out in the adjoining room. She had told Brinkman she'd pay for the extra room if he wouldn't. He did.

Her new Number Two didn't see Cindy for six days. In the interim, he gathered data on the Camelback Killer's latest victim who had been found in an arroyo below the hump, his favorite dump site. He preferred teenage boys. Phoenix PD wanted him stopped badly. The new mayor's son was gay and terrified to go out of the house.

The new TASK agent proved helpful, analyzing data, giving decent if not specific parameters regarding his profile of the unsub to the chief. But when Cindy finally showed up on day seven to give hers, even he was impressed. She perfectly described their main suspect— the one PPD had recently dismissed as a suspect and who had gone missing.

"Snooze, ya lose," was all Cindy said on her way out the door.

The new guy said a few kind words on Cindy's behalf then ran out after her to find that Cindy and the loaner sedan were already gone. "How the hell'd she do that?" he said to himself, then walked to lunch alone. At least it wasn't raining.

Chapter 35 – The Truth about Everyone

Cindy's new partner knocked on her door for several minutes before finally getting a bellman to let him in. He'd had no word from Cindy in three days. Not a peep. He thought she was dead in there for sure, Riverbend having come back to finish what he started in Houston.

The room was neat as a pin. Agent Baker was gone.

He called Brinkman vexed and angry, then sat in silence as Brinkman ranted for ten minutes about "getting rid of one rolling goddam cannon for a-goddam-nother." He did love his rocking boat analogies. But even Brinkman couldn't find her.

Cindy was in Seattle. Where it all started.

She'd gone to Les's house. No one seemed to be home, so she staked it out for thirty-six hours, across the street and down some. On the second day, after waking from an unintended nap in her car, Cindy found a note pinned to her *sweater*.

Nice try, Baker, but leave me alone. Not interested.

Good luck on your case. L.

Cindy was so angry she pounded on his door until her knuckles were rawer than her ego and she started around back.

Then she had second thoughts. Knowing Les, there might be booby traps.

At any rate, there was no point in hanging around any longer. He would be seen when he wanted to be seen. Until then, Cindy should take his advice and get on with her case.

Which was exactly what she did.

***

"Where were you on these dates?" Lead FBI TASK Force Special Agent Cyndra Lynn Baker flung a photocopied list of SKK hit dates onto the desk of King County Sheriff Major Frederick Jonas Bondini. At the top of list was Merfinridge.

Bondini's reaction conveyed somehow that had Cindy not been Les's friend, he might have saved Riverbend the trouble and shot her right there in his office. She saw it in his eyes.

Then he willed it away and said, "Do I look like a 145-pound woman to you, Agent Baker?" Before she could reply, he added, "I don't even look like a 145-pound *man*." Going nearly a hundred pounds more than that, he had a point.

"That was a wild guess from an assistant-assistant medical examiner," Cindy said, not about to back down so soon.

Bondini sucked his teeth, probably how he always did when he wasn't sure whether to start making phone calls to DC or just answer the question. Then he cautioned, "You know, Les and I go way back."

"I know," Cindy said. "That's why I came here and asked you directly."

Professional courtesy.

Bondini sighed, "Okay. Let me see."

He picked up the list, and for the next hour-plus, pored over his daybook, schedule apps, and travel records. As with anyone, the major had several windows of opportunity, along with a few lapses in memory. But for two of the key SKK hits—the Jupiter Killer and Boston's Star of David nutball—Bondini was out of the country with his family and three others from his church, never out of somebody's sight "for longer than a good shit," as he put it, obviously trying to get her goat. (It didn't work. Brothers.) And, while the Windy Killer was getting whacked—forensics was able to give a narrow window of time, less than two hours—Bondini was giving a pep-talk to five hundred highway patrolmen in Hilton Head. All other hits corresponded to similarly unassailable alibis.

Fred Bondini was no longer a viable suspect.

"Had to ask," Cindy said with a shrug, not surprised. And not caring whether he agreed that she had a professional responsibility to look under every rock or not.

Bondini surprised her and said, "I suppose you did."

Feeling empowered, Cindy tried out her pet theory on him. "What do you think of Phil Brinkman?" she said.

"As a person or an insect?" Bondini said, providing the answer without actually saying it.

"As a suspect."

Bondini laughed nearly as hard and long as Les had.

"I'll take that as a no," Cindy said, and he laughed some more. But she ended his mirth sharply with, "What about Les?"

Really ended it.

Bondini pointed to the door. He never said a word, just bent over his work and started writing something—probably a note ratting her out to Brinkman. Or Les.

Cindy sighed heavily. "Sorry," she said, mostly meaning it, and gathered her paperwork. "Had to ask that, too. Part of the protocol."

Bondini let go a small huff, crumpled up the piece of paper with the scratchy sketch of a duck and tossed it into his trashcan, rebounding it off a small backboard that read "The Buck Stops Here" over an arrow which pointed down into the basket.

With her things repacked, Cindy asked, "You wouldn't happen to know where I could find Detective Anne Lorman, would you?" The desk sergeant had told Cindy she'd have to ask Bondini about Lorman.

The major looked up. "What do you want with her?"

"Same thing," Cindy said. She had, many times, regretted leaving Lorman out of her initial rewrite of Les's Riverbend report, back in the trailer in the Pitt. Now, she would have to dance around her omission to get at the truth—whatever it was.

Bondini leaned back in his chair. "Who told you?"

"Told me what?"

He squinted as if unsure whether she was jerking him around. "About her record."

"Her record is sealed." Cindy had already tried.

"Well, thank God for minor miracles," Bondini said. "At least some things are still sacred." He sighed again and said, "Close the door. Please."

Cindy did, came back, and sat down across from the major as he proceeded to tell her about Detective Lorman's "overly aggressive field tactics." She had apparently taken to beating up any man she arrested for crimes against women. The size or shape of the perp didn't faze her. "She thumped 'em, pretty bad," he said.

"She was a big woman. Strong," Cindy recalled. "Probably did some damage."

"To the tune of fifteen million in pending lawsuits."

"You put her on suspension?"

"I fired her." He didn't sound like he'd had any second thoughts or remorse.

Cindy leaned forward, interested. "And?"

"She blew town."

"Skipped bail?"

"No bail. Formal charges hadn't been filed."

"So, you don't know where I can find her." Statement as question, a Les Moore tactic if her there was one.

Bondini said, "Oh, I know."

He went to a file cabinet, opened a drawer, pulled out a newspaper clipping and handed it to Agent Baker. "It's from her hometown. Wide place in the road north of Boise." The headline read, "Former Policewoman Dies in Car Crash."

Bondini synopsized. "Ran into a tree, alone on an empty highway. No signs of drinking or drugs." He paused. "Her family thinks it was suicide."

Cindy guessed, "They're suing you, too."

"Why not? Care to join in? I'm sure there's still a sawbuck in the budget somewhere."

Cindy laid the clipping on his desk and said, "You think there's any reason I should trace her timeline?"

He said, "Anne Lorman was never anywhere but three places—on the job, in the gym, or in bed with another officer who shall remain nameless but who vouched."

Cindy thought perhaps the officer shouldn't remain unnamed. "Chris Hines?"

Bondini shook his head without a thought. "Married, three kids, moved them all to the Big Island last month after Lorman checked out. Said it wasn't worth it anymore." Bondini nodded as if he empathized. "His wife's a physical therapist. Got a job at a hospital in Hilo and Chris is crewing on a charter boat. Game fish."

Cindy noticed how Bondini got misty-eyed talking about his old employee's new life. Nothing strange there, she thought; she'd had the same dreams, only without the fish.

But Hines packed up and left, "Just like that?"

"He had his twenty in."

"He didn't look like he had *ten* in. Barely looked old enough to shave." Cindy thought back to Hines standing over her at the diner counter.

"Some of us age better than others," Bondini allowed, as if knowing he wasn't part of that group.

"So, I'm assuming you're ruling him out as my unsub as well."

"*Way* out. But you're the prosecutor."

Cindy let the little dig slide, choosing to accept Bondini's assessment of Lorman and Hines for the moment. "Okay. What about this Megan person, at the coroner's office?"

"That'd be where you'd find her," Bondini said, standing. "But if you ask me, you're barking up the wrong tree there. Megan's as sweet as they come. Little bit of a flirt, maybe, but other than that, a straight arrow far as I can tell."

"You go in much for archery?" Cindy asked. Bondini said he didn't. "A blade of grass can knock an arrow off course. A single, narrow blade of grass. Bullet too, if it's a small caliber."

Bondini raised an eyebrow. "You're saying?"

"Any traumatic event can be a stressor. And the victim doesn't necessarily talk about it. Sometimes they act out. Find victims of their own."

"Do you know something, or are you postulating?"

"Just asking the questions no one else wants to."

Bondini sucked his teeth again briefly, then said, "She does travel a lot. Never talks about it either. Can't pry it out of her." He went pensive. Then he shook his head. "Damn, listen to me. I'm starting to sound like you and Les."

"Speaking of Les," Cindy said. "Have you seen him lately?"

"Just once," was all Bondini would say.

***

As it turned out, assistant coroner Megan Foley was every bit as sweet as Bondini had said, going so far as to split her low-cal lunch with Cindy who suddenly found herself famished and shaking. After a short chat about girl stuff over tofu egg salad and carrot sticks, Cindy decided Bondini was right. Megan was about as pleasant a person as she'd ever met.

But she did travel a lot—alone—and she couldn't, even wouldn't, offer any details.

Cindy chose a different tack. "You put the killer of Merfinridge at 145, probably female."

"A guess," Megan shrugged. "I only had two prints to work with," she said, showing the plaster impressions to Cindy, who noted they were the same foot.

"Two rights," Megan said. "Must've been a good dancer."

Cindy chuckled — until she noted the poor quality of the casts.

"Soft soil" had caused the imprints to sag on the sides, Megan said. "The ground stays wet around the river there," distorting footprints and making precise determinations difficult.

Unaware of Cindy's prior relationship with Les, Megan asked how he was doing.

"Don't know. Haven't seen him," Cindy half-lied.

"He's off the case?" Megan asked, sounding surprised.

"Yeah," Cindy said with little emotion. Or so she thought.

"You had something going with him?"

Megan had apparently done more than flirt with men to pick up on something so subtle. Maybe she was hooking in those other towns, on a lark; for danger's sake, for the rush. The money. *No, she's too —*

"Because, if you did," Megan continued, "I can understand it. There's something about his manner..." she said, drifting away dreamily. Then she snapped back into focus with, "And that *smile.* Killer!" She made a *phew!* sound, as if she was getting revved just thinking about him. Then she turned away, shaking her head.

For Cindy, the effect was similar to being pinched on the butt by Brinkman.

"Where were you on the night of June 15th?" she asked abruptly.

"Don't remember," Megan said, unruffled, putting the casts away. "Do I need a lawyer?"

"I don't know, do you?"

"I don't think so."

"Then you probably don't," Cindy said. "Could the person who wore those shoes be heavier?"

"Could weigh a ton for all I know."

"I don't understand."

Megan explained, "A person could put a shoe on their hand, press it into the soil here and there where the ground's soft, and who would know? We guess a 145-pound woman based on shoe style and size, depth of impression versus texture and moisture content of the soil at the time the imprint was made. Doesn't mean it's accurate. Just conjecture at this point. Plus, where are the lefts? If anything, that would tend to support the hand theory. Not many peg-legged serial killers hobbling around the deep woods these days."

Cindy slid past the levity. "You're saying the perp might not have even been wearing the shoes?"

"That's it," Megan said, sitting in her castered chair, the one she rolled from cabinet to cabinet.

Cindy thought a moment, pacing, then turned back with a direct, "Could you have been wearing those shoes?"

"Could have, but wasn't," Megan said, seemingly unflappable. "The imprint was made by a nine-and-a-half wide. My size. But as you can see, I have a right foot *and* a left foot." She then rolled over in front of Cindy and looked up at her.

"Agent Baker, I appreciate what you're doing here. I know you've got a job to do. A tough job. But I'm just not the killer type. Sure, I can cut open a dead body if I have to. The pay's not bad. Not many people want this work. But cut open a living person? Or shoot them in the head? I have a hard enough time squishing a spider in my own kitchen. I'm not your murder suspect, I promise. You can check out the dates if you want, but you're wasting your time."

Cindy looked deep into the pretty assistant coroner's upturned, dark brown eyes and felt that she was probably telling the truth. Anyone who said she had trouble squishing a bug probably wasn't a murderer. She'd take Megan off the list — for now.

***

Back in the Best Western, Cindy started removing other unsubs from her list while the phone rang incessantly and she ignored it. Probably her new partner.

What was his name?

In no time at all Cindy had a short list. Her SKK had to be someone with a direct line into the system, someone with inside knowledge of each case. Someone like Les. And she still wasn't sure it *wasn't* Les.

But he hadn't shown sufficient mettle when the chips were down. He'd given up. And not just given up the chase; he'd given up access to information crucial to determining Riverbend's identity and movements. So, it wasn't Les. He wasn't that stupid.

That meant only one possibility remained, no matter how much everyone laughed at her when she brought it up. She booked her flight to DC.

Chapter 36 – The Big Showdown

"I'm not the fucking SSK, Baker!" Brinkman shouted from behind his desk. Jesus Christ, what're you on? And what the hell are you doing here on a Saturday?"

He sported a natty, pink Pierre Cardin polo shirt, collar up, looking for all the world like an eighties bourbon ad shot on a golf course with a Lincoln Excalibur Phaeton in the background.

Cindy had taken the red-eye from Seattle just to confront him face to face. "What the hell are *you* doing here on a Saturday?" she shot right back.

"Trying to figure out what the fuck I'm supposed to be doing here before I get my fat ass fired for not doing it!" Brinkman shouted while shuffling some two-year-old papers, no doubt left there for effect. He didn't appear to have any idea what they were or what to do with them.

"But you know what?" he said, puffed up with choler and cholesterol. "You want to march up there and tell the Old Man I am, you go right ahead. And I will happily sign your discharge papers when he throws you out on your pretty little ass!"

Pudge muffined out around his waist under the pink shirt.

He swept up every paper and file on his desk and threw them in the trash. "There!"

He looked at his lead TASK agent for an endorsement.

"First off, Phil," Cindy said, unimpressed, "it's SKK, not SSK. Serial-Killer Killer, not Serial-Serial Killer."

"Big deal, Miss Rookie. Whatever the hell it is, I ain't it!" he shouted. Then, thinking better of his actions, he started rooting around in his wastebasket to make sure he hadn't thrown away anything important.

Miss Rookie?

"Second of all, and most importantly," Cindy said, "if you refer to my 'pretty little ass' even once more, you won't have time to figure out what you're supposed to be doing here because you're gonna be up to your self-described fat ass in depositions."

Brinkman stopped riffling the papers in his trashcan to yowl, "Baker, you're accusing me of *murder*. You think I'm worried about a silly little sex harassment suit? Sue me! Please! I'd love to get your pretty little ass in court and countersue the shit out of it!"

"For?" Cindy said, incredulous.

"Slander!" her boss screamed at her.

"Phil," Cindy said, almost crestfallen. "There's only the two of us here. Slander requires a third party."

"Then take your shot and get out," he said. "I have work to do. Apparently!"

He sat, helplessly shuffling the aged papers without any apparent clue as to what was on any of them or what he might accomplish by sorting them. So, he threw them away again.

Cindy shook her head and took her shot. "Fine. Yes. I think you're the SKK."

Brinkman looked at his desk, rubbed the back of his neck, and said, "My neck's tighter than Bette Midler's bra in the bathhouse years." Then he looked up. "You've got nothing. So, just... go away, Baker. We'll pretend this never happened."

Cincy wasn't about to do either. "I've got charts, Phil," she said. "Charts and graphs, and you're on every one." She took out color Xeroxes and spread them out on his desk.

Brinkman looked over her presentation, clearly having no idea what they were—what they purported to prove—but seeing his name emblazoned all over them sent him into a foaming frenzy. "Okay, that's it!" he said, standing. "Either you go up there and tell the Old Man what you *think* you know, or you walk out of this office and never, and I mean *never* come in here again with bullshit like this, or your career in law enforcement is as dead as Les's!"

Cindy said, "Oh, come on, Phil. Les could come back any minute and you'd kiss his ass all the way up to OPR and back, and have a great time the whole way."

"He ain't comin' back!" Brinkman declared.

"Then, you're *it*!" Cindy jabbed her finger at his name on the charts.

"Fine!" her boss said and sat again. He rocked back in his chair, looking as if he actually knew what he was doing and how to do it, and said, "Prove it. Make me the Killer."

Cindy stared—for the briefest moment unsure in the face of his sudden poise, a wholly new experience—then she said, "Okay," took a breath, and began. "One," she said, "you have access to every file about every SK who ever worked in the United States."

"So do you," Brinkman said. "Next."

After an arrested moment, Cindy moved to, "Two," still feeling confident, "you have repeatedly shown no sense of remorse when an SK is assassinated. Hell, you're happy about it."

"So are 99.9 percent of the 330-*million* people in this country. Next!"

He wasn't buckling. More surprisingly, he even sounded like he might have known at one time how to think through an actual case.

Cindy was thrown, stunned really, but she kept up the pace, anyway. "Three. The SKK has struck almost exclusively on weekends."

"So?" What the hell does—

"You have not been here on weekends."

"We're closed!"

"You're here today!"

Brinkman looked at Cindy with exasperation and befuddlement. "Argue one side of your case or the other, Baker. I thought you went to law school, for Chrissake."

"I quit. And this is an anomaly. You know that."

"So, I'm not here most weekends. So what?"

"Not *here* here. In *town*, here," Cindy persisted. "You haven't been in town." She put her finger to the graph, tapping each date for which he had no alibi. "Not one of these dates."

Brinkman had turned red enough to indicate rage, but he had gone quiet, which might indicate guilt. Cindy watched as his eyes shot from date to date as if he only now understood the pictographic representation of how he had spent his free time. The worry showed.

"Ah-ha!" Cindy said. Oh, did this feel good. "And don't tell me you were in your cabin in the woods either, because you weren't."

Cindy shifted her incriminating documentation around and poked at several weekend squares marked with yellow. "These dates, yes," she said, then pointed at several other weekend blocks highlighted in red. "But these, the ones that count. No."

Brinkman looked up as if in shock, stunned silent. His jaw moved, but nothing came out. Then finally, he stammered, "H-how..." He took three more gulps to get out. "H-how did you know about the c-cabin? No one... knows about the c-cabin."

Brinkman reduced to stuttering? Too fabulous!

"Oh, *I* do," Cindy stated unequivocally, and charged right ahead. "You closed escrow on a Friday, August 23rd. Exactly four weekends later, you shot that poor horse-dicked son of a bitch Merfinridge in the woods at Riverbend, caught a red-eye back here, and put me on the case, along with Les, who you have tried to railroad out of a job, for doing his job ever since this whole goddam sham began! You're our SSK, Phil!" she shouted—then heard herself.

"Goddammit! SKK!"

With her terminology straight, she concluded, "If you're not specifically, that secret friend of yours is. Maybe you did the research, and he pulled the trigger." And, the cul-de-sac: "Either way, I got your fat ass, and you're going down for this, Bossman!"

Bossman? And it had been going so well.

But Brinkman had paled, all the red gone, now more closely matching his faded pink Polo. Cindy knew she had him cold. "Truth hurts, doesn't it?"

She gloated. "So. You wanna move aside so I can call the Old Man at home?"

Cindy nodded toward his phone with a sarcastic arrogance he had obviously never seen in her before and didn't much like now. She heard herself, saw his reaction, and felt even more empowered, and let her gaze bore into him.

Brinkman glanced at the phone. He was sweating. *Sweating!*

"H... how do you know all this?" he said shakily, eyes darting.

Cindy had won. She said, cockily, "You were easy. You—"

He screamed, "How do you know about the goddam cabin and my goddam schedule, goddammit?!" He had gone red again, really red, and returned to shouting just fine. Fully recovered, headed for a stroke.

"Phil, for chrissakes, we're the FBI," Cindy said. "You, me, Les, the Old Man. We're trained to find out where people are and where they aren't. You *trained* me, you fucking moron." She was on a roll. Why not? "You weren't there!"

Brinkman looked at her with paretic alarm. "Y-you can't call me a fucking moron."

"I just did, and you weren't there. I *know*."

Brinkman half-glared, half-pouted as his mind seemed to be searching for some effective verbal subterfuge. But all that came out was, "Just because I wasn't... here, doesn't... mean I did it... and that... that I... killed people and... stuff. It... it doesn't."

Babbling! Phil Brinkman, author and master of *Brinkmanship*. Hardly the reaction Cindy would have expected from a stone-cold killer of killers.

On the other hand, she had done stellar work, if she did think so, herself.

She told Les she wasn't going to let go of the idea of Phil Brinkman being their SKK, and she'd done her homework, discreetly and thoroughly. It hadn't been easy, essentially spying on a fellow agent, her boss, but she'd persevered and now she had him by the short hairs. There was no point in him denying it or trying one of his patented detect and deflect moves. Cindy was too much on her game. She had her full hand around his shriveled nut sack and was squeezing for all she was worth. Why *shouldn't* he babble?

"You'll need more than that," he finally said, softly.

"Why? What else do I need? You're FBI, Phil. The American people have entrusted you with a solemn purpose. A sacred pact. You took an oath. Now you take it upon yourself to go vigilante? To kill the people you can't arrest, because you're so damn inept—"

"You don't have enough!"

Brinkman shouted so loudly Cindy was sure someone would hear all the way out at the front desk and come running. But no one did. Maybe this was a typical Saturday with Phil Brinkman at the office. Everyone stayed away.

"Okay, fine," Cindy said, patronizingly. "What do I need, Phil? You buy this cabin for an excuse, only you never use it. Oh sure, a few weekends here and there maybe. Go fishing with your friends, make it look legit. But on the weekends that count, you weren't there. So where were you? We've got motive, we've got opportunity—"

"You don't have a weapon," Brinkman said, pitifully.

"I don't need one, Phil. I've got *you*. Motive, opportunity, access to profiles, no fucking alibi. That's all I need! That's all anyone needs to open the door. To check you out. And when that door *is* opened, and they *do* check you out, they're going to find out that you're—"

"Gay."

"No!" Cindy said, irritated and refusing to be derailed. "That you... that you're..."

Her mind seized up. Refused to work. Her body spasmed. She finally spluttered, with a mixture of utter incredulity and outright offense, "What?"

"I'm gay!" Brinkman yawped. "There you have it! Destroy my career. Ruin me. Go ahead! Do you think I'll ever make director when they find out I date men? No! I don't think so, Agent Baker. Thanks so-fucking-much. Twenty-two years down the fucking toilet because of your ridiculous, stupid meddling. Who asked you?"

"You did!" Cindy screamed. "You hired me!"

"Not for this!"

"Jesus," Cindy shook her head. "If you think I'm falling for that line'a crap, you're a crazy killer, Phil. Not any old-fashioned kind either, but a fucking crazy, idiotic dope!" She laughed. "Gay! Please. You were married! We all know that! You talk about her all the time. What the hell's her name? Millicent! Millicent Northridge! Gay. You can do better than that, Phil. Much better."

Maybe he couldn't. He was starting to shake and yes, cry.

Cindy looked him over, wagged her head as if trying to shake off a bad daydream. "Phil, goddammit, it isn't gonna work. You're not gay." He wasn't responding. Just shaking and crying more. "Phil?"

"It's true," he said weakly. "I am." And he wept like a baby.

"No, no, no," Cindy repeated, trying to reaffirm her position— mainly to herself. "You're a killer. You killed them all. You're the SKK, or your partner is—"

"No, goddammit, you meddling twat!" Brinkman shrieked. "I'm a practicing homosexual! I date men! I have sex with men! I'm gay! I'm a queer! A fag! A cocksucking FBI faggot! And now I'm fucked in the ass for real, not just for pleasure!"

At least he was consistent with his debasing nomenclature.

Sobbing, Brinkman pulled out his wallet and showed Cindy the photo of a man he had always said was his nephew. "See this? This is not my nephew. This is my lover, Carlo. We've been together fifteen years. Since I left Millicent." He was bawling. "Tell the world! Ruin me!" He waved the wallet again. Credit cards and IDs flew everywhere.

Cindy suddenly had to sit down.

He said, "And those fishing parties you thought you found out about?"

"Don't tell me," she implored.

"Yes! Group sex. Group gay sex!"

"I asked you not to tell me."

"Well, I have to, now! You've exposed me!" He shouted so shrilly, with such panicked commitment, his entire body went red. His fingertips.

Cindy got up and tried to calm him down. "Phil, sit."

"I don't want to sit!"

"Sit, please. Before you have a stroke."

"I only had safe sex. I don't take chances," he avowed, fully out of control. "Except with my career! Oh, Christ. I'm finished!"

Cindy stared in disbelief as yet another block in her ideological foundation crumbled to dust. "But, Phil..." Try as she may, Cindy couldn't get her brain wrapped around the concept. "You're so... awful. So... truly *god*-awful."

"I know! It's all just a front! I had to be. Don't you see?" Pleading.

"But, Phil, I mean, really. You were a misogynistic asshole."

"I know, I know, I know!" Whining.

"A sexist, homophobic pig!"

"I know!" Wailing again.

He left his office.

Cindy took her own advice and sat — hard — bewildered. Breakers were tripping left and right in her neurotransmitter circuit box. For the first time in years, she didn't know what to do. At all. Had she just sunk her own career? *Christ.* Could this have gone any worse?

She heard wailing around the corner, then solid thumps and louder wailing.

What now?

She jumped up, ran through Peggy's ante-office into the hall, to find their boss, Phil Brinkman, standing on a marble bench, pounding his head into a mural of the director — *The* Director — staring down as stern and antihomosexual as ever a director could be.

Brinkman then pulled back and screamed at the painted face. "You hypocritical son of a bitch! You queer bastard!"

Cindy said, "Phil?"

He ignored her to continue his screed. "You goddam cross-dressing hypocritical freak! The FBI was my life! You were my idol! I did everything by the book. By your book! I even kept secret sex files on people. Hell, I've still got yours on Forrest Tucker. Forrest-fucking-Tucker! From fucking *F-Troop*!

"But I did it. Did it all. And because of you, because of your goddam silent policies, my career is over, you sick... fucking... diseased..."

Completely out of control, Brinkman suddenly yanked out his keys and started stabbing at the mural, slashing the canvas.

Before Cindy could get to him and stop the destruction, it was a done deal. He then ripped the painting off the wall and assaulted a potted ficus with it, venting a lifetime of frustration, fear, and rage.

"Phil! Stop it!" Cindy grabbed him, shouting in his red face, "Phil! Goddammit! Stop it!"

Phil stopped. And he looked at her, sweat pouring, eyes blinking, eerily motionless. Then he said, quietly, "I don't feel so good," and collapsed.

Cindy said, "Oh Jesus," and tried to break his fall before going down under his considerable heft, onto the floor, sure she'd be crushed alive.

It took all her strength to roll him off her and stand. He looked like a beached whale, in a pink big-man's Pierre Cardin polo. She climbed aboard, straddling him, and looked down into his glassy eyes for signs of life. "Phil? Are you okay? Phil! Talk to me."

She slapped his cheek like she'd seen in movies.

Brinkman's eyes rolled around in his head, then he whimpered, "I did everything..." For a moment Cindy thought maybe this was going to be his big confession, but Brinkman finished, "... for him."

She followed his eyes and found Hoover peering around the leafless ficus, bare twigs growing out of his forehead. Somehow, he still looked intimidating.

"Look at it this way," Cindy said, turning back. "Maybe you're a lot more alike than you thought."

"I never wore a dress," was all Brinkman could muster.

"Okay," Cindy said, standing. "I'm going to call an ambulance. Stay put."

Realizing this was a pointless instruction—he was barely breathing—Cindy ran back to his office and dialed 9-1-1 on his landline rather than her cell so they'd know where he was. At least she was thinking clearly again.

She then hurried back, sat on the floor, and cradled his large head in her lap to pet his wet hair. Which came off in her hand.

Les had been right about the wig too.

***

The ambulance arrived in under eight minutes. When she heard the siren outside, Cindy told her boss, "I'm not going to say anything about this, okay?" His eyes looked hopeful. "You're gonna be okay, and no one's going to know what I found out. It'll be our little secret. Okay?" Brinkman stared, too weak to respond.

Cindy positioned the soggy toupee on his slick, sweaty pate the best she could and forewarned him. "But if you come back to work," she said, gently defining the terms of their unfolding agreement, "you're going to have to be nice to people. Even if it kills you."

Brinkman's panic increased. His eyes bulged again as if having to be nice to his employees might kill him quicker and deader than coming out and having a whatever-this-was he was having.

"You want me to keep this our little secret, don't you?" Cindy said. His eyes bulged less, and his brow furrowed more, something resembling consent.

As EMTs clattered up the hallway with their gurney, she said, sounding like her mother catching her doing something she didn't want her dad to know, "Do we have a deal?"

Brinkman glanced down the hall—without moving his head— then back to the person holding his head in her lap, this special agent he had personally selected and groomed to carry out his mission to keep watch on the most dangerous agent in the Bureau, and possibly ferret out a serial killer or two, this dauntless agent who had come back to uncover his most deeply held secrets, his secret life—to *out* him— and he folded down into his soul. She saw it happen.

Then he gave the tiniest nod of assent Cindy had ever seen. A tear fell and he looked... relieved. The charade was over.

***

A few minutes later, Brinkman was on a stretcher, paramedics about to wheel him out. When they turned away to wrap up their gear, he motioned Cindy closer with his eyes.

His words were barely audible. "Les said... there was a knife."

Keeping her eyes on the EMTs, busy closing up their crash kits, Cindy screwed her face into a clear question and leaned closer. "What? I'm—"

Brinkman whispered, "In the Pitt. The... Slasher's van."

Cindy still didn't understand. Or didn't want to.

He spelled it out. "Les... knew the knife...was there... before I told him. Before... the report."

Cindy pulled back sharply and stared at the pathetic bloated figure below her who looked proud and broken at the same time. "I noticed that," he said weakly — maybe the first case detail he had ever noticed — even if he hadn't probably wanted to because he knew he might have to tell someone someday, and he knew he wouldn't want to say it when the time came.

That was nothing compared to how much Cindy didn't want to hear it.

Chapter 37 – The War Room

Cindy hoped no neighbors heard the tinkling glass.

Wearing non-latex surgical gloves for this operation, she had broken into Les's kitchen via the windowed Dutch door. "Les?"

She had her gun out.

Seeing it in her hand, Cindy thought back to the first time Les observed her service weapon. "Glock, huh? Sounds like something you chuck up and spit out."

She remembered defending the Glock 17 as "the weapon of choice for most of law enforcement for three decades." How he scoffed at the inability of the masses to think for themselves and said, "So, how come you carry a model 35?"

"More than twice as good," she'd said and grinned at him. Truth was, the 35 was better-balanced, built for competition shooting. Whatever edge she could get.

How he gave her a polite smile and said, "I think I'll stick with Bill Ruger's design."

His P-85 had never let him down, Les claimed. "Never jammed once in twelve years of heavy use."

How she nodded at the *heavy use* bit and said, "Ruger, yeah. That sounds better. More like a dog choking."

How Les gave in and they shared their first laugh. And finally, how Cindy wondered now, in a showdown, if it would be the Glock or the Ruger.

"Les, it's me. Are you home?"

Only Sinatra came back, from somewhere in the back of the house, saying how he was seventeen again, full of piss and vinegar, ready to take on the world one last time. He sounded angry.

"Les, it's Cindy," she called out one last time and stepped inside.

The one-story brick rambler was a disaster. In the kitchen, take-out containers and dishes were piled high. Garbage spilled from mountains of black plastic bags. Flies buzzed.

Cindy covered her nose and mouth and let her Glock lead her around the corner into the laundry room where dirty clothes were piled so high the washer and dryer had disappeared.

She checked the pantry, but his cupboard lay bare.

In the dining room Cindy found chairs but no table, an open hutch, mostly empty, and more garbage, bags and bags of it. The living room looked as if Hurricane Lesley had veered northwest and blown through. Newspaper lay strewn everywhere mixed with dozens of books.

Cindy picked one up, *In Cold Blood*. The cover had blood on it and was cold. She set the book back down on an empty cover of *Madame Bovary*, pages all torn out. The wife dies in the end. Disney's *The Parent Trap!* had a 9mm hole through it.

"Les? It's me, Cindy. I'm in the house."

Sinatra saying he was older now and things just weren't the same.

Cindy stood in the center looking around, clutter everywhere, the fireplace raked high with coals holding bits of books, pieces of clothing, garden tools, and a transistor radio. This wasn't home to any Les Moore Cindy had ever known. This was the psycho Les.

Then she saw the den. Les had stripped the family room entirely — the one he'd had refurbished — then crammed in every table he could hijack from the rest of the house, all blanketed with file folders and scraps of paper — hundreds of them, maybe thousands — along with rows of audio- and videotapes, CDs, DVDs, thumb drives, stacks of letters and official affidavits, "miscellaneous" quotes, "missing" reports and "lost" interviews. He had ripped out the carpet and hung it over the windows. No light came in; no thoughts escaped. No one heard.

He had plastered the walls with photos of Riverbend's victims. Cindy recognized a few, enough to know who they were. But many, she had never seen before — including a half dozen shots of Marjorie and Melissa Ann that weren't in any official records. At least anymore. Close-ups of their bodies, transgressed beyond anyone's worst imaginings. Pale, smeared, debased, their genitals —

Cindy turned away. She had wondered how Les went on living at all and here was the answer: in madness. Here, where he had tried to force order from chaos. An impossible task in the best of times and circumstance. But this?

She now saw that he had made copies—or stolen originals—of everything to do with Riverbend and every other SK case he'd ever worked in his career, and then some. A large room, a long career, a *lot* of files. Some lay open, some closed, in stacks and piles, on the floor, under the tables, on cabinets and chairs. One hung from the ceiling fan, rotating indifferently.

Cindy turned a slow circle, looking up, only then seeing that Les had papered the ceiling with photos too, at least half of them new to her. At first glance, they appeared to be victims of SKs. But how many might *be* SKs, their runs ended by Les?

Back there somewhere, Sinatra, now old and bitter.

Cindy understood. Les hadn't given up any access to information at all. He'd gotten all he needed. He was flush. When Riverbend finally gave him a reason to resign, he took it. Les didn't need the Bureau anymore, the access, so he left and came here to finish it His Way.

This was Les's Command Central, running his goddamned Operation Whack Riverbend campaign out of this very room, empty but for the voices calling to him for finality from countless graves. Two in particular.

But how many were there in all? Cindy saw more than a dozen case names she knew nothing about, had never heard mentioned. There might well be another dozen if she took the time to look and think back, but she found herself staring at a photo mural on the wall—what was obviously supposed to be a comical double-exposure of a stressed-out, wide-eyed, screaming nutcase in a straitjacket with the caption, "I may be schizophrenic, but at least I'm never alone."

Cindy didn't laugh. Maybe it was too close to home, here in Les's inner world of self-generated electroshock, post-regressive, vengeance therapy and need for things unspeakable. He hadn't told Cindy, that was for sure. Or had he, and she hadn't been listening? Didn't want to listen, was more like it. Who would want to hear this?

Sinatra near the end of his life, back there, done with it all.

Feeling an urgent and sudden need to check the rest of the house before digging any further into Les's private cache of death data, Cindy eased down the hall, halfway expecting to find Les hanging from a ceiling fixture or a shower rod. Over a door. But she didn't find Les, just more of his noir-nouveau interior decoration.

On the bedroom wall, over the king-sized bed—mussed only on one side, *his* side—he'd hung photos of those three dissected coeds and the butchered family of five from Provo. In his closet, his dresses, wigs (damn good ones, she noted), pantyhose, purses, heels, along with various leather and latex accessories. In the master bath, enough Lancombe and Clinique to service a brood of starlets with a high-end line of Trashy Lingerie drying in the shower.

Lots of razors.

Cindy felt her knees give way at one point and just caught herself on a door handle. She slid down the wall onto the tan berber in tears before she knew what hit her.

***

When Cindy had gathered enough courage and blown her nose twice — pocketing the Kleenex — she located the shelf-stereo in Melissa Ann's old room, set on replay. She silenced Sinatra, finally, and went to work.

Much of the paperwork Cindy recognized but much she didn't. Files on Riverbend that she had no clue even existed and reports that had never made it into official records — letters, handwriting samples, fingerprints, photos. X-rays! All for Les's eyes only.

Like the one on Ginger the dog. Les had been allowed to remove their eight-year-old golden from the crime scene before forensics got a thorough look. Sure, they cataloged the wounds, position of the carcass, the usual, but they never got to run serum tests, or hair and fiber. So, they never knew that a blond human hair was found on Ginger. Les did the forensic work in his garage. Neither Marjorie nor Melissa Ann had ever been blonde.

"That's why he fucking wasn't surprised to find out Riverbend was blond," Cindy muttered angrily. Les had said he knew because *He knew*. Because *he stole the fucking evidence!*

Cindy thought of the eight-by-tens Les had asked her to forget about up in Montana and, a few folders down, there they sat. She cussed again, this time like all three brothers at once. Drunk.

Digging more, faster, Cindy discovered the results of a vacuum metal deposition test run on some partials a few years back by RCMP up in Vancouver. Lifted from a tough and shiny holly leaf, one of them, the right ring finger, was clear enough to run through IAFIS — which Les had done on his own. He had received no hits, so it wasn't in a file and meant nothing. Still, if Les had kept the print, it must be Riverbend's. Cindy stared at the stolen evidence and muttered something she hoped her mother couldn't hear in heaven.

Next, she discovered a report from Cellmark Diagnostics that Les had managed to cadge and crib away. Cindy was dumbfounded to find that Bureau pathologists had found traces of semen in the "oral cavity" of Jerry, the kid Riverbend raped and killed in the cabin. That wasn't in any goddam report! Apparently, Les had intercepted the sample and kept it for himself. And for good reason. He had it run against Riverbend's... *blood?*

Cindy stared down, astounded, at a toxicology report comparing both trace samples. A note in Les's hand cross-referenced the Cellmark test. The DNA had matched.

How the hell did he get Riverbend's blood?

She dug on and gleaned that it had happened four years earlier. The body of a thirty-three-year-old woman was found near a Mt. Tamalpais hiking trail, north of San Francisco. She had been savagely slashed to death and thrown off a cliff with a yellow ribbon tied around her neck to accent her blood-soaked L.L. Bean socks. During the attack, while kicking at Riverbend with her hiking boot, the mother of three had apparently managed to deflect the Killer's blade back into his own leg. When he pulled it out and turned it back on her, minute drops of his blood fanned her thigh. Noting the different spatter pattern at the dump site, Les secretly removed the Killer's blood with a gauze patch soaked in EDTA and had it analyzed — off the record — by a friend of his, an old schoolmate who had become an ME in a small city in the South. Les had mentioned to Cindy how his friend had cheated on his civil service exam and how Les would bring that up when he needed a favor. Now, she understood the darker depths of that favor. Typical Les.

Les had been sitting on this evidence — *critical DNA evidence* no one else in the Bureau knew about — for *four years.* "Christ."

It only got worse.

Cindy next found the unofficial statement Les took from an emergency room intern in Durango. The ER nurse — another male — who triaged Riverbend had written, "Trauma to upper arm/right shoulder from automobile accident," in the hospital file. But the young female intern who sewed the Killer up wrote in her personal journal (a document Cindy was now reading for the first time which had not made its way into any official report, thanks to Les): "Wound appeared as re-injury. Muscle torn in manner consistent with bullet entry/exit." Being new, with two years to go, she hadn't wanted to make any wild speculations officially, but Les had gotten it out of her.

"I *did* hit him in the van. I knew it!" Cindy said aloud. *Sonofabitch.*

Hoping to get a description, Cindy read on. But sadly, neither the male nurse nor the female intern nor anyone else had any concrete memory of Riverbend's appearance. "Dark-haired and rugged" was all they said. *Dyed his hair and grew a beard. Of course.*

Finally, Cindy unearthed The File. On top were Les's notes on the Strip Killer, listing the date Les had killed him and detailing the burial site—not fifty feet from where Nipple Bar's body had been discovered.

No wonder Les had gone so pale when he looked down at Helen "Bitsy" Miller's body in the muck. The blue dress meant for Cindy hadn't rattled him. No! Les had realized at that instant that Riverbend knew Les had killed the Strip Killer and had buried him out by the *dike* in the Everglades. *For Christ's fucking sake! No wonder he blanched and went all stoic.*

To make his point, Riverbend then killed Nipple Bar—that was bad enough—but then he deposited her body less than thirty feet from where Les had buried Strippie. Cindy thought how if rain hadn't obscured the shallow grave dug by Les, Riverbend would have left Nipple Bar right on *top* of the Strip Killer's body. That would have clanged the blustery Broward detective's nuts. "A hundred feet due west from the second bend in the levee, two feet under," Cindy read in a disquieted burst.

For the moment, she couldn't grasp why Les would write any of this anywhere, but then she remembered: Sinatra. This journal was Les singing about his own life, in his own way, saying, "Here it is; here's what I did; take it or leave it; I don't care. What matters is: I did it." *That's what they'll remember* was how Les put it in the red Dodge Avenger.

And he didn't go passively; he kept at it until the end. Past the end. The end was quitting. This, here, was well beyond that. Beyond reason and sanity, even obsession. All the way to epic ballad. He just didn't care. Les and Frank. Sing it one way, mean it the other; say you're done, but go out kicking and screaming.

And he wasn't done yet. Cindy stared at the confessional and she understood. Les wanted someone, maybe even everyone, to know everything—probably not right now, but someday. To cleanse his conscience. Whatever was left of it.

Cindy next found Les's notes on the Pittsburgh Slasher, complete with date and dump site. "Three Rivers. Van in water. Clean." Later, he had added, "Forgot knife." A note in the margin.

Brinkman had heard right. "Bless his poor dark heart," Cindy muttered.

Les also took credit for Jupiter, Two-Step, the one in New Orleans — where Les had been spotted briefly, as he had in Gainesville by the elderly woman in the hospital lot — and *the Bayside Mauler*. Les's confession over breakfast in Miami had been *real*!

An arctic floe clogged Cindy's veins. She had taken his confession over Cuban steak and hash browns and had laughed it off. "Good Christ," she groused, certain she was headed for unemployment come Monday. If not extradition. "How could I..."

She couldn't even finish the thought.

The remainder of the SKK hits had been Riverbend's. Gainesville's Predator, the phony granpa/grandson team in Iowa, the Boston and Portland hits, Windy, and one other in Reno that Cindy had suspected all along. Les had cataloged each of them as carefully as his own, almost as if Les and Riverbend were...

A team?

Cindy gasped sharply, sucking saliva down her windpipe and straight into her lungs. In seconds, she was hacking like a consumptive on a cheap cigar. She coughed and gagged and choked and put her hands on her knees.

When that didn't work, she stood up. But seeing the files and the dates and the dumpsites and the photos on the walls and the unfunny schizoid poster only made her cough harder, so she turned around to flee the War Room and...

Les said, "Hi." He smiled as if no time had passed, no bad feelings, no sex — no lies.

Cindy couldn't move, couldn't speak. She became a pillar of salt. She had dared to look back into Les's personal Sodom and Gomorrah and had paid the price.

Les said, "I hate to do this." He held up thick black tie-wraps for her wrists and ankles.

Now, Cindy could move. She reached for her gun.

Les coldcocked her.

She heard a smudgy, "It's for the best, Missy."

Then the lights went out.

Chapter 38 – Slow Ride

Cruising the Strip in a classic Eldorado—black, with red leather and a moon roof—Seattle shrouded, cold and cheerless. Dusk is past. No headlines this week means the girls are back.

"Hey, you're not a cop, are you?" the blond driver asks his hooker.

"No," Les says. Not anymore.

***

When Cindy came to, she found herself bound and gagged on the floor, her weapon across the room. But this time, she came prepared. She slammed her beige pump down and the heel popped off, exposing the short, sharp blade she had planted in there.

That's what you do with a ruined shoe.

In less than a minute, Cindy had her pistol in one hand and was rifling Les's files again with the other. She didn't know what she was looking for, only that she was determined to find it.

Only then did she hear it. Les had put Sinatra back on Melissa's stereo before leaving. Was it "Fools Rush In" or "Send in the Clowns"?

No. It was "All or Nothing at All."

***

Les takes in the accoutrements of his favorite car, a 1976 Eldorado. Be better if it was a ragtop—last year of the classic American convertibles—only two hundred were made—but the moon roof helps. And white would be better than black, but who's complaining? It's the right year. And what's even better:

Riverbend is at the wheel.

"You got any Sinatra?" Les as the hooker asks, low and breathy. He worked a full year to get the voice down, the walk. That perfect blend of sluttiness and mystery.

"No," the Killer of Les's wife and daughter says, other things on his mind. Past pleasures, future longings.

Les can read his mind better than he could Cindy's.

"I've got some in my purse. You mind?" the hooker says.

"No." The Killer looks over, then back to the road ahead.

Les opens a gaudy little red clutch to retrieve his *Solid Gold Sinatra* tape. Pops it in the dash. "Old Blue Eyes," the girlish side of him drawls as Frank launches into "Mack the Knife." Sharks biting, bees stinging.

Killers killing.

Les's red come-fuck-me pump bobs and swings as he moans like a woman in love, pushing back to feel Bill Ruger's classic P-85 Mark-2 nestled in the small of his back—up under the red tube top and matching sequined jacket.

Riverbend had felt everywhere else. Les knew he would, so he didn't let the search begin until he was all the way in the car and pressed hard against the seatback.

The Ruger offers comfort in discomfort, not like sitting on all God gave him as a man, taped-back and under. But he's gotten used to it. Like they say: Location is everything.

Only eight miles to Riverbend.

***

Standing in the middle of Les's War Room, Cindy realized he hadn't moved a page, hidden a thing. Either he didn't think she'd get free, or he was planning on returning soon. That, or he truly didn't care anymore.

Frank urging, "Come Fly with Me."

To keep her mind from locking up again, Cindy dug through the files, searching for anything that might give her an idea as to what Les was thinking or where he might have gone. She found two tidbits of evidence absolutely no one knew about.

One was a charred sliver of black plastic with foil on it from the burned-out cabin in Montana that Les had apparently spotted and pocketed it when no one was looking. The other was an interview he had done with an adult bookstore clerk a few weeks before he quit the Bureau. Les had scribbled, "dragon tat/left fore. check if nec."

According to his detailed account, after the adult bookstore episode in Chicago, Les had the black plastic and foil analyzed. It turned out to be a DVD case, as he'd thought. He then made the short leap that Riverbend had probably picked up the cabin kid in a similar porn store in his college town. So, Les visited every one until he found a clerk who remembered Jerry Carver.

"Goddammit," Cindy said aloud. Les had so cavalierly shot down her suggestion to do just that. Shot her down because he'd already done it.

In the margin of the file, Les had written, "Refer to Tape 43, Side B, Footage Mark 129." No time for transcription.

Cindy located the audiotape and player in seconds. Seconds later, she was listening to Les's covert interrogation of two young men who were obviously unaware they were being recorded. He even asked them to turn down the heavy metal on the stereo because it was giving him a headache, obscuring his illegal warrant-free taping. When they refused, he asked one of them, a friend of the clerk who was apparently busy sketching highly accurate, detailed studies of female genitalia from the many *wide-open-the-way-you-like-it* magazines surrounding him, if he'd "killed or robbed anyone I should know about?"

"Not lately," came the reply. Then the music went down.

The clerk recognized Cabin Jerry from a color photo Les had 'borrowed' from girlfriend Melody's dorm wall. But when Les offered laser-print copies of the police renderings of Riverbend—Ernesto's six best recollections—the guy with the fire-breathing tattoo said, "No. Just the eyes."

Cindy nodded. *Just the eyes.*

On the tape, Les asked if the buddy with the sketchpad might, with some guidance, be able to enhance the police renderings and make the face look more like the face the clerk had seen. The "goochie *artiste*," as the clerk called his friend, said he thought he could, and started making alterations.

After a few minutes of "No, not so much on the chin," "smaller ears," and "longer hair"—which Cindy fast-forwarded through—the clerk finally said, "Yeah. Good one, Richie."

But, wait. He had seen Riverbend clearly and *lived*? How was this possible? Cindy had to know. So had Les.

"I was in the back, cleaning out the booths," the clerk said on the tape. "You should see what some of these dipshits leave for me back there. Anyway, the kid was coming out of one. I heard him watching some bisexual shit. You know, guys doin' guys while some skank pretends she's interested. Doesn't do anything for me."

Richie agreed; it didn't do anything for him, either.

"I was around the corner back there," the inartistic one continued, "when I saw this blond guy standing outside the kid's booth, listening to what he was watching. He acted all inconspicuous and shit and when the kid came out, he waited a second then followed him out. I figured he was a fag or somethin', wantin' to get some college kid to suck him off in the alley or in his car or whatever. Happens all the time. We run 'em off in packs. Call the cops three times a week, at least."

Richie echoed, "At least."

Les asked, "And you're sure this is what he looked like?"

"Pretty sure. Yeah. I got a good memory for faces. Names? Forget it. But faces—"

Cindy hit Stop and scurried back to the file. Three pages down she found the drawing. Her heart was racing. Her chest was tight.

She was staring at Riverbend.

***

The old sign hasn't changed, nor has the population. Still zero. That won't change tonight when all is said and done.

The heavy Eldorado, its satisfying rumble, glides effortlessly up onto the old bridge, the single bare bulb shifting ever so slightly in the silent, invisible chill.

One unguarded moment is all it will take. One bullet through the Killer's eye—then one more to be sure—and silence will return to Riverbend.

Peace, elusive.

***

Cindy ran to the bedroom for a quick inventory. The red sequined outfit was missing. She remembered seeing it an hour before, hanging from the closet door in a fresh dry-clean bag. The wire hanger was bare now, the plasticine bag empty on the floor.

Cindy spun, angry with herself and slapped the wall, cursing wildly. Les was gone, and with a decisive head start. He could be anywhere by now.

Feeling hopelessly incompetent and illustriously defeated, Cindy started to turn away when something caught her eye in the wide mirror above the twin chiffoniers across the room. A photograph was taped to the opposite wall, over Les's bed — what he went to sleep under every night — no doubt what he dreamed about. The three headless, limbless coeds. Cindy had noticed the picture earlier, but something about it looked different in the mirrors, in reverse. As things do. Like reviewing one's own past in fast-reverse.

Cindy crept toward the tall dressers until the still shot — a sideways eight-by-ten color enlargement of the three savaged torsos — was centered and clear so that she could now see how the letters, reflected backward in the mirror, spelled not "l-a-W" but...

Wal.

The blood drained from Cindy's skin, the breath from her throat. "Shit, oh shit, what were we thinking?"

Whatever she had been thinking, she realized now with resounding regret what Les had been thinking the moment he saw it. Riverbend was luring him back to the Walmart, back to where it all began.

Then Cindy saw Les's wall calendar, marked in red — exactly four years ago, "Today" — the fourth anniversary of the night Les lost Marjorie and Melissa Ann to the Riverbend Killer.

Cindy checked her watch.

They'd been abducted from the parking lot around seven thirty in the evening. Mickey's little hand was on the — "Eight. Shit!"

Cindy looked up, around. Was her heart pounding, or had it stopped completely? The pictures, the wardrobe, the mirror — and Cindy staring back at herself. She knew now where Les was and what he was planning.

Cocksucking murderous little fuckbug.

***

The woods stay dark and lonely along the Black River. Ghosts out here could scare even Riverbend, given the right conditions. Les the hooker, idly looking over, asks, "This the place?"

"Always," the Killer says, stopping in the deep and soft, the always wet, heavy highway grass. He lifts the shifter into Park and his arm to the seatback.

Leaves the engine running. This won't take long.

Side A of the tape is over. Les looks down at the player, then out. "End of the line," he says. No question, no doubt.

"Yeah. End of the line..." Riverbend agrees. "Les."

***

Cindy took the turn off the Strip sideways, clipping a red Honda wagon across from the old motel. This was *not* going down on her shift.

***

Realizing too late that this has been Riverbend's night all along, Les reaches for his Ruger.

Riverbend is faster. As the tape reverses and Frank is stating his case on Side B, of which Les is certain, the Killer states his, sending a powerful blow to Les's left temple, driving his head into the right-side window.

Dazed for a split second, Les forgets where he is. He stands sharply, reaching back for a better angle at his weapon. His head finds the hard, glass roof. Pops his neck. Almost knocks him out. *Goddam hardtop!* He forgot. His hands drop like polio.

Riverbend has the Ruger.

The next few seconds are a blur. The gun going off. Side glass blown out. Cracks in the windshield. Punching. Scrambling. Fighting for his life.

More shots?

Les slings a backhand fist into the Killer's nose and follows with an enormous right hook to the same spot—*make him fight the pain, not you*—spreading it flat. The Killer's head snaps back like a Zapruder clip. Erupts in red.

His door falls open and they're out in the road, in the rain, on the ground, gun skittering over the side as—

A big Chrysler almost runs them both over. Wide tires on wet asphalt, grabbing, sliding, threatening, as Les and his Killer go over the edge, tumbling tank top over miniskirt after the Ruger. The big car doesn't stop.

***

Cindy was traveling way too fast, well beyond her ability to control the car on a rain-slicked, curvy course. It had to happen sooner or later.

The new Chevy Malibu—nice, but no SS Impala—went squirrely on a reverse-banked left and quickly ended up in the far rail. Fortunately, there *was* one, and the silver midsize hit the low steel mostly tail first, not hard enough to deploy the airbags, but enough to crumple the quarter panel, rip off some side molding and make her *slow down!*

Cindy knew she was no good to anyone wrapped around a tree out in the boonies, to be body-bagged by Megan the next morning under Fred Bondini's doleful eye.

Riverbend dead and Les gone—or worse.

Cindy checked her weapon and her backup weapon, and her backup-backup, a Glock 19 with the optional thirty-three-round clip. All loaded, chambered, with six clips in reserve. Each. That should be enough for anyone. Even Riverbend.

Les would go peacefully. Wouldn't he?

***

Les can't take his hands away or Riverbend will crush his larynx like an empty egg. He brings a fishnet knee up. The Killer rolls. One more and he's up and gone, free to do as he pleases.

Home again.

Les scuttles on hands and knees, scratching in the dark for his weapon, his faith—only a dim glow from the interior lights of the idling black Eldorado above, door open, key in the ignition, tolling *pding—pding—pding*.

And Sinatra. How he's lived a full life, planned his careful steps, traveled all those highways. Les ending up on this one, beside and below.

Looking up and listening, because suddenly, bizarrely, Frank is more important. Sure, he's had his regrets, but they're too few too mention. Les's are too many to list. But he understands. He's achieved parity. He's finally gotten there.

Here.

They both did what they had to do, bit off more than they could chew. They ate it up, they spat it out, they stood like men. Neither shy nor hesitant. They said what they believed, said it clear if not loud. They saw it through and paid a price. Had their share of losing, of loss. They laughed, they cried. Had their loves, their doubts. Had their fill, and now they're done.

Frank finds it amusing. Les finds a smile. Because he can hear it now, over the rain, the rumble, what he thought was arrogance, sheer audacity, solid brass-balled *certainty* was really acceptance.

Letting go.

Frank, sensing terminus for the first time. How it's not so far away as it used to be. How it leaves you longing and afraid but resigned. How it takes guts, grit, supreme will — *something* — not to quit when you come up against it, not to give up. Never to give up. But how it does come, that day. That one day when it's just there — and how a man knows.

All a man has is himself, nothing more. *Nothing*, Les. For better or worse. Frank knows. And now Les does, too. It's all come down to this.

The long, heavy Eldorado door slams shut above. Frank is finished. The engine doesn't rev, the car doesn't move. Riverbend isn't running away. He's up there waiting with his big .44. Les down here digging in the mud and cold for his nine.

What a lousy way to die.

***

The big Chrysler came around the turn on Cindy's side of the yellow line. The fog thick, the lights dim. Cindy found the ditch and soft earth. Her tires spun and her tears came without warning, fast and nerve-jarring, but there was no time for it.

She did like her brothers taught her and rocked the car from Drive to Reverse, Drive to Reverse, Reverse to Drive, and she prayed for the first time in a long time. She prayed like hell.

What could it hurt?

***

Les finds his Ruger. He clears the chamber and racks a fresh one to be sure. Rips what's left of his sequined jacket away, the skirt, reaching up and under to yank the tape off.

A man again!

Time has arrived; Les can no longer hold it back. What the hell. It wasn't such a damned good year after all.

Les climbs the bank onto the highway, creeping low for the Eldo. Doors closed, lights off, engine idling, fog hanging still and thick.

The lone dim light on the bridge.

Before he knows it, Les is dead in the middle of the road — a bad place to get caught with your pantyhose down. Backup lights clack on and the big V-8 redlines.

The big black Caddy is coming fast.

Les tries but doesn't make it. The bumper catches his knees, breaking both instantly and flinging him onto the trunk. The rear window collapses under his weight as his upper body catches the trailing edge of the smooth roof, snapping his left collarbone and four ribs below.

Reflexes wound tight, Les fires a wild shot which does no harm, no good. Two more drill the backseat. Red leather doesn't bleed, just looks like it.

Up and over the roof, the long, slick hood jetting back out from under, spilling him onto the pavement like black magic. His right arm breaks in two places; jagged ribs puncture a lung; his head bounces off the pavement like a bowling ball.

He senses only pain, deep and sharp and frightening, as the long, low coupe slides almost off the far shoulder, brakes locked in sibilant defiance.

Then it's coming back.

Les looks up in a concussive muddle, tries to move out of the way, but his body won't cooperate. He'll have to take it.

The sexy black Eldo stops two feet from his hip and idles.

Purrs really, Les thinks; the Caddy's big beautiful eight — 500 cubic inches of American pride. Such a tease. And such a shame to waste it on the useless likes of Riverbend. He'll just burn it later to erase the evidence.

Pity.

To console himself, Les remembers *it was the biggest, but the weakest,* that 500, its last year — slowly, incrementally diminished in horsepower to half what it once was. It's fitting in a sad way. A barbed laugh deep in his spleen.

And a quick inventory.

Awake means alive, but nothing works, nothing will move. Brain functioning enough to know it's bad. His pain is awful — the kind that turns quickly to numbness, debilitating. Still, Les calculates, if it doesn't get worse, he can survive this. He's seen men much worse who lived on. If they could, so can he.

But where is his gun? He can't feel it; can't feel anything with his right arm. So, he's reaching across with his left, fighting the pain like jagged glass...

"Looking for this?"

Riverbend steps into the glow of the headlights, Les's Ruger in hand. He fires down. The pain is double because Les has been, "Shot with his own gun. How sad is that?"

The Killer shakes his head, as if any of this means anything to him at all, and shoots Les again. The first one was in the gut, to one side; the second in the opposite hip. Nothing fatal, not yet.

So, it's going to go like this.

Les hopes maybe Cindy's gotten loose and figured it out. On her way with the cavalry! *Come on, Cindy. You can do it. You're smart. I trained you. Left you plenty of clues. So, come on! Help me —*

The next shot finds his good arm.

"Penny for your thoughts," Riverbend says, and shoots again, this time in Les's good shoulder. The Killer knows how much a victim can take before fading out, before giving up and *going for the light.* Before all light ceases to be.

He leans down. His nose is putty, spread with blood, grotesque. "You didn't really think you could win, did you? Not with a name like *Leslie*?"

Les asks, "Why?" quietly, recalling the cabin in Montana, the kid, and what the Killer did to get noticed. "What's your name, you pitiful butt-fucking faggot?" He doesn't care, doesn't judge; even if he knows the Killer will.

Riverbend shoots him again, this time without bothering to stand. It's more humiliating that way. He's saying, *Why bother?* And his answer is, "Riverbend. You should know, you named me."

There is only the soft folding of the river for a moment. Then the Riverbend Killer says by way of a compliment, even appreciation, "You clean up pretty good as a woman, Les. I never would've known... if I hadn't known. It's no wonder that Merfinridge idiot let you kill him out here. That *was* you, wasn't it?"

Les doesn't give him the satisfaction; but the Killer knows. He's been here all along. Les now knows that.

"You know," his Killer waxes warmly, "I fucked your little girl right over there." Pointing with Les's favorite dependable Mark-2. "Fucked her dead body. Little bitch shit all over me."

It all runs together, then and now, and Les cries. What else is there?

"There you go, whimper like the little baby you are," Riverbend pampers. "And I thought you were gonna be a problem."

He yells, "You took every piece a' bait I threw out like trout in a drought! What the fuck is wrong with you, Moore?" He sounds disappointed. "What were you thinking?"

"Killing you," is all Les can say. The pain is fading. He almost didn't feel the last shot.

"Well, you were obviously thinking about the wrong fucking thing." The Killer stands and shoots down again.

The numb thud feels good. Les, thinking about Marjorie and Melissa Ann. How he let them down. How they died here and now he will. How it's good. Right. The way things were meant to be all along. Now he can see that.

Riverbend rages. "Look at you. You lost! I killed your wife, fucked your daughter. Fucked your wife, killed your daughter. Who cares? It's all the same!" Waving Les's Ruger. The next shot could be the last.

Then, polar-switched calm. "Can't say as I'll miss you. You've been a pain in my ass. If I had to do it all over again, I'd probably pass them right by." He looks over into the dark, wooded glen, apparently recalling the great pleasure had from raping and slaughtering Marjorie and Melissa Ann. Ginger. Moore blood.

"Then again, maybe not," he allows with a sigh.

He looks back and lights up. "Hey, how about Chicago, though? I had you all going, huh? That was sweet."

Les understands immediately. Riverbend targeted the politicians' women, killed them, and created Windy's journal. Then he killed some poor loner to tie it all together, duplicated his handwriting and gave the PD a gift wrapped in yellow ribbon. *Of course* Henry John Freeman couldn't have killed them all. He didn't. Riverbend did.

Les feels sorry for the simpleton; his obsession with serial sex-killers got him killed by one.

Les can relate.

Their Killer shakes his head and looks up the highway. "Cindy should be coming along any minute now. I'd love to stick around and kill her, too, but... she's a little more unpredictable than you."

Yeah. She *shot* him.

Bondini told Les he'd gotten predictable. Les thinks now how he should've listened—everything so clear in hindsight—and a Brinkmanism comes to mind.

"Everything's twenty-twenty ex post facto, Les," he used to say.

What has the world come to? Brinkman right about something, and Les quoting him while dying on the road in Riverbend in the rain. Always the goddam rain.

Riverbend shoots Les a last time, a meaningless hit just to do it, and the slide locks out, empty. "How about that," he says, playing at surprise.

But Les knows. Riverbend knew; he kept better count. That's why he's standing, ready to walk away, and Les is on the ground bleeding to death.

The Killer wipes off Les's Ruger and drops it on the ground, already in a better mood. "See, if I leave the gun, they'll think it was a suicide."

Les smiles, weakly. He can't feel the pain anymore, and Riverbend made him laugh. Maybe they're not so different after all.

"That's better," the Killer compliments, pulling gloves from his pocket—and a length of three-quarter-inch wide antique yellow ribbon, ends trimmed at forty-fives.

Bending down, slipping it under Les's neck.

"I've been waiting a long time for this," he says, deftly tying a double square knot with a bow, left-over-right loop—then sitting back on his heels to admire his signature handiwork.

Then, a frown. "Doesn't feel as great as I thought it would." And a facial shrug. "Still, all things considered, better 'n a poke in the eye with a sharp stick."

One more look around and he's done. "Well, buddy, gotta roll," he says and starts to stand, but something catches his interest. "I'll take the Rolex," he says. His one concession.

He slips it on, admires it a moment, its weight, then says, "You have a good one, okay." He smiles, walks back, and climbs in the phallic Eldo.

Sinatra clatters onto the wet pavement, under the tire, then the Killer mashes the gas, running over the tape and Les's pelvis, crushing both—a final *There's nothing you can do. Nothing you could ever do. I won.* His final fuck you.

Les's Final Curtain.

***

As the seductive roar of his favorite vintage V-8 faded away, Les Moore lay thought-free in the silent rain, life draining, slow and steady. Even if someone were to find him, it wouldn't matter. He won't make it. Not now. A man just knows.

Within thirty seconds, a plain late-model sedan clattered across Riverbend Bridge at a good clip, having come out of the fog a half-mile back. At the last possible second, the driver saw a motionless lump in the road and cut right, then corrected left, losing all control, and going over the side, backward.

Halfway down the bank, the right rear bumper caught soft earth and flipped the rental end over end, with a twist in the middle, so that it landed against the trees on the driver's side—hard enough to blow out the windows and deploy the airbags—then slid to the ground on its wheels, facing the bridge.

A noisy, violent crash. Then everything went quiet again. Les had just enough life left in him to roll his eyes to the side and pray it wasn't who he thought it was.

Seconds later, Cindy scrambled up over the bank, the Malibu's high beams ricocheting up hard behind her. Blood trickled down the left side of her face, scratches from flying glass, but otherwise she seemed fine—until she saw who was lying in the middle of the road.

***

"Les!"

Cindy had hoped it was Riverbend, but hoping hadn't helped. "Oh my God." Tears erupted before the words were free of her mouth. As she carefully lifted Les's head and slipped a hand under to cradle him in her lap, he looked up with milky eyes and a faint smile.

"What took... so long?" he asked in a haunted whisper.

"Oh, Les. Oh, Jesus Christ." Cindy had never felt pain like this. Not when her mother died, not even in the Killer's van crash. Those were nothing; she'd gotten through them. But this, losing Les? This, she might not survive.

"I see you're getting... my knack... with cars," he said.

Cindy managed an aching smile. "You're a good teacher. The best." It was hard to be strong, here, now, but she was determined.

Les nodded, then whispered, "I'm your SKK... Missy."

"I know," Cindy whispered back. Still, it felt like a shiv being jammed into her spine, hearing him say it.

"Pittsburgh," Les began. "Found him watching coeds... in a laundromat... chewing blue Bic pen caps." He smiled weakly to recognize Cindy's contribution. She returned it through the tears. "No... victims had washers... at home," he said.

Cindy nodded and thought how the solution was usually something simple, if you knew where to look, and how to interpret what you saw. Les was a pro. She *had* learned from the best.

"The two in Florida," he whispered on. "New Orleans, San Diego... all mine."

"I know," Cindy said, crying harder. She couldn't stop it. Any of it.

"Don't... mind?" he asked.

Cindy shook her head. What difference did it make at this point? Besides, "They all deserved to die." She then said, "But you don't," and shook her head as if that could undo all that had been done tonight. Could anything else hurt like this? It didn't seem possible.

"Started with... Julio Charman... For Hap," Les said. "Left the country... came back disguised as... normal person." They shared a smile. Les Moore normal? *Never*. "Then... left again... came back as... real me."

"Les, save your energy," Cindy coached. Pleaded, really. Though they both knew.

With great effort, Les told her to, "Tell Bondini... sorry I left... Merfin... ridge's car in... impound yard. Little joke."

"I'll tell him," Cindy said, laughing behind increasing tears.

"I..." He was almost gone.

"It's okay," Cindy forgave and encouraged at the same time.

"No..." he said. "Not... okay." His eyes closed, fluttered then rolled back open. From somewhere beyond life, Les found the strength to give one of those smiles of his and say, "Most... important... thing."

His brain and body were trying to die, but Les wasn't leaving until he'd said what he had to say. "From here... first time... saw you... to here... last time... I see..."

With his last breath, Les forced the finish. "Love... Agent Baker."

Then his eyes closed, and Les was no more.

Cindy held him close, her own cold body convulsing with each clench of pain, each spasm of tears. How could she have ever known that when she finally heard those most important words, the words she had lived a lifetime to hear, from the one man who meant them so completely — that hearing them would cause her the deepest pain she could ever imagine.

Cindy knew right then that love itself would die with Les.

She let out a wailing howl of denial from so deep inside her soul that she thought her body might shatter into a million pieces on the empty blood-soaked highway, then melt away in the rain. She hoped it would.

But when the last echo faded in her mind, she was still there, and Les was still dead.

At least it was over.

Federal Bureau of Investigation Special Agent Cyndra Lynn Baker would never be the same again. A woman just knows.

***

Under a predawn sky going pink behind the gray, Cindy removed Les's makeup, located the wig and the skirt, the shoes and the Sinatra tape, tied them all in a ball, weighted them down with a rock and consigned them to the dark waters of the Black River which flowed full and ever patient under the Riverbend Bridge. The currents were fast and deep through here, and the bundle would be a good mile downstream before it started scraping bottom. A few days later, it would be in the ocean, Les's secret safe with it, the rain having finally done him some good.

By the time someone came along, got to a phone (Cindy made sure hers was underneath the wrecked Chevy), called the sheriff's department and some fifty police and emergency vehicles showed up, the crime scene was clean. They found Les naked in the road, most trace evidence washed away by the rain, the rest by Cindy's tears. Everyone assumed Riverbend had stalked Les, found him, brought him here and killed him—or killed him first and brought him here. With all the rain and wet, no one could ever know for sure. But what did it matter? There would be no question as to who had killed him—though there might be a few as to how Les got in this mess to begin with.

Any answers to those questions disappeared later the same day when a mysterious and very hot fire swept through Les's house, destroying everything. Fire inspectors determined the cause to be arson, but no suspects were ever named.

Fred Bondini made sure of it.

As a favor to Cindy—one he figured he owed—Phil Brinkman later managed to make a few files disappear, with Peggy's help. So ultimately, all the SKK hits were attributed to Riverbend. If unfair in a grand sense, it was all very neat.

Les received full reinstatement in the Bureau and several posthumous commendations—a star, a shield, a medal, another medal, and another star. Since he had no living relatives, Cindy accepted them all, and a flag, at his burial ceremony in the Quantico National Cemetery with full military honors. The epitaph on his headstone read.

"O that thou hadst hearkened to my commandments!
then had thy peace been as a river,
and thy righteousness as the waves of the sea."
Isaiah 49:18

Les had never been a religious man, but Cindy thought he would have appreciated the sentiment as well as the irony. She had them play Sinatra's cover of "River, Stay 'way from My Door" from a boom box by the podium after Director Wilstrong made his kind remarks.

Cindy smiled, turned her face to the sun, closed her eyes, and thought of Les as the lyrics floated so effortlessly across the empty cemetery on the warm, blue day. The Sinatra CD from Melissa Ann's old room was the one thing Cindy still had of his.

That, and his Ruger.

Shannon Creamer attended. Tall and ranch strong, she wore black and felt the loss. She hugged Cindy tightly but couldn't find more than half a dozen words of sorrow then left early, eyes filled with tears for someone she barely knew. Cindy guessed it would be a long ride home for the young videographer with the keen eye for death's memories.

Brinkman attended in a wheelchair. As it turned out, he'd had a minor heart attack *and* a mild stroke. He didn't get his speech back for a few days, but his first words were to thank Cindy. Carlo was at his side the whole time, playing the ersatz nephew.

Brinkman even took Cindy's hand when she could hold back the hurt no longer and her tears broke free as the gleaming white casket was lowered into a hole in the ground. For the first time ever, she was grateful to have Brinkman by her side.

Afterward, Phil and Carlo went on an extended vacation and when they returned, Brinkman was *nice*. No one knew how to act around him anymore.

Peggy took early retirement.

Special Agent Cyndra Lynn Baker received a general commendation for her good work on the Riverbend case, and a few others, some of which were finally solved on her shift. But she never forgot Riverbend. And she never forgave Les Moore.

Chapter 39 – Riverbend Redux

Dusk on the Boulevard, the Sea-Tac Strip. Endless soft rain doesn't keep the hookers inside. Nor does the *Times* headline.

RIVERBEND KILLER FINALLY DONE?
Prostitutes Safe for a Full Year

It's no longer a false confidence that brings the girls out. *They're here in droves*, Fred Bondini notes as he drives past. He doesn't care. Being a cop isn't fun anymore, not with Les gone and everything so different.

The county commissioners will find his faxed resignation Monday morning. Two more Mondays and he's riding his new John Deere on the ranch he bought outside Flagstaff, down there where it doesn't rain so goddam much. He won't miss it.

***

A gray 2001 Town Car slows, checking out the competition. He's blond, forty, flashing a white gold Rolex and a tentative smile that put together reads, *Big wallet and a small dick*.

As intended. The whores swarm.

A white girl in a black blunt-cut and fashion shades gets there first. "Hey, sailor. Lookin' to rock the boat?" No disguised male voice; this one's a hundred percent. And aggressive.

A real cunt, he thinks.

Perfect.

One year to the day. His nose is flatter than it used to be, but other than that, nothing's obvious. Nobody knows what to look for, anyway; he left no one to report back.

Les dead on the highway.

The Killer got away clean. Torched the black Eldorado outside Olympia. Burned it to the ground. And with no more *psycho* off-duty agents...

Speaking of which. "Are you an officer of the law, sweetheart?"

"Shit," the hooker bitches, turning away. "Asshole." Carping to the other girls who wag their heads and walk off. Who needs that shit on a rainy night?

Riverbend doesn't give up so easily. He calls out the open window, "It was a joke, honey, c'mon. I don't care if you are. I'm not offerin' money for sex anyway."

"Then what *are* you offerin'?" she wonders, wandering back. Putting on. "I ain't out here in this weather for my health, ya know." Always the *fucking* rain.

"How about a ride in a nice warm car and some friendly conversation," is his answer.

"Yeah?" she says, gazing across his roof for other prospects. "About what?" Everyone looking, no one stopping.

"About whatever you like," he says. *Be nice; turn her around.*

With no other takers, she leans low to charm him with a peep down her top. No bra. *See, these are real.* When she sees that he sees them: "How much you willin' to pay for this *conversation*?"

"How much you want?"

"How much you got?"

Now, *he's* off. "Forget it." Creeping his gray Lincoln ahead, for the other girls. He started with a hooker sixteen years ago. Tonight will be full circle, to get things going again.

Any one will do. But, one leg over the other, crossing sideways to stay with him — what it does for her ass — this one knows what to say. "They don't like talkers either."

He stops, waiting to hear what else she has to say. Any deal is her call now.

"I have to ask," she tells him. "Because of all the creeps out there. You know. Some guy says all he wants to do is talk, what he really wants is to chop you up with a hatchet."

"I understand," Riverbend says, empathizing. He used a hatchet once.

"A girl can't be too careful these days is all I'm saying," she says — and she's in the car, quick, before he changes his mind.

"I understand," he says again. "Everyone's gotta be careful, make a living." He drives off past the other girls already flagging down better prospects.

They won't remember anything.

The old motel's been closed two years now. She watches it slip past, and the sign that still reads "Riverbend - 8."

It's raining harder now, so he takes the wipers off Pulse. The slapping steady now.

"C'mere," he tells her, hands roaming, checking the small of her back when she slides over. He won't make *that* mistake again.

"You feelin' me up or friskin' me?" she says but doesn't seem to mind either way.

"Little a' both," the Killer says, and finishes with his hand between her legs, up high—to be sure she doesn't have something lashed up there he doesn't want.

He won't make that mistake again either.

She lets him up under the edge of her lace before her knees slap shut. *Pop!* "First you pay, *then* we play," she tells him. It's all rehearsed, all the same.

He doesn't care; she's clean. And, even better, "Someone's smooth as a ten-year-old."

A sly smile on her lips; head turned down, eyes up. The little nod. The pop of the gum.

The expectation.

"Damned if I don't love a slick kitty almost as much as I love a new gun," he swears honestly.

"Then you're gonna *love* what I got for you, baby." Her knees swinging out and back. The little girl look. The lips. The lust.

The act.

It's hard, driving and looking—and getting harder. Thinking how good she'll look with a yellow ribbon around her limp neck. "You like it in the backdoor, baby?"

Not that he cares one way or the other. But she says, "Like it? No. But for an extra twenty, I'll pretend."

"That's cheap," he figures. "Sure you're not a cop?"

"Per *inch*," she comes back with.

Any appreciation he had for her dies. "I gotta pay extra you're funny?"

It's more of a threat, but she knows what to do, how to handle him. "Helps pass time until the Big Bang." With the Big Face to match—nudging closer, too—all eyebrows and lips, and an extra-loud Double-Bubble *pop!*

Winning him back. "Is that what you call it?" He can hardly believe what he's hearing from this one.

"Just wait, sugarplum," she testifies like her hand's on a Bible. "Back a' your head's gonna explode right off. Pow!" Eyes going wide under her dark glasses with a cutesy little smile to match.

Cruel laughter runs wild and unchecked inside his crowded head. *More like the back a' your head, you stupid cunt*, is what he thinks.

His plan.

Smacking her gum, looking out the window, *oblivious*, she asks, "So, where we goin', sweetie?"

Then, getting *a face*. Concern. Turning it back on him. "Hey, you're not that... Riverbend psycho are you?" Puzzling over his face. "They said he was gone."

He grunts, seeing another Marjorie, a Melissa Ann. Ginger the dog. A dozen others. But he says. "Do I look like a serial killer, baby?" Half-joking, half-insulted. Ever calm.

"Yeah," she says honestly, but it doesn't seem to bother her. And out the window again, and with the gum.

He can't help but laugh. "Jesus." *They get dumber every year.*

Now it's her turn. Up against him, roaming his chest with her small hands. His hips, legs. A smiley-face squeeze where it matters most, then the quick drop, face to thigh, hands to his ankles and back, fast, and flipping the hair.

Sitting up with the *crazy* smile. The damn gum, the hands. "You friskin' *me* now?" he says, not hiding his ire.

"Now, why would I do that? Are you dangerous? Do you rob banks or somethin'?" Eyes wide again. Smile. Gum pop.

Jesus fucking...

And finding the scar on his arm. "What's this?" Followed by the Scolding Mommy voice. "Has someone been a bad boy? *Figh*-ting?"

The Killer looks over, dully. *They always go too far.* That's why he always has to kill them.

***

A new sign says the old bridge has finally been scheduled for demolition. The end of an era. It's about time.

And timing.

Clattering loud and lonely over the disturbed waters of a tired river boiling dark and deep, she's suddenly excited. "Oh! Pull over! Pull over here! Ooo, Ooo!"

Bitch can't wait any longer.

Here where it all started, and where it all will end someday.

He knows it's out there somewhere — The End — knows he'll recognize it when he sees it. Maybe even here in Riverbend. But for the moment...

Green silk panties slide down smooth calves on fingernails of intentional red, then she *kicks!* them off, never giving away her slick trick or revealing her deepest secrets. Saving that for the payoff.

Sleight of hand from a sex magician.

One leg goes up then under and she's on her knees, wig to window, tailbone high, lips pulled back, twitching with breathless, feral desire. Practiced makes perfect.

He hates her.

"Move your hand, bitch."

She's in control, pushing him to his limits. "No hair down there. I'm *bare* down there." The strip joint sonnet is cheap but effective. They all know it.

The Killer growls low.

"Are you gettin' hot, baby?"

He's getting real hot.

"Are you ready, baby?"

He's ready to *kill*. Panting like a fast mile, surprised at enjoying her game so much, giving up so much control.

She's got it all. Tantric promises rising behind a Midwest smile as honest as what this night's really all about. Luring him with her soft sell into his own life of vice.

"Isn't it nice?" she says, showing him almost everything.

"You got one helluva body, bitch," he has to tell her.

"I swim," she says. And... *Now.*

"Aaaaaahhh!" A gasping clutch, a throttled scream barely held, and she's back against the door, knees to her chest, clutching all that's important, gaping past him, out his window, glasses torn away to *see!*

And the look in her eyes.

Heart racing, he spins, no longer the killer. Just a scared little boy in his mother's basement.

What's out there? Is it her? Is it Les come back from the grave? The others? The cops? The FBI? Is it finally over?

It's none of that and all of that.

He hears the click and turns back to find the over-under derringer in her hand. Chrome barrels glisten wet and smell like sex. "Say hi to Les if you see him," she says.

Epilogue

A woman's hand grabbed up a complimentary *USA Today* from the hotel carpet. The story was big news everywhere.

> SEATTLE (API) — *Spokespersons for the Federal Bureau of Investigation, along with retiring King County Sheriff Major Frederick J. Bondini, held a press conference today to announce the discovery of yet another body in the area known as Riverbend Township.*
>
> *According to the new King County Medical Examiner, Megan Foley, the latest victim, John Leslie Aaronson, had been shot twice, once through the right eye and once behind the left ear, execution style, and died instantly. Major Bondini said he hopes, "This will be the last one we find out there."*
>
> *Workers preparing to replace the old bridge, in the heart of Riverbend, discovered Aaronson's body in the woods nude but for a yellow ribbon tied around his neck. Preliminary tests indicate the ribbon is identical to the type and style used by the Riverbend Killer as a "signature" to identify his hits, an FBI source said.*
>
> *In a Washington, D.C., press conference held yesterday afternoon, the FBI's new deputy assistant director, Philip Brinkman — the Bureau's first openly gay agent to reach such a high-level assignment — said no clues had been left as to the identity of Aaronson's assassin. However, agents suspect it was the unknown man, or woman, referred to within the Bureau as SKK, or Serial-Killer Killer.*
>
> *Brinkman further stated that, though this case will remain officially open, the FBI has no plans to pursue it at this time. Nevertheless, he did say he's certain the controversy won't die with Riverbend.*

Cindy closed the paper, flashed a smile at her new partner, checked her men's white gold Rolex Oyster Perpetual with the President band — her one concession — and said, "Lunch?"

But it wasn't really a question.

THE END

ABOUT THE AUTHOR

Author Glenn A. Bruce, MFA, is an award-winning writer-director who began his career in Hollywood, where he wrote the hit movie Kickboxer as well as episodes of Walker: Texas Ranger, Baywatch, plus many more. He's had over fifty short stories and essays published internationally, and recently completed his 42nd novel. Glenn taught screenwriting at Appalachian State University for over a dozen years, and recently returned to his home state to once again be a Florida Man.

You can follow Glenn online at:
Website: www.GlennABruce.com
Goodreads: Glenn A. Bruce
IMDb: Glenn A. Bruce
Facebook: @GlennArdenBruce
Instagram: @GlennArdenBruce
Twitter: @GlennArdenBruce

MORE FROM GLENN A. BRUCE

BANANA REPUBLIC: RICHIE'S RUN
When criminal elements collide, the rules of the jungle will prevail, and those unprepared will pay the highest price.

RACE!: A HEI$T STORY
This white-knuckle chase crosses three decades and as many continents, a wild ride rife with countless twists and surprises at every turn, all wrapped up in the sexy world of fast cars, smart women, and high-stakes capers.

RUBRIC
Detective Mark Young is caustic, dark, and funny... when he's in a good mood. If not, he's downright dangerous—especially to himself.

THE MAN
He thought he was free to leave his old life behind, but The Man receives a clear message that his old "friends" have found him and will do anything to get revenge—even kidnap his daughter or murder his wife.

VERSIONS OF THE TRUTH
The sex is as hot as the tropics, the body count as high as the temperature, and the intrigue as thick as a red tide. No one is safe—especially from themselves.

MORE FROM EVOLVED PUBLISHING

We offer great books across multiple genres, featuring high-quality editing (which we believe is second-to-none) and fantastic covers.

As a hybrid small press, your support as loyal readers is so important to us, and we have strived, with tireless dedication and sheer determination, to deliver on the promise of our motto:
QUALITY IS PRIORITY #1!

Please check out all of our great books,
which you can find at this link:
www.EvolvedPub.com/Catalog/

Thank you!